HEADSPACE

HEADSPACE

JD EDWIN

———————————

Hey reader! Want a free book? Get one when you sign up for J.D.
Edwin's newsletter. Sign up at jdedwin.com.

Read. Dream. Repeat.

- RICHELLE E. GOODRICH

CONTENTS

CHAPTER 1

THE ORB SEIZED THE WORLD'S ATTENTION INSTANTLY despite arriving without flourish or fanfare. The first image, taken by a weather satellite, was thirstily grappled over and shared by news programs, tabloid blogs, and every wannabe social media celebrity. Roughly on par in size to a football stadium, colored close to Vantablack, with a sheen like an oil slick, it already had over a hundred Twitter accounts and followers in the tens of thousands by its second hour of existence.

Save for chatter, very little happened on the first day. The Canadian Prime Minister accused Russia of violating international treaties with unapproved space program tests. The UN hypothesized it to be a military tactic by obscure African countries under martial law. Activist groups ranging from treehuggers to skinheads tried to claim credit, though each proved to be short-lived. Comedians went into overdrive pumping out jokes and skits, desperate to be on the front lines of relevance, and Buzzfeed mined clickbait gold at unprecedented speed with *Everything You Need to Know about the Orb*. Every politician facing potential reelection extended their "hopes and prayers to those affected," though no one was quite sure who the "affected" were. The orb did nothing. It meditated in the center of the Atlantic as the populace buzzed around it.

The first video appeared exactly twenty-four hours post its arrival. Two more were discovered a day later. By the end of the week seven versions made their rounds on the web.

The original began with a colorless city. A middle-aged, bored-looking woman in khakis and flannel trudged through a bustling downtown, head down. A beacon of light illuminated her from above. Her steps slowed as she lifted her gaze to the light. Color appeared on her face, over her clothes, bled to her surroundings, and people stopped to face the light, following her example. Her face lit up and the camera panned up to her smile, though the reason for that smile remained a mystery. A soothing, disembodied female voice cooed, "Ready for the spotlight to shine on *you*?" The scene faded to white, leaving a single line of clean black text on the screen.

www.headspace@theorb.com

The second version featured a thin, nervous teen in suspenders and a bowtie awkwardly hovering behind red velvet curtains. Shuffling his feet and running fingers through his curly hair restlessly, he took a deep breath. Others could be seen behind him, rehearsing a variety of talents—singing, dancing, gymnastics . . . After a moment, the boy took a step forward, pulled open the curtains, and was greeted by a cheering audience. He smiled, and the lights hit him center stage. The same line was spoken, though this time by the voice of a teenage boy.

Ready for the spotlight to shine on you?

The differences between the seven versions were negligible, following the same theme to the letter. A homeless octogenarian down on his luck; a rice field worker in a straw hat; a weary musician playing jazz to a drunk audience in a near-empty bar; a tired-looking young mother tending to her children; a grandfather in a wheelchair. Seven people, seven ages, seven ethnicities, seven lives, seven voices.

Seven faces lit by the same light, and seven identical looks of hope and excitement. One question asked seven times in thousands of languages—admittedly an incredible feat on the part of the enigmatic producers—and one curious website with an address that by all accounts should not even work. The commercials trended rapidly, gaining hashtags faster than Kardashian marriages ended, but the one that took the lead was the eighth video, which greeted visitors to the website itself.

THE SITE, upon initial arrival, was a black screen that stood silent just long enough to evoke suspicion in the viewer that they'd been tricked after all, that maybe they ought to go make a cup of tea and have a laugh. Then the music began, and any and all speakers, earpods, and wireless headphones within a twenty-foot radius sprang to life on their own, as if answering its call. Reports even existed of sound emitting from baby monitors and metal dentures. It began loudly, a welcoming fanfare, then quickly faded as the screen dissolved to white, followed by the echoing sound of heavy heels against a marble floor. A figure appeared in the center of the screen, walking on what first looked like nothing, but upon closer inspection was revealed to be a white floor under a white ceiling. The white was so pure, bright, and slippery that the eye could not help but slide toward the approaching newcomer.

Whatever one expected, this person—figure—thing—probably wasn't it. Tall, slender, and clad in a rich burgundy Edwardian suit complete with long coat and white gloves, they sauntered into view, a silver-topped walking stick dancing around the long fingers of their right hand and left hand in their pocket. Their walk was almost a tune, each click of the heel a note or word complementing the music around them. The walking stick spun effortlessly till the hand gave it a casual flick into the air, caught the silver-coated handle, and slammed the other end into the floor with a punctuating "thunk." The figure stopped moving and swiveled to meet the audience, and at this point their headlessness usually became a trifle unnerving, though not for very long. From the hole inside the pressed collar emitted a fan of light, not too unlike the display of a holographic alarm clock. In that fan of light were the three symbols that formed the bare minimum that passed for a face—two short lines for eyes and a half circle for a smiling mouth. This emoji face winked at the viewer, and the smiling mouth line did not move as it spoke.

"*Do you want to be a star?*" they said, an androgynous voice that matched its androgynous body, too melodic to be digital yet too synthesized to be human. The spoken language was different based on the primary language configuration of each device it played on. "*The stars are where we've come from, in search of* you." They pointed the walking stick at the screen, straight at the viewer. Many later reported that they felt a physical tap on their bodies, as if the stick struck them through the screen. The figure then lowered the stick and began to walk slowly, gesturing at the white space around it. "*This arena is unlike any other. This is a place that tests not your strength or speed, but yourself. Here, you will stand on equal grounds with geniuses, athletes, and prodigies. Here, your chances are as good as anybody's. Here, the world will know your name and see your face. Here, you can and will emerge a star, on a stage grander than your wildest imagination.*"

They stopped and clacked their heels together like a soldier coming to attention, throwing their arms out to the side like the ringmaster that they were. "*Welcome,*" they proclaimed, "*to Headspace.*"

The video faded away at this point, and all

speakers, baby monitors, and vibrating dentures fell silent. A logo appeared on the screen—a black orb half-sunk in blue waves. Then this, too, faded. What remained was a simple button that said "Enter." Clicking on it brought up a form with a few paragraphs of instructions at the top. This, like the video, appeared in the primary language of the display device. Paraphrased, they boiled down to this:

- Contestant must be at least 17 years of age
- Contestant must be of sound mind (though not necessarily of sound body)
- Contestant cannot be pregnant (as fetus is not over 17 years of age)
- Contestants will be selected at random

The form was strangely sparse as well—name, primary language of communication, and birthday. No space was provided for contact information, physical address, or even general geographic location.

HOW SILLY, some jeered. To have gone to such lengths on advertising and then produced such an unproductive entry form. How would they even get ahold of the people who entered? Someone ought to fire their marketing department. It's some television show sure to flop after a ridiculously lofty buildup. It's a hoax, a joke that even the party behind it was too embarrassed to own up to.

And yet, that little voice whispered. In every ear, in every heart, it whispered. Few spoke it out loud, but we all heard it in our heads.

What if it's not?

The number of entrants grew by the day, by the hour. Call it curiosity, call it absurdity, call it foolishness, but it grew. Every day more names were typed into that short, simple form. Despite the thousands of conspiracy theories buzzing through the airwaves, no one came any closer to unveiling the truth. All that sustained was that little "what if."

"LIKE *E.T.* BUT WITH GAME SHOWS."

I felt around the cluttered kitchen counter half-heartedly, only to remember that all the napkins were still packed. I settled for the ragged edge of a damp paper towel.

"Can't be." I wiped the pizza grease from my mouth and turned back to the phone. Buy napkins. Add it to the list. "It's never that."

"It has to be. Did you see that one episode of *Doctor Who*? With the black ball? It's just like that."

"Not even close. Didn't they say it's several hundred feet high?"

"The part over the water, yes. And it's *floating*."

"It's not *E.T.*" The paper plate went in the trash, though the gesture felt futile considering the state of the rest of the house. "You didn't enter, did you?"

"No," Hannah sighed, comically bitter. "I just *had* to go and get pregnant now." On the phone's glowing screen, I could see the light changing as she moved around her bathroom, turning sideways to check out her bulging belly in the mirror. "A few more months and I would've been able to."

My feet tangled themselves in a pile of mismatched shoes as I rounded the kitchen island and I just managed to avoid a spectacular faceplant. Put those away—add it to the list. "Why? It's obviously some joke or a game show."

"*Extraterrestrial* game show."

"Let's say it is," I relented. "Would you really want to enter? You don't know what they'll do to you. What the hell are they doing here anyway?"

"Who knows? Isn't that the fun?"

"What if they probe you on TV?"

"Some people like that. Don't judge." Hannah

giggled—a giggle I recognized as the same one that usually preceded a tour of the principal's office way back in the day. "Maybe they're promoting a movie. Remember *Starship Excelsior* with Crish Michaels? They had a lottery for a walk-on role. Maybe it's like that. Are you really not going to enter?"

"Nope." Turning the camera around, I gave her a fetching panorama of the boxes of toiletries, half-open containers with clothes pulled out to hang then left to sit when well-meaning intentions ran out halfway through, and the brand-new refrigerator that so far contained four cans of soda, a bottle of barbeque sauce, and the dregs of an abominable kale smoothie. I had yet to finish the rousing debate with myself on whether to finish the disgusting concoction for health and economic reasons or relent and leave it to its ultimate date with the trash. "I have enough to do. There's no internet and I've been eating the same pizza for two days."

"Mm-hmm." Hannah pursed her lips. "Set up your library, though."

I turned to the only immaculate corner of the house, a small nook with rows of floating shelves now filled neatly with books, alphabetized and organized by size and genre, the result of two sleepless nights right after moving in. Viewed with blinders, it could be right out of *Housekeeping* magazine, if one could ignore the piles of half-unpacked boxes that I had to go through to find each and every book.

"Well, yes."

"Feel like a homeowner yet?"

I thought for a moment. "You know how people always say when your dreams come true it's never like how you imagined?"

"No, but go on."

"It's exactly how I imagined—shit tons of work, everything's dirty, and there's no one to make me dinner." I turned the camera back around and grabbed the glass of whiskey I'd been sipping from next to the Domino's Pizza box. "But I get to stay up as late as I want and no one tells me I can't start drinking at 11 a.m."

"So it's amazing?"

"The best."

"Tell you what," Hannah said, moving out of the bathroom. I saw her sit down in front of a glowing screen. "I'll enter for you."

"God no. I don't want to be involved in that."

"One of us should have some excitement. You don't have any internet anyway, right?"

"Are you serious?"

"Yep."

"No."

"Gonna do it. Love you." She blew a kiss at the screen and hung up. I shook my head and sighed.

The house felt empty without the sound of her voice. Its newness echoed loudly at me. I stepped over two open clear plastic bins—one filled with half-used notebooks and the other with pastel towels I didn't remember buying—and maneuvered myself to my little library, past the living room couch which currently held a dozen wrinkled magazines as well as every pillow I owned, plus a week's worth of work clothes I hadn't managed to wash. Buy washer and dryer—add it to the list. Underneath it all was the comforter I'd been sleeping with, as I had yet to unpack the bedsheets and refused to sleep on a bare mattress—add it to the list. Dad had called earlier to check in. He'd asked if I planned to visit him in Florida, a formality of every one of our sparse conversations. I gave the same answer as the last four years —*when I find the time*. The rest of our conversation was stilted as usual, but he did remind me to wrap the outside pipes—add that to the list, too. Just thinking about it made me want another drink, but I'd just drunk the last of the whiskey. Stop at the liquor store—add that to the list, too. The list was growing fast and at some point I'd have to get started.

But before all that, a break. As I sat down on the floor of my little library, something wedged itself under my thigh. I felt around and came up with a transparent super ball, an old carnival prize from days gone by. A little green alien figure with a bulbous head and pointed eyes smiled and waved from its center. I set the toy down on the edge of the shelf and congratulated myself for putting something away, then ran my hands over my neat, clean books all in a line. Looking at them, I could almost ignore the rest of the chaos around me. I grabbed a book at random, which turned out to be an old geology textbook from college, and turned the pages lazily. I could lose the day with a book in my lap, just perusing facts about sand and sediment and the properties of diamonds, but I had all the time in the world. A few more nights on the couch seemed unimportant.

There was always tomorrow.

CHAPTER 2

PUNCTUAL AND PUT-TOGETHER AS EVER, ADDISON WAS already waiting when I arrived for our usual morning coffee. As I shambled into line behind her at the counter, she gave my wrinkled blouse and uncombed hair a once-over and offered a sympathetic smile.

"All settled in?"

I yawned widely as the barista rang up a pair of extra-shot cappuccinos. Mondays were her turn to pay—good thing, too, seeing how I'd forgotten my wallet in my rush out the door. "Not even close."

A pair of screens glowed from the walls. News anchors droned on about the hot topic of the week, which was the same as last week and the week before. Addison pushed one of the cups to me as we settled at a corner table. I nodded a thanks and grimaced as my tongue burned from the hot drink. Addison toyed with her own cup and kept her eyes on the screens.

"Have you seen the new commercial?"

I took a long, painful gulp. The need for caffeine beat out the searing pain in my mouth. "There's a new one? What is that now? Eight or nine?"

"It's different." She fished her phone out of her purse and with a few quick taps pulled up a video. From what I could make out on the tiny screen, the video centered around the figure in the Edwardian suit. "Came out last night."

The figure walked across the screen, then disappeared and repeated the same walk. I took an embarrassingly long time to realize the video was cycling the same few seconds repeatedly.

"Is that all?"

"It's really short." Addison pushed the phone closer to me. "He just walks around and says one line."

"He?"

"I mean, I guess. The name sounds like a 'he.'"

"What name?"

"They gave him a name. You haven't heard?"

"I haven't cared." My stomach growled. Oversleeping meant no breakfast. I wondered if Addison might lend me a few dollars for a croissant. "What is it?"

"Cheshire."

"Like *Alice in Wonderland*?"

"Because of the face, I guess. Don't know what his name actually is, but that's what it is now." She pulled the phone toward herself and squinted. "Could be a 'she.' But it's a robot or something, right?" She arched a brow at me. "Have you entered?"

I shook my head. "Nope. Did you?"

"Haven't decided. My sister did. She doesn't think she'll win or anything but she thought it might be fun to be on TV. I think this might be the last commercial."

"I couldn't hear it. What does it say?"

"It's just him walking around and saying—"

"*ARE YOU READY?*"

I nearly jumped out of my seat, as did most of the café. Addison gave me a confused look.

"Was that *my* phone?" she asked hesitantly.

"*ARE YOU READY?*"

Louder this time. Addison slowly held up her phone. The voice had indeed come from it, but it wasn't the only one. I heard it, as we all did—the voice had spoken from every phone in the room.

Half a dozen pedestrians outside the storefront window stopped in their tracks to pull out their phones. If I were outside, I was certain I would have heard that voice come out of their phones as well. Every phone in the vicinity had spoken at once, in a single voice. For a long moment none of us could think of the proper reaction, and I hoped irrationationally that no one would ask me about it.

"*I SAID*," the phones barked again in unison, taking on a loud, rolling tone not unlike that of a Spanish soccer commentator, "*ARE. YOU. READYYYYYY?*"

Each word grew louder than the one before. As the final word resonated through the room, the screens on the walls—along with every iPhone, Blackberry, and Android in the place—roared a raucous fanfare that filled the tiny space to its brim. The news program disappeared, replaced by a painfully white screen, and a figure, now familiar to most of the civilized world, oiled into view.

"*HELLO, WORLD!*" they said, their emoji face displaying a broad, openmouthed smile. Polished boots spun on the edgeless white floor as the silver-topped walking stick did its dance in graceful gloved fingers. Then, with a startling "thunk," the stick struck the floor and the figure—Cheshire, if a name

17

must be used—halted in an elegant "A" stance before facing the camera. *"Welcome,"* they purred like a jazz club crooner, *"to Headspace."*

"What the hell is going on?" someone shouted over the noise. The morning commuters had abandoned their cappuccinos and espressos to crowd around the screens, wide-eyed and open-mouthed.

"First things first," Cheshire said—"said" being a term used loosely. Their voice, melodic with a slight mechanical buzz, could easily be piped from elsewhere to match their movements. *"In case you're wondering—yes, we are broadcasting from within the sphere. And no, this is not a hoax, or a joke, or a conspiracy. This is real. The games are about to start. So get comfortable, folks, because this ride is going to be wild."*

Walking stick twirling slick circles in one hand, Cheshire paced in large, almost comical steps from one side of the screen to the other. *"Let's start with the basics, shall we? The name of the game is Headspace, and the rules are simple—enter the arena; use your head. It's unfair, you see, that we should all be born with different bodies. We can't all be athletes or superstars, and that isn't fair, is it? But we're all born with heads."* They raised a hand as if to tap their nonexistent noggin, then gave a mechanical, unsettling chuckle. *"Well, almost all of us. And in our heads, we are equal. In our heads, we can fly and scheme and invent and do all the things everyone else can in* their *heads. And in this game, your head is all you will need. No hands? No problem! Two left feet? Who cares! Coordination of a three-legged donkey in heat? Not an issue! All you need is your head, and your chances are as good as anyone else's."*

I tore my eyes away from the screen and looked around the café, hoping to catch someone's amused chortle or shrug, but not a single pair of eyes met mine. Addison's cup teetered on the very edge of the table. I grabbed it before it fell into a sopping mess in her lap.

"Some of you may be asking, is it too late to enter the game, now that we've started? The answer is a resounding NO!" The walls vibrated with the impact of the last word. *"You have until the end of the trial rounds to enter the contest, so keep those entries coming. What are the trial rounds? We'll get to that in a second. First, let's welcome the first batch of contestants to the arena."*

Slender fingers snapped crisply and the white landscape began to change. Flawless black appeared behind them, splitting the white horizon and pixelating across the floor. Seconds later Cheshire's polished boots presided over a velvet-black grounding. Then, from above, came the lights. They were difficult to see at first, thin and bright like hanging threads from heaven. But as they increased in number, their presence became hard to miss. As they struck the ground, each one began to pulse back and forth in rapid succession, like the heads of laser printers. But what they printed were not blocked letters or tiny wax figures. The lights printed people.

In the moment of quiet during this spectacle, I heard the room around me begin to bustle. Everyone shook themselves as if waking up from a fog. I heard fingers tap on laptops keyboards and phones being whipped out—Cheshire's voice emitting from them did not appear to impede the devices' normal function. Someone muttered that the same video was being broadcast all over the world, in dozens of languages. Another asked aloud if we ought to turn it off, but no one answered. The café suddenly felt small and claustrophobic as voices, pointing fingers, and wafting body odors assaulted me from all directions. Addison stared at the screen with her mouth slightly open. I nudged her arm.

"Let's get out of here. We're late for work."

She raised a hand and pointed to the edge of the screen. Several of the contestants had already been printed in full. Eyes wide and faces blanked by confusion, they turned this way and that, trying to make sense of the strange space around them.

"Addy?"

"That's my sister."

NO TWO FACES WERE ALIKE, though they all wore the same perplexed expression. I saw a woman with a half-shaved hairdo, an older man in a suit who looked like he just stepped of a metro subway, a matronly lady with lines on her face and a name tag that read "Beth," an androgynous youth dressed like a barista, a dark-skinned man with tribal markings, a woman sporting an elegant updo and a mermaid-style wedding dress . . . and among them, a young woman barely out of her teens in a jean jacket and black tights, wide eyes peeking out from beneath a long braided weave.

"Right there," Addison said urgently. "That's Maddy. That's my sister!"

"They didn't seriously just teleport them in?" someone behind me said at the same time.

Before I could decide which piece of absurdity to focus on, Cheshire moved again. The new arrivals—contestants, I assumed—had begun to find their footing. They gave Cheshire a wide berth, splitting their ranks like the Red Sea parting. I hadn't given much consideration to Cheshire's size before, but now, surrounded by people, I saw that they stood head and shoulders above the others, easily surpassing seven feet. The wary group gazed up at the smiling digital face apprehensively.

"*Welcome, contestants,*" said Cheshire. A few nervous smiles crept in here and there. "*The one hundred of you have been selected from a pool of millions to participate in the very first round of Headspace. Give yourselves a hand!*" Tucking the walking stick under their arm, Cheshire raised their gloved hands and resolutely began to clap. A moment later others joined in, and soon there were cheers and whistles all around the arena. The group in the café also began to murmur in excitement. Cheshire raised a hand, and the contestants fell quiet.

"*Allow me to explain a few things.*" They swept one long, skinny arm toward the horizon, where white met black. The contestants hung onto every word and motion. As did, I assumed, the rest of the world. "*The name of the game is Headspace, and the purpose of the game is fun. This is going to be the most fun you ever have.*" The emoji face winked and the majority of the contestants hooted in excitement. Maddy, barely visible on the edge of the camera, did not. Like Addison, she seemed to be trying to make up her mind about the situation. "*We will be broadcasting once a week for the trial rounds. Once the trial rounds conclude, we will be making some scheduling changes.*

"*You are probably wondering what the trial rounds are. They are, shall we say, practice, for all of you to get a grip on how the game works. A challenge will be presented, and those who cannot complete it will be eliminated. The early rounds may be difficult. You folks here today will be the pioneers, so set a good example for the kiddos at home. As contestants are eliminated, new ones will be selected to fill the slots for the next round. So, as I said before, keep those entries coming. Once we have one or more contestants survive a trial round, the real games will begin.*"

Addison drummed her fingers on the table. The novelty of the whole thing was already wearing off for me. Cheshire strolled among the contestants, who grew less worried and more excited with each passing moment.

"*In the game, every challenge will be a little different. You'll be given instructions for every round. Just do your best, use your heads, and you'll be just fine. You'll laugh. You'll cry. There will be drama and comedy and intrigue. It'll be a jolly good time!*"

"What do we win?" someone shouted. Laughter

rippled through the crowd, coupled with expectant gazes.

"*Excellent question, contestant,*" Cheshire replied cheerily. "*After we conclude the trial rounds, scoring will begin. In order to win the game, a contestant must score a minimum of one hundred points as well as be the last contestant standing after the final elimination round. Points are awarded based on the criteria for each round, such as targets eliminated, time taken to reach the goal, and so on. Bonus points may be awarded for style, so don't be afraid to throw a little flair into your performance during the competition. The winner has much to claim. Fame! Fortune! Power!*"—a wink—"*Immortality!*"

The contestants chuckled in good humor. The crowd in the café did the same. Cheshire scanned the group and singled out the woman in the wedding dress.

"*You look a bit preoccupied.*"

The woman blushed. Her meticulous updo had started to droop in the commotion. "It's just . . ." she began. "It's my wedding day."

"*Don't worry your pretty head about it. Win the game, and you'll have the wedding of the century.*"

She smiled shyly among cheers and hoots. Cheshire continued their unhurried stroll.

"*The losers, well, the losers lose. If the winner of the final elimination is unable to amass a hundred points, everyone loses. Well, except for the winner. The winner gets to watch while we blow it up.*"

An awkward silence fell. The bride's smile froze on her face, as if time suddenly stopped. The flickering emoji face scanned the crowd. Then, they touched the tips of their long fingers together and pulled them apart with a snapping motion.

"*That's right. We blow up the planet. Boom!*"

Silence. On the screen, contestants were smiling, nervous and expectant, waiting for the punchline. Someone behind me asked, "What'd he say?"

"*If no one wins, we also blow up the planet. Boom!*"

The emoji face turned to the camera and for the first time, showed an unsmiling expression. The mouth blinked off for a moment then returned as a flat line. A blank, serious expression.

"*Little message for the folks at home,*" they said, the game show-host voice suddenly gone. That buzzy, melodic voice turned a shade darker as they addressed the other side of the screen. "*We're familiar with your knee-jerk responses. It would be unwise to interrupt the game, especially with aggressive means. Sure, you might think, sacrifice a hundred to save the billions, but it takes a lot of, shall we say,* energy to split *a planet, and to save the trouble of multiple trips, we've packed it all with us.*" One gloved hand pointed to the floor beneath their feet. Several contestants yelped in terror and actually hopped as if playing an impromptu game of the-floor-is-lava. The excited smiles and cheers were replaced by frightened cries and angry shouts. Cheshire dipped their head and stared down at a man who was angrily shouting in their direction. Their mouth blinked off and returned as a curved smile once more.

"*Why?*" they said, amused. "*Well, contestant, I'm afraid I can't answer that at this time. You see, answers are a winner's privilege. We've got to keep some suspense to make things interesting, don't we?*"

The silence lasted longer this time. In truth, it was probably no more than a second, but the air thickened with millions of unspoken thoughts. Then, Cheshire clapped their hands together, and the sound jolted the human race collectively out of their momentary trance.

"*Now then, let's get started, shall we? No time like the present. Round One—*" A crisp finger snap.

Was no one going to say "gotcha"?

"*Rat Maze.*"

Walls exploded out of the black floor. White, flawless enclosures towered over the contestants, neatly segmenting the space between them. Shouts of surprises and fear rose from the narrow halls where they now stood, alone or two to three together. Cheshire stood atop the endless white maze, balancing effortlessly on surfaces no wider than the bottom of their boot, peering down at the panicking people. The smile never left their face.

"*The rules are simple.*"

The camera panned over the maze, an aerial view of fearful faces and searching eyes.

"*Keep moving and watch out for the marbles.*"

Marbles. A deceptively harmless word.

"*Time limit is one hour.*"

Enormous red letters appeared on the white ceiling, reminiscent of old digital clocks.

1:00:00

"*Survive, and you will proceed to the next round and make your people proud.*"

"This is a joke." Someone said this, though no one believed it.

"*Ready?*"

"No." Voices rose. Panic. Confusion.

"*Set.*"

"Oh god."

"*Go!*"

The first one crushed the bride—one moment

anxious and radiant, the next a puddle of blood and lace.

SURVIVE.

Addison was on her feet, pushing through the crowd to get closer to the screen, shaking, fingers held up awkwardly in front of her as if she didn't know what to do with them.

"Maddy," she kept saying. "Oh god, Maddy."

Cheshire had used that word. It clanked around in my head like a forgotten penny in an empty jar. *Survive*, in its rawest form, as an alternative to death.

Red stood out starkly against white. Streaks and splatters painted the floors and walls into a macabre art exhibition. Cameras zoomed from one terrified face to another. Who was working them? Who was calmly pointing their lenses at wet eyes and panicked sweat and necks craning to see how far behind inevitable doom was?

Five minutes passed. I made a valiant effort to retreat into denial, until the cameras treated us to an intimate close-up of a man rolled out like so much pancake batter after slipping on whatever was left of the person who came before him. The number of contestants had been reduced by half.

The metal "marbles" were the size of minibuses, rust colored and sporting single, searching red mechanical eyes that zeroed in on any sign of movement within sight. I counted four, though there might have been more, rolling their way through the maze with expert precision, crushing every contestant in their path with the smoothness of steamrollers plowing over pudding. Several people had already turned away from the screen, horrified eyes buried in their hands, but most couldn't tear their gaze away from the horror show.

Addison wasn't blinking. She looked like she was trying to resist clawing her way into the screen. Her teeth ground audibly. Only five left now. Less than fifteen minutes had passed. Her sister, the surprisingly sprightly Maddy, was still sprinting through the maze, chest pumping rapidly as she struggled to catch her breath. Exhaustion and fear had begun to weigh down her body and drag her feet. One of her legs was moving a hair slower than the other—her ankle might have turned but she couldn't allow herself the luxury of resting.

Another one went down. Only four left now.

The camera followed Maddy. She glanced through the screen briefly, sweat dripping from her face. We all ran with her, staring at unnerving, endless white walls that went on forever, trying not to drown in the scent of the blood that drenched the walls and floors. She sobbed, and held one hand over her mouth to hold in her breakfast as she passed one bloody pond after another.

One of the marbles crossed her path and stopped. The red eye rotated to face her. Addison drew a sharp breath.

"No."

It came for her with purposeful speed. Maddy spun around and took off in the opposite direction as fast as her legs could carry her.

"*Run, Maddy! Run!*"

She was fast, but many of them were.

"*Run!*"

She went under. No screams, just like the bride. The camera zoomed in just as the last of her disappeared underneath the smooth metal surface, catching a split-second glimpse of her sparkling brown eyes popping out of their sockets like a rubber squeeze toy.

Then there were three. Then two. Then one.

Then silence.

Then, like some demented joke, two words appeared across the screen in cheery yellow letters followed by a sad-faced emoji.

GAME OVER

The walls disappeared back into the floor. The metal marbles rose back toward the ceiling and out of view. Cheshire reappeared on screen, taking careful steps to avoid the remnants of the massacre. The emoji face had changed to an amused expression, a flat mouth with a mischievous curve at one end.

"*Well*," they said. "*How disappointing. I hope nobody placed any solid bets on those folks. Nobody used their heads, it seems.*" A shrug, facing the camera. "*Shame, shame. But the first round's usually a bit rough. I hope you folks get the hang of the game soon.*" A pause, a glance away, then back.

"*I might have neglected to mention,*" they continued, slow and thoughtful, leaning on the walking stick casually as if having a leisurely afternoon stroll and chat, "*that the producers of Headspace have a finite amount of patience. You see, a planet full of losers is a boring planet, and a boring planet is a useless planet. You folks get five trial rounds to prove you're worthy entertainment. If you can't produce at least one survivor at the end of the five rounds . . .*" They lifted one hand, fingers tented together at the tip, then spread them dramatically. "*Boom.*"

The screens turned off. Every device in the room fell silent. No one spoke. Then, slowly, Addison turned away from the screen, eyes wide and dazed. She managed a single stumbling step before her knees gave out. On the floor on all fours, she felt around as if blind, then, following a hideous retch, vomited.

CHAPTER 3

THE REST OF THE DAY WAS A BLUR. SAME FOR THE DAY after. For the dozen or so days that followed, much of the world churned on a combination of despair and pure denial. This time would come to be known as the Near End of Days, a haze of noise and fear. News advisories warned of riots and looting and chaos in the streets of major cities. Panicked citizens were demanding that government officials act on the "alien threat" immediately, though what that entailed was anyone's guess. Governments, officials, celebrities, and anyone with an opinion and a voice sounded off, loudly and publicly. The airwaves were filled with feuding voices, but as time ticked by, no one seemed any closer to figuring out an answer to the real question.

How is the game won?

A few facts came to light quickly. They were these:

- The broadcast was received worldwide, with the languages used varying by region.
- Post hoc analysis revealed that the contestants in the arena spoke different languages even though Cheshire addressed several of them directly; the theory was that Cheshire's voice was superimposed on the video based on region, and they spoke different languages to each contestant. However, as there were no survivors, this could not be confirmed.
- The contestant list was posted on the Headspace website five minutes prior to the start of the game. Due to the short notice, it went largely unnoticed. The list contained only full names, age, and an image of each contestant, most of which appeared to be headshots pulled from driver's licenses, passports, and various social media databases.

- The list now showed each contestant's photo with a red "X" over it.
- All contestants were awarded zero points.
- External scans revealed nothing about the orb. Whether it did indeed contain enough explosives to split the planet could not be confirmed.
- An entry point to the orb also could not be found. Planes and submarines were equally unsuccessful.
- Family and friends of the contestants told identical stories of "teleportation." One moment they were there; the next they were not. There was no fanfare, no flashes of light, nor any further dramatics.
- No communication with the orb could be established.

Dad called. He had little to say. Sounding weary and sweaty, he managed to ask how I was, then reminded me, again, to wrap my pipes, mumbled about troubles in the cities, and hung up.

Work called. The office was closed for the remainder of the week.

Hannah called. I didn't answer. She left several messages that I didn't listen to. She probably thought I was angry with her, which wouldn't be too far from the truth. She sent text messages, consumed with guilt, but guilt wasn't going to absolve me from the hellish lottery. I didn't want to hear her apologies, but anger was not the main reason—the thought of talking about it was simply too much. There would be time to talk, I told myself, when this all blew over.

For several days I couldn't bring myself to do much of anything as the world outside plunged into turmoil. If it weren't for the fact that every media outlet was clamoring about the orb, I'd kill time watching TV or surfing the net, but instead, when I got tired of Netflix, I unpacked. Opening boxes and sorting through clothes and books managed to keep me from sinking into a panicked restlessness. I dusted off end tables and folded sheets and told myself that my chances were one in millions, smaller than being struck by lightning. Something would change before then. This was a belief I always held —something would change before it affected me. As an unknown and unremarkable person, surely I would never experience my own world change.

Four trial rounds remained.

. . .

THEN THREE.

ADDISON RETURNED to work an ashen husk of herself two weeks after the grisly first round. When offered a smile, she looked back blankly, as if having forgotten how to mimic the expression. She spent much of her time sitting at her desk, eyes fixated on nothing in particular, as if the sight of her sister's eyeballs escaping their sockets played before her again and again, rewinding and fast-forwarding like an old VHS. When the broadcasts came through, blasting Cheshire's voice through every phone, computer, and anything with a speaker on it through the building, she stood up quietly, went to the bathroom, and dropped her phone into the toilet.

The death toll after round three was three hundred—one hundred per round. By this point most of the population had decided on how to spend their last days on Earth. Some chose to give in to their baser instincts and indulged in the things they'd spent their lives deprived of for one reason or another—drink, food, sex, drugs. The entrepreneurial types had begun to cash in with "End Days Club" operations that provided these vices for exorbitant prices, making a mint just in case the world didn't end after five weeks. Rumors spread of macabre "viewing parties" where the rich and powerful placed bets on how long each contestant would last. An ex-boyfriend from college called offering an "end of the world" booty call, but gave up after I listed out places he could shove it in alphabetical order.

"DISAPPOINTING," Cheshire quipped, stepping over yet another puddle of blood, mouth curved downward mockingly. Round four had just concluded. "So disappointing."

HANNAH STILL TEXTED to apologize every day or two. I texted back once, "It's OK."

THE POWERS that ran the world met in secret often. Rumor had it there was a finger hovering over the nuke button, ready to drop at the same time as the final contestant. Days etched by, clawing ever closer to what felt like certain doom. I couldn't lose track of time if I wanted to. Every day that passed was one more day since the last broadcast, and one more day until the next. Every person on the street, at bus stops, in grocery stores carried a black cloud.

FLIPPING through the old geology book, I tried hard to pretend I wasn't watching the clock. The morning was clear and cool, but a bleak quiet hung over the world. I called in to work, though it was a formality. No one went to work. Every pair of eyes was glued to a screen, waiting.

Anticipating the end of the world was a funny feeling. It was almost an itch, a phantom pain on the body, the sort elicited by the sight of a needle approaching the skin or videos of dental surgery. The urge to scratch was there, though there was nothing to scratch. Three invites to "doomsday parties" had come to my mailbox, but I wasn't sure I wanted to spend my possibly last day on Earth mired in drunken chatter. My television and computer were both unplugged and I'd intentionally let the tablet run out of battery.

Hannah texted. I hadn't decided whether to text back. Not talking about it kept it from being real. The world spiraled rapidly downward and I was in my own little world. Instead of unpacking, I idled in my library. Despite the number of boxes I'd opened, I hadn't organized much. After all, if the world were to end, a few boxes of old magazines hardly mattered. But at the moment, this little house with its little library felt like my entire existence.

Hannah called.

What time is it?

I refused to check—I'd know when Cheshire's voice started blaring through my phone. My plan was to throw it out the window when it did. When this round was over, I would talk to Hannah.

I flipped through the geology book, nonchalantly glancing at sediment charts and stone properties and pointedly ignoring the noises from my phone. The news alerts must be coming through, as they did every time a broadcast drew near. Folks in the Eastern Hemisphere were surely staying up late tonight. Sleeping was for the dead.

Hannah called again.

Then the text messages began. Not just from her, but from everyone.

Are you OK? —Hannah

Oh my god. Are you alright? Did you see? —Addison

Hang in there. We're pulling for you. —Nicholas

I'm sorry. —Hannah

Don't be scared. —Dad

Just saw. You OK? —Cooper

Don't worry. You got this. —unknown number. Who even was this?

Good luck —Cousin Jen, whom I hadn't spoken to in years

I'm so sorry —Hannah

Praying for you —Aunt Gloria, who at last Thanksgiving said I would find a husband a lot faster if I spent more time "touching up" and less time sharing "mimis."

Oh god I'm so sorry —Hannah

I had just enough time to read and wonder about these texts before the phone shouted in my face.

"*ARE. YOU. READYYYYY?*"

Then, black.

MY EYES SAW white and for a dizzying moment my extremities couldn't locate the rest of me. A long second passed before I was able to look down at the ground beneath me, so dark it swallowed the light itself. The white dome above was infinite and endless. My right hand was still curled, holding the air where my phone no longer was. I was barefoot, still in the oversized T-shirt and pajama pants I hadn't bothered to change out of this morning. I quickly crossed my arms to conceal the fact that I wasn't wearing a bra. Suddenly, I was very grateful that I hadn't slept in less.

Disoriented, I bumped into a warm body and mumbled an apology, then quickly realized the person I bumped into wasn't paying attention. He was in his fifties, wearing a dark sweater, running pants, sneakers, and a face wrinkled with tears.

"I'm never gonna see her again," he sobbed, face buried in his hands. "It was the last time. I'm not ready for this."

"Fuck!"

I jumped, my feet nearly losing their grip on the slippery floor. Another man, this one quite a bit younger, was standing a few feet away in flannel, old worn jeans, and work boots.

"I had it in my hand and it's not fucking here!"

"You think you're the first person to try bringing a gun in here?" someone else was saying. Other people were stepping into my view and I couldn't tell who spoke. "They don't let you bring anything in here. Don't you read the news? Whatever you're holding gets left behind!"

A weapon. I hadn't thought of that. Would I have

thought of that if I knew this was happening? I would've at least worn shoes. Someone else bumped into me and nearly knocked me over. I pushed my way through the crying, shouting, babbling, ranting crowd and managed to get out of everyone's way. Very few people were conversing, though many were praying in a variety of languages I couldn't identify.

Though I understood them.

Syllables and phrases assaulted my ears from all directions. French, Japanese, Spanish, Hindi . . . I couldn't distinguish one word from another and yet I understood them. Each person spoke with two voices, yet both were their own, as if they were performing their own voice-overs in a foreign film. The sensation was disorienting.

An old woman was on her knees, weeping. Her lips formed words in what might be Greek but I heard the second voice in English. She was saying goodbye to her children and grandchildren. She had a grandbaby barely a week old. What kind of world would she grow up in, and without grandma? She prayed for her family, for the new baby. She hoped that if she were to die today, at least someone else would win. My heart sank with a heaviness that was nearly audible at the thought of the baby that Hannah had yet to hold in her arms.

A hand grabbed my arm. I started and turned to face a dark-skinned woman in her late thirties. She made a series of gestures with her hands, staring at me intently.

"Can you sign?" she asked, practically shouting, pointing at her ears as she spoke. I winced and shook my head. "Shit," she exclaimed, and moved onto the next person. Each person she approached shrugged her off in fear and annoyance, but she persisted.

"HELLO CONTESTANTS!"

My bones rattled. I didn't see where Cheshire appeared from, but suddenly they were there. Those nearest to them jumped out of the way in fright. The emoji face, smiling as always, surveyed us. Up close, their inhumanity was more obvious than ever. Their body was much too thin, little more than a wire frame with a suit draped over it. Long fingers and joints moved with an oily sway as if held together with ball bearings. Their walk was a smooth, agile one, but one that was wrong, as if someone who didn't quite know how humans walked tried to program a machine to mimic the motion. Shiny boots and walking cane clinked against the floor as the dotted eyes surveyed us. In person, their height was intimidating.

"*Well, well, well. Lucky number five, eh?*" they teased, threading their slender body between the nervous contestants. I was suddenly very aware of my bare feet against the cold floor. "*How are we all feeling today? Spry?*"

I heard their voice in two languages—the only two languages I knew fluently—though a few words fell off here and there in each. Whatever this place was, it seemed to take away just enough of the language barriers. Cheshire glided past me and I shivered.

"*I hope you're all ready to play*," they said, cheery as ever. "*But I must say, there have been a lot of disappointments. The producers aren't terribly pleased with you folks. If you don't tighten it up, we might have to—*"

They stopped mid sentence. The smiling mouth changed to a flat line. The deaf woman was waving to them. She gestured at her ear as Cheshire regarded her.

"I can't hear," she called to them. "Can't hear you."

"*Ugh,*" Cheshire grumbled, shaking their nonexistent head. "*What a pain. This is why I keep telling them to get more specific with the entry forms.*" They raised their hands and clapped the palms together twice. "*Eleven! Come handle this!*"

There was a worried mutter through the crowd, then I heard a few surprised gasps. Several people scrambled out of the way as a second robotic figure cut through the crowd. This one was smaller than Cheshire, only about half a head taller than the tallest human contestant, and built like a soldier out of cyberpunk films, covered in dull, chinked armored plates that followed the subtle curves of their body. Compared to the flamboyant Cheshire, they were much more subdued in design and seemed built for function. Their face, sleek and expressionless, turned up to Cheshire, who pointed to the deaf woman with distaste.

The crowd backed away with apprehension as this newcomer—Eleven—stepped in front of her. The woman looked up and ran her hard black eyes over the alien armor, and for an unnerving moment I thought she was going to be executed before the game even began for her disability. Watching the massacre on a screen was one thing, but I wasn't sure I could handle the sight of someone being killed in front of me.

Then, Eleven raised their hands and began to sign. The contestant watched for a moment, then nodded.

"*There*," Cheshire said, sounding irritated at the

interruption. Eleven signed to the contestant as Cheshire spoke. "*As I was saying, we need quality entertainment. Entertainment you people haven't managed to deliver so far. This is your last chance. So get loose, shape up, and remember, use your heads!*"

Eleven signed as Cheshire spoke. The deaf woman watched intently. Something was off, though I couldn't put my finger on it. I squinted to get a closer look, and a white wall shot up right in front of my face, nearly shearing my nose off. I stumbled backwards and my back struck a second wall. The space was narrow, claustrophobic, and I was suddenly very aware that I could no longer see any of the other contestants. I looked up and there was nothing but white sky and towering white walls. Blood drummed in my ears.

I'm going to die.

A marble boomed into the middle of the maze. I didn't see it, though I felt the floor tremble from its impact. The first tremor was followed by three more, and the game was on.

TIME LOST ALL MEANING. All I saw were white corners and white walls, and every once in a while a dark round shape whizzing past. Screams of fear and pain attacked me from every direction but I couldn't pinpoint where they came from. Then there was the rumbling, the movement of the rust-colored metal marbles, always on the other side of the wall, always just one wrong turn away.

My lungs struggled to inflate themselves and my heart pumped like a rusty machine, thudding away noisily as I rounded yet another glaring white corner, just in time to see a head of blond hair disappear between the black floor and the barreling sphere. The single red eye turned and I threw myself out of its sight line just in time, not daring to scream or look down as I stepped in a slippery puddle of metallic-smelling substance. Something jabbed my bare heel and I bit the inside of my cheek to keep from crying out as the marble rumbled past me, mere inches away, and disappeared down another hall. I allowed myself just enough time to pull the bloody tooth from my foot.

Nearly every path I turned down was a nightmare of blood and gore. I was soaked up to my knees and my fingers were stained with red after carelessly leaning on the nearest wall. I'd stepped in things I could go my entire life without looking at. Tears or sweat or both were sliding down my face, and I didn't dare wipe them away with my blood-streaked hands.

The ominous red timer overhead counted down steadily. Less than seven minutes had passed. Frankly, I was surprised I'd lasted as long as that. More sounds to my left. Wet, squelching sounds. Crunching sounds. Sounds that were almost inhuman, then cut off short.

Would my eyeballs pop out of my head as the metal marbles rolled over me, like Maddy's did? Was Dad watching, wishing we'd gotten closer before I fell to this gruesome and embarrassing fate? In between running for my life and praying death wouldn't hurt too much, I found a sliver of a second to be grateful that if the world ended today, at least there would be no one left to remember me sweating and crying, stumbling through a rat maze with pajamas pasted to my skin with someone else's blood.

The amount of screaming around me had gone down. Fewer mouths were left to scream and the ones remaining—assuming any were remaining— were hiding. The marbles patrolled nearby. The floor carried the vibrations from their weight.

Ten minutes had passed.

I willed myself to breathe quietly, to move

nimbly, and not to look at the soft masses of red and pink all around me. Whether they could hear me was uncertain, but it was also not something I wanted to test. Cowering with my back against one of the few scraps of clean wall left, I tried to catch my breath when a movement above caught my eye. At first I thought it was Cheshire, but the figure was crouching.

A sharp crack rang through the air, like the snap of a massive whip. My skeleton made a momentary effort to leap out of its skin sack. Lifting my gaze upward, I saw the figure dart away and quickly followed it. Perhaps catching my movement, it stopped and turned toward me.

It was the deaf woman. Our eyes locked for a moment and she turned away, looking over her shoulder. Then, turning back toward me, she raised a finger to her lips, gesturing for me to keep quiet before disappearing again. Another thunderous crack rang through the air. I heard her shuffle atop the wall, hopping nimbly from one wall to another. I had no idea how she managed to scale the slippery, ten-foot wall in the first place. Was there a ladder somewhere I'd missed? Or a trick to the walls I didn't notice? I thought about this—a grave mistake, as it turned out, as the hundred-ton metal marble bore down on me in the single second I took my eyes off it.

Half an hour ago I was home, flipping through a geology book, reading about the properties of diamonds.

It came at me. I couldn't run. My legs quivered and bent.

Life was funny like that.

It moved in slow motion. I saw the red eye roll to the top of the marble, then down toward me as it came.

BOOM.

I curled up into myself.

BOOM.

The world was shaking and I didn't dare look up.

BOOM.

Was I still alive?

BOOM.

BOOM.

BOOM.

Time passed, though I didn't know how much.

I raised my head. My limbs creaked like old machines trying to rumble to life through layers of rust and dust after a long slumber. Leaden feet pushed against the black floor. My body, heavy and lumbering, unfolded itself with effort. Silence had fallen.

I took a step but went nowhere. My feet were stuck in place. I tugged and they came loose abruptly. I stumbled forward and a red-stained floor rushed toward me. I braced myself, but the impact never came. A strong arm had caught me across the chest. The surreal two-toned space was spinning.

"Thanks," I muttered. Further words caught in my throat when I noticed the mechanical arm that had caught me. I looked up into the expressionless face of Eleven looming over me. A gasp escaped and I pushed them away, only to slip backwards and nearly fall again. Eleven reached forward and steadied me with steel fingers that burned hot. I cried out as my bicep sizzled in their grip.

"Let go; you're hurting her," a voice said from behind. The vice grip released, leaving red welts on my skin. I started to turn around but a gentle hand laid across my shoulders. "Don't look. It's not pretty."

I looked into hard, tired brown eyes. Eyes that watched my lips.

"You're okay," the deaf woman said. She spoke English with a heavy accent I couldn't pinpoint. She pointed to her ears. "Enunciate if you can. Hearing aids didn't make it. Also—lipreading, not great."

"Okay," I said shakily.

She walked me past Eleven. An unnerving tremble coursed through my body. Everything shook. My bones were brittle. Every nerve and tendon in my body tightened like an overstrung harp.

"*Well, well, well!*"

The slender form stepped into our path and the flickering emoji face dipped down uncomfortably close before us. The hand around my shoulder tightened protectively.

"*Finally, some true contenders,*" Cheshire mused, studying us and sounding truly pleased. "*Just in time, too. Here I thought we were going to have to pack up the gear and give up on this place.*" They circled us. Something buzzed around them, tiny and mechanical and chirping softly. Cameras. They couldn't be seen during broadcast, but now that the chaos had died down and the walls cleared, I saw that they were everywhere, no bigger than fruit flies, zooming from one spot to another like hummingbirds.

"Get away," said the hard-eyed woman. I heard two languages. She had switched back to her native language, and the arena was translating in my ears. "We've had enough of you."

"*Ooh, feisty,*" Cheshire cooed. They shoved their dotted eyes into our faces. I cowered and looked away, but the woman did not back away. "*You have potential,*" they said, one finger curved and tapping their nonexistent chin thoughtfully. "*Alexis Monroe, age 37. Hailing from Scotland. Figured out the game just in the nick of time, did you? Very impressive. I have high hopes for you. But* you." They turned to me. "*That was an interesting move. Unusual, but interesting. Donna Ching, from the United States of America. The producers were very amused. Props to you, too.*"

What did I do? I had no idea.

Cheshire pulled away and turned toward the nearest camera. "*There you have it, folks!*" they announced, turning the game show-host voice up to max, booming through the thick silence like a ramrod. "*You've got two new champions. Now things will really get interesting. Will the champions' reign last, or will they tap out by their second round? Make sure you tune in soon to Headspace!*"

They paused, then looked back to us.

"*And we're out,*" they said, and clapped their hands together a few times, almost sarcastically. The arena was filled to the brim with a sickeningly sweet, warm metallic smell. My stomach brought itself almost all the way up and out, then snapped back like a rubber band. "*To tell you the truth, I was starting to worry this was going to be one really boring season. But hey, you gals pulled it together. You got potential after all. Fair warning, now that you know how to play the game, it's only going to get harder.*"

"What the hell does that mean?" snapped Alexis Monroe as Eleven finished translating in sign, not a hint of fear in her voice. "What is all this shit for? You better start answering some questions or—"

"*Oh! Too bad,*" Cheshire said, interrupting her. "*Answers are for winners, which you are not yet. But hey, keep playing and you may get there. Till then, see you next time!*"

The world turned black.

MY PHONE BUZZED. I was convinced for a moment that I was lying in darkness, until I realized my eyes were still closed. My neck craned awkwardly against a stack of dusty cardboard boxes and a hard corner of something dug into my back. Groaning, I bent my arm behind my back, wincing as every joint creaked its protest, pulled a hardback book out from underneath my torso, and dropped it unceremoniously on the floor.

Water. I need water.

The phone buzzed again. I willed my arms to lift my shoulders off the ground. The welts Eleven had left on my arm were still there and looking rather red and angry. A wave of nausea overtook me as my head gained altitude. Calls came through. Every person I knew was calling, but I couldn't bring myself to answer. My tongue was sandpaper and I had no clue what time of day it was.

I coughed, which turned into a gag. My body begged to crawl into bed and sleep for a week.

Water.

I stumbled into the kitchen, turned the faucet to full blast, and drank directly from the spray, soaking my bloodstained clothing. The water was lukewarm and tasteless, but it did the job. Satiated, I picked up the phone and rejected the latest call. There was something I had to know first. I opened the web browser, typed in the address, and scrolled past the face of the old praying woman, now marked with a red X. I thought for a moment that she must be happy to know her grandbaby would live, then remembered that she was now a puddle on the arena floor. Resolutely, I moved on until I reached the first face not crossed out. Alexis Monroe looked back at me from a mildly blurry headshot that might have been a passport photo. I studied her smooth, maple-colored skin and short, dark hair. In the photo, she was smiling tightly and confidently.

46. Alexis Mae Monroe. Point total: 20

I scrolled a few dozen names down.

79. Donna Astra Ching. Point total: 5

Five points. I didn't know what to think about that. I had survived the game, though I could not for the life of me remember how. I rubbed my face hard. I should call someone. I should call Hannah. I should call Dad. I should call into work and see if I should come in tomorrow, now that there was going to be a tomorrow.

An urgent pounding thumped through my head and I winced. I shook my head and it came again. Someone was knocking on my door. I groaned. Opening the door to strangers might not be the best idea, but good judgement was far in the back of my mind and I just wanted the pounding to stop.

I pulled open the door a little too hard. The chain holding it to the frame held taut and I nearly lost my grip on the handle. Sunlight stunned my eyes. Through the gap and the dots slowly easing themselves out of my vision, I saw two men in what looked like police uniforms.

"Donna Ching?"

I nodded. The motion made me dizzy. "Yes. That's me."

"Please come with us."

CHAPTER 4

THE TWO POLICEMEN, A BLOND YOUTH AND AN OLDER man sporting a pot belly and a generous collection of wrinkles around his eyes, lingered awkwardly outside my bedroom door as if afraid I might go out the window—though I had neither a place to go nor the strength to open a window. They whispered uneasily to each other. For all I knew, they were judging the disastrous state of my house. It wasn't until the young one eyed my legs pointedly that I remembered I was still half-covered in blood. I wanted to take a shower, but they insisted that time was in short order and I had to hurry, so I was only allowed time to wipe off and change clothes. As my shaky hands failed again to button up the jeans I struggled into, I considered the possibility that I'd just allowed dangerous strangers masquerading as police into my house. But with the past hour still fresh on my mind, strangers seemed the least of my worries.

The bloody clothes I shoved into a bag in the corner for lack of a better way to deal with them. My right arm stung where Eleven's hand had left a multitude of angry red welts. I couldn't find any ointment so I made do with running cold water over them. I was allowed to grab my purse, phone, and keys while the two men fidgeted, tapped their feet, and cast paranoid glances outside. At the door, I considered once again that maybe this was a bad idea, but their hands on my arms, just a hair tighter than they needed to be, told me it didn't matter. Once I was ushered outside into the black police cruiser, they both relaxed visibly. I sat in the back, blankly counting the holes in the steel mesh dividing me and them. Just as we pulled around the block, several vans and cars sped by in the opposite direction.

"Reporters," the older man spat. "Fucking piranhas."

We kept driving.

For what felt like an eternity, no one said anything, though I caught the two men sneaking curious glances at me. Their gaze made me want to rummage through my innards.

"Excuse me."

The young officer turned around. He had soft eyes but I could tell he was wary. "Yes?"

"Where are you taking me?"

He shook his head with genuine regret. "Sorry, ma'am. Can't tell you. We're just following orders. All I can say is, we're taking you someplace safe." He glanced at the purse laying at my side. "Please don't text or make any calls. Meant to tell you that earlier. The world is a dangerous place right now. Can't take any risks."

"Risks of what?"

He chewed his lip for a moment. "Listen," he said, slowly as if searching for the right words, "I know you're probably shook up, after—"

His partner clicked his tongue loudly. The young officer paused. "They said don't talk to her," I heard the older man hiss. "You wanna get us in trouble?"

The young officer looked to his partner, then gave me a shrug that said the conversation was over. I watched the busy streets reel by and marveled at how nothing looked different. In my exhaustion, I could almost convince myself it was all a hallucination if not for the dried blood still under my fingernails.

The cruiser merged onto the freeway. I pressed my head against the cold glass window and slept.

I JERKED out of a fitful doze filled with white walls and red blood, convinced my skull was being crushed under a rust-colored boulder only to realize it was my head bumping against the window. I pulled myself upright and nearly collapsed to the other side. The sound of slamming doors, then the front seats were empty. Pushing the weight of sleep from my eyes, I looked outside to both officers standing a few yards away, conversing with people whose faces I didn't recognize. We had arrived at what appeared to be an airport, a very small one just outside the city. A row of small planes could be seen if I craned my neck hard enough. As I tried to make sense of the new surroundings, the two officers stepped aside. A woman with a face as tight as her twig-colored ponytail in a dark gray pantsuit stepped between them. She glanced in my direction briefly and said a few more words to the officers. The young blond officer walked back to the cruiser. There was a click as the doors unlocked. I hadn't noticed until then that they had me locked in.

He pulled the door open for me. I clutched my purse like a shield and stepped out. The woman approached and extended one hand.

"Lydia Porter," she said with practiced formality. "It's an honor to meet you, Miss Ching."

"Honor" wasn't the word I would've expected her to use, but I shook her hand anyway. Her grip was tight, too.

"Hi," I managed.

"I imagine you're a little confused right now."

"Very."

"You are safe, I assure you." She gestured at the nearest plane—a sleek, tiny, unmarked jet; the kind of thing I'd only seen in movies. "But for now, we are pressed for time. Please board the plane."

I looked toward the plane. It seemed strange, almost alien, as if I would enter another world and never return if I were to step inside. I took a deep breath and met Lydia Porter's eyes.

"What happens," I said, "if I say no?"

She pursed her lips and looked down for a moment, as if trying to find the best way to break the worst news. "If you resist," she said, "we would have to employ necessary means of getting you onboard.

I'm sorry, but this is now a matter of national security and it's in your best interest to cooperate."

"National security."

"Correct."

I turned to the plane again. The pilot waved toward us, indicating he was ready to go.

"Shotgun," I said. No one laughed.

FEAR SEEMED LOGICAL, though looking out the oval window at the spools of unraveling clouds, I felt none. I had no idea where we were headed, but the farther I got from the bloody pile of clothes in my house, the better.

The inside of the plane was unnervingly luxurious. Two recliners wrapped in rich white leather faced each other, a fold-down tray in between. Across the walkway was a long couch, also in white leather. To one end of the cabin was the doorway to the pilot's cabin, next to which was a well-stocked bar, and to the other end was another door, where I'd been led through after boarding. It was locked. Every door I stepped through seemed to lock behind me lately. Whoever these people were, they were very worried that I would run off, even a thousand feet in the air. Judging by the rustling coming from behind closed doors, there were more people onboard than the pilot, Lydia Porter, and me, but I saw none of them. I sat tensely in one of the recliners—the couch was inviting but sitting on it felt too much like letting down my guard. The stark-white space smelled like leather and disinfectant, a scent that mingled uncomfortably with the acrid scent of blood that stubbornly clung to my skin.

I opened my purse and retrieved my phone—two dozen missed calls and hundreds of text messages. Lydia stepped through the door on the far end of the cabin just as I debated whether to delete everything without reading.

"I wouldn't do that," she said. She was holding a white plastic box with a red cross on the lid. "Not that it matters. No Wi-Fi or signal on this flight. But we were given strict instructions to prevent you from giving away your location, and that includes cell communications or accessing social media from your phone."

I set the phone down on the tray table as she took a seat across from me in the other recliner.

"Help yourself," she said. "I imagine you might need something to calm your nerves. Do you drink?"

"Yes," I said. "Whiskey."

Her brow arched slightly as she opened the first

aid kit. "Strong drink for someone your age." She slid a tube of Alocane across the table. "For your burns."

As I slathered the slippery gel over my arm, she rose and poured me a drink from the bar—whiskey, neat. It tasted smooth and clean but hot going down. Lydia watched me with interest.

"Can I at least call my dad?"

"We will communicate with him," she said in a tone that shut down any further discussion. "Please rest assured that what we're doing right now has your best interest in mind. We're trying to ensure your safety."

"Safety from what? The game?"

"No. We have not yet figured out how to prevent people from being taken into the orb."

"Then from who?"

"Get some rest." She stood. "Your handler will meet with you at the destination."

"What handler?"

She was already gone. I helped myself to another shot of whiskey. Then another.

THE PLANE ARRIVED at its destination in the early evening. A chilly breeze caught me off guard as I stepped off. The purple sky cast its murky light over glowing orange trees on rolling hills. A nondescript gray car with heavily tinted windows pulled up. The driver stepped out and though he tried to hide it, I caught him casting an awed, incredulous glance in my direction before opening the back door. It yawned open like the mouth of a waiting beast and I suddenly felt the urge to run, though I had a feeling the suited men and women milling about would restrain me like a 1930's asylum ward and force me inside if I did. I got in. Lydia followed.

"Where are we?" I asked as we passed a military cemetery. Rows of white tombstones gaped back at me from immaculate columns and rows.

"Outside Washington D.C. I can't be more specific than that."

"I don't know what you're good for then," I said. The part of me that wasn't exhausted was angry, though I didn't know what at.

A sleepy seaside town scrolled by outside. The sight of little gas station diners and seafood restaurants reminded me that I hadn't eaten since breakfast, which felt like an entire lifetime ago—a different lifetime when the world was ending but my life was still four walls, a shelf of books, and piles of boxes. My stomach rumbled its emptiness but thoughts of food turned inevitably to images of meat, blood, and smears of red on glaring white walls.

The car eased onto a dimly lit street and stopped in a dispirited little neighborhood. I stepped out and through dense, salty air heard the distant crashing of hefty waves. A lonely little house with dust-colored walls and a gray roof covered with dead leaves loomed in the night, bathing in the murky light of a single flickering street lamp. Other houses, equally silent and colorless, flanked it. I counted six on one side of the street, five on the other.

"It's not much," said Lydia, stepping up beside me, "but it's the safest place for you right now."

She walked toward the sun-bleached front door but I couldn't bring myself to follow. This was not my little house with brick walls and gable roof, and the little library that I'd spent most of my youth dreaming about. That house—home—was very far away. Lydia opened the door—a keypad lock, I noticed, instead of a keyhole—and was waiting for me expectantly. I marched my reluctant legs toward her.

The inside of the house was as bland and spirit-less as the outside. Lydia closed the door behind us and flicked on the first light switch we came across.

Stark white light washed over peaks and valleys of gray and tan that, upon closer inspection, turned out to be furniture draped in heavy drop cloths. Lydia grasped the nearest one and pulled. A veil of dust rose into the air as an old floral couch was revealed.

"This place hasn't been used in a while." A chipped coffee table, a TV stand, and a distressed end table were soon uncovered. "We haven't had time to get it prepped, but luckily it's clean enough."

"Clean enough," I repeated dully.

"It's poorly stocked right now, but we brought a few things. After you settle in, you can figure out what other things you might need." She was looking at me, trying to gauge my reaction to the place. Whatever she saw on my face made her look away and clear her throat. "I'll go help the driver bring the bags in. Why don't you look around?"

With that she was gone. Silence echoed around me. Except it wasn't quite the same as the silence in my own house—a slow, lazy silence filled with colors of life and things waiting to be done. This silence was abrasive, heavy, suffocating. It swelled up around me like balloons, pressing against my skin and squeezing me until I had trouble pushing air from my own lungs. I forced myself to move, taking slow steps around the house, clutching my purse tightly, the only familiar thing within a thousand miles. It was a small space, perhaps a thousand square feet give or take a hundred, and old. The kitchen was reasonably spacious, with a linoleum-topped island large enough to eat on. The gas stove was covered in dust and looked like it hadn't seen a hot pan for many seasons. A yellowing Formica table accompanied by two retro-yellow chrome chairs occupied a tiny breakfast nook. There were three bedrooms, equal size rather than the expected master and two smaller rooms. Each one had an attached bathroom, tiny with just barely enough space for a sink, toilet, and shower stall. Single beds covered in thin white cotton sheets occupied the corners, two to a room like a dormitory. Each room also housed a closet and a short, squat dresser. I walked my fingers over one of the beds. The plastic mattress, stiff and unyielding, crinkled underneath.

"Making yourself at home?" I looked up. Lydia stood at the bedroom doorway. Behind her, I could see the driver setting a pair of brown duffle bags in the front hall. She reached out and held something out to me. "Here."

I took it. "This is my phone." I opened my purse and dug through it. "When did you take this?"

"While you were dozing on the plane."

"You went through my purse?"

"We needed to make sure you didn't give away your location. It's mostly untouched. We just had to do a hard disable on location and network services. Don't worry; we'll lend you a tablet for entertainment. Just remember your activities will be monitored."

"Why?" I said, a little too loudly. "Why am I even here? Where is this?"

"I can't answer everything right now. But tomorrow . . ."

"*No*," I snapped, interrupting her. The anger that had been slowly drumming away in my chest was bubbling up. I paced back and forth along the floral couch. My hands ached to reach out and shake someone. "You have to tell me *something*. You just dragged me out of my home and flew me across the country. The world was going to *end* this morning. You can't just leave me here and tell me nothing!"

Lydia hesitated. She glanced behind her and nodded to the driver, who nodded back and walked out the front door. She turned back to me.

"There has been an order to protect you."

"Order from who?"

"Very high up."

"That means nothing to me."

"I can't say more than that, but it was issued this morning, as soon as you survived the Rat Maze. The order was very clear—ensure your safety, keep you out of the public eye, prevent your location from being found."

"So you're hiding me here?" I cast a disgusted look at the brittle little house. "In this place?"

"Don't be fooled by the way this place looks. It's one of the most secure locations we have." She gestured to the windows on the wall. "Bulletproof glass, reinforced walls, and every entry point is monitored, surveyed twenty-four hours a day, seven days a week. The houses to either side of you are occupied by people who are watching and guarding the house. They monitor the video feed, but don't worry; they can only see you if you're very close to the doors and windows." She pointed to a small white device mounted on the far wall that I hadn't noticed. "Alarms are always active for fire, monoxide, and breaking glass. By morning every house on the block will be stationed with guards. All persons and vehicles within five miles will be redirected away from you."

I shivered at the idea of so many eyes around me, watching unseen. This was, unquestionably, a jail sentence.

"We've brought a few necessities to get you through the night. Your things will be delivered in the next day or two."

"My things?" I looked down at the purse in my hand. "What do you mean, my things?"

"They've sent people to your house to pack up some essentials to help you get settled in for the long term."

"How long do you expect to keep me here?"

"I can't answer that."

"*Fine*," I seethed. "But *why*? Why am I here? Why do you need to do this? I'm nobody."

"I don't think you grasp the magnitude of the situation."

"I want to go home."

"That's quite impossible."

"I'll keep quiet. I'll stay home. I don't need you to hide me."

Lydia shook her head. She removed a phone from her pocket and tapped on it rapidly. "Like I said, you don't understand. You are here for your own safety. Have you actually thought about the implications of what happened this morning, besides keeping the world from ending?" She handed the phone to me.

I took it with shaking hands, unsure what to

expect. She had Googled my name. Staring back at me were my own face and hundreds of results.

Thousands.

Millions.

Every news site clamored about me and Alexis Monroe. Our names trended on every social media website. Pictures of me from college, high school, even as a child, had been dug up and posted across the internet. The world was splitting my life open and dicing it up for public consumption. My face burned and suddenly I was very thankful that I never got drunk enough to streak at that one Halloween party in college. The anger welling up just a moment ago deflated into a heavy, nauseating sensation.

"There are already cults starting in your name," Lydia said. Her voice sounded very far away. "Every person in the world has an opinion about you. The hobo in the park knows what you ate for dinner two weeks ago and the last time you got your teeth cleaned. Miss Ching, you are the most famous person in the world."

THE BED WAS as hard and uncomfortable to lie on as I imagined. My spine protested the rough surface.

Though exhausted, my brain felt like a cheap windup toy one crank away from splintering to pieces. I counted the bumps on the ceiling, head propped up on the only pillow I could find in the house.

The duffle bags contained some basic gas station-variety food items, a bag of toiletries commonly seen in roadside motels, a set of ill-fitting pajamas, and most importantly, a last-generation tablet and charger. When sleep failed to come, I turned it on, plugged it into one of the few working outlets, and sat on the hard floor reading late into the night.

I began with the news articles, but graphic descriptions of the Rat Maze turned my already-sour stomach. Next I skimmed blogs, stories about the deceased, reports of vigils being held, and coverage of crowds in the streets celebrating that the Earth had survived to see another day. I read until I could rehash the day's events no more, then I logged onto Facebook. Over a hundred thousand messages waited for me, as well as thousands of friend requests. My name was tagged in dozens of status updates. Videos of me, barefooted and half-drenched in blood, were everywhere. Everyone was talking about me, claiming credit for knowing me, and showering praise on me. Knowing my every move was monitored, I couldn't respond or comment —not that I had any desire to. I watched the conversations go on without me, a deep, sinking feeling in my stomach.

I scrolled past at least ten video posts before I remembered that I still had no idea what I did this morning to escape the Rat Maze. I had numerous means to watch it at my fingertips, and yet I found myself resisting. The idea of seeing that arena again made my skin crawl. I debated, went back and forth, but curiosity killed the cat in the end and I pressed Play.

Cheshire's voice blared through the room. I winced and turned down the volume. The camera panned through the crowd. It focused on me briefly, confused and dazed, arms around myself and looking around like a startled rabbit. I saw Alexis Monroe and the robot designated Eleven signing to her. Then, it was on.

Two of the four marbles crushed contestants the moment they landed. In the midst of things, I saw very little. Now, I was seeing it in startling clarity. I averted my eyes and felt around the screen to fast forward, but still couldn't avoid seeing the gruesome close-ups in short glimpses. I was very glad I hadn't eaten for most of the day.

Alexis Monroe skipped into view. I stopped the fast forward. It seemed that none of the cameras caught her climbing up the wall, but now that she was up, they focused their attention on her. I watched her crouch atop the wall, carefully balanced, and follow the moving marbles with a steady eye. Most of the contestants were smears on the walls and floors by this point. The camera shifted, and I saw Cheshire some distance away from her, perched with their usual effortless grace. Alexis tossed them a scathing glance, raised one hand, and extended her middle finger. If they were offended, they gave no sign. Then, Alexis moved on. Nimbly and silently, she navigated the walls, though once or twice I saw her nearly lose her footing. She watched the marbles with entranced concentration. One was rolling her way, red eye searching this way and that, but never quite looking up. As I watched, she carefully maneuvered herself into a cross-shaped corner, set one knee down to steady herself, and raised her hands, one held in the classic finger-gun position and the other supporting it, taking aim at the marble as it rolled closer. The camera zoomed in on her face. I saw her mouth open to form a silent word.

"*Bang.*"

A crack rang through the air. I recognized the sound. I'd heard it from inside the maze. The marble jerked to one side, bounced back and forth against the white walls, and lolled to a stop. Where the red eye once glowed was now a ragged hole.

Before I could figure out what had happened, she took aim at another marble making its way over and took it out with another crack. My mind struggled to comprehend the events before me, but the view suddenly changed. I was now looking at myself, disheveled, sweaty, with puffy, bloodshot eyes. Hair pasted to my forehead and up to my knees in blood, I ran, stumbled, and tried to run again, like a terrified child lost in a haunted house. I was the second to last one still inside the maze. Then, on the other side of the wall directly to my left, one of the remaining marbles rolled over a red-haired woman who went down without a sound, and I was the last one. Luck, nothing more.

The marble bore down on me. On this side of the screen, my teeth threatened to bite through my lip and I forced my jaw to unlock. It rolled over me and my stomach did a nauseating flip-flop at the sight. The volume was all the way down but I would always remember that sound.

BOOM

It rolled away from me. Then, making a sharp one-eighty, it turned around again, back in my direction.

BOOM

It rolled over me again. The camera zoomed in.

I laid on the ground in a fetal position. At least it looked like me. I could barely make out the outline of my body through the thick layer of ice covering it. The marble came at me again.

BOOM

Not a scratch. My entire body was concealed and the clear substance appeared to be growing, reaching higher and higher with jagged points.

Diamond had sprouted from my body, growing and reaching toward the white dome, covering my entire body in a thick, crystallized layer. The marble came again, red eye turning in its socket and zooming in on me. If it had a face, it would look confused.

It rammed into me again. And again. The crystal, now a jagged six-foot monolith, was unscathed and still growing. I couldn't see my own body inside the diamond prison. The marble kept at its task, though it could no longer roll over me. It reared back to gain momentum, then came again.

BANG

A shot split the screen and I jumped. Time paused for a moment. Then, the ball slowed and rolled to an awkward stop. Its red eye rolled into view and the camera flew to it. Like the others, where its pupil used to be was now a gaping hole. The camera panned up, and I saw Alexis Monroe, perched on the edge of the nearest wall, finger raised. Above her, the looming red numbers had stopped their countdown. The game was over.

The walls dropped into the ground. Alexis got to her feet, looking around with a paranoid expression on her face. All around us was red on black. Then, Cheshire clapped.

"*Wonderful,*" they said, approaching Alexis. She looked up at the diamond monolith, where I was entombed, took a protective step between it and Cheshire, and raised her finger gun. "*Oh no, that won't work on me. You're welcome to try, though. Knock yourself out.*" She hesitated, then slowly lowered her hands. Cheshire snapped their fingers. "*Eleven, make yourself useful and dig the other one out.*"

Eleven stepped into view. I watch them approach the diamond structure, now nearly ten feet. One metal hand lifted and steel-plated fingers touched its surface. The crystal's surface cracked, then burst into gleaming shards like a pane of sugar. I saw myself emerge from the wreckage, pull my foot out from crystals still holding me, and nearly fall. One metal-covered arm reached out and caught me.

I stopped the video and considered the possibility that I had gone mad.

Despite the suffocating quiet around me, I was overwhelmingly aware of how noisy the world had become. I let the tablet fall from my lap and stood to look out into the starless night. A tiny camera looked down at me from the wall and I gave it the most scathing glance I could manage. They all wanted to watch me now, I supposed. Yesterday I was no one; today they all wanted to watch me.

Was Dad wondering where I was? We'd spoken maybe a dozen times in the last four years.

I never talked to Hannah.

Did Addison watch me? Did it bring back bad memories of Maddy?

I took a shower. The water was tepid and the pressure was weak. I ate a bag of Cheetos and forced myself to swallow without thinking. I laid down on the hard bed with the thin blanket over my body and again failed to sleep. Instead, I scrolled through pictures and videos on my phone. Pictures of school days, of my mother before the cancer won, of my father before her death drove an invisible wedge between us, of Hannah and me at the water park, of my college graduation, of the day I signed the deed to my new house . . . a whole lifetime and one endless day ago.

CHAPTER 5

THE MAN WITH THE DOMINO-BRICK FACE AND starched suit didn't so much enter the house as apparated inside it. When I rolled out of bed, shaking loose fragments of white and red and black from my addled mind, he was sitting on the living room couch, legs crossed, a brown leather satchel in his lap. He looked up as soon as I walked out of the bedroom. Disapproving brown eyes raked over my nose stud and choppy haircut. I could almost hear him calculating my weight, height, and unimpressive measurements in a near-medical manner.

"Donna Ching, I presume?" His hair was combed to perfection and his voice was even and measured with the slightest edge.

"Astra," I said.

"Your file says Donna." He opened the satchel

and removed a tan-colored folder. Inside was a stack of printed sheets that he quickly scanned. "Ah, there. Donna Astra Ching. Hippie parents?"

"My mother was into astronomy."

"And where's she?" He scanned the pages again. "Right. Dead. Well, no matter. We've already notified your family within the country of the situation. Looks like that's just your father. The rest of them are—let's see here—China. Funny, I would've guessed Korean."

"Chinese. On my father's side."

He shuffled the pages back into the folder and stood. The couch's ancient springs groaned as he moved. "So, Donna," he said. "We have a lot to talk about. Would you care to freshen up first?"

I looked down at the wrinkled, ill-fitting pajamas and pulled my fingers out of my tangled hair. The amount of useful sleep I got between the plastic mattress and the disorienting dreams was roughly zero, and I could feel my dry, irritated skin pulling and cracking, my toiletry kit not having included moisturizer. For a moment, tired and weary, I felt embarrassed at my appearance, then embarrassed for being embarrassed.

"No," I said, trying to meet his eyes, but he was already heading to settle down at the Formica breakfast table. "I don't have another change of clothes. Your people brought me here with nothing and you walked in without knocking. I don't know what you expect me to do."

He tossed me a brisk, uncaring glance as if it made no difference to him whatsoever, and turned back to his paper. "Alright, have a seat," he said, gesturing nonchalantly at the empty chair across from him. Scowling, I plodded over and dropped into it. For a long minute neither of us spoke. He was preoccupied with his papers and I sat, arms crossed, stubbornly refusing to speak first. Finally, as if finally remembering I was there, he closed his folder and looked up at me.

"So, Donna," he said. "Let me explain your situation."

I nodded shortly. "Someone should."

He leaned back in his seat. "The world is dealing with something unprecedented in history. Whatever this 'Headspace'"—he raised his fingers in air quotes —"is, it's an equal threat to all states, nations, and people. Now, the workings in the upper levels is not something you need to understand. Just know that, being one of the first to survive this thing, you're now the equivalent of a national treasure and will be treated as such." He tucked the folders back into his satchel. "Austin Heath, by the way. I'll be your primary handler going forward."

I didn't comment on the fact that treasures were usually locked away in boxes, nor ask what exactly he meant by "handler." Something told me this man wasn't going to indulge me.

"I can't tell you where you are, but you don't need to know that either. This house technically does not exist. It sounds like something out of a movie, but sometimes those things hit close to home. These houses were used for witness protection in the past, usually people with pretty steep prices on their heads. Now, it's used to protect you. Your fame has attracted quite a bit of attention. You've logged onto the tablet already, haven't you?"

"You know I have."

"Then you've seen the media hubbub. Your home is surrounded by news choppers around the clock. Every person you've crossed paths with on a bus or in a grocery store has been hunted down and questioned. Every nobody out there is trying to get rich and famous by pretending to know you. If you've got a speck of dirt, you can bet there's a million eyes waiting to see it."

"I don't have any dirt," I said, though even as those words left my mouth I could feel my confidence wavering. Was there something I'd forgotten? Some picture I'd overlooked? Some person I'd wronged eager to tear me apart?

Heath—I couldn't quite bring myself to think of this man as "Austin"—sighed. It was the kind of sigh children heard in the principal's office, one of disappointment and defeat. "It doesn't have to be dirt." He removed a smartphone from his pocket, tapped on it rapidly, and held it out to me. A headline screamed back at me.

HAS HEADSPACE WINNER ALWAYS BEEN ALIEN-OBSESSED? THE ANSWER MAY SURPRISE YOU!

I TOOK the phone and scrolled, my hands shaking. The article was full of clickbait, ads, and random buttons linking to unrelated websites, but through it all was a flimsy story whose central exhibits were half a dozen Facebook posts I had made nearly half a decade ago, spanning months of time. I could barely remember making them, but now, strung together, they appeared to be telling a different story.

Rereading Little Green Men. One of my faves :)

Watching Alien vs. Predator. Nobody likes this movie but me!

Avatar was alright, loved the look of the Na'vi though. Such beautiful design <3

The story went on to paint a picture of me—a me I didn't recognize. Someone obsessed with the supernatural and aliens and who preferred the company of fiction over people. Just reading the story, I sounded like some oddball outcast of society, head full of alien abduction dreams under my tinfoil hat. Heath took the phone out of my hand and turned off the screen.

"That's a mild one," he said. "I don't have the heart to show you the bad ones. You should be grateful though—they're making up worse shit about the other one."

My head snapped up. "Alexis?"

"Alexis Monroe, yes. She's a bit more . . . shall we say *colorful* than you. Nothing too exciting, but certainly more for the tabloids to work with. Do you understand now? You don't have to do *anything*. Anyone will take any word you say, any move you make, and run with it. The world is full of sensationalists and shortsighted people. They will hunt you down and tear you to shreds for their entertainment. If you were out there right now, there would be a dozen cameras aimed at your face, trying to see if you've popped a zit overnight, and a dozen more shoved up your skirt, trying to get the color of your underthings. Do you really think you can live like that?"

I shook my head numbly.

"Now, I trust Lydia has briefed you on this already, but while you are free to surf the internet and entertain yourself on the tablet, you are not to post information, input anything on websites, or order anything to be delivered. Anything you need or want, you can get through she and I. Your activity on the tablet is monitored to prevent any mishaps, and if we feel you can't be trusted, we will have to remove the tablet."

"You want me to be a prisoner."

"Unfortunately, until we know more about how and why you and Alexis Monroe survived the game, your safety outweighs your comfort. The entire world hinges on you two. This may not be the most hospitable situation for you, but your safety and anonymity *are* guaranteed. You are immeasurably valuable right now not only to the country, but to the world. We can't have you kidnapped or incapacitated or worse—run off and sign some contract for a reality show."

"Okay," I said. I had a nagging headache. The room was crowded with a million invisible people, all whispering and pointing at me. "Fine. I'll stay here."

"You don't have much of a choice, but I appreciate that." Heath checked his watch. "Your things should get there this afternoon. Before we talk further about the logistics of your living here, there is one more thing we need to do, and it's just about time. Please fetch your tablet."

"My tablet?"

"Yes." He tossed me an impatient look. "Go get it."

I went to the bedroom, unplugged the tablet from the wall socket, and set it up on the Formica table. Heath turned it on and opened up an app I had noticed the night before but hadn't bothered to mess with. He typed in a few letters and digits into open fields.

"This app was created as a secure channel for communication between a few select parties. I will give you the login information, but be aware that it will not allow you to communicate with anyone but the designated persons. Right now that is only myself, Lydia Porter, and ..."

A video screen popped up and a loud, warm, familiar voice interrupted him.

"*Hello??*"

I grimaced at the high volume.

"Oh, sorry; am I shouting?" said the grainy face swimming into focus. There was some fumbling and static, then I saw her, big-eyed and wide-smiled, maple skin slightly discolored by the screen. Out of the arena, not surrounded by blood and screams and panic, Alexis Monroe looked incredibly, unsettlingly normal.

She might have thought the same about me. The first look on her face once she saw me clearly was a mix of surprise and recognition, which quickly melted into relief.

"Hi there!" she said, still a bit loudly. Her accent I now recognized as distinctively Scottish. "Glad to see you! I was worried you'd be poorly after that whole ordeal, but you're looking alright."

Before I could answer, Heath pulled the screen from me. "Ms. Monroe," he said, "I'd like to speak to your handler, please."

"My what?" Alexis frowned. "Oh, you mean Paul. No."

I saw a flicker of surprise in Heath's mud-brown eyes. "I beg your pardon?"

"Not yet. I want to talk to *her* first."

"Ms. Monroe," Heath said with the enunciation of someone with paper-thin patience, "please understand that before we allow you to converse—"

"*Allow?*" Alexis repeated, with exaggerated, almost comical offense. "You're going to *allow* us to talk to each other?"

"Given the circumstances, there is a process to be followed an—"

"You wouldn't *have* a process," Alexis interrupted again, biting each word, "if it weren't for her and me. In case you haven't noticed, we are the reason you're still here, going on about your *process*. That girl you got there is the only person in the world who knows how to defend herself against those alien things. And I'm the only one who's taken one down. We may have been nobody before, but right here, right now, we're important and we have rights. This guy" —she shifted the screen to show the man next to her, a skinny drink of water in a suit who was looking rather uncomfortable—"has been giving me the runaround since I got picked up. It's always 'we can't tell you this,' 'we can't tell you that.' Well, what *can* you tell me? I've been here a day and a half, I left my family behind, and I don't even know where 'here' is. I can't imagine what you've put *that* poor girl through. We deserve better than this. Now if you'll excuse me, I'd like to have a conversation with her, without you people in the room."

Heath gave me a stern look, like a father expecting a child to give a preapproved response. But seeing Alexis bolstered me slightly. I sat up a little straighter and looked him in the eye.

"If you don't mind," I said.

He shook his head and gave me a dismissive wave. I grabbed the tablet, went into the bedroom I had slept in, and closed the door behind me.

"Hey," said the friendly voice on the tablet. "Are you okay?"

I nodded and sat down on the bed. "I am."

"They'll be recording us. Not that it makes any difference."

"I know."

For a long moment we studied at each other, unsure of where to begin. Then, she spoke. "I'm Alexis Monroe. But you already know that, don't you?"

"Yeah," I said. "I'm Donna Ching. I go by my middle name though—Astra."

"That works for me. You can call me Lexi."

"Okay."

"So."

"So."

ALEXIS "LEXI" Monroe was thirty-seven years old, the military daughter of a military family, now working in technology. There was little she could freely tell me of her time in the military, though she showed me her stylish, candy apple-red hearing aids. "Souvenirs from an IED. Blew my ears right out," she said with good humor. "Got discharged after that. No regrets, to be honest." Since then, she'd finished her degree and settled into a desk job.

"Pays well enough," she told me. "But boring as hell. Still, it puts food on the table, pays the hydro bill, and leaves enough to get Bella a tutor on the weekend. She's eight. She's got a mouth on her but I love her to death. Danielle's got more patience with her than me. Kids, you know?"

I gave her a quick summary of my life, though being a twenty-five-year-old accountant had never felt so dull. She asked if accounting was as dull as technology and we shared a quick laugh. For the first time in these long few days, I felt a weight on my chest lighten. We chatted about her daughter, exchanged gripes about our jobs, and traded complaints about our current living conditions. Unfortunately, we could only pretend for so long.

"We have to talk about it, right?" I said eventually.

Lexi nodded grimly, broad smile shrinking from her lips. "Can't keep pretending it didn't happen. Where should we start?"

I thought for a moment. "How did you . . ." I held up my hands, one in a finger gun, the other supporting it.

Lexi looked away. "I don't know how to explain it completely," she said, her face tight with concentration. "But when those walls came up, I had this thought. I was looking up, and I saw that thing—Cheshire—up there, and I thought, if I had some stairs, I could get up there. I had this picture in my head, like a bureau with drawers you could pull out." She curved her fingers as if hooking them to the underside of something and mimed a pulling motion. "Like if I could pull out these steps, one at a time, like drawers, I could climb up. Then the craziest thing happened." Her hand flattened, as if feeling along a wall. "I put my hand on the wall, and I heard this hum. It's so hard to explain, like the wall was *responding* to me. I kept feeling it until I found this notch. It wasn't there before—I know that for sure. Even when I looked at it, I couldn't see it at first. I felt it, *then* I saw it. Like I asked the wall for a notch and it gave me one. I pulled it out and it was a step. Then I pulled out another one, and another. It was that easy. So I stood on them and climbed up."

She gave me a probing look, as if inviting me to question her. I didn't.

"I couldn't believe it once I got up there." I saw her suppress a shudder. "I could see so many people running, and dying. I tried yelling to them, but no one heard me. My brain was just . . . a cluster, just looking for something to focus on. And I thought about my dad. I don't know why. Comfort, I guess. He loved guns. I wasn't a huge fan but when I was little, he was obsessed with teaching me. Not just how to shoot one, but how to clean one, how the parts worked, how to take one apart and put it back together. And in that moment all I could think about was the parts of this 9mm he bought once. He sat me out in the yard and showed me all the parts of it and how they all worked with each other. I started thinking about how I wished I had something like that. And then . . ." She trailed off, thinking hard. "I can't even put this part into words. I *felt* it. Like it was part of me. It was *in* my arm, like my bones rearranged. And I put *force* into it. Because a handgun can't do that, I was thinking. It needs to be more. Something that pierces, goes right through. It's all a blur right now, looking back on it. It wasn't so much thought as . . . a feeling."

She fell silent. I could tell by her face that even as the story came out of her mouth, it sounded absurd to her own ears.

"I sound mental," she said after a moment, and let out a half-sigh, half-laugh. "This is all . . . I don't even know the right word. Nuts. Barmy. How about you? What happened? All I saw was the ball coming for you, then it bounced off. Then there was that crystal."

"Diamond," I said. And, as she said, it sounded *barmy* as soon as it left my mouth. "At least, I think it was."

Lexi arched a brow. "Really."

"I had been reading a book. This old geology book, and I was reading about diamonds. And when that thing came toward me, all I could think about, at that moment, was how I wished I could be indestructible." My hand had closed itself into a fist. I forced it open again.

"Like a diamond."

"Not in those words. More like—"

"Pictures."

"Feelings." I shook my head. "It's so hard to explain, like everything I'd read about diamonds flooded my head for a second. I don't remember much else."

"It's funny," Lexi said, studying her hand. "I can still feel it. Not just to have a gun but to become it. My arm was the barrel. My shoulder was the hammer. The trigger was somewhere inside my head. When I pulled it, there was a recoil through my whole body. I felt it in my bones."

Did I feel like that? I flexed my own hands. I hadn't thought about it until now, but there was a crackle in my joints, as if tiny crystals were being broken as I moved and bent. I'd thought it was just part of being exhausted, but now I was wondering whether I would bleed diamond dust if a vein opened.

"Me, too," I murmured, more to myself than Lexi. I turned my wrist this way and that, mesmerized by the sound of crackling crystals.

"They did tell us the rules."

"Rules?"

"On the first day. They said it. *Use your head.* Just none of us were listening."

"You think this is what they meant?"

"What else could it be?" She sounded so sure of herself. I couldn't help feeling reassured. "It was even on the form, wasn't it? Sound mind is required, but not sound body, because you can make whatever you want of your body. You can make stairs out of walls, or make guns out of your body, or make diamonds out of nothing. As long as you know what it is you're trying to make."

Lifting my head, I shifted my gaze to the window. I hadn't noticed until now that I could see the ocean. Just outside was a weed-covered slope that led down to a muddy shore lapped lazily by gray waves.

"Alright?"

"I don't know."

"Feels like the world should look different right now, and it's odd that it doesn't, right?"

I nodded. "I don't know what's next."

"Well," she said, and looked off screen for a moment. "Chances are our handlers are already working on getting this bit of knowledge out there. That's all they really need us for—to figure out how this game works and get it out there so more people can play to win." She paused for a moment. "Astra."

"Yes?"

"I know I'm not your mum and I'm not in any

place to give you advice, but I do want to say one thing to you, if you don't mind."

"No, please," I said, almost desperately. Truthfully, having someone tell me what to do at that moment was the most I could hope for.

"Don't let them under your skin."

"Who?"

"Any of them. The aliens, the news rag, your *handlers*. Don't let them under. A lot of them are going to try, but hold yourself tight. We're closed off, far from everybody and everything. It's all we've got right now."

My things arrived that afternoon, meticulously boxed into plastic shipping crates. I was initially pleased to see they appeared to have taken some care with my belongings, until I remembered that it meant every item I owned now had strangers' fingerprints on them. I unpacked and pushed away images of people I'd never met sorting through the Hello Kitty underwear I'd bought because they were on sale and comfortable, or having a laugh at the box of embarrassing old high school poetry. Not under my skin, not today. Taking out my things and setting them up was an odd, out-of-body experience. When I'd packed them away, I'd pictured setting them up in my new home, the first place that was all my own. Instead, I was here, and I had no idea where "here" was.

Somehow, though my own house sat cluttered for weeks, I couldn't stomach the idea of leaving my things in boxes in this depressing little house. I unpacked through the night, filled with a strange, almost desperate drive to turn this sad space into a home. I even dusted off the dresser and bathroom before setting up my own clothes and toiletries, though I couldn't recall the last time I'd dusted anything in my life.

Grocery requests were made in text through the messenger app to Lydia Porter and dropped off soundlessly by a driver whose face I never saw. It was beginning to feel like a theme, the mysterious, unseen hands moving the pieces of my life. Cooking was the last thing I wanted to do, but I forced myself to fix a proper meal, hoping the act of doing so would impose some sort of normality on the situation. To relieve the silence, I left Netflix running on the tablet—nearly every channel on television was plastered with my face.

As I picked at my halfhearted attempt at a

chicken stir fry, the messenger app rang for video. Heath's face appeared.

"Have your things arrived?" he asked, wasting no time with greetings.

"Yes," I said. "It's here."

"If you need anything else, message Lydia."

"I know."

"A few more things will be sent to you tomorrow. Look through them and make sure they fit."

"Fit?"

"I'll be back tomorrow morning. We need to go over a few more things before communications are made to the world at large. Get yourself settled, and remember, do not attempt to make contact with anyone."

"I know," I said, annoyed. "I haven't—"

"There are a lot of people out there who would love to get their hands on you right now. You're a valuable commodity. Keep yourself safe. I'll see you tomorrow. Rest up for the next round."

Then he was gone. I pushed the cooling plate away, appetite suddenly gone. It hadn't occurred to me until that moment that I was going to have to play again.

CHAPTER 6

THE FIRST WORLDWIDE BROADCAST WAS RELEASED. Despite the shortage of time, strings were being pulled with impressive speed behind the scenes. Lexi and I were both questioned—interrogated— time and time again after our initial conversation. We recounted the same things we told each other over and over. By the end of my third day in the safe house, I was very weary, but being able to converse with Lexi freely—albeit monitored—helped. I wasn't alone in the madness.

The information we provided was broken down into a few easy-to-digest bullets and placed on a simple blue slide with white text, then translated into every language imaginable. Clear, friendly voices narrated the slide, teaching the public about the meaning of "using your head." The broadcast was repeated on every channel every fifteen minutes. Hotlines, social media posts, and pamphlets were made widely available.

Aside from the information released to the public, Heath badgered me relentlessly on the workings of the arena, Cheshire, and the helper, Eleven. He was unabashedly disappointed in what I provided, but the truth was I had little to offer outside of what was already visible in the broadcasts. I described the white domed ceiling and smooth floors, the chill air, and Cheshire's odd, robotic joints. I couldn't tell him how the maze was formed, what machinery might be operating underneath the floors, or what technology was being used to manipulate the marbles or Cheshire's body. And of course I could not begin to tell him whether the orb was indeed capable of splitting the planet in half.

Then the "trainers" came, stiff-faced men and women laden with charts, books, and lists who wasted no time with pleasantries. They marched into the house, opened their laptops, and force-fed me information. Guns, weapons, basic combat, survival equipment, first aid . . . I took in as much as I could, but it was rather like drinking from a fire hose on full blast. Despite what they seemed to think, they couldn't make me into a firearms expert or survival specialist or any sort of competent fighter in a few short days. I saw the frustration on their faces as I failed, again and again, to memorize the inner workings of a semiautomatic pistol. Lexi was surely having an easier time with this.

The "things" Heath had sent to me turned out to be a tracksuit. Or rather, what I initially assumed to be a tracksuit. He gave a rather condescending sneer when I asked him if that was what it was, then gave a lengthy, wordy explanation full of technical terms I couldn't quite grasp. Long story short, it was a heat-resistant, flame-retardant, cold-resistant, anti-shock —the list went on but I would fail if quizzed on it— piece that cost more than five years' worth of my paychecks. It had been special rush-ordered, made of some material usually only privy to NASA-esque operations, and delivered to Lexi and me, along with specially made footwear made for athletic endeavors commonly reserved for seasoned Olympians.

"It feels nice, huh?" Lexi was saying. Five days into our imprisonment, we'd formed a fast friendship. We'd spent some time getting used to our suits, with her lamenting that she couldn't show it off to her daughter.

"Have you spoken to her?"

She shook her head. "Not allowed. They're letting me send some simple messages, but no direct contact. What about you? Talk to anyone?"

"No. Can't think of what to say." I sighed. "I wish I could talk to a friend, but what can I say in a two-line message? I don't even know where to start."

"How about your mom?"

"She passed away a few years ago."

"Sorry. Dad?"

I shrugged. "We're not what you'd call close. Seems after Mom died we had nothing left in common."

"I'm sure he's still worried."

"I know." I nodded. "I just don't know where to start with him either." I looked at the bed next to me, where the suit lay neatly folded. To pile it with the rest of the laundry felt like an insult. "Look at this thing—what exactly do they expect us to walk into?"

Lexi chuckled. Her laugh relaxed me slightly "Who knows? But we'll at least look good doing it."

THE SILENCE LASTED TWO WEEKS.

For fourteen long, anticipation-filled days, nothing happened. The world learned about how to play the game. The tabloids screamed our names and threw out conspiracy theories left and right. A live feed monitored the orb around the clock, but nothing of interest took place. The first week passed, and the world grew more agitated with each additional day in which nothing happened. I was instructed—ordered rather—to keep the suit on at all times in case the game suddenly began with no warning. I did this, less out of obedience and more out of fear and paranoia. The burns on my arms blistered, then drained and left behind pink welts.

Between training sessions, I passed time reading and researching, though I could never be sure exactly what it was I was looking for. There was still much about the rules of the arena that I didn't know. I looked up the elemental makeup of fire, water, and various minerals, though I couldn't begin to figure out how to use them in a pinch. My research even led me down the paths of animals, mythical creatures, even Harry Potter-esque magic spells, though I had no idea if those things could be replicated in useful ways in the arena's environment. A gun was one thing, but magic was uncharted territory, with no solid rhyme or reason to be applied and no one to tell me how it should feel. I watched movies; action movies with a lot of fighting and shooting starring Crish Michaels. But watching and being an action hero were vastly different. I had no idea whether I could replicate sharpshooting and gallant parkour in the arena. And so the days were spent aimlessly jumping from one topic to another, though I did spend a little extra time brushing up on the properties of diamonds.

After the second week passed, the world calmed slightly, and I did also. There was a whisper, a soft murmur that perhaps it was over. Perhaps we'd won and that was it. Maybe the aliens were satisfied with our performance and had abandoned the orb to rot. I even allowed myself a few minutes out of what I'd come to think of as the "battle suit."

And, of course, that was when it happened.

THE TELEPORTATION INTO THE ARENA—WHICH I'd gotten used to thinking of as "3D printing"—did not quite catch me off guard this time, but was no less disorienting. I recognized the onset dizziness shortly after stepping out of the shower and black dots began to swim in front of my eyes. Thankfully I had already begun to dress myself and I had just enough time to struggle into my pants and grab the shirt and shoes before everything went back. The world fell out of existence for a moment and then, after a long, dizzying second, was replaced with the endless black floor and white dome above.

Except not quite. After shaking off the vertigo, I realized the ground beneath my feet was white. Above me arched a bright blue sky that reached into infinity in all directions, where it met the horizon, blue on blue.

We were surrounded by water.

I was barefoot and there was nothing covering my upper body except my old, frayed sports bra. I quickly shrugged into the rest of the suit and slipped on the shoes.

"Hey."

I spun around and was enveloped in a tight hug. Lexi looked me up and down. She was wearing the same suit, but somehow on her it looked more straight and pressed, almost militant. Over her ears were the spines of her red hearing aids.

"They let me keep these this time," she said, noticing me looking. "Suppose they figured out I need it." She looked around. "Bit different this time."

I nodded. "Is this the real sea?"

"Maybe."

"I hope this isn't too hard." I glanced around self-consciously, then lowered my voice in embarrassment. "I can't swim."

Lexi squeezed my shoulder. "Don't worry too much. Remember, things work differently here." She glanced behind her. "Looks like the new folks are arriving. We were first. Winners' privilege."

Thin, white beams of light busily printed new figures one after another. Soon the platform, roughly the size of half a basketball court, was filled with bodies, all varying in size, age, and shape. But, I noticed, the atmosphere was different. Most were nervous, a few seemed on edge, some were calm, but no one was crying this time. No one was screaming. Some looked in our direction and gave us nods of acknowledgement. A man gave us a mock salute. His T-shirt read "**#UseYourHead**."

A single beam of light descended to the very edge of the platform. The others instinctively moved a few steps farther from it. Eleven lifted their faceless mask as they were printed into the arena. After a chaotic few days, I had forgotten the burns they left on my arm. But now, the welts stung at the sight of their robotic form. Eleven turned in our direction and I looked away. Lexi met their gaze, tapped her hearing aids, and gave a thumbs up.

"Guess no work for the helper today," she said, then raised her voice. "Hey!" I jumped a little. The new contestants looked our way as one. "Stay calm; use your heads; we can do this."

A few people cheered. Most stayed quiet but I saw their chests rise slightly and some stood a little taller. At least a dozen came toward us. Lexi shook their hands readily while I stood back and watched the last of the contestants arrive.

The final one to be printed was a short, stocky girl noticeably younger than the rest. I wondered for a moment if a mistake had been made and she was not yet seventeen. After finding her footing, she looked around with panicked almond eyes, swinging her head sharply in one direction, then another, sending stringy blond hair flying over her face. Before I could pinpoint what was different about her, a familiar voice cut the air.

"*Hello, contestants!*"

Dozens of heads snapped as one to the source. Cheshire strolled into view, tall and slender and strange as ever. They stepped to the center of the contestants and scanned us, emoji face smiling wide.

"*Welcome to the new course!*" They gestured around us at the sprawling sea. "*I must admit, for a second there I thought you folks were done for, but you pulled through and cut it close. Now, the real fun begins. And speaking of which—*" They bent, dropping their flickering "face" in front of Lexi and me. "*Welcome back, reigning champs! I've got high hopes for you. Setting up for this round took a little extra time. Did you miss us?*"

I shrank back from the emoji face, but Lexi stood her ground, arms crossed. Cheshire gave her a wink and walked off again, zigzagging their way among the contestants, checking them out, posing them to the cameras, and teasing them. Their presence had always been unnerving, but this time, perhaps bolstered by Lexi's presence, the contestants regarded Cheshire with annoyance and refused to feed into their baiting.

"*What a spirited group,*" Cheshire quipped as they stopped at the edge of the platform. "*I am eager to see you folks perform. The rules are a little different this time —reach the target within the hour, and you'll score a place in the next round.*"

I surveyed the horizon, expecting to see an island, or a coastline, or maybe even a comical bullseye, but saw only water and more water. My mind rattled off options in a panic. Boats. Submarines. Floating foam noodles.

"*Ready?*"

Scuba suit. Did I know anything about scuba diving?

"*Set.*"

How long could I hold my breath?

"*And go!*" The floor disappeared. For a brief, terrifying moment there was nothing but air beneath my feet. Then the sea, cold and suffocating, swallowed me whole.

I WAS DROWNING.

I couldn't see anything and my entire body thrashed helplessly. Water pressed me from all sides. I lost track of up and down. The sea strangled me and I didn't dare breath. My lungs burned and my hands struggled to find anything to hold on to. I forced my eyes open and saw nothing but darkness.

And one spot of light.

I focused on it. The world swam into view. There was a single spot of light deep down, toward the ocean floor. Blinking, beckoning.

And it was shaped like a bullseye.

The absurdity of it managed to calm me for a very brief moment. My body floated and drifted upward. Instead of fighting it, I recalled the feeling of crackling crystals in my veins. Then, as it came to me, I grabbed hold of it and molded it, shaping it.

Images flooded my mind. I reached out and seized one, hanging on for dear life.

My spine creaked and lengthened, as if manipulated by invisible hands that pulled it loose and added new joints. My legs pumped up and down, a strangely natural motion, moving as one. I opened my mouth and the last of the air escaped. Water drew into my body, then flowed out. I was breathing.

A figure swam into sight. I blinked. My vision had changed. The water before my face moved in magnified waves. Lexi gave me a thumbs up. Her hair drifted with the water. I saw her as if through a fish-eye lens. Her entire lower body had elongated into the silvery shape of a fish, with blue back and white stripes. When she turned, I saw the enormous sail on her back. Her eyes were glassy and round and she darted through the water like an arrow fresh sprung off a bow. I wasn't sure what I looked like, but I didn't dare look down at myself for fear that whatever was holding my shape would vanish.

She jabbed a finger toward the target, then to the side. I followed her pointing. Some of the contestants were adapting. Several had created various forms of scuba and diving apparatus. One was wearing an old-fashioned diving suit. One man even grew long, frog-like feet. They were heading to the bottom, slowly making their way toward the target.

But not everyone.

Lexi spun around sharply in the water, heading towards a man who appeared to be conjuring up various mechanical parts around himself, but none of which fit together. He was flailing and sinking, and whatever he was trying to construct was not coming together. Lexi launched herself through the water toward him and pushed him to the surface. Her action inspired a few of the other contestants, who turned in their descent to help the ones struggling. I watched them, waiting to see who was still without aid—aid I was hoping I wouldn't have to give.

Someone was panicking. I waited for Lexi to help, but she was occupied above the water. I swam a little closer.

The girl who arrived last was thrashing like a dying toad, eyes wide and frightened. Someone would help her, I hoped. I waited one second, then a second longer, glancing toward the target below me. Someone else would help her. It didn't have to be me.

No one saw her.

I started down, glanced back. She was still struggling.

Damn it.

I swam toward her, slid my hands under her armpits, and dragged her upward. My legs—tail fin—parted the water rapidly. She was in a panicked frenzy, twisting this way and that in my arms and clawing at the water and me. We broke the water surface with a splash and I immediately heard Lexi's voice.

"Use your heads!" she was shouting. "Think about what you need and it will happen! Hurry!"

With that she was gone again. I struggled to keep a good grip on the panicking girl, who was kicking, splashing, and shouting, practically trying to climb on top of me to get out of the water.

"Calm down!" I shouted over the noise, nearly losing my grip as she accidentally kneed me in the stomach. "You have to stay calm!"

"*Ca swa!*" she was yelling. "*Ca swa!*"

I pressed her against me until she finally stopped fighting. As she caught her breath, fingers digging into my arms hard enough to draw blood, I finally took a good look and realized what was different about her sweet face.

"You're okay," I said, enunciating clearly, hoping

she would understand. She looked at me frightfully, fingers clutching my arms so hard her knuckles were turning white. "You are okay."

"Ca—" she started, then stopped. Her mouth moved awkwardly as if she couldn't quite control her tongue. "Ca. Swa."

I swiveled my head around, looking for Lexi, but she had her hands full counseling the other contestants, who were making their way back underneath the water one by one. Several nodded to me as if seeking reassurance before they disappeared under. I wished one of them would tell me how to deal with this girl clinging to me like a barnacle. Time passed rapidly and my heart sank as Lexi gave me a nod and disappeared under as well.

"Ca swa," the girl said again.

"You can't swim?"

She shook her head, almond eyes pink with tears. We were the last ones above the surface. However frightened I was, she looked ten times worse, shivering so hard I thought her bones might come apart. I gave her a reassuring squeeze and tried to sound as hopeful as I could.

"It's fine," I told her, feeling like I was lying through my teeth. "I can't swim either. Just think hard. Think of something that can swim."

Her face was blank and confused and for a moment I feared she had no idea what I was saying. Then, tentatively, she loosened one hand off my arm, pressed the fingers together, and made a motion like a fish dipping up and down in waves.

"Yes!" I exclaimed. "Good! Now, try to imagine you're a fish. Think about . . ." Think about what? I racked my brain. "Think about how it would feel to *be* a fish."

Tentatively, she slid her fingers over my neck, touching the gills that had formed. It was an alien sensation, the feeling of being touched on organs not previously there. Time was running out fast, but she was calm and concentrating, and I dared not interrupt her.

Then, slowly, she released me. Her hand went to her own neck and a moment later gills appeared—tiny, fleshy slits that cut into her skin in parallel. Her eyes were unblinking and had taken on a milky sheen. I didn't know what she was thinking of, but it seemed to be doing the trick.

She squeezed my hand and slowly, slowly dipped beneath the water. No one else was surfacing. I dropped back into the water, still holding her hand. Her lower half, I now saw, had formed into clumsy, crude, but functional shape, bulky and round with a single clamshell-shaped flipper almost like a manatee. My gills flared open. I hadn't realized until now that they had closed when I rose above to speak. My body was adjusting to the changes as if they were second nature.

A screaming face floated in front of us. The girl opened her mouth in a shriek that came out as only bubbles. A woman with red hair, eyes and mouth open wide in shock, drifted through the waves. There was another not too far away, an older man suspended in the water with his shirt half-open, face unsettlingly serene. Unlucky ones. I swallowed thickly and pushed past them, pulling the frightened girl behind me. My tail parted the water expertly as if I'd had it all my life. We dove deeper, deeper, into the dark sea toward the glowing target.

THE SWIM WAS long and unbearably slow. The target appeared to be moving farther from us the more we approached it. More bodies crossed our paths. Every time the girl holding my hand turned toward one, I yanked her arm and forced her gaze back to the target. Dead, glassy eyes watched us as we descended through the silent waters.

Keep moving.

Another body, fingers curled, as if trying to claw their way out of the water.

Don't look.

Another one, face and torso encased in metal and rubber. Whatever they had been trying to form had failed and suffocated them instead.

Focus.

Half a body suspended listlessly in the water, blood and entrails swaying like a jumble of seaweed.

I halted my descent. The girl did the same. She pointed at the half-body, pulling on my arm frantically with her other hand. My heart hammered against my chest as I scanned our surroundings. Lexi was not far from us. She had seen the body, too, and was swiveling her head rapidly this way and that. It didn't take long for me to realize what she was looking at—almost none of the other contestants could be seen. Below me, I could only see three or four people, the closest being a tall man dressed in a wetsuit. A few others were off in the distance, but not more than a dozen.

She looked down and our eyes met. Though we could not speak under the murky water, I knew we were thinking the same thing. She dropped down to my side and we advanced slowly. Out of the corner of my eye, familiar shapes darted through the water. Cameras. They'd followed us even down here.

The sea's silence was deafening as we descended, a complete contrast from the chaotic arena of the previous rounds. I kept my fingers wrapped tightly around the girl's hand. The thought of her becoming one of those floating bodies was somehow more frightening than whatever danger might be awaiting me.

Something shot through the water and I jerked to the side, shoving the girl out of its way. Lexi was already on the move, darting off and toward the nearest contestants. I watched her shove one of them out of the way. The other was not so lucky. He raised his head just in time to see the thing coming at him. He struggled briefly and disappeared, swallowed by a dark, inky cloud.

I opened my mouth to shout but nothing came out except bubbles. From the dark cloud emerged a tangle of gray, fleshy tentacles covered in suckers, reaching for the contestants.

The ones remaining were picking up speed, swimming as fast as their bodies could manage. Rather than going down, I saw Lexi going up, gliding her body just out of the reach of the creature, circling it and baiting it while everyone else made their way out of its range. The girl had stopped moving and was staring slack-jawed at the spectacle. I grabbed her arm and forcefully dragged her downward as fast as my body could manage. Something was chasing me but I couldn't allow myself to be distracted. Something rubbery touched my fin—hadn't realized I had a fin until now—and I bolted forward, pulling away.

The girl had regained her composure, but try as she might, manatees were not made for speed. I dragged her behind me, pushing through the water at breakneck speed. The thing was just behind us. We passed the man in scuba gear. I reached out to grab him, too, but he brushed me off.

I paused just long enough to see him pull out a dive knife and with a swift strike slice through the gray flesh. It recoiled and snapped back. The man turned and gestured for us to move on as more wriggling forms came toward us. I hesitated, but he gave us a thumbs up. I kept moving.

The bullseye was much larger than it looked from above. Sunk into the ocean floor, it glowed and hummed, pulsating with red light. I dragged the girl toward it, pushing through that last hundred feet just as something rubbery and sticky wrapped around my tail fin. I reached and my fingers bathed in the red glow. My lower body collapsed in on itself. My spine unraveled like a spool of thread and water gushed into my lungs.

I COUGHED AND SPUTTERED. An endless stream of salty water gushed out of me. It seemed to keep going forever until I felt like I'd emptied my body of all of its internal organs. Finally, I drew a deep breath.

The girl next to me, now without her manatee half, was doing the same. More contestants were making their appearance, dripping wet, gagging, and looking generally waterlogged. We were back in the arena. I sat up shakily on the slippery black floor, soggy clothes clinging to my skin. A large hand laid on my back.

"Are you OK?"

I nodded. "I'm fine. Thank you. I—"

My voice caught in my throat as I looked up at the face looking down at me. There was pointing and gasping. He was wearing a cap when we entered the arena, and in the excitement of the moment, no one had taken a good look at his face. Under the sea, his face was obscured by the scuba mask. But now, the dirty-blond hair, chiseled chin, and high, iconic cheekbones were on display for all to see. My heart was pounding for a very different reason now. He looked just like he did in the movies.

"Are you . . ."

He smiled, wide with flawless white teeth. "Yes, Crish Michaels."

"Oh," I said. He offered me his hand and helped me to my feet. "Thank you. For earlier. With the . . . thing."

"My pleasure," he replied smoothly, gallant like a prince. I was lost for a moment. Then, I remembered where I was and who was still missing.

Eleven stood some distance away. I glossed over them and counted the contestants.

Nine . . . ten . . .

A few more came in.

Eleven . . . twelve . . .

For a terrible moment no one appeared in the arena. Panic welled up in my throat just as Lexi was printed in. She flopped ungracefully onto her stomach, propped herself up, and vomited up what looked like several gallons of water. Then, wiping her mouth, she lifted her head and found me with her eyes. She gave me a tired smile. I let out a sigh of relief.

Thirteen of us survived the round.

CHAPTER 7

Her name was Evie. The orb had arrived on her seventeenth birthday.

They dropped her off at the safe house unceremoniously less than a day after we dragged ourselves out of the murky ocean. She arrived close to midnight, but I was awake, restless and insomniac after the game. Lydia Porter accompanied the disheveled, disoriented girl, who refused to enter the house until she saw me, at which point she dashed inside and clung to my arm with soft, tiny fingers. Lydia gave a sigh that told me the trip here had been less than smooth.

"She has a speech impediment," she told me after giving me a quick rundown on Evie. She was a small, stocky thing, head buried in my shoulder as if trying to hide from the world. "She can sign, but mostly she communicates with typing. We're in the process of procuring a device for her. Meanwhile, if you don't mind, she'll be bunking with you. We can get someone to help out if you need."

I shook my head. Having one of *them* in the house felt like an intrusion. "No," I said. "We'll manage."

"Austin will be over to check on both of you tomorrow." Lydia pointed over her shoulder at the house across the street. A flat, blue structure that had been dark since I arrived. "The other contestant will be staying over there."

Other contestant. I felt my face flush. I pictured Crish Michaels walking through that door across the way and waving good morning to me. Tall, handsome, famous Crish Michaels.

"Okay," I said, trying not to sound too eager. Lydia turned to Evie.

"*I will go now,*" she said, loudly and enunciating each word clearly. "*You stay here. Okay?*"

Evie clung to me and said nothing. Lydia shook her head and left. A moment later, the driver dropped a duffel bag at the door, identical to the one left for me on my first night, and that was it. Evie and I were on our own.

I offered to fix her something to eat, but she

refused. I asked if she could get herself cleaned up and change her clothes, and she nodded yes. I waited for her to shower and rather than the ill-fitting pajamas they provided, found her an over-sized T-shirt out of my own stash to wear. When I held it out in front of her, Evie laid eyes on the big Hello Kitty face on its front and finally cracked the first smile I'd seen since our first meeting in the arena.

Despite having three rooms to choose from, Evie chose the empty bed in my room and was asleep within minutes of laying her head down. I watched her chest rise and fall, and though sleep still didn't come easily, it was nice not to be alone.

I SAT at the Formica table, which was a little more crowded today with the new additions to our group.

Heath was across from me, with his leather satchel and folders full of papers. To my right was Evie, stringy hair hanging over her face and dark circles under her eyes. I'd heard her toss and turn last night, muttering in her sleep. Whatever sleep she got was far from restful. I had yet to check myself in a mirror, but knew I was probably a horrendous sight myself, which normally wouldn't bother me except for the person to my left.

Crish Michaels leaned back in his chair, broad chest wrapped in a simple white cotton T-shirt. Every time he looked toward me some embarrassingly girlish part of me wanted to blush and giggle. If any of this didn't feel surreal enough, his presence truly made me want to pinch myself. I found myself periodically drifting off, daydreaming of myself as his femme fatale.

"Down Syndrome, apraxia, and learning disabilities." Heath's voice cut into my fantasies. He was talking not so much to Evie as at her. "They picked you up from a group home. Right." He closed his file, linked his fingers, and adopted the same overenunciated tone that Lydia used. "Do you *understand* what's going on?"

"She can hear you just fine," I said. Heath ignored me.

Evie nodded and held out one hand. She tapped the table's surface, mimicking typing on a keyboard. Heath gave an impatient wave of his hand.

"Yes, we have a communication device ready for you," he said, and reached into his satchel, where he retrieved what looked very much like a black, heavy-duty tablet. He turned it on and handed it to Evie. It displayed a keyboard with aggressively large keys. "Try it out. If you need help spelling something, I'm sure Donna here can help you." He turned to Crish as Evie fiddled with the device. The corner of his thin lips curved into the first almost-smile I'd seen since meeting him. "Mr. Michaels. Pleasure."

"Crish, please." That smile was as dazzling in this dingy house as it was on the red carpet.

"I hope your accommodations are adequate."

"It's just fine."

"Your performance in the game was impressive yesterday." Heath retrieved his phone and pulled up the Headspace website. "You now command the top score in the game after just one round."

This was true. I'd confirmed it myself yesterday, killing time waiting for Evie to arrive. Out of the thirteen who survived the round, Crish ranked at the very top, and judging by video replay, it was because he had landed more hits than everyone else combined on the thing in the water. The stunning footage easily surpassed any number of sci-fi flicks with bloated special effects budgets. Crish was born for this game. Lexi now ranked second, and I—

Well, I would be dead last if not for Evie. We had been pushed to the very bottom of the list.

My new ranking, however, was something of a

blessing. By this morning the news media had already lost interest in me and taken on a brand new frenzy over Crish. The "**Who is Donna Ching?**" headlines had been replaced by profiles of Crish Michaels and his incredible life and career. He shone over the masses like a beacon of hope and I couldn't help but feel a little mesmerized.

Heath had set up a pair of tablets on the table. From the screens, ten faces greeted us. Lexi sat with an older French gentleman. A woman in a hijab waved to us from Abu Dhabi. A man and two women from Ghana wished us good morning via a translator. A young man who looked to be about my age was attending from Mexico City. A woman in her sixties with fierce silver hair sent her well wishes from Chile. A portly middle-aged man and a slender woman were the last to arrive, dialing in from Australia though the woman introduced herself as a native New Zealander.

After initial introductions and some translations, there was an awkward moment where no one knew what to say. They all looked sleep-deprived and shell-shocked, two feelings I was intimately familiar with.

"If you don't mind," Lexi said, interrupting the silence, "I would like to ask the handlers to please refrain from butting into this conversation unless you need to translate. I think those of us who just came out of this alive have plenty to talk about."

There was grumbling, but I could tell the contestants were relieved. Some glanced warily at their handlers. Heath shook his head in disdain. I snuck a peek at Crish, wondering what he made of all this, but he was focused on the screens, his expression one of intense concentration.

"Thank you," Lexi said. Then, she looked around the display in front of her, and her voice softened. "I'm sure you're all feeling a little tired right now. You've been through a lot. And trust me, I understand. But unfortunately we don't have a lot of time. We don't know when the next round might happen."

"D-do you have a plan?" the portly Australian man asked. I was still trying to remember everyone's names and at the moment his escaped me.

"I do," Lexi replied. "I know I've only got one round on all of you. Well, most of you." She winked at me. "But I have had some time to think and I've figured a few things out. If you're all willing to hear me out, I think it will make our chances better going forward."

The others nodded. I nodded. Evie did the same.

Crish dipped his head slightly, blue eyes hard and focused.

"Astra." My head snapped up. I had hoped not to be put on the spot, but it was inevitable. "Interesting form you took—shark, was it?"

I hadn't said this out loud yet, nor allowed myself to think too hard about it. Even when I rewatched the recording, it was hard to look directly at myself on the screen, as if a closer inspection would retroactively erase the magic that held everything together. But Lexi was looking at me expectantly, as was everyone else.

"Mako shark," I said.

"Is it?" The voice startled me. Crish was looking at me with interest. "How did you come up with that?"

My face burned. I couldn't look him in the eye. "It's one of those things that sticks in your mind from school."

He looked genuinely impressed. "That's amazing," he said, and smiled. I couldn't help returning it.

"And you?" Lexi cut in. "Evie, right?"

Evie straightened slightly and nodded with uncertainty.

"You chose a manatee, but combined it with gills."

Evie paused. Then, slowly, she typed on her device. "**Yes**," it said in a stiff, mechanical voice when she finished.

"That's a clever choice. Why did you pick manatee?"

She typed again, a little faster this time. "**Cute.**"

Someone chortled. I scanned the screen to see the man from Mexico City stifling a laugh behind his hand—Sergio, his name was. He looked to be about twenty-five, tan-skinned, with a set of dog tags around his neck. Lexi rounded on him without missing a beat.

"Don't you laugh at her," she growled like a mama bear. "She's alive, isn't she? She did what worked for her and she's here with us."

"I'm sorry," said the man, still chortling. He was the only one who didn't wear that weary, tired look. "It's just a little funny. I mean, it's obvious why she picked a manatee, right? Look at her."

Lexi's brown eyes narrowed slightly as Evie shrank into herself. "Sergio Lopez, right?"

"What of it?"

"I remember you. Diving helmet. Not exactly creative."

"Was creativity the point?" Sergio asked, tilting his head teasingly. "I thought it was about saving the world and all that jazz. But that's just me. You go on."

Everyone's eyes were on Lexi. I ground my teeth and hoped she didn't take the bait.

"As I was saying," she continued, turning away from him. "There are a lot of things we don't know about the arena. But it does seem that following our instincts goes over best. We can't just think up whatever we want. Things that we have a more intimate understanding of will work better. Draw on what you know and don't force it. There's also consideration for offense versus defense. You all saw Astra's diamond shield. That's obviously one way to do it. I th—"

"Excuse me." Sergio raised his hand mockingly. "I was just wondering, what do you do?"

"I'm sorry?"

"I'm just wondering," he said, one finger on his chin. "Seeing how you've appointed yourself our glorious leader, we should know what your qualifications are. How about it? What do you do? Bake, maybe? You answer phones? Stay home with the kids?"

Once again, Lexi did not dignify him with an answer. I wasn't sure I would've been able to keep my cool quite so well. I started working up my courage to say something, but before I could, the older gentleman next to her cut in.

"She," he said with a thick French accent, "has taken down more of those things than you. I'd like to hear what she has to say, if you please."

Others muttered in agreement. Sergio smiled and put his hands up.

"Alright, alright," he said, still sporting that teasing smile. "I didn't mean to cause any offense. Please go on."

Lexi continued. She laid out plans for collecting information and finding out everyone's personal expertise and making use of them for constructing weapons, shields, and escape methods. Protecting new contestants was also a priority, she stated, and everyone hung on to her every word, though Sergio's curved smile never left his face. But despite his flippancy, we all sat a little taller and felt a little more confident by the end. Even Evie looked more relaxed.

I snuck looks at Crish periodically, wondering what he was thinking, but his expression never changed, nor did he speak up again the rest of the meeting. He seemed to be watching, and thinking. I also caught Heath looking toward Crish, with a look I could only describe as measured satisfaction.

.   .   .

EVIE'S THINGS arrived later in the day. She had very little to her name and was attached to even less of it. She sat cross-legged on the floor and unpacked her meager belongings with practiced efficiency, as if completely accustomed to putting them in boxes and taking them out again. I sat on my bed, watched her go about her task, and decided it would be in bad taste to ask what she'd gone through in life to give her this skill. Since the meeting, she had said very little.

"You okay?" She looked at me for a moment, then scooted across the room and grabbed her device.

"**Tired.**"

"It's a lot to take in." I ran a hand over the mattress under me. "These beds sure don't help."

"**Too hard.**" A pause. "**But harder back home.**"

"What did you think of Lexi?"

"**Cool.**"

"And what about Crish Michaels?" I gave her a smile. "Can you believe he's actually here? It's unreal."

Evie looked at me, long and seriously, before she typed. "**Strange. Him.**"

"How so?" She shrugged and wasn't terribly interested in elaborating. "What about Heath? What'd you think of him?"

Evie tapped her chin with two fingers, then typed purposefully on the device. "**What an ass.**"

I burst out laughing. She grinned mischievously. It was one of very few moments in those hard months to come that I almost felt like things were going to be okay.

CHAPTER 8

EVIE AND CRISH LENT A SENSE OF NORMALCY TO THE dreary safe house. Before their arrival, I'd spent much of my time in a state of agitated anticipation, pacing the house, reading odds and ends on the internet, and pinching myself hoping to end this waking nightmare. I'd stopped sleeping on any schedule resembling normal and ate the bare minimum to stay alive.

But Evie was calm—or withdrawn, I couldn't quite tell which. The only things she requested from Lydia were crafting supplies—scissors, glue, construction paper. She spent hours meticulously cutting apart the paper and gluing them into intricate collages. As far as I could tell, this was an activity she was taught in the group home to pass time, and over time became something of a coping mechanism. I watched her work in between reading and cooking meals—though it wasn't my responsibility, I felt like I would somehow be failing as a person if she didn't get proper meals and bedtimes. We talked, or rather I talked and she listened. I told her about Addison and Maddy, about my mother's short but intense battle with cancer, about growing further and further from my father after her death, and about Hannah's surprise baby after struggling with infertility. She always listened intently, though she had little to say.

Meanwhile the world fell quickly and violently in love with Crish Michaels. Overnight, he had moved on from a run-of-the-mill celebrity to the hero of the world. He was, by all accounts, a remarkable man. Up until now he hadn't been real to me, the same way any celebrity that frequented movie screens and magazines carried a mirage-like presence. But now he was here, across the street and stopping by often with his bright smile to check if we were alright. I had never taken a vested interest in him before beyond a mild and distant admiration, but now I couldn't help reading what all the news blogs and gossip sites were saying about his brilliant career, impressive portfolio of talents, and pet projects, which mainly consisted of charity work for brain-injured children. He was like a storybook hero, the world's knight in shining armor.

Every time he showed up at our door, I struggled to keep myself from blushing and blubbering like an idiot. Sitting at the Formica table and looking completely at home, Crish regaled me with stories of eventful travels, movie sets, and people of all shapes and kinds he'd encountered in his illustrious career. He was never boastful, but seemed eager to have a chance to hear his own voice after being trapped in his gray box of a house, much like our own.

Evie, on the other hand, was less than impressed. She watched Crish out of the corner of her eye and gave him little more than a glancing acknowledgement. In all honesty, I was selfishly glad not to have to share Crish's attention. I listened to him and quietly nursed my schoolgirl crush, mesmerized and glad for the escape.

I LANDED FAIRLY STEADILY on my feet this time despite the vertigo. Evie appeared next to me a moment later, eyes darting nervously until they found a target. I followed her uneasy gaze and spotted Eleven standing some distance away, silent and motionless as usual.

We were ready this time. As the days ticked by and the week mark passed, we began to leave the tablet running, automatically refreshing the Headspace website with a macro command Heath helped us set up. This time it took ten days before the list of contestants was posted, and within a minute of it posting, Crish was at our door, dressed to the nines in his "battle suit." I couldn't help but notice how well it hugged his broad form and strong legs. He didn't come empty handed.

"I asked for this the day I arrived," he said, showing me the half-empty bottle of scotch in his hand. "I don't know if you're a drinker, but it calms the nerves. What do you—"

I grabbed it out of his hand before he could finish the question, upcapped it, and took a swig. It was the first drink I'd had since the plane ride with Lydia, and it left a nostalgic, bittersweet, burning sensation going down. Crish looked surprised and amused. I couldn't say if it calmed my nerves or not, but as I stood here once again, a little voice in my head restlessly whispered *do or die*.

Evie's hand brushed my arm, her fingers tracing over the fabric covering the remnants of the burn welts left by Eleven on that fateful first round. She glanced at Eleven again, and made a sign that I'd

141

come to understand as a question. I shook my head dismissively. There were more important things for her to worry about.

More contestants appeared. The members of the surviving thirteen nodded to each other as we spotted each other in the crowd. The newcomers looked around, uneasy. A few made a beeline for the veterans, as if seeking safety. The younger ones gravitated toward Crish right away. Among them was Sergio, who had pushed his way through the others and was eagerly shaking Crish's hand and gushing his admiration. A fan, I supposed.

Evie tugged on my sleeve. She made a sweeping gesture at the contestants and did a sign I didn't recognize. Seeing my confusion, she raised one hand with five fingers splayed and the other she curled into a circle.

"Fifty?" She nodded. "There's only fifty?"

She was right. The group was only half the size of past ones. What this meant I wasn't certain.

"Squad leaders, raise your hands," came Lexi's authoritative voice. Eight hands went up. Gathering my courage, fueled by the shot of scotch, I raised my own. I'd never wanted to lead, but Lexi was insistent. The thirteen of us had been divided into nine teams, some choosing to pair up. I would be lying if I said I didn't wish I could've paired up with Crish, for the sake of having someone more capable to lean on if nothing else, but looking at the gaggle of starry-eyed new arrivals around him, I decided I was probably better off with Evie.

"The people you see with their hands up have survived at least one round and have volunteered to help out newcomers," Lexi was saying, her own hand raised. "Hurry and find your way to one of them. Try to divide up evenly, four or five per group. They will brief you on what to expect and what you need to do. Stick close to them if you can and they may be able to help you during the game."

The spots next to Lexi were immediately claimed. A few came toward me, but most glanced our way, mentally sized up Evie, and suddenly seemed to change their mind. In the end, only two others joined us.

"You're Donna Ching!" one of them gushed, a matronly woman in floral pants. "I'm Vanessa. You're amazing. I saw you do the . . ."—she gestured at her legs—"the shark thing. It was in-*cre*-dible."

"Thanks," I replied awkwardly.

"I'm Aaron," said the nervous-looking man. He was big and burly, but his eyes betrayed a quivering vulnerability. "Can you get me back to my kids?

That's all I want. I'll do anything you say. Just please get me back to my kids. I can't leave them without a daddy."

All I managed to say was, "I'll do my best."

I laid out Lexi's plan as quickly and clearly as I could, trying hard not to stammer over my words or talk too fast. The concept was simple—stick to your group, use what you know, be aware of your environment, and if something works, hold on to it. Leadership and public speaking were not things I prided myself on. The other group leaders all looked much more sure of themselves, particularly Lexi, who rang the image of a true leader from every angle. The group around her was hanging on to her every word.

"*Hello contestants!*"

Cheshire's voice blared into the echoing space just as I finished going over the plan. The contestants tensed visibly as they strolled into view, walking stick and heels clicking rhythmically against the floor. This time, I noticed, very few of the contestants jumped or stepped back.

"*Look at you all, plotting among yourselves*," they quipped. "*You're all so cute. Are you whispering secrets? What are they? Care to tell the cameras? Anything for ratings.*"

"We don't have to tell you anything," announced

a strong, raised voice. I looked to the source of the voice and was somewhat unsurprised to find Sergio, chest puffed and chin raised, peacocking for all to see. "We're here to fight for the fate of our planet, and we're going to win. Now stop wasting our time and get on with it."

"*Ooh, tough guy*," Cheshire cooed. They gestured toward Eleven. "*Keep it in your pants, big boy. Or Eleven might have to lay you out. I think you'll find that rather deflating for your ego. But, as you wish. Let's get this game started.*"

I passed a glance at Crish, standing just behind Sergio. Something made me think the little "fight for the planet" schtick was for his benefit. But if he was impressed by Sergio's bravado, he gave no sign. Before I could think much more on it, the ground shook. Cries of surprise and fear rose through the crowd. I instinctively grabbed Evie.

A massive structure tore free of the black floor and the contestants scrambled to get out of its way, scattering in all directions. The quaking went on forever. When it finally stopped, we all took a deep, tentative breath, and looked up.

A pyramid stood in the center of the arena floor. Though on the surface it resembled the worn sandstone pyramids of Egypt, it was infinitely taller, reaching endlessly into the sky that had now faded from white to solid black. Enormous red countdown numbers appeared. The sight of them gave me a gnawing feeling in the pit of my stomach.

60:00

Sixty minutes until what?

"*Welcome to the Pyramid Climb,*" Cheshire announced with their usual flair. "*When the clock starts, you'll climb. Make it to the top by the end of the hour, and you'll survive the round. The faster you climb it, the higher your score. Other . . .* opportunities *to score may present themselves. But you'll figure it out. Easy enough, yeah?*"

A murmur rippled through the arena.

"It can't be that simple," I heard Aaron mutter to himself.

"Don't worry," said Vanessa. She gave me an exaggerated, almost comical wink. "I was hoping for something like this. I came prepared."

I had no idea what she had in mind, but her confidence was infectious. I squeezed Evie's hand.

"*Take your places, folks,*" Cheshire called, clapping their gloved hands together. "*Hop on.*"

Lexi took a resolute step onto the pyramid. She nodded to the squad leaders and we did the same.

The sandstone step was hard and warm, as if it had been baking for centuries under a hot alien sun.

"*Ready?*"

Most of the other contestants also stepped on. A few put on only one foot. The rest stayed hesitantly just off the edge of it.

"*Set!*"

"Watch this," Vanessa said, beaming with excitement.

"*Go!*"

A pair of long wings burst out of her back, hitting me with a faceful of feathers. The other contestants stared in disbelief as Vanessa shook herself out like a bird, long, gray feathers rustling. She tossed me a triumphant smile, crouched down, and with a half-sprint, half-leap launched herself into the air. For a moment I feared she was going to fall, but then the wings gave a powerful pump and carried her upward. Her silver hair shimmered as she rose and in flight she was almost angelic. Cheers rang out all around us. Evie tugged on my arm with excitement, pointing and signing.

BANG

The sound took a moment to register. Vanessa halted in midair for a moment as her torso snapped backward, then down she came in a tangle of feathers and limbs, spine meeting the steps of the pyramid with a sickening *crack*. She rolled to the bottom, one broken wing wrapped around her body. I dashed down after her, but even before I could brush the feathers from her face, I knew she was dead. The gaping hole in her chest gushed liberally, painting gray feathers and brown stone with hideous red. Her neck bent at an unnatural angle and her eyes were wide open with surprise.

Cheshire lowered their hand, held in the shape of a finger gun. Their face was still smiling, but the sight of that simple curved mouth line sent a shiver down my spine.

"*Sorry,*" they said, sounding almost regretful. "*No flying. I thought that would be obvious. Bad sportsmanship and all.*"

Whatever confidence was instilled in me by the scotch was rapidly draining, much like the color on the contestants' faces. I tore my eyes from the broken form and faced Cheshire.

"You didn't have to do that," I said, my voice a shaky mutter instead of the stern authority I was going for.

"*No, I didn't,*" Cheshire replied with a shrug. "*But isn't this so much more dramatic? And by the way, with that little infraction, you've lost some time. Now your head start is gone."*

A piercing scream rang out, followed by several more. My head snapped left and right, searching for the source. Several yards away, a woman screamed and flailed. I needed only to look down to see the reason.

The black floor had taken on the texture of fine sand. The woman's feet were already completely buried. Her group members quickly grabbed her hand and pulled frantically. Half a dozen others were in the same predicament. Helping hands tried their best, but to no avail. Their legs were buried within seconds, and sand rapidly rose to their chests, pulling them in like a creature swallowing its prey.

Then, with a gutteral rumble, the pyramid began to sink into the soft sand. The people who didn't step on lost their grips and the rest of us watched as their faces, pale with terror, sank beneath the black surface.

"*Climb!*" came Lexi's commanding voice. We turned as one and began scrambling up the pyramid.

. . .

THE SINKING WAS THANKFULLY SLOW, and we made headway right away. Several people were already making use of the ability the arena offered them, though no one dared to fly again. The Australian man's group had transformed their hands into bird-like claws that gripped the sandstone as they ascended. The woman from Abu Dhabi was bounding ahead on mountain goat legs, herding her group upward. I made sure Evie stayed ahead of me. The shoes given to us with our suits luckily provided excellent grip. Our little group of three moved up, putting step after step behind us, not daring to look back.

The climb was exhausting and increasingly difficult the higher we went. The stone steps increased in size and twenty minutes in we were hauling each other up and over them.

"Here," said Aaron. "Try this." He raised one hand and placed it against the surface of the stone. His fingers elongated and widened. Ridges appeared on the underside of his hands. He reached over the top of an especially tall step and hauled himself up with relative ease. "Geckos. Best climber out there. Helped my son with a science project with them. Never thought it'd be any real use."

"You can thank him when you get home," I said,

and followed his example. Evie hesitated. I reached my hand down to her. "Come on. I'll help you."

Slowly, as if lost in thought, she raised both hands and looked at them. A moment later a white substance oozed from her fingertips and quickly coated both hands like thick, sticky mittens. She grabbed the top of the stone; the white substance stuck and held strong. Aaron and I helped her pull up.

"What is that?" I asked her as we moved on. She thought for a moment, then made a gesture like her fingers were stuck together, then pulled apart.

"Glue, I think she means," Aaron said. Evie nodded with a smile. "Smart girl."

I held out my hand. Evie gave me an eager high five, and we continued on.

THE RED NUMBERS in the sky read **30:15**. The black sand was far below us. The other groups were moving along. There had been no lives lost since the initial unfortunate few.

Evie made a gesture at me, wiped away the sweat on her forehead, and sat heavily down on the step above me. I nodded. I was exhausted, too.

"One minute," I said. "Then we keep going."

For a brief, almost peaceful moment we sat on the stone steps. Several other groups also paused their ascent, panting as they slumped on the nearest surface to rest. I craned my neck upward and found Lexi, who waved at me. I waved back.

"It hasn't been that long, has it?" Aaron said incredulously, gazing into the black horizon with a bemused look in his eyes. "Since this whole thing started. Even though I'm here I still don't believe it. I mean, what are we doing? Who'd ever believe this?"

I hadn't actually thought about it in those terms, but hearing it spoken out loud nailed the absurdity of it. Aaron looked at me with his deep brown eyes.

"You've been hiding, eh?" he asked. "Everyone's wondering where you folks have been, the ones who survived. If you're hiding, I can't say I blame you. It's crazy out there."

"Is it?"

"There's people coming outta the woodworks left and right, claiming to know one of you or been involved with you in some way. Every politician you can think of is using your names to get votes. That Crish Michaels guy—the movie star—his face is all over the place. Can't walk down the street without hearing his name." A thin smile crept over his face. "You didn't really make a sexy video with a bunch of guys dressed like little green aliens in college, did you?"

"*What?*" I couldn't hide the abject horror on my face. "Is that what they're saying about me?"

Aaron chuckled. "Didn't think so. Don't worry, they're making up new stories every day. That one already came and went. They can't help it—too easy to sell a magazine with one of your names on the cover."

I shook my head, trying to clear the mental images that conjured up. "Let's keep moving," I said, getting to my feet. "I don't want to think about this."

"I hope I get to tell my grandkids about this someday," Aaron said wistfully. "I'll write a book and read it to them. Might even draw pictures."

"Can you leave out the little green aliens?"

"Sure, and when—"

A new rumbling cut him off and the ground beneath us slipped down several feet in a jarring shudder. Evie let out a cry of surprise and nearly tumbled off the steps. Aaron reached out and grabbed her shoulder before she could fall.

The pyramid picked up speed, descending faster than before. The black sand rose at frightening speed.

"*Go!*" I shouted, and we scrambled up the pyramid, pulling ourselves up step after step. A number of tiny cameras flew by our faces, trying to capture our terrified expressions. *Ratings*, as Cheshire would say.

Evie shrieked, jabbing a finger downward behind us.

Several shapes, black as the desert itself, had pulled themselves from the sand. Slithering and shapeless as liquid, they oiled up the pyramid steps. Most of the contestants hadn't noticed them. To my left, two groups, led by Crish and Mia, the woman from New Zealand, were climbing without a look back.

"Heads up!" I called, pointing toward the foot of the pyramid as they looked toward me. Their eyes widened as they spotted the creatures and immediately the pyramid was filled with shouting and calls as the groups alerted each other. I turned upward to warn Lexi, but she was already looking down, brow furrowed. She lifted one hand, finger pointed in the gun pose, and narrowed her eyes.

BANG

One of the creatures splattered apart, oozing down the steps like an oil spill. The others paused momentarily, as if surprised, then began to zigzag their way upward at double speed.

"Keep climbing!" Lexi shouted. "Squad leaders, protect your group!"

My chest clenched. Aaron and Evie looked to me hopefully. I gritted my teeth and took a moment to gather myself.

"Go," I said, and waved them on. Evie gave me a hesitant look. I returned a smile that I hoped was brave. "Go ahead. I got this."

Except I didn't believe that. As Aaron helped Evie in their ascent, I took a deep breath and let it out. The other squad leaders also stood their ground. The black shapes snaked their way toward us.

Another shot rang out—this time from Crish. Several of the others fired as well. Not all the shots found targets. In fact, a few of them were quite far off. But they served as enough of a warning to slow the creatures' pace. Lexi, true to her military background, was picking them off one after another. Crish and Sergio weren't too shabby either. The women from Ghana were impressive as well, every shot meditated and precise.

I raised my finger.

Muzzle. Barrel. Slide. Hammer.

Misfire. I felt an uncomfortable jolt through my shoulder.

Muzzle. Barrel. Magazine? Release?

My fingers let out a weak spark. Try as I might, I couldn't formulate the weapon in my mind. I struggled to remember what the stiff-faced trainers taught me, but my body refused to cooperate. The crash courses were simply not enough to bridge the gaps in my knowledge.

Muzzle. Barrel . . .

"Astra!"

Lexi's voice cut through my mind like a knife. My head snapped up just in time to see a black, oily shadow tower over me. My arms raised reflexively to protect my face and it threw itself over me like a falling parachute. Its weight pinned me to the ground and the back of my head connected painfully with the sandstone steps. I saw stars. The black form folded over my face, suffocating me. I heard Lexi's voice calling me over and over as I struggled underneath it.

I couldn't breath. It weighed me down, enveloping me. Swallowing me. Tiny tendrils fingered my mouth and nose as if looking for a way in. Panic choked me.

Something.

I couldn't scream. I couldn't think.

Anything.

Suddenly the weight was off me. I drew a deep, desperate breath. The back of my head was slick with blood.

The black creature was still above me, wiggling and trying to get at me. Diamond spikes had sprouted from the ground all around me, some so close they had cut my skin in their emergence. Their pointed tips pierced the creature, holding it immobile above me. It made one last desperate attempt to struggle before falling apart in a wet splatter, coating me with a black, gritty slime.

"Astra!"

I peeked through the spikes of diamond to see Lexi's concerned face.

"Alright? Can you get out?"

I nodded, which was difficult with the little wiggle room I had. I closed my eyes and concentrated. The diamond spikes shattered all around me. I got shakily to my feet and Lexi grabbed my arm.

"Hurry."

The other contestants had gone on ahead. The black creatures, perhaps wary of our resistance, had stayed back for the moment, hovering roughly twenty steps down. The clock had counted down to less than twenty minutes. We kept climbing. My body ached and the gecko-skin textures on my fingers were deteriorating.

"Look!" someone shouted. "I see the top!"

The top of the pyramid was indeed visible. The tip ended in a small, flat platform. Eleven stood at its edge, peering down at the climbers with their expressionless face. The contestants redoubled their efforts and moved upward. I glanced over at Lexi and saw a glimmer of joy.

Then, with a rumble, nearly a quarter of the pyramid collapsed.

Three groups tumbled down among the falling rocks. Desperate hands reached out and grasped empty as they fell. Several people lost control of their form in panic and reverted back to their unmodified bodies. The teen from Vietnam made a desperate attempt upward and a pair of scraggly wings sprouted from his back. He managed a few weak flaps and just barely got his fingers onto the edge of the remaining rock surface. A shot pierced his forehead before he could pull himself back up and he joined the others in the darkness below.

No flying.

More of the pyramid fell away. The ground beneath Lexi and me cracked. Another group made a desperate lunge out of the fall zone but half failed to make the cross. Victor, the old French man, lost his footing as the ground beneath him gave away. He reached out and managed to seize the edge with one hand. Crish shouted to his group and Sergio sprang forward and grabbed the old man's hand. For a precarious moment they dangled over the edge, then Victor joined the others, falling into the black abyss.

"*GO!*" Lexi screamed. We sprinted upward, trying to ignore the rumbling beneath our feet. The pyramid crumbled fast. My fingers were raw and bleeding from gripping stone. The back of my head ached but I couldn't afford to stop.

The contestants who had made it to the platform leaned over and shouted encouragement from the side. I let out a sigh of relief as Evie climbed her way over the last step. My brief tangle with the sand creature had slowed me down, and Lexi and I were among the last ones.

The ground fell from under me and my foot stepped empty. I let out a cry and for a moment felt myself falling. As my head tilted back I saw Eleven on the platform above. My mind snapped to the burns on my arm, to the metal hand that left them there. My own fingers stiffened and I threw my arm upward to the nearest edge. The metal claw that was once my hand sank hard into the stone and my body jerked to a stop. Lexi grabbed my arm and hauled me back over the edge.

"Come on," she panted. "Almost there."

We continued upward, toward the sound of encouraging voices.

"I wonder if my baby girl is watching," Lexi said, her face coated with dust and sweat. "I hope not, but if she is, I hope she knows Mama's coming home to her."

I looked up and saw Aaron leaning over the edge of the platform, gesturing eagerly at us. "Yeah," I said. "I hope so, too."

The clock in the sky had only a few seconds left as we reached the platform. Lexi, one step above me, grabbed my hand and pulled me up in front of her, just as the ground under her crumbled to dust.

I instinctively tightened my fingers around hers. My other hand gripped its metal fingers around the edge of the platform. A scream escaped me as Lexi's weight dislocated my shoulder. There was nothing but air around us.

The clock in the sky ticked down. **0:00**

"Help!" I cried, or tried to. The pain in my shoulder was blinding and holding on to her hand took everything in me. The very few seconds I hung there were an eternity.

A strong hand gripped my arm and lifted me effortlessly over the edge. I gritted my teeth and counted to five before I let go. Lexi and I landed heavily on the platform, panting. My right arm hung limply as I lay on my side, afraid to move.

"Thanks," Lexi panted. I rolled onto my back with a groan. Eleven stood over us. Their metal hand had left indents on my arm, but at least no burns this time.

"Yeah," I breathed, hissing at the pain in my shoulder. "Thanks."

Eleven knelt down beside me. I eyed them nervously. They were intimidatingly tall and nothing but metal as far as the eye could see. Suddenly, I was afraid. Had we lost? We weren't technically on the platform when the clock finished. Cheshire shot two people for flying. Was Eleven now going to throw us over the edge for not standing on the platform with both feet when the time ended?

They took my arm firmly in one hand and with a jarring *snap* set it back into place. A scream burst out of me but was cut short as I tried to catch my breath.

"Are you alright?"

For a moment I couldn't figure out who had asked the question.

"You talk?" I managed between shallow breaths.

Eleven nodded. A single, efficient motion. Their voice was low with a buzzing quality, as if produced through some sort of synthesizer.

"Yes, I'm fine," I said, shifting my arm carefully. "Thank you."

Evie pushed through the group and embraced me tightly. Eleven rose and stepped away from us. I scanned the platform blearily. The contestants slumped on the ground in various forms, resting, smiling, and congratulating each other. The surviving squad leaders looked a little more worn than the rest, but everyone was relieved and thankful, at least for the moment. I should have been relieved, too, but somehow I didn't quite feel it. Over Evie's shoulder, I found Crish's group.

Crish was hugging the women in his group and no doubt giving them sweet words of encouragement. Next to him stood Sergio, looking relieved and pleased with himself. He turned slightly my way and I quickly looked away, pretending my eyes hadn't caught his. My heart pounded. Did I really see him tear Victor's hand from the ledge?

CHAPTER 9

A TIGHT-LIPPED DOCTOR PATCHED UP MY HEAD, checked my eyes, and inspected my shoulder, all under Lydia's watchful eye. Cuts and scratches were bandaged up and he informed me tersely how lucky I was that Eleven hadn't done any damage resetting my shoulder, as if it was my fault. He left as quietly as he came and I sank into the floral couch, head draped limply over the back. The quiet of the house was eerie after the chaotic hour. As I stared at the colorless ceiling, the pyramid, black sand, and creeping black slime felt like a bad dream.

Thirty-one of us survived the Pyramid Climb. Though I didn't want to think of the nineteen that didn't, Vanessa's bent wings and broken body haunted me. Sleep was near impossible so I spent much time restlessly pacing. Evie followed me silently, carrying her tablet and crafting supplies and staying within earshot as she worked, completely engrossed with her papers and glue. Though we spoke little, I appreciated her company—being alone would probably drive me to madness.

Crish scored exceptionally well in the Pyramid Climb, as did Lexi. My own score languished at the bottom, though I couldn't care less. In fact, I was thrilled that no one was counting on me to cross the score line for saving the planet.

The number of surviving contestants based in the United States had risen to six. The other three were being housed in a similar facility somewhere on the West Coast. The higher-ups, whomever they were, decided to spread us out for safety. We were introduced via teleconference, and meetings were held with Lexi leading the discussion nearly every day. The thirty-one of us hailed from fifteen different countries. Languages, time zones, and cultural barriers made communication a challenge in itself. But one thing we silently agreed on was to listen to Lexi. Unwavering in her positivity and determination, she was every bit our fearless leader, though the suitcases under her eyes told a different story. For her resilience I was grateful. She held us together.

The media dubbed me "Diamond Donna," a nickname I was not partial to. A chat chain started in the messenger app comparing the absurd stories in the tabloids. Someone mentioned that a company in Asia had begun to create trading cards based on each of us. My skin crawled at the thought of millions of strangers playing with little pieces of paper bearing my likeness.

The fact that we all grew accustomed to this lifestyle spoke volumes to the adaptability of humans. Perhaps the increasing number of survivors relaxed the newcomers. They seemed a little less nervous and a little more excited. The one who bubbled with the most excitement over our shared fame was Sergio. Not a day went by without messages from him, linking us to yet another tabloid story, most of the time about himself or Crish. He was the only one who seemed truly and genuinely happy to be a part of the game, a joy that both dismayed and vexed me.

"HE'S JUST EXCITED."

"I suppose," I said noncommittally, measuring out two teaspoons of sugar for Crish's coffee, very aware of his watchful eyes on me.

"Thank you," he said, smiling. I still couldn't

help hiding my blush in his company. "How are you sleeping?"

"Not well. Hard to keep my head quiet."

"Are you still meeting with the trainers?"

"Yes. Didn't help me in that last round, though."

"So guns aren't your strong suit. Big deal. Work with what you know."

"You must know a lot. From acting, I mean."

"You could say I've picked up a few things." I set the coffee in front of him. Whenever he became lost in thought, he cupped his mug in both hands, as if warming his fingers. "Jack of all trades, master of none. Some of the stage combat and weaponry training has been useful, which was really just luck." He nodded to the closed bedroom door behind me, where Evie usually sequestered herself during his visits. "How's Evie?"

"Fine," I said, then added, "I think."

"Still doesn't like me, huh?"

"It's not your fault. She doesn't like people. Have you been talking to—" I stopped myself.

"Yes?"

I bit my tongue. Sergio's name was at the tip of it, but the questions were difficult to form.

"Heath," I said, picking the first name that came to mind. "Austin."

Crish lowered his gaze. "So you heard."

"Heard what?"

"The campaign."

"What campaign?"

He pursed his lips hesitantly. "They want me to film a series of clips to be broadcast worldwide. Public service announcement kind of thing, to reassure the general public that we have things under control and to hold course and keep peace. People are in a constant panic that the world might end. They figure some reassurance from someone in the game will help."

"That's great!" He arched a brow in surprise. "You're perfect for it, with your background and all."

"You think so? I wasn't sure. I told them the message should come from the original survivors, you and Alexis."

I shook my head. "God, no. I can't imagine putting myself out there like that. Just having everyone gossiping about me is too much. I want to get this whole thing over with and go back to my normal life."

"I don't know," Crish said, tapping one finger on his mug. "Do you think everything will ever be normal again?"

"I haven't thought about it," I said honestly. "If I overthink it, I might go crazy."

He chuckled. "Fair enough." A pause. "Are you sure it doesn't bother you?"

"Not at all." I smiled at him. "Go for it. You'll be brilliant."

Crish leaned forward over the table and laid one of his hands, still warm from the coffee mug, over mine. Something inside me flip-flopped and before I could decide how to react, the door behind me opened. My hand pulled back reflexively. Evie emerged from the bedroom waving my tablet in her hand and signing. Seeing Crish was still here, she stopped in her tracks and looked from me to him.

Crish got to his feet. "I should go," he said. Then, leaning down, he pecked me on the cheek. "I'll see you later, Astra."

My face burned hot. Even as he closed the door behind him, I could still feel his lips on my face. I turned to Evie, feeling a little irritated at her inter- ruption, and saw she looked as annoyed with me as I was with her.

"Don't like him."

"You don't have to," I said, a little flippantly, though I wasn't sure if she was declaring her own dislike for Crish or telling me not to like him. "What's up?"

She shoved the tablet at me. The Headspace website glowed on the screen. I scrolled through and quickly saw what she was trying to show me.

"Is this right?"

She reached over my shoulder and scrolled the page back to the top, jabbing her finger where she wanted me to look. A line of red text had been added to the top of the page, followed by a countdown.

BONUS ROUND IN 14:46:10

"That's tonight!" I exclaimed, leaping to my feet and scrolling as fast as the tablet would allow. "It's too soon. And this list—" The screen sprang to a stop as I reached the bottom. "There aren't any new people."

Evie nodded vigorously.

Before I could think about what this meant, the messenger app rang. Messages flooded in. One after another, and another, and another.

Midnight.

Wet, lightless skyscrapers loomed over us like dead giants. An unpleasant moisture seeped over every surface. Flickering street lamps cast a dirty yellow glow over the streets. Something shrieked in the distance. The contestants drifted close to each other, seeking comfort in numbers. Almost all of us were dressed in some form of protective gear, provided by our respective handlers. We looked like a ragtag, haphazard group of superhero washouts.

"You know what this reminds me of?" Lexi said, her voice low as if wary of disturbing the thick, clammy air. "Playgrounds in horror movies. Where the seesaw squeaks but there's no one on it."

I nodded. The hair on the back of my neck stood at attention. Dark buildings and empty streets stretched in every direction. I folded my arms in front of me, rubbing the phantom chill from them, feeling exposed.

"Well," Aaron said, stepping next to me, casting nervous glances at the sky. "I don't think I can get used to this. This is only my second round, but I can't imagine the next one, or the one after that."

"One at a time," I said, half to myself. "Don't worry about the next one. Just focus on this one."

"This is your fourth one, isn't it?"

It was. I hadn't realized. I didn't like to think about it.

A clicking sound drew our attention, growing closer as the tall, slender form of Cheshire emerged into view, tap-dancing between the islands of light from the street lamps, walking stick spinning in one hand. And, in case the slasher film vibe hadn't been fully driven home, they were headless.

"*Hello, contestants*," Cheshire greeted us as they approached, the glowing blue emoji face flashing on. "*How are we doing on this very fine night?*"

No one answered.

"*Tsk. Such a solemn bunch.*" Cheshire spread their arms and gestured at the gloomy buildings behind them. "*Welcome to the Hollow City!*"

"Get on with it."

Cheshire lowered their arms and regarded Lexi with interest. "*Reigning champion stepping up. Very nice. You are very popular, you know.*" They strolled forward and walked a slow circle around her. The rest of us backed away uncomfortably. "*The producers are very pleased with you. Tell me, are you curious?*"

"About what?"

"*Life, the universe, everything.*" Cheshire let out a snorting laugh and slapped their knee. "*Oh, I crack myself up. But seriously, you're not wondering at all?*"

"About *what*?"

"*Why there's only thirty-one of you? Why there's no one else here?*"

"You'll tell us if you want to."

One of Cheshire's eyes turned into an asterisk for a moment, then turned back—a wink. "*So smart! And that is correct. Lucky for you, I have every intention of telling you. We only need thirty of you for the next round, but you managed thirty-one. You guys are getting good at this. Especially you, Glorious Leader. So, after talking to the producers, we decided to add a bonus round. This one is going to be special.*"

They turned away from Lexi and addressed the rest of us.

"*The goal of this round will be a little different. You see, no matter what, we need to reduce the number of contestants to thirty. There are two ways to do so. The first is simple—for one of you to die. Once one person is eliminated, the game will be over.*

"*The second is to take out the target. Whoever takes out the target gets to take the one-way train out.*" A thick silence fell over the group. "*Let that sink in for a moment.*"

Excitement stirred in the air.

"*That's right,*" they said, before anyone could ask. "*Take out the target, and you'll get to go home, no strings attached.*"

My heart pounded. I didn't dare let myself think of the possibility, but I could hear the thought echo in every voice around me.

I could go back to my life.

"*Now the rules of Hollow City. There's a simple reason for the name—everything you see around you is hollow.*" Cheshire held up a hand in gun shape and fired at a building half a block away. The shot cracked through the air and the skyscraper crumbled like a dry biscuit. Rock and dirt tumbled to the ground in an avalanche. "*They're all ready to fall with a stiff breeze. If you don't want to trap yourself or get buried, I'd be careful with those shots.*"

A nervous rumble. Cheshire went on.

"*Of course, the buildings aren't your main concern. As you move around, watch out for the spider.*"

As if on cue, something dashed through the air behind them, leaping from one building to the next, disappearing into the shadows before any of us got a good look.

"*The spider is a tricky one. She likes the shadows and she moves quietly. Stay in the light, and she might not get you. But, if you want that ticket out of here, you'll have to brave those shadows to take her down.*" The emoji face scanned us, enjoying our apprehension.

Evie grabbed my hand nervously. "Stay in the light," I whispered.

Cheshire's gaze landed on us. "*Oh,*" they said, "*one more thing—you won't be starting from here. Ready? Go!*"

The world went black. A split second later it swam back into focus and I was alone. I looked frantically around but could see no one. Blood pounded in my ears as I started to call out Evie's name, then stopped myself. The dark city closed in around me and I heard nothing but dripping water.

A movement to my left, leaping through the air from wall to wall. I broke into a run toward the nearest street lamp and stepped into its protective light just as the moving shape landed on the side of a nearby building.

It wasn't quite what I expected a spider to look like. I had imagined a crawling creature with eight scraggly legs creeping up and down the skyscrapers. This thing looked human, thin with long, delicate limbs, crouching on the flat surface as if the laws of gravity were irrelevant. It turned its faceless head toward me, then tilted to one side, as if studying me in curiosity. I didn't dare move. It was black from head to toe, as if made of shadow itself. A long, tense moment later, it turned away, scaled the wall in a manner straight out of Spider-Man comics, and disappeared around the corner. I waited far too long before working up the nerve to step out of the light and keep moving. I had to find Evie.

The crack of a shot fired took me off guard. Then, the building right next to me, where the spider had just perched, began to crumble.

WHEN THE DUST CLEARED, I was still shaking. Sprawled in a puddle on the cold concrete, I looked back at the remnants of the collapsed structure. It was my sheer luck that it wasn't one of the larger buildings. I had managed to run out of the crash range just in time. I got to my feet, just as another shot zipped past my face and hit the concrete.

Someone was shooting at *me*.

I broke into a run as the shots came at me one after another. Was it the spider? Somehow I didn't think so. They stopped as soon as I rounded a corner and pressed myself against the wall. Whoever was aiming at me knew I was out of range.

Why would someone open fire at me? They couldn't possibly have mistaken me for the spider. Breathing hard, I kept moving, putting as much distance between myself and the shooter as possible. I had no idea where they were, but I could keep moving in the opposite direction from where the bullets came from. The spider was in the shadows and the shooter would spot me in the light. I picked up the pace, staying in the dark but keeping the lights close.

Time eked by and I couldn't find any trace of Evie. Once, I spotted someone at the end of a block, but they disappeared down an alley before I could catch up. No more shots came at me, but I stayed vigilant. I didn't see the spider either. The only sounds were dribbles of rainwater falling from gutters and overhangs.

A scream stopped me in my tracks, followed by

panicked shouts and a shot that brought down another building. A shape zipped through the air onto the side of another building and disappeared. A pair of figures stepped into view.

"*Astra!*"

Relief washed over me as I saw their faces. Lexi rushed over and wrapped me in a tight, brief hug. Aaron followed on her heels.

"We got split up," she said, breathless. "All of us. This place is huge. We haven't found anyone else."

"Me—" I started, then remembered the person shooting at me. "Me either. I think."

"Did you see it?" she asked, head whipping around in all directions. "We had it cornered but it got away when the building came down."

"Almost got me, too," Aaron said, hissing as he rubbed his neck. I saw his hand come away with blood. "Landed on me from behind and I swear to god it was trying to peel off the back of my head. Thank hell Lexi here was close by."

"No time to lose," Lexi snapped. "Which way did it go?"

"There." I pointed down the block where it had disappeared. Lexi and Aaron were off immediately. I followed after a moment of hesitation.

It was another three blocks before we spotted its

shadowy form again, zipping along the walls and leaping from building to building. Every now and then it paused and looked down, emitting a chittering laugh as if teasing us. It was small and thin, like a prepubescent girl, with no face that I could see nor any other discernible features, scaling impossible surfaces easily with its graceful limbs. Lexi leveled her gun at it several times, but each time the shot proved too risky to take, with the danger of bringing the enormous buildings down on our own heads.

"We have to try something else," she said. We stopped our chase, and the spider stopped, too. It leered down at us and chittered. Our boldness had drawn its interest, but it was reluctant to attack while outnumbered. It also showed no intention of coming within reach of us. While it stuck close to us, at least, I could be sure that Evie was safe from it.

Evie.

"I may have an idea," I said, keeping the spider in sight.

THE SPIDER, as expected, did not move from its spot when I left the group. It was focused on Lexi, perhaps sensing her to be the worthiest prey. I rounded the corner and pressed my hands against the building it was perched on. The preparation would take a bit of time, and I hoped Lexi and Aaron could keep it engaged.

Out of the corner of my eye I saw Lexi pacing back and forth, her eyes never leaving the spider, as if daring it to make a move. Aaron had taken some steps back. The spider watched, head turning this and that, following Lexi curiously. It surely noticed that I was not around, but given that I had run from it earlier, it probably assumed that I was no threat.

Several nerve-wracking minutes later, I was ready. If this worked, I told myself, I was going to owe Evie a big favor. I extended one arm over the side of the building, took a deep breath, and made a gesture to Lexi.

In a second she whipped out her gun and fired to the spider's right. It dove to the left and ran. What came from the shot, however, was only the sound. No bullet struck the building, but it was enough to startle the spider around the corner and toward me. It came around the corner and I crossed my fingers, hoping it wouldn't leap onto the next building. It didn't. Instead, it landed right onto the side wall, which was now completely covered in glue.

It wouldn't hold it—I didn't expect it to. It was

only crafting glue, after all—the only glue I was familiar with enough to produce due to Evie's near-constant crafting. But the sticky substance surprised it just enough to pause in its movement. In the short second it took to examine what was under its feet, Aaron came around and his right arm shot out toward it, extending in segments as it did. The spider let out a yelp that was unsettlingly human-like as Aaron's hand wrapped around its ankle and yanked it off the building.

"Inspector Gadget!" he yelled to me. "My kids love that show!"

The spider landed on the ground and Lexi was immediately on it. It flailed and shrieked and clawed at her face and neck, but she held tight.

"Shoot it!" Aaron was shouting. Lexi's hand leveled into its gun pose and aimed at the spider's face.

"Mommy, no."

The voice brought all of us to a halt. Lexi froze. I wondered for a moment if I was hallucinating.

Then, the featureless black face peeled away, receding like water from the shore to reveal the face underneath. A child's face, a girl with familiar maple-colored skin. She looked up at Lexi with fear in her watery brown eyes.

"Mommy, please," she said.

Lexi shook visibly.

"Bella?"

"Mommy," the thing with her daughter's face said. "I'm scared."

"Hold steady, Lex," Aaron said. "That's not your kid."

But there was uncertainty in his voice. He was wavering. I couldn't speak. Had they really brought her daughter here, wrapped her in black goo, and sent her to crawl the walls?

"Where am I, Mommy?"

"Baby," Lexi said, her voice quivering. Her hand dropped from its forehead. "I don't . . . I—"

Her voice cut off. The spider's arm, now a seamless black spike, disappeared into her chin and reappeared at the top of her head. Her body shook briefly, then fell limp, crumbling to one side like a marionette with cut strings. The spider threw her to the side, stood, and laughed its chittering laugh. The sound echoed loudly in my head.

CHAPTER 11

I JERKED OUT OF UNCONSCIOUSNESS WITH THE IMPACT of a crashing semi. What felt like a scream welled up, then disappeared into a thin whimper. I coughed and felt pain in my raw throat. I tried to stand and fell right off my bed. Fumbling for the lights, I pulled myself up by the edge of the mattress.

Was it a dream?

Nausea overtook me as the image of the black spike sticking out of the top of Lexi's head swam back. I shambled into the bathroom and gagged over the toilet. Very little came out. I felt my way to the sink and rinsed out my mouth, breathing hard.

The mirror hanging over the sink reflected a face that I didn't initially take for mine. Gingerly, I brought one hand up and touched my cheek. My right eye was swollen, purple and shiny like a ripe plum. Bruises covered my face and my lower lip was fat and bleeding. Following my damaged face downward, I saw cuts and bruises riding up and down my arms and shoulders. My neck felt tender and I brushed my hair aside to see deep red welts along both sides of it. The suit was torn all over, parts barely hanging on. My head spun as I tried to think but a wave of dizziness hit me. Slowly, weakly, I leaned my back against the nearest wall and slid to the floor.

Lexi.

I buried my head in my hands. Something was pounding. It took me a moment to realize it was coming from the door and not my head. I opened the bathroom door to see Evie, eyes wide and gesturing wildly.

"What's wrong?" I asked, my voice a dry croak.

She grabbed my hand and yanked me through the house to the front door. As soon as I opened it, flashing lights and voices assaulted me from all sides. A rumbling gust nearly knocked me over as a chopper flew by overhead, spotlight aimed at our doorstep. The digital clicks of camera shutters chattered like descending locusts. Policemen in blue uniforms were trying to hold back the swarming paparazzi, but they became near-frenzied once they spotted me.

"*Diamond Donna!*" someone was shouting. "*Over here!*"

"*Give us a wave!*"

"*Can you answer some questions about what happened tonight? Look this way!*"

My first instinct was to turn back into the house and slam the door behind me, but as my vision cleared from the flashing lights, something else caught my eye.

"*Hey, robot! Look this way!*"

"*Yo, Eleven! Say something!*"

Standing in the middle of the road, looking somewhat lost, was Eleven. I had to rub my eyes to make sure I was seeing correctly. Seeing them out of the arena was surreal. Behind them, I saw Crish rush out of his house toward us. The cameras turned to him immediately.

"*Crish! Look this way!*"

"*It's Crish Michaels!*"

"*How's it feel being America's hero, Crish?*"

Crish rushed to Evie and I, giving Eleven a wide berth as he crossed the street, and stood between us and them protectively. Eleven regarded the three of us.

"I need to speak with Astra Ching."

My entire body tensed up.

"What do you want?" Crish asked, raising his voice. Cameras clicked, loving every moment.

Eleven tilted their head slightly and looked from Crish to me. "It does not concern you," they said. "I need to speak with Astra Ching."

Evie was gripping my arm tightly, as if afraid someone might rip me away. I patted her hand and she loosened her grip.

"Stay here," I told her. Crish gave me a worried look.

"You sure about this?"

"If they wanted to kill me," I said, keeping my gaze on Eleven, "they would have already."

Crish didn't seem convinced, but I took a deep breath and stepped past him into the street. The hubbub died down somewhat, but the clicking shutters continued their chatter as I approached Eleven. Dozens and dozens of eyes widened in expectation as we stood facing each other. Up close, I saw that the armor plating covering their body was coated in a generous layer of dents and scratches.

"Okay," I said. "I'm here."

A metal-clad hand reached out and I nearly flinched, but it took hold of my chin gently and shifted my head to the side. It took me a moment to realize Eleven was studying the wounds on my face. "You should seek medical attention," they said evenly. "Splintering is hard on the body."

I pulled my head back out of their grasp. "Please don't touch me."

"I apologize," Eleven said, and withdrew their hand. I crossed my arms in front of myself, feeling foolishly like a defiant teen but unable to think of what else to do.

"You couldn't be more discreet?" I asked, glancing at the leering photogs.

"There was an issue in my attempt to pinpoint your location, resulting in me having to trek through several small towns to arrive here. It was not my intention to rouse attention."

"Well, you failed," I said, unable to bite back my sarcasm. "So what do you want?"

The metal hand reached out again, but this time it was holding something. I had to blink twice when I saw it, glistening like a mirage. The light from flashing cameras bounced off it. It was roughly two inches long, not too much bigger than the average army man toy, and appeared to be gilded or carved from gold. I stared at it. Cheshire's golden form, smiling its emoji smile and posed ridiculously like

John Travolta's iconic dance pose in *Saturday Night Fever*, stared back.

"What is this supposed to be?"

"The token to exit the game."

"Oh," I said, my voice thin and breathy. I looked up at Eleven. "Is this for me?"

"Yes."

"Why?"

"You took down the target. Even though the contestant total had already been reduced with the elimination of Alexis Monroe, you still took down the spider in the Hollow City; therefore it was decided that you have earned the prize."

"I—" A thousand emotions flooded me at once but no memories. "I did?"

"It's to be expected that your memory of the event would be sparse—splintering often causes short-term memory loss, especially on the first occurrence." They held the token a little closer to me. I couldn't stop staring at it, but neither could I bring myself to take it. To be perfectly honest, I didn't want to touch anything shaped like Cheshire. But for a moment my life flashed before me. My old life. My house and my job and my family. Hanging out with Hannah and falling asleep reading on Friday nights. Coffee with Addison before work. But as quickly as it came, it extinguished.

"What does that mean? Splintering?"

"It is a state triggered by heightened emotion. Your compatriots surely recorded the event. It can be jarring to see. I recommend you concentrate on recovery before watching it." They gestured at the welts around my neck. "I hope you are not in pain. There are only so many ways to break the splintered state, and that was unfortunately the tamest of them."

"Okay," I said. This was too much for me to think about right now. Eleven was still holding the token out to me. I glanced behind me at Crish and Evie.

"Can I pass it to someone else?"

Eleven's hand drew back a touch. They were surprised, which wasn't an emotion I thought a machine was capable of. "Yes," they said, "if you wish."

"Aaron Hale. He helped take the spider down, and he has four children waiting for him. Please take it to him."

"Are you certain this is what you want?"

"Yes. Go before I change my mind."

The metal hand withdrew, taking the token with

it. I felt like I was watching the light at the end of my tunnel disappear.

"That is noble of you," Eleven said.

"Thanks," I said tiredly.

They glanced toward the flashing cameras briefly. "I should go. I have overstayed my—" They paused. "Excuse me; I am still unfamiliar with the nuances of your language."

"Welcome," I say.

"Welcome?"

"That's the saying. You've overstayed your welcome."

"Right." They nodded. "One more thing—I am sorry for your loss."

"What?"

"Alexis Monroe. She was dear to you, was she not?"

Lexi's name sent a pang through my chest. "Not as dear as she was to her family."

"Of course." Raising a hand, they pointed at my arm. "And also for that." I looked down at the red welts on my arm, left there by his armor on my first round. "I needed to use heat to break through your crystal, and the cool down was not as instantaneous as it should have been. I apologize for that as well."

I chuckled bleakly. "At least they programmed you to be polite."

"No one programmed me. I am what you would call a biological entity."

The bitter smile froze on my lips. "What?"

"This suit is for my convenience—the air on your planet is not optimal for my physiology, and your natives do not generally react well to the sight of what you call 'extraterrestrials.'"

"Oh," I said awkwardly. "I just assumed . . . I mean, Cheshire is . . ."

"A very different being."

"Okay," I said weakly and rubbed my face with one hand. "It's been a very long night."

"Of course," said Eleven. "Goodnight."

Then they were gone. The noises of the paparazzi screamed to life again. I turned my back on them and hurried back to the house with Crish and Evie, shutting the door on the clicking cameras.

As soon as the streets were cleared of reporters, the move began.

By the time dawn drew near, we were coasting down a seaside road in an unmarked black SUV with tinted windows. Crish dozed in front next to the driver. Evie was asleep as well, head pillowed against my shoulder. We were all exhausted, physically and emotionally. We hadn't had time to catch a breath, much less talk about Lexi and the spider. I had no idea where we were headed, and I couldn't bring myself to care. As long as it put distance between me and the flashing cameras, I was happy.

Well, happy wasn't the right word.

I clicked on the tablet and slipped headphones into my ears as ocean waves and stringy clouds billowed past. The video of the bonus round was posted on numerous websites, but I had a hard time pushing Play, dreading watching Lexi's death once more. I argued with myself, worked up my nerve then lost it again, and finally relented when the sun began to peek over the horizon.

Most of the footage consisted of the contestants running through the city in a panic, dodging from light to light. I saw Evie looking around from a street corner, Crish trying to scale a wall to get to a better vantage point, and Aaron feeling his way along a long alley. There were one or two quick shots of me, but no camera captured the shots from the hidden sniper. I shuddered at the memory.

Finally, the camera centered on Aaron, Lexi, and me. Seeing Lexi's bright, determined eyes brought on a wave of bitterness. I bit my lip and tried not to focus on the fact that she was gone.

Lexi was on the spider the moment it hit the ground.

It twisted its face into Bella's and whispered, "Mama."

I heard Lexi say "baby" before it stabbed clear through her skull. She crumpled and the spider threw her aside. It got to its feet. I hadn't gotten a truly clear look at it until this moment. It was dark and sleek, as if covered in oil. Its face was still peeled back to reveal the little girl's soft features, but the face no longer looked human. The mouth pulled back into a smile too wide, revealing hound-like teeth. The chittering laugh sent a chill down my spine.

"Oh god, no," I heard Aaron say. Face buried in his hands, he seemed to be sobbing. The me in the video stood silent and still as if in shock. I had no memory of any of this.

"*Well!*" exclaimed Cheshire's voice. The slender form strolled out of the shadows and hovered over Lexi, poking her side with one finger. "*Yep, she's dead. But hey, good news for the rest of you, you'll live to play another day!*"

Aaron's fists clenched and shook. I still hadn't

moved. Cheshire glided over to the spider and patted it on the head. Bella's face relaxed into a grinning purr.

"How'd you like my pet? Sweet little thing, isn't she? So many tricks up her sleeve. But don't worry—we only trot her out for special occasions. You won't have to play with her again. You know—" Cheshire paused. I followed their gaze and saw their attention was on me. I had hunched over a bit, face hidden behind a curtain of hair. Cheshire dipped their head down, trying to peek at my face. *"Hello, hello."*

I didn't move.

"You alive? We'll have to pick someone else if you're dead."

Then, without warning, I lashed out. Cheshire dodged to the side and for a fraction of a second, though that digital face didn't change, I thought I saw surprise in their usually gleeful expression. The spider took a hop back in alarm.

The me on the screen took a step forward and finally lifted her head. The hair fell away, revealing her face.

My throat clenched.

Like a zombie, she took a few shambling steps then dropped to one knee, eyes rolled back and mouth halfway open. A second passed.

She leapt into the air, so high and fast the camera was half a second behind to react. By the time it caught on, she had landed. Cheshire had stepped out of the way again, but they weren't her target. My zombie self had landed right on top of the spider.

The entire right side of her body was swollen and protruding in points. Her fist struck squarely on the spider's body and pounded it half way into the ground. A shrieking sound filled my ears and I nearly yanked the earbuds out of my head. It was *screaming*. Even worse, it was screaming with Bella's voice. The sounds coming out of it were those of a distressed child.

The figure that was starting to look less and less like me shuddered visibly. The protrusions on her body grew. A moment later small, sharp, glistening specks appeared all over her visible skin, through her clothing. Diamond crystals broke out, growing in clusters. They coated her shoulder, right arm, and face. She raised her left hand, grabbed one of the creature's arms, and pulled. It shrieked in agony, its other arm scratching at whatever came within its reach.

With a sickening, wet tear the arm came off. Black ooze poured out of its body. The diamond-crusted zombie threw the dead limb aside. Blades in the shape of cats' claws sprouted from her fingertips. She brought her hand down on the spider and raked the claws from its throat to its belly. The screaming stopped but the struggling didn't. Aaron was staring in abject horror. Bella's eyes were wide and rolled back. It coughed and black ooze came out of its mouth, convulsing as the diamond-crusted creature cut its torso to ribbons.

Finally, it laid still. The cameras zoomed in on its face—the face that looked too much like a dead child. Its killer—*me*—*it*—stood slowly and turned toward Cheshire. I suppressed a cry. Diamonds were growing out of her right eye, and all over her right cheek. Glassy threads appeared amongst her dark hair. Cheshire let out a raucous laugh and clapped their hands.

"*Now there's something to see!*" they cheered. "*Hey, cameras! Make sure you get that! Diamond Donna, true to her name. Isn't she a beaut?*"

The diamond creature lunged at him. The crystals coating her right arm and hand were reshaping to resemble a crude mallet. Cheshire dodged easily. The creature crouched down, blank eyes following their movement.

Just as she sprinted upward, Eleven slammed

into her side. The two fell sprawling as Cheshire chuckled in amusement. I watched as Eleven pinned the thing down by the throat. My fingers felt back to my neck, over the welts from their fingers. She put up a fierce fight, diamonds clashing against metal armor relentlessly. I gasped as the diamond mallet caught Eleven on the side of the head, nearly knocking them off, but they held tight.

Slowly, after what seemed like an eternity, she stopped struggling. The diamonds began to fall away from her face, dropping in large shards onto the ground. Eleven laid their free hand on the diamond-coated arm and a moment later the crystals growing there shattered and fell away, too. Bit by bit, I could recognize myself again. I watched Eleven tentatively let go of my neck and brush strands of hair—now back to its normal dark brown—out of my face, and open each eye to check them.

I stopped the video.

CHAPTER 12

CRISH'S CAMPAIGN FOR PEACE AIRED SHORTLY AFTER the Hollow City debacle, but its effect was somewhat diminished, as the populace was much more interested in talking about Diamond Donna, the freakshow who tore apart a screaming child while the world looked on.

The replacement for our seaside dwelling was an old apartment complex. Our things followed us in haphazardly packed boxes. The movers brought by Lydia to deliver our things cast odd, uncomfortable glances at me out of the corners of their eyes as they worked. The gist of the place was mostly the same—securely locked and monitored entry points, guards residing in the nearby units. The outside walls were coated with old bricks the color of dried blood, and the inside was filled with two-bedroom units that smelled of wet dust. Due to short notice, the units were unfurnished, and for several days we slept on air mattresses and heated up canned soup in coffee mugs. Ironic, considering several tabloids were in the process of theorizing what kind of five-star treatment from the government the "champions of the Earth" had been enjoying in secrecy.

I'd never thought I would miss the dreary little seaside abode, but in those short few weeks it had begun to feel like home. The new dwellings gave off an eerie feeling of abandonment and I picked up a persistent wet lump in my throat from the moment we moved in. Evie took the whole thing in stride, though she took her crafting and gluing to a whole new level. It began from the moment we settled in and continued from morning to night. I spent a lot of time watching her, because at least when my eyes were on her instead of the tablet screen, I could pretend that the entire world wasn't talking about me.

Though no one knew where we were, security had been increased around us. Eleven's cavalier stroll through town had shaken the confidence of our handlers. Crish was given a unit in the building opposite ours. We could see each other through the bedroom windows, and sometimes we waved. I saw

Heath's car come through the complex several times, but he rarely visited Evie and me. He and Crish holed up, talking constantly, and when I asked Crish what it was about, he always became sheepish and awkward.

He described it as damage control—regardless of what had taken place, what the world saw was me, unhinged and inhuman, tearing apart something that looked like a child. Looking past the spider's wide, innocent eyes was difficult for most, and whatever peace his campaign could've brought was now moot, as the populace had begun to grow fearful of the contestants in general, thinking we were all becoming unstable and that the game was turning us into monsters. There was much speculation about Eleven's visit, and it didn't help that the tabloids got hold of dozens of photos of the encounter, some of which consisted of Eleven's hand "caressing" my cheek. Questions about our "relationship" were raised, the winner's token conveniently buried in a mountain of clickbait. Pictures and videos went viral before we even left the safe house. Theories flew left and right. Worthless, idle gossip, but gossip that unsettled the public nonetheless.

I wondered if Aaron got his token, but had no way of knowing at the moment. Whoever his handlers were, they'd done well keeping his status under wraps. The doctor came back and checked me over, declared my wounds were superficial, and left without looking me in the eye. He returned once more, a few days later, with medication to help me sleep, after it became evident that the nightmares and panic attacks were here to stay.

THE FIRST MEETING of the contestants after the loss of Lexi took place a few days after relocation. Lydia facilitated for Evie and me—I had the distinct feeling Heath had pawned me off on Lydia, now that my reputation was a liability.

The medication left me sluggish and weak during the day. Lydia cast concerned glances at me as she set up the conference.

"You feeling okay?" she asked.

I shook my head. "No."

I could tell she didn't know what to say. No one seemed to know what to say to me, though there was plenty being said *about* me. "If there's anything you need, just let me know."

"Okay," I said stiffly as the other contestants flickered into view one by one. They were all looking at me while pretending not to, trying to make up their mind about me and my bruised face. Aaron Hale was absent, which allowed me a small sigh of relief. I held on to the thought that he was home, safe with his children.

No one spoke for a long moment. Lexi's absence left something of a vacuum. Without her taking charge, no one was quite sure how to start.

"I know we're all sad about Alexis."

The voice belonged to Crish. I turned to his image on the screen. He was sitting straight, shoulders squared, face grim.

"But we have the world to think about."

The others nodded in agreement.

"Let's not dwell on what happened and let Lexi's sacrifice be in vain. We don't know what's ahead of us and that's what we should be thinking about right now."

There was a sense of relief, like a breath simultaneously held by all had been let out as he spoke. The void was filled for the moment. Not a word was said to or by me in that meeting. I accepted, for now, my new role as The Elephant in the Room.

AFTER EVIE FELL ASLEEP, I turned on my phone for the first time in over a week. I began by checking social media, which quickly proved to be a mistake as nearly every person I knew was talking about me in some capacity. I was about to close it when a single message from Hannah, dated two days ago, caught my eye.

I DON'T KNOW **how you're doing. No one tells me. I hope you're OK. You're our hero no matter what those bastards are saying :) This is baby Erin. She came too early. The doctors worry she won't make it. 23 weeks is not ideal. But I know my girl is strong. I hope she gets to meet her Auntie Astra soon. Kisses**

ATTACHED WAS a photo of the tiniest baby I'd ever seen, nearly completely hidden from view inside its isolette by tubes and wires sticking out of its fragile, pink body. It looked like it could fit in my hand, this little, defenseless being born too soon into this noisy world.

CHAPTER 13

I STOPPED TAKING SLEEP AIDS THE NIGHT BEFORE THE next round. There was no announcement and no countdown, but somehow I had a feeling it was coming. Headspace appeared to follow no specified schedule and happened at the whim of Cheshire or whoever was pulling their strings behind the scenes. The air was still warm with late-summer heat when this had all started. Now, the skies had turned gray and cool. Halloween came and went and Evie covered our bedroom walls with paper cutouts of pumpkins and skulls. I lay in bed that sleepless night, looking at the crooked smiles of jack-o'-lanterns, and drifted off for a few fitful hours around dawn, dreaming of diamonds and metal fingers around my throat.

I entered the arena just in time to hear someone

say, ". . . and just leave her and the retard . . ." The words cut off when the speaker spotted me. I pretended not to hear.

The space we occupied was surprisingly small. For a moment I wondered if there was some sort of mistake. In stark contrast to the pristine white arena with its shiny black floors, the structure was a small, gray, concrete cube, dimly lit by bulbs concealed behind metal cages, like those found in industrial mines. A narrow, unlit pathway opened on each of the four walls, giving way to silent darkness. A stale, musty smell permeated the air. In the distance, water dripped.

Minus Lexi and Aaron, there were twenty-nine of us. Compared to the initial one hundred, the group felt significantly smaller, which made the apprehension the others had about me glaringly obvious. No one spoke to me and everyone was pretending not to notice me. Evie sidled over to my side and stood by me, wordless as usual. Crish, the newly acknowledged leader, gave me an encouraging smile through the gaps in the group. The others looked to him to protect and guide them now.

And what of Evie and me, the "retard" and the "monster"? I hated those words, but I didn't have time to worry about it before rapid footsteps echoed from the nearest tunnel. Cheshire tap-danced their way out of the shadows, fingers twirling the walking stick as usual. Eleven followed quietly behind and took up a spot against the far wall.

"*Hello, contestants!*" Cheshire said in good cheer. They scanned the nervous group until they found me. The others gave them a wide berth as they stepped in front of me. "*Well, well, well. Diamond Donna returns. Gave away your token, did you? That's a new one. Most people jump at the chance to get out of here, but you must be really having fun.*"

I could think of no clever response, so I decided to be honest. "Fuck off."

"*Ouch! Some sharp teeth she's got.*" Cheshire chuckled mockingly and backed away. "*Now, I'm sure that you've noticed that due to special circumstances, we are down to twenty-nine contestants rather than the thirty that we originally intended. As a result, we will be drafting one additional person to round out the numbers. Say hello to your new teammate, folks.*"

A single beam of light came from above and a new person was printed into the arena feet first—a tall, broad figure with a radiant tan and large hands. Jaws dropped all around the room as the chiseled face came into view.

"What?" he said, looking around at us, blinking

in confusion. He was wearing a sports jersey bearing a logo vaguely familiar to me but I couldn't quite identify. "What's going on? I was just—" Seeing Cheshire's smiling emoji face, his face went pale from forehead to collarbone. "Oh god no."

"*Welcome to the arena, contestant,*" Cheshire said with all the manners of a gracious host. "*Looks like the rest of them already know you. Someone care to enlighten me?*"

"That's the basketball player!" someone said hotly. "Mikale James!"

"*A big deal, is he?*"

Several people began eagerly rattling off stats and dates. The numbers meant nothing to me, but I did recognize the man as gracing the covers of *Time*, *People*, and, most recently, *Rolling Stone*. A big deal he certainly was, with professional athlete, businessman, philanthropist, and music producer being just a few items on his very impressive résumé. Right now, however, he looked nervous and confused. His gaze ran over the group until it landed on me.

"Holy shit," he said, a little too loudly. "You're that—"

"Mikale," Crish said, cutting him off. He stepped in front of the group, took Mikale's hand, and shook it. Mikale looked him up and down. "Crish Michaels. We met at the Met Gala."

"Right!" Mikale said, fumbling but visibly relieved. "Of course. I mean, everyone knows who you are these days."

Crish tossed a glance toward Cheshire, who was watching them with amusement. "Sorry we're not reuniting under better circumstances, but don't worry. We'll get through this."

"*Well isn't this heartwarming*," Cheshire said, dripping with sarcasm. "*Sorry, Mr. Basketball Player, but we have to move on.*" They made a slow circle around the cubic room, pointedly ignoring Mikale James, as if irritated by the attention he had attracted. "*Today's game is Sewer Crawl. Where you are currently standing is the finish line. As you can see, there are multiple ways for you to reach this point. There are six starting points, all of which will eventually converge in the maze to reach here. You will be divided into six groups of five, though whether you choose to cooperate or go off on your own is up to you. Your time limit is two hours this time. Oh, and watch out for the rats.*"

The moment Cheshire's voice dropped away, I found myself in a different room. The sudden transition was jarring and I doubted I would ever get used to it. Though very much like the previous one, it was much smaller, and instead of four tunnels leading into darkness, there were only two. The dirty gray walls were covered with smiley faces sprayed in dripping yellow paint.

Four others were in the room with me—two women and two men, including Sergio.

"So," I said awkwardly, wringing my hands. "Two doors."

The others looked at each other. I peered down the nearest tunnel. It was pitch black, with a single, dim light far down in the distance. I heard a draft blow through, as well as a faint, unsettling chatter.

"Can you believe Mikale James is here?" someone said behind me. "I couldn't believe it."

"I know," replied another quietly. "Here I thought having Crish Michaels was a big deal, but damn. Wonder where he is now."

"Who knows, but I'd rather have . . ." the voice dropped low and I could hear no more. It didn't matter—I knew anyone would rather have Mikale James than me.

"Astra."

I spun around. Sergio stood behind me. He gave me a cordial, untrustworthy smile. "Let's just head in. We'll split into two groups. No time to waste."

"Oh," I said. "Okay."

He didn't speak, but that smile stayed on his face, and it took me a moment to realize what he was waiting for. Four pairs of eyes were glued to my back as I took a tentative step into the tunnel, and I was not the least bit surprised when no one followed.

THE SPACE WAS CLAUSTROPHOBICALLY narrow and low, and light sources were few and far between. I could extend both arms and touch walls on either side with elbows still bent. Reaching up, I could touch the ceiling with my fingertips. There was nowhere to go but forward and I couldn't help but feel the walls close in. I felt my way along, touching the walls to reassure myself that the space wasn't getting smaller and trying not to think about the slimy spots that my fingers struck every now and then.

Chittering to my left. Then to my right. A split in the road and both paths pitch black. There was a distinct smell in the air, one that reminded me clearly of the name of the game. I coughed and gagged. The smell was stronger from one tunnel than the other, but I couldn't see a thing down either.

Could I produce a light? I tried to think of a flashlight. Several useless parts appeared in my hand

and dropped to the floor—I simply didn't know the inner workings of one. A torch? Fire in this closed-in space might not be wise. Night vision goggles? I couldn't begin to fathom how to create one of those. Cold sweat covered my forehead. Was it really going to end this soon, at the first fork? Would I have to feel my way blindly the rest of the way? If only I could see in the dark. If only . . .

I closed my eyes.

The image that appeared before me was my old home, the little house with gray brick walls that we lived in before my mother fell ill. I guided my mental gaze through the house, at the old bookshelf filled with comics, the combo TV/VCR that my father was so fond of using even as it rapidly went out of style, to the fireplace that we never lit. In front of the fireplace, lounging in his usual spot, was Murphy.

Here, Murphy.

The old, arthritic, overweight ball of fur got to his feet and waddled over to me. I scratched his head as he looked up at me with his deep green eyes. Toward his final days, they were nearly fully covered by cataracts, but in my memory, his eyes would always be bright and kitten-clear.

I opened my eyes.

The first thing I saw was gray. Everything was

gray as if filmed through a black-and-white camera. Almost all colors had washed out. But the tunnels, pitch black just a moment ago, now stood clear and open. I looked down one, then the other, my newly contracted cat eyes adjusting quickly. The tunnel to my right was long and narrow, even narrower than the one I stood in now. I would have to turn sideways and shuffle my way like a crab. The other was wider by far, but the ceiling dropped quickly after a few feet. Beneath that low ceiling was the source of the acrid smell and I was immediately glad I thought to look before stepping. Less than two feet into the tunnel, the floor gave away to a thick, murky filth that could barely be called water. The floating foam and solids turned my stomach violently. I retched. There was no way through the low space, nothing to cling onto. The ceiling was too low and the only way to get through would be on hands and knees.

Swallowing hard, I ventured down the narrow pathway. At first I thought my nerves were getting the best of me, but as my back and chest touched the sides of the tunnel simultaneously, I had to admit the space was growing narrower as I went. The road before me was endless and a dozen more steps would leave me stuck. I backtracked, but the thought of crawling through sewage was too much. If I went back to the starting point, I could take the other door out, the one everyone else took, and try a different path. I was determined, set on this plan, until I came to a dead end.

It was as if the room we started in never existed. The tunnel ended at a blank wall. A yellow smiley face stared at me mockingly with its dripping eye dots. I suddenly felt tightness in my chest, like I was suffocating in this tight, stinking space. I forced myself to breathe. And breathe. And breathe.

They want to see me crawl.

Who? a part of me asked. It was not something I'd given much thought to until now. I went back to the filth-filled tunnel, knelt down, and was immediately overcome by the stench.

Was the Earth really eager to see me swim in shit? Somehow I doubted that. Humans had our limits. But then, they never said the show was made for human consumption, did they? For the first time, I wondered who else was watching, but now was not the time for introspection. I grimaced at the thought of Evie, frightened and alone, facing a tunnel like this one. I would give anything for her not to have to touch the reeking sewage. I couldn't help her during the bonus round, and I couldn't help her now. Thank goodness the spider didn't . . .

I paused. The tunnel stretched endlessly before me. I got down on my hands and knees and peered through it.

I'll crawl. But not through the sewage.

I thought of the Hollow City, of the spider perched on the side of the brittle buildings. I put one hand on the low ceiling of the tunnel and willed it to stick, the same way I willed my fins to swim in the ocean stage. It stuck. I added my other hand, tentatively dragged myself forward, and soon my knees were on the ceiling. I was on my hands and knees, defying the laws of gravity that I was trying hard to keep out of my subconscious.

My hair fell over my shoulders and I felt the tips drag in the filthy water. The thought of touching the sewage nearly rattled me. I slammed the thought out of my mind and moved forward. The sensation was disconcerting, as if gravity itself had changed and the sewage was flowing above me rather than below. I kept moving and didn't look toward it, focused on keeping my grip on the damp concrete against my palms, fighting against my mind that wanted to argue the illogic of clinging to nothing.

After what felt like an eternity through the winding path, the crawl ended in another tunnel that ran perpendicular. I let out a breath and eased myself out onto the ground. My knees nearly buckled as I stood, but I made it.

A voice caught my attention to the left. I turned to see a faint light at the end of the tunnel. I hurried to it and nearly tumbled to my death as the path came to an abrupt end. Clinging to the walls, I peered out.

This tunnel ended at what appeared to be an opening on a high wall. Squinting, I could make out figures moving below, two or three stories down, in an open, rectangular room roughly twice the size of the one we started in. I saw the tall, easily recognizable figure of Mikale James and a woman whose face I couldn't quite make out, her body glowing like a bioluminescent jellyfish.

"Is this the way?" I heard her say to Mikale.

"Your guess is as good as mine," he replied. I crouched, peering down at them.

"Hey, where'd they go?"

Mikale looked around. "They were just here. Maybe they went back in the—" He stopped and looked to the end of the room as another person emerged from a tunnel opening. "Hey, there you are. Where's Cliff? Wasn't he with you?"

The newcomer said nothing. I squinted but couldn't make out who it was. Before I could decide whether to look for a way down, the man raised one hand, forefinger and middle finger pointed, and pressed the tips to Mikale's temple.

"What are y—"

The *BANG* that followed was deafening. The woman let out a shriek of terror that was cut short by a bullet through her forehead. She collapsed to the ground next to Mikale, her light fading slowly. I drew a sharp breath and the shooter's head snapped up. I threw myself back into the safety of the shadows, but not before I saw his face, clear as day to my feline eyes.

Sergio.

I was breathing too loudly. Did he see me? I held my hands over my mouth, scrambled to my feet, and fled in the opposite direction. My heart thudded loudly in my ears.

Shooting each other was against the rules.

Wasn't it?

A chill ran down my spine as I thought back to the fateful bonus round. Did Cheshire say, at any point, that the one doing the eliminating had to be the spider?

I kept running, putting as much distance between us as possible. I heard a scrape behind me and didn't dare look back. I kept moving until something hard and solid stepped into my path. I smacked right into it and fell backwards. A hand grabbed my arm and kept me from hitting the ground.

"You are off course."

I breathed hard, stars dancing before my eyes. When they cleared, I looked up at Eleven's metal-clad form.

"What?" I stammered, looking behind me anxiously. "I . . . I just . . ."

"You are off course," they repeated, a little slower this time.

"Wh-what does that mean?" I panted. "Back there, I saw—" I stopped myself. I couldn't trust this person, robot or alien or whatever they were. "I mean, what are you doing here?"

"You and a few others have gone too far to the edge of the maze. The cameras are having difficulty locating you. I need to escort you to a location more convenient for them."

"Oh," I said, wondering if having Eleven around would at least keep Sergio from picking me off in the dark. "Okay."

Eleven led and I followed. They navigated the maze expertly, taking me toward what I assumed was closer to the center of the maze. The silence made me uneasy. I hadn't thought about it since we last met, standing in the street surrounded by flashing cameras, but there were so many questions I wanted to ask.

"Why do you do this?"

Eleven's steps slowed momentarily. "What?"

"This game. It's so . . ." I thought hard. Could I risk offending them? I decided I didn't care. "Sadistic. This whole thing. Why do your people do this?"

"The ones behind the games are not my people."

"Oh." I didn't know what to do with that information. "Then who is—"

"I cannot answer that."

"Why do you work for them?"

"I cannot answer that either. I am merely a contractor. The inner workings of Headspace are reserved for those who complete the game."

"You mean the winners?"

"Yes."

"Alright," I said, irritated. Seemed all everyone said to me since this whole thing started was they couldn't tell me anything. "So," I pressed, "where are *you* from?"

Eleven glanced back at me, as if surprised by the question. "A planet in a different quadrant of the galaxy."

"What's it called?"

They replied with a word that would likely herniate my tongue. "What's it like?" No reply came. "Fine, don't tell me."

"I am thinking," Eleven said. "Describing an entire planet in a few short sentences is difficult."

Their response surprised me. I waited patiently, suddenly excited to hear a firsthand account of an actual alien planet.

"It was much like yours," they said thoughtfully after a while. "Though the landscape was dominated by deserts. Cities and towns were built in tropical areas, and transportation was developed around traveling over sand. Most biological life was evolved to be adept at surviving in dry environments. Habitation—"

"No," I said.

"No?"

"That's not what I meant. I didn't mean read me the Wikipedia article. I asked you what it's like. It's your home. Can't you tell me something more interesting than that?"

Eleven went quiet. Just when I thought I'd pushed it too far, they spoke again.

"As a child, I resided in one of the dwelling communities far in the desert. It was popular among families who wanted a life quiet from the bustles of the cities. The way into the city from the remote dwellings was through underground transport, similar to what you would refer to as . . ." they thought for a moment. "Subway, I believe.

"The subway system was vast and old, and the elders would often tell the children of their history. I would listen to these stories with my childhood friend, awed at all that went into building them. Then one day I came out of my home to the sight of my friend digging fervently at the ground. I asked what she was doing, and she declared she was going to dig a hole to the subway path, so she could look down and see it pass by every day.

"We dug for days. The hole was deep. We were sure we were close, until a sandstorm blew through and filled the hole overnight. The next day I woke and could not find her and became convinced she had fallen through the hole and become trapped. I roused the adults and there was a massive hubbub for days as they attempted to reopen the hole to rescue her. It was only after they'd exhausted all resources that I learned she had actually gone away with family on short notice."

I chuckled. "Did you get in trouble?"

"They never let me forget it."

"That's a great story," I said, grinning. "You know, when I was seven, I—"

The words caught in my throat as we rounded a corner. I stopped in my tracks and clasped my hands over my mouth as my internal organs fought to leap out. The ghastly sight before me suddenly reminded me where I was.

There was too little of the head left for me to identify. A bite too big to have been done by the jaws of any predator I knew had been taken out of the side. Red innards spilled out in a puddle. Enormous rats with pink, naked tails feasted on what was left. A rat the size of a Pomeranian skittered past me, an eyeball in its teeth. I tried to catch my breath but the smell of blood and feces permeated the air.

"Oh god," I gasped. "Oh my god."

Eleven steered me away from the grotesque view with a hand on my back. "Do not look."

"Cheshire said it," I muttered between gasps. "Watch out for the rats."

"They are only rats," Eleven said flatly, ushering me down yet another hall.

"They're huge!"

"It does not change what they are." They stopped abruptly.

"What are you doing?"

"You are back in range of the cameras."

"You're leaving me by myself?"

"You will be fine," Eleven said. "You already have what you need. Do not let them see your fear."

I looked down the dark tunnel with uncertainty. When I turned back, they were gone.

I LEARNED QUICKLY that the closer I went toward the center of the maze, the more rats there were. To find my way, I simply had to brave their nests—easier said than done. I kept quiet, sneaking past as they followed me with their beady little eyes. Aside from one unnerving incident in which one of them attempted to scale my hair while I crawled upside down through yet another shit-filled sewer, they left me alone. Whether it was luck or something else, I couldn't be sure. Several times they approached me, teeth chattering threateningly, but ultimately backed away before their little claws could touch my shoe. I kept moving.

Voices could be heard occasionally, but after witnessing what took place between Sergio and Mikale, I was too afraid to seek out anyone else. In fact, the other contestants frightened me more than the rats. Two hours had never felt so torturously long.

I made my way down a wide hall, the widest one yet. I could stretch out my arms to the fullest and not touch the wall on either side. Rats skittered off left and right. A light appeared in the distance and I broke into a run, hope welling up in my throat. I could see bodies moving, and hear many voices—others who had made their way here. It was almost over. I'd made it.

A shape blocked my path. I skidded to a halt as a rat easily mistakable for a brown bear turned to study me, red eyes glowing in the dark. The fur around its jaw dripped red, a jaw that was just about the same size as the bite on the side of the first body.

It took a step toward me. I took a step back. Would anyone come if I shouted? It hissed. I started to step back again, then remembered Eleven's advice and stood my ground despite my quaking knees. How could I not show fear to this thing? It could tear me to shreds in a moment. But it hadn't yet. It was studying me. Would I be lucky enough for it to leave me alone? All the other ones did.

The realization hit me like a ton of bricks. I was so dense.

The enormous rat took another step. I crouched down, faced it, bared my teeth, and hissed.

It flinched. The smaller rats scattered for cover. I got down on all fours and arched my back, mimicking an angry cat the best I could. It was never luck, not for a moment. To them, with my slitted pupils, I had always been a cat.

I hissed again and crawled forward. The rat began to back away. I thought back to Murphy, and the time he spent the afternoon torturing a half-dead rabbit in the back yard. By the time we got to it, it was too late to save, but Murply, good old Murphy, was so proud of his hunting skills he strutted around for days.

A yowl escaped my lips. The rat hissed back but I could tell I was gaining ground. It was afraid. Large though it might be, as Eleven said, it was only a rat, and its rat brain was telling it that I was the predator.

It stared.

I stared back.

It bared its teeth.

I pulled back slightly and made a motion as if to leap for its throat.

It let out a squeak and skittered into the darkness.

I got to my feet and ran as fast as my shaking legs could carry me.

CHESHIRE GLANCED in my direction as I emerged from the tunnel, panting. Evie ran up and enveloped me in a tight hug before I could catch my breath. I looked over her shoulder and spotted Crish, who gave me a nod and a thumbs up.

"Kept her safe, don't worry," he said.

I smiled gratefully, held Evie tight, and surveyed the ones who had made it so far. It was obvious that quite a few of them had had to make the unpleasant crawl at least once. By my count, there were nineteen in the room including me.

"Hey."

A hand landed on my shoulder as Evie finally let go. My entire body tensed up in alarm.

Twenty.

"Thought I saw you in there," said Sergio. The hand he laid on my shoulder tightened. I was almost afraid to face him. "Lost you pretty early. Glad to see you got out."

His fingers sank into my flesh, digging between my bones. I fought not to grimace. The smile on his lips was eerie, chilling, and did not reach his eyes. He leaned close to my ear.

"See a lot of rats in there?"

Suddenly, his grip was lifted. I let out a small breath of relief and turned to see Eleven next to us. I didn't even hear them approach. They had snatched Sergio's hand off me and were gripping it in one metal-clad hand. I thought I heard Sergio's knuckles creak.

"Hey now," Sergio said, unsuccessfully concealing a grimace of pain behind his tight smile. He yanked his hand out of Eleven's grip. "Just talking to my fellow contestant here."

Eleven looked toward me briefly, looked back at Sergio, then walked away without a word. Cheshire clapped their hands, drawing the attention of all in the room.

"*Let's see here*," they said. "*One, two, three ... Twenty. Not bad! Not bad at all. Time is just about up. Let's see how the rest of them are doing.*" A transparent blue screen appeared in midair with a snap of Cheshire's fingers. On it was a map of the sewer maze. Ten red dots were spread across it, some moving and some still. I looked to the lower right corner of the screen, where two red dots were in a room together, unmoving.

"Well, there's less than a minute left and I doubt they'll get here by then. Guess they're out of the game." Cheshire snapped their fingers again and the screen disappeared.

For a moment my exhausted mind thought of how lucky those contestants were, to be brought out of the maze without having to traipse through any more rat nests. Then Cheshire clapped their hands and with a thunderous rumble every tunnel in the maze collapsed.

CHAPTER 14

I WOKE WITH A START, STILL FEELING THE RUMBLE OF falling concrete under my feet. I drew a deep, desperate breath and sat up.

Some part of me had been in denial. Even though I knew how the game worked, even though I'd seen Cheshire shoot two contestants on the pyramid in cold blood, I had somehow held on to the notion that losing the game led to something other than certain death. But the sight of Cheshire burying the remaining contestants without a hint of hesitation rattled me more than anything had so far. I could take the thought of fighting for survival, but the possibility of being killed in such a cavalier manner was hard to swallow.

And Sergio.

Just the thought of him drove a shiver down my spine. I'd witnessed him kill two fellow contestants, maybe three. And there was no doubt in my mind he was the one who shot at me in the Hollow City. Did the cameras catch him in the act? Unlikely if, as Eleven said, we were too far out of the cameras' range. Did Sergio know that? Did Eleven and Cheshire know and simply not care?

I grabbed the tablet, opened the first browser I saw, and searched fervently. I hadn't checked the news in weeks in an attempt to avoid reading about myself, but I had to know if someone saw. One of the cameras had to have caught him in the act. It had to.

I found a photo of Sergio, but the accompanying headline made my stomach drop.

DONNA ASTRA CHING FURTHERS ALIEN AFFAIR RUMORS! IS SHE ALREADY AN ALIEN CONCUBINE??

The photo was of Sergio, Eleven, and me, right after Eleven pulled Sergio's hand off my shoulder. The article went on to make mountains out of mole-hills, claiming Eleven acted out of possessiveness because Sergio had made a harmless physical contact with me. Theories followed of exactly how far things had gone and whether I had already been brainwashed by the enemy. I couldn't bring myself to finish the article. Though we had only left the arena less than an hour ago, this piece of trash was already making the rounds. I buried my face in my hands and gave serious consideration to the benefits of the human race's extinction.

"You're asking a lot of me."

"I know," I said. "I'm asking for one day, a few hours. I'll wear a disguise if you want me to. I'll only stay for one hour. Please."

Austin Heath pursed his lips. This was our first in-person meeting in several weeks. He hadn't stopped in to check on Evie and me since moving to the new location. With all the promotions and campaigns for peace with Crish, he had mostly forgotten about me except as "damage control." "I'm not sure this is a risk we can afford to take. Getting you in and out of here will take approval from the upper authorities, and we've already had one incident of your location being exposed."

"Only because Eleven led them here. It won't be like that this time."

He shook his head. "I'm sorry, but no. We can't

risk letting you off the premises."

I bit my lip, chewing so hard I tasted blood. "I'm going to lose my mind. I don't know what I'm going to do with myself if you keep me locked up here."

"There's already been enough dubious press about you out there. I don't know what's going on between you and that *alien*, but your image affects the entire country."

"There is *nothing* going on," I seethed. "They're making a big deal out of nothing."

"It doesn't change the fact that your safety is a matter of national security. I am trying to keep you *safe*."

"Which is why I trust you would keep me safe out there, for a few hours."

"This isn't up for debate. The answer is no."

"Fine," I said through gritted teeth. "But if, as you said, my image affects the entire country, you should probably be more invested in keeping me mentally sound."

Heath's eyes narrowed. "What exactly are you implying?"

"That in the next round, when the cameras are on me, I don't know what I might do."

The look he gave me told me that he was increasingly finding me to be more trouble than I was worth. I was bluffing—I had no idea what I could possibly do for the cameras. But I knew this was a sore point for Heath, since what went on in the arena was the only thing he had no control over.

"I am not having this conversation," he said, and stood in a huff. I didn't stand to see him off. If I did, I might've thrown something hard and breakable at his head.

WHICH WAS WHY, when Lydia Porter appeared at my door later the same day, I was completely taken by surprise.

"Are you ready to go?"

"Go where?" I asked incredulously.

"To see your friend."

"Heath already said I couldn't go."

"I know," she replied. I waited for an explanation but got none.

"I won't attract too much attention?"

She shook her head. "Everyone is too busy mourning Mikale James. Are you coming, or not?"

"I am!" I exclaimed. "I am. But . . . why?"

"Do you want an answer, or do you want to go?"

I chose the latter.

THE SKY LOOKED DIFFERENT, though I was sitting on the same plane, in the same seat.

The situation still made no sense—I had no idea why Lydia was helping me get out of the complex, but she had remained tight lipped and silent since we departed and I didn't have the energy or interest to pry. I could only hope that, whatever her reason, it wouldn't bite me in the ass later.

In those few short months, the world changed. Or perhaps it changed from the day the orb arrived and I just never noticed. From the moment we pulled out of the airport, billboards covered with the faces of the contestants were everywhere. I saw posters and T-shirts on the street and pedestrians wearing baseball hats with the Headspace logo on them. Businesses and politicians alike appeared to be trying to cash in on our names. Crish's face was plastered around every corner, and in most of them he was smiling and lifting his face into the light like some revolutionary hero. Preachers on street corners shouted loudly that the game was God's way of punishing us for our sins. The sides of highways and bridges bore graffiti in the form of hashtags. I saw at least a dozen that read "#TeamDiamondDonna," one of which had been crossed out. Next to it in red letters were the words "alien fucker."

And yet, in some ways, everything looked the same. Purpose-driven cars filled with purpose-driven people passed us. Everyone was still coming home from work and shopping for the holidays. Skyscrapers were being built and little diners hung ornaments in their windows for the upcoming festivities. Strands of lights illuminated roadside trees. I used to love the holiday season, but this year it never even crossed my mind. Normalcy was another lifetime ago.

Lydia sat next to me in the back. We were riding in a medium-sized blue Sedan—a nice, inconspicuous car—and we were dressed in street clothes. Seeing her out of her usual black, starched getup was unsettling.

"You alright?" she asked, surprising me. She hadn't said much on the trip and appeared to be deep in thought, perhaps trying to figure out exactly how much trouble she might get in for letting me out.

I nodded. "Trying to take it all in, I guess. I haven't been home in a long time."

"Okay." I could tell she was trying to be nice to me but couldn't think of anything to say. "I know you were hoping to be able to meet your friend at the hospital where her baby is staying, but after studying the logistics, it looks like the hospital is too public a place and you showing your face there would be too big a risk. Not to mention it could cause disruption to the other patients, which would just put another black mark on your image."

"Sure," I muttered.

"You shouldn't let them get you down," Lydia said. She was studying me, trying to see whether I was disturbed by the posters and graffiti.

"They don't."

"And Mikale James was not your fault."

"Are they saying it was?"

"You didn't hear."

"I don't read the news much."

"I see."

"What are they saying?"

"There is a school of thought—not a majority, just a vocal one—that Mikale James would never have been selected for the game, and subsequently died, if you weren't given the token after . . ."

"After I went unhinged like a lunatic," I said blankly, quoting several dozen articles. "Sure."

"It's not your fault. He was very famous and fame attracts idle talk. There was talk about one of his foundations being shut down. People are just upset and need someone to blame."

"It's fine," I said, and turned back to the window, my mind replaying Sergio's bullet splattering Mikale's brains all over the concrete floors. My eyes followed the repetitive peaks and valleys of the power lines. I ought to have been upset, but couldn't muster up the strength. "People can say what they like."

There was a moment of silence. "So this friend of yours."

"Yes?"

"Why did you choose to see her?"

"She's my best friend."

"I just figured if you wanted to see someone, it would be family."

I didn't pull my gaze from the window. I could explain that most of my family wasn't in the country, or go into how my father and I drifted apart after my mother died, but it felt like a whole lot of effort to avoid giving her the real answer. So I did.

"She entered me for Headspace."

She shifted. "Did she?"

"It was a joke. She said I needed some excitement in my life so she put my name in. She had no way to know this is how it would turn out. I haven't spoken to her since before the first round."

"Did you resent her for doing it?"

"Not really." We were approaching our destination now, turning down a familiar highway. "I was just stressed and didn't want to talk to anyone. Then I was drafted for the game and I *couldn't* talk to anyone. I'm sure she's been watching, and feeling awful that I'm there because of her."

"You want to tell her you're OK?"

I looked at Lydia. She'd seemed so intimidating at our first meeting, so worldly and mysterious like the rest of my "handlers." Now, somehow, she was a little more real.

"I might die." Now that I said it, I felt strangely calm. "If I do, I want to tell her face-to-face that it's not her fault. Then, I hope she'll lie to me."

"Lie?"

"By telling me everything's okay."

She said nothing else. Turning into Hannah's neighborhood was like traveling back in time. In this old suburb, where Hannah had lived since her childhood, now in her parents' house that she'd bought from them when they retired, it was as if the past few months were nothing but a bad dream. The corner

Exxon with chipped paint on its price sign glowed the same fluorescent light as when we passed it every morning walking to school. The old oaks and rose bushes stood completely unperturbed by the chaos that took hold of the rest of the world. Light poured from bay windows as the people inside went about their lives, protected by their safe brick walls. It was as if a protective bubble held this piece of the Earth in stasis, unchanging, undisturbed. Somewhere among the madness, I had forgotten that life went on.

"One hour," Lydia said as we pulled up in front of Hannah's house. "We'll wait here. If anything goes wrong, we will have to pull you."

"Fine," I said, and got out. Here in the south, the weather was still warm and dry. Everything smelled like it had been freshly kissed by the sun. I looked up at Hannah's house, the house where we'd had dozens of sleepovers, watched hundreds of movies, talked about our school days and worked on science fair projects. I was back, and I didn't realize until that moment that I had never expected to see it again.

I walked up the front stoop and rang the doorbell. For a moment I worried she wasn't home and all this was for nothing. Then, the door opened. A man looked me up and down.

"Holy shit," he said, and turned back into the house. "Hannah! Hannah, get down here!"

He stepped aside and waved me frantically into the house. Though I'd been here many times, I looked at it with different eyes. Was it always so warm, and so colorful? I didn't have much time to take it all in before I heard Hannah's footsteps.

She looked older.

Perhaps it was the bags under her eyes, from long hours of work, followed by long evenings at the hospital. Perhaps it was the constant hint of worry that lined her face, as her life rotated between her fragile daughter, the precarious future of the world, and the sight of her best friend crawling through a sewer while a rat used her hair for a climbing rope. Or perhaps it was merely that my view of the world had changed. She paused when she came down the stairs and our eyes met for the first time since this whole mess began.

"Oh my god," she said. "You look like shit."

A laugh escaped me. She dashed down the rest of the stairs and wrapped her arms around me. Her long blond hair tickled my face and smelled like home.

"So do you," I said, and the tears flowed with a will of their own.

. . .

I HAD no idea what exactly I planned to say. Truthfully, I hadn't expected to make it this far. Even now, sitting on her old couch, in the same living room where we used to spend late nights watching silly teen films and giggling under a blanket, I found myself drawing a blank. But as it turned out, Hannah knew me better than I knew myself.

"I'm sorry," she said.

"It's not your fault."

"I know. But I'm still sorry."

She showed me pictures of her little girl, who had doubled her weight and was meeting milestones like a champ. She was growing and thriving despite the odds laid against her and I couldn't help looking at her tiny, three-pound body in awe. The glint of pride in Hannah's eyes was unmistakable.

"Isn't she perfect?" she asked me.

"I'd crawl through a million more sewers for her."

She told me about her traumatic delivery and her exhausting new schedule. She talked about the gossip at work and the people who continued to ask her about me every day, and how she eventually hung a sign on her office door stating she would no longer talk about "Diamond Donna." She told me about the reporters who came to her, and the exorbitant amount of money she'd been offered—the money that countless other people had been offered —to talk about me. She went on and on about the ups and downs she'd had with Jeffery, her live-in boyfriend and Erin's father, who was currently in the kitchen, sneaking awed peeks at me as he pretended to do the dishes. As long as I stayed silent, she chatted away, and I found solace in the sound of her voice. I knew she was whiling away the time, filling the silence and waiting for me to be ready.

"It's been unreal."

She fell quiet.

"Now that I'm here, it doesn't feel real." I scanned her cozy, peaceful home. "I wish I could stay."

Hannah bit her lip. "Don't take this the wrong way," she said slowly, "but I think they're doing the right thing. You're better off hiding. Everyone wants a piece of you out here."

I nodded. "I know. It's just . . . very lonely."

"You lost weight."

"I've seen a lot of shit."

"You never get to leave the complex?"

"This is the first time."

"At least you get to bunk with Crish Michaels,

right?" she asked, giving me a wink. "Is he that hot in person?"

I flushed slightly. "He's a nice person."

"Some people think you're doing him."

"Everyone thinks the contestants are doing each other."

"True enough." She paused. "So are you doing the alien or no?"

I sputtered. "What?"

"You can tell me. Is it good? Does it feel like— you know—human?"

I shook my head hard. "No. God no. That's all false. And ridiculous. I've talked to them twice. They touched me once and the tabloids went nuts."

"Oh." Hannah was so genuinely disappointed I couldn't help but smile. "I was hoping for something juicy."

"I think there's enough excitement without that."

Hannah laid a hand on my leg. For a moment neither of us spoke.

"Are you okay?" she asked, and I knew she was avoiding asking the real question.

"I'm trying to be."

"We're all rooting for you. Don't worry about what the tabloids are saying. Nobody cares about Mikale James."

"That's not true."

"Okay, it's not. But it doesn't matter. He couldn't have been very good if he died in his first round. It's not your fault. And I hate that no one talks about how you let the other guy have the token. That was amazing."

"He had four kids. He needed it more."

"You're so good." Hannah rested her head on my shoulder. "You're going to be okay."

I pillowed my head against hers. "I know."

"When this is all done, you'll be able to meet Erin in person. She needs to know her auntie."

"I'm looking forward to it."

"You know—" She stopped. I watched in confusion as she lifted her head to the ceiling, squinting.

"What's wrong?"

"Do you hear that?"

"Hear what?"

"Shh."

For a moment I couldn't hear a thing. Then, it came. A shiver went down my spine. It was a sound I knew. I leapt to my feet just as the front door flew open.

"We have to go!" Lydia shouted.

"What's going on?" Hannah cried as the sound poured through the open door, along with a gust of wind that nearly took Lydia off her feet. "Is that a *helicopter*?"

"Damn it!" a voice from the kitchen said. I swerved around to see Jeff rushing out. "I only posted that two minutes ago. How could they already be here!"

"What did you *do*?" Hannah shouted over the noise.

"I-I just—" Jeff stammered as Lydia rushed me out the door. "I just took a picture and put it on Facebook. I figured she was leaving soon anyway and—"

Hannah smacked him upside the head. "You idiot! Astra, be careful!"

I didn't have time to answer before Lydia dragged me outside. The driver waved us over urgently, but our path was immediately blocked. Flashing lights blinded me and I was very much aware that, away from the safe houses, there was no one to shield us from the reporters.

"*Hey! Diamond Donna! Over here!*"

"*Let's have a smile! Look this way!*"

"*Can we get a statement?*"

I shielded my face from the flashes as Lydia led the way. I didn't even say goodbye to Hannah. Eager hands pawed at us and I yanked my arm out of persistent grips more than once as we pushed through the crowd.

"*You feel bad about Mikale?*"

That one gave me pause but I kept moving. Lydia shoved a camera out of our way.

"*Hey! You like doing it E.T.-style?*" A hand grabbed the back of my collar. I pulled forward, nearly choking myself, but it let go. *Keep going. Just get out of here.*

"*What you got to say about yer bastard sister?*"

"What?" My hand dropped away. The cameras immediately went wild. I searched the crowd for the source of the question but couldn't make out a single face among the flashing lights. "Who said that?"

"Come on!" Lydia gave me a hard yank toward the car, but I resisted. Panic welled up inside my chest as I frantically searched the crowd.

"Who said that?" I yelled.

"*Yer a ho just like yer daddy!*" someone shouted back. It was the last thing I heard before the driver's hand clamped around my arm and practically threw me into the back of the car. I went sprawling as Lydia climbed in behind me and slammed the door shut.

"Drive," she said to the driver. The shouts and camera flashes were muffled. I righted myself into the nearest seat, mind spinning.

"What are they talking about?" I asked no one in particular. My imagination ran wild, and I couldn't stop picturing some buxom girl with heavy makeup and "evil stepsister" eyebrows out to make a buck off my unwanted fame. "What sister? I don't have a sister."

No answer.

"Well?" I asked a little more loudly. The driver and Lydia exchanged a look through the rearview mirror.

"We thought you knew," Lydia said.

"About what?" I snapped. "Someone tell me what's going on!"

Lydia pulled out her own phone, made a few quick taps, and handed it to me. Glowing on the screen was what I initially mistook to be an old photo of me.

But it wasn't. The girl in the picture looked to be about six years old, with my round face and slightly upturned nose. But her lips were thinner, and her hair a lighter shade of brown, longer than I'd ever worn mine as a child. The picture was obviously cropped from a larger photo. The girl was looking at the camera, eyes wide with surprise and mouth slightly parted as if to speak. Whoever took this photo had caught her off guard. She held the hand of a woman who had been cropped out, looking confused and scared.

I scrolled up to the headline.

DIAMOND DONNA'S FATHER HIDES SECRET LOVE CHILD!

The world spun. I stared at the headline, unable to comprehend what I was seeing. Had the world truly gone mad in the little time I was locked away? I scrolled down to the little girl's face again. My fingers were moving on their own and before I knew what I was doing, they had already found the keypad and dialed my father's number.

"What are you doing?" Lydia asked.

I ignored her. My hand was shaking. He answered on the third ring.

"Hello?"

"It's me," I said.

"*Astra?*"

His voice was so full of emotion that for a moment I lost my voice. I was so used to hearing him speak to me in that awkward, distant manner that his shaky voice drained my anger almost completely.

"Astra, is that you?" he asked, voice trembling. "Oh my god. Is that—"

"Is it true?"

He stopped. In that moment of silence my rage and confusion boiled over again.

"How could you?"

"Sweetheart, please—"

"Don't call me that!" I screamed into the phone. "Who the hell is she? How old is this kid? *Did you have her when Mom was still alive?!*"

"Please let me explain," he said. The calmer he was, the more angry I became. I couldn't stop.

"Do you know what I'm doing?" I yelled. One of my fists struck the window and Lydia flinched. "I'm trying to save the goddamn world! I just crawled on my hands and knees through sewers full of shit! And all anyone can do is make up lies about me! Then I find out about *this*?"

"I know; just let me—"

"*You couldn't keep it in your fucking pants while your wife was dying?*"

"Astra."

The chill in his voice halted my ranting. It was the same voice I remembered from childhood, the one that told me I was in trouble.

"I am sorry this is how you found out," he said. "But it's not what you think. They've twisted everything. Will you please let me explain?"

I took a deep breath.

"No," I said, and hung up. I handed the phone back to Lydia, who looked a little shell-shocked at my outburst. I was suddenly very tired. All the warmth that Hannah's presence had offered me was gone. The winter night grew colder as we drove in silence.

CHAPTER 15

Days passed in a blur of turbulent emotions and restless sleep. I couldn't remember how I got through the days that followed leaving Hannah's house, but it involved a lot of pacing, drinking, and late nights ranting to Evie. I felt like I was going mad, unable to stop replaying that night, and no amount of alcohol and sleeping pills stopped the loop in my head. The arrival of the next round was almost a welcome distraction.

Though that sentiment was short lived when I arrived in the arena and found myself in a dark, narrow space. Closer inspection revealed that what I initially took to be walls were actually towering shelves of books reaching toward the ceiling with dizzying height. I scanned the rows of cold, motion-less tomes. Books used to calm me. Just being in their presence gave me a sense of unparalleled peace. But this was not the cozy library in my sweet little house. Never before had I thought that books could feel menacing.

Seconds ticked by and no one else appeared. Carefully, quietly, I made my way to the end of the stacks and peeked around the corner. Endless rows of shelves greeted me in eerie silence. A thin, gray mist filled the air. If there was an end to these stacks, it was lost in the haze. I saw no ceiling above, but there was just enough light to illuminate the space between the shelves. A few camera bots flew by overhead. Several shelves down, a familiar shape stood at the top of one of the tall shelves. I quickly hid behind the nearest stack as Eleven turned in my direction, in case staying out of sight was part of the game.

"Hello?"

I turned toward the sound of the voice.

"Is someone there?"

I opened my mouth to answer, but something stopped me. I made my way in their direction on tiptoes. Something else rustled through the stacks. Something not human.

"*HELLO CONTESTANTS!*" I winced at the sound and looked up, but there was nothing above save for tendrils of mist and fog playing about the tops of the shelves.

"*Welcome to the Library*," Cheshire's voice said. "*This challenge is going to be a fun one. Are you ready?*"

I never was, but it made no difference. What could I do here? I couldn't see a thing and there was only enough space between the shelves for one person to move through. Field of vision was nonexistent.

"*You're free to do whatever you want in the Library, but be careful, the bookworm is on the prowl. Make too much noise and he'll get you. Stay still, well, he'll still get you. You might have noticed that you've already been scattered for this challenge.*"

A rustle to my right. I quickly pressed my back against the nearest shelf. The rustling faded into the distance.

"*This is so you don't draw attention to yourselves and get gulped up before the game even begins. Remember, more people means more noise, and a bigger meal for the bookworm.*"

A shriek far to my left pierced the misty air then was cut short. My heart pounded and I hoped desperately that it wasn't Evie.

"*Oops, looks like he couldn't wait.*" Cheshire chuckled from beyond the fog. "*Guess we're down to nineteen. One quick note before you get started—anybody notice we haven't drafted anyone new for this round?*" Another laugh. "*What am I saying? You can't even see each other. Anyway, we won't be adding any more new contestants to the games. You lot are the finalists. Give yourselves a hand!*" Silence. "*Look at you all, so smart. I was hoping at least one of you would clap. Anyway, your hour starts now. Enjoy!*"

Enormous red numbers appeared in the darkness overhead, illuminating the mist eerily. I swallowed thickly and proceeded through the stacks as quietly as I could, hoping I was somehow getting closer to Evie.

Another sound. This time a slither. I pressed my back against the shelf again. Should I change? Create something? A shield? A weapon? A disguise?

Before I could decide, something slid through the fog. From the shadows where I hid, I barely made out the mass of sickly gray flesh. The segmented, wriggling body resembled an earthworm but moved like a snake. Its bulbous front portion reared up in the air. Roughly the size of several semi trucks connected end to end, sides covered in fleshy, segmented appendages, it coated the ground in a thin, transparent slime as it passed. Rows of eyes blinked on its flank, searching for prey.

Every muscle in my body clenched in cold, cutting terror. I tried to think of something useful but nothing came to mind. All I could do, once the bookworm disappeared, was move as quickly and quietly as possible in the opposite direction.

The fog thickened as time ticked by. I could barely see more than three or four shelves down. Once in a while I heard rustling or scraping behind nearby shelves, but was too afraid to call out, not being able to tell whether it came from human feet or a fleshy appendage. I heard no other voices. No one dared speak.

Another scream in the distance, though I couldn't quite tell in what direction. The disorienting shelves trapped me like a lost rabbit. I could vaguely figure out my orientation using the countdown in the sky, but no matter how long I headed in one direction, I never reached an end, and that dreadful slithering always sounded too close for comfort.

Shouting, followed by gunfire. Someone— several someones by the sound of it—was fighting back. Another scream cut short, followed by more gunfire. Could I even create a gun if I needed it? I still had no faith in my ability to do so. I looked down at my hand and concentrated. A layer of diamond crystals grew over my hand and formed into cat-claw points over my fingertips. Old Murphy came through again. It would have to do in a pinch.

A rustle above me. My head snapped up, for a moment fearing I'd see a gaping mouth attached to a mountain of pale flesh lunging down at me. But only a single camera bot flew overhead, toward the sound of gunfire.

A metal-clad hand reached out of the top of the nearest shelf and grabbed the camera out of the air. A moment later Eleven peered over the edge down at me. They looked over one shoulder, then the other, in the direction of the commotion, and crushed the camera bot. Then, they reached down over the top of the shelf, tapped the books that filled the top layer, nodded toward me, and disappeared back over the edge.

The gunfire stopped. Whoever encountered the bookworm had either escaped or been eliminated. I shuddered. Not even twenty minutes had passed. I glanced at the books in front of me.

They came in all different shapes and sizes, most in languages I couldn't identify. Was I supposed to look for a specific one? I couldn't understand, and Eleven was nowhere to be seen now. Tentatively, I ran my fingers over their spines.

Voices filled my head instantly. A million different languages flooded my mind like a firehose filling a balloon. I gasped and pulled away. The silence that followed was deafening.

Another slither to my right. I pressed my body to the shelf and held my breath. Something emerged from the fog into the space between the stacks where I hid. It felt around the floor, at the books and shelves, mere inches from my ankles. Could it hear my heart beating? Pressed against the books, I wished desperately that something would distract it before it found me.

Suddenly, without warning, an avalanche of books came tumbling from the middle of the opposite shelf. Enormous volumes crushed thunderously to the ground, some landing heavily onto the fleshy appendage. It jerked in surprise and pulled back as the books continued to fall, creating a small mountain between it and me. I heard it feel its way along the book pile, then retreat away into silence.

As my heart struggled to slow down, I heard the voices again, this time a low hum. Was this what Eleven meant? I could only guess. Was it a puzzle I was supposed to solve, or something simpler I was missing? I found myself missing Lexi, as I often did. She would help me figure it out.

Except she already had.

I heard a hum. I asked for a notch and it gave me one.

I looked at the pile of books on the floor. Then, slowly, politely, I put my hand on the shelf and asked.

Ladder. Please.

The books on the shelf to my right popped themselves out of their slots, spaced perfectly for climbing. I looked up at steps they formed, all the way to the top, then grabbed one and tested it. It held tight. Carefully, quietly, I climbed.

The tops of the shelves were wider than I expected, but I still felt unsteady standing so high. I peered through the fog at the rows and rows of shelves, panting from the long climb. Eleven was nowhere in sight, but what I did see was the center of the library. What I had originally thought to be an arrangement of parallel rows turned out to be a concentric circle—hundreds upon hundreds of shelves all arranged to point toward a center clearing.

Several of the bookworm's appendages snaked over the top of the shelves. I quickly lowered myself and stayed still. They pulled back after a few moments and through the mist I could vaguely see the pale gray body swimming through the aisles.

What now? I was debating whether I should just stay put until time ran out when the bookworm suddenly changed direction. It swerved around the stacks, nearly knocking one of the shelves over, and made a beeline toward the center clearing. Dread sank through me. I crouched, reached down, and laid my hand over the nearest book.

Bridge.

Several dozen books leapt out of their slots and formed a floating bridge to the next shelf. I eyed the precarious structure and gingerly stepped on the first one. It sank down slightly at my weight and I quickly pulled back, unable to stop picturing myself plunging into the foggy depth, just as a shrill scream cut through the air.

"*Hal!*"

My head snapped up at the sound of Evie's voice. In two steps I was over the shaky bridge and on top of the next shelf. The bookworm weaved through the stacks, knocking down books left and right as its bloated body slammed into the shelves. I followed it, one shelf to the next. The book bridges built themselves and I willed myself to move faster, leap farther. My muscles pumped and strained. In my terror, I felt alive.

The row of shelves ended without warning and I

nearly tumbled off the last one into the clearing. Evie emerged from the mist. I dropped to my knees just in time to see her dash into the clearing, the bookworm, a mess of scrambling appendages, close behind.

"Evie!"

She looked up at me, then the bookworm was on her. She raised her hand and I heard two misfires before the bookworm blocked my view.

Could I jump? Not without breaking something.

She screamed again, calling for help with her garbled words. Sweat coated my forehead and hands. A train of jumbled thoughts barreled through my mind and I seized the nearest one.

Bird.

The book bridges disassembled themselves and soared into the air, flapping their pages like wings. They flew over the clearing and dove like bomber planes. The worm reared up, taking notice of the newcomers just long enough for Evie to scramble out of its reach. I took the chance to make a new ladder and descended as quickly as my shaking legs would allow. Evie ran towards the center of the clearing. The space was roughly the size of a baseball diamond and she was halfway through before the worm turned toward her again. I begged the shelves for more birds but it cost me the ladder, which crumbled and left me grasping at thin air.

Evie screamed again. I landed painfully on the hard floor and my right leg buckled under me. My ankle popped audibly, just as the worm's appendages shot out and wrapped around Evie's leg, pulling her back. Her fingers scraped against the slippery floors. Dozens of teeth emerged from the bookworm's yawning maw as it dragged her closer. I heard screaming but couldn't tell whether it was me or her. I dragged myself to the nearest shelf and grabbed the hard book spines.

Birds, I begged. *Birds. Birds. BIRDS.*

Every book in the library lifted off their place. My head exploded with millions of voices shouting in different languages, pushing my skull outward like air in a balloon. I held on to consciousness that threatened to slip away. The sound of rustling paper filled the air and the ceiling disappeared behind a storm of flying books. I fought to hold on to their presence, as if each book was tethered to my mind with an unseen thread. They moved toward the center clearing, pages flapping rapidly.

Just a little longer.

The ones at the center of the clearing dove at the

worm. It reared up and swatted several out of the sky.

"*Take cover!*" I screamed to Evie, but she was already on it. A white substance oozed from all around her and curved itself into a dome over her, like half an eggshell.

Thousands of books dove. Millions more followed. The worm fought to get out of the clearing and hide from the barrage between the stacks, but the weight of the books slammed into its bulky body. The volumes around it began to pile up and it grappled with difficulty to maneuver itself over hard edges and corners.

My vision blurred, but I hung on. I kept the books going. If they fell, I wouldn't be able to make them fly again. Pain shot from my ankle through my leg. Books rained from the sky, some already weakening and falling before they could reach the clearing. I covered my head but few landed on my back and nearly knocked the breath from me.

Books covered the entire clearing now. The worm's movement slowed. The noise in my head was taking over and my eyes yearned to close. The book pile grew rapidly. I hoped that Evie's shell was enough to keep her from being crushed.

Finally, as the last book fell onto the top of the

pile, all movement stopped. The bookworm's last few visible appendages shivered weakly and fell still in its final attempt to dig out of the tomb of books. The world went dark.

THE SOUND of movement woke me. I tried to sit up and something rolled off my back. I blinked the mist out of my eyes and saw the **00:00** glowing in the sky. With a disappointed groan I realized I was still in the arena. Books sat like a mountain before me. Several of the contestants were moving around it and on top of it.

On the side of the slope was Eleven, kneeling over the books and digging rapidly. A moment later they reached inside with one arm and reemerged holding another hand. Evie crawled out from under the heavy pile with their assistance. Crish rushed to help her.

Eleven stood and turned toward me. I sat up and grimaced at the pain in my ankle. In a few nimble steps they were off the slope. I raised my hand expecting them to help me stand, but a strong arm slid under me and I felt myself lifted off the floor before I could protest. Next thing I knew, Eleven was carrying me bridal style toward the corner of the clearing where the other contestants were gathered.

About fifteen others had ventured here, talking amongst themselves. As Eleven approached, they turned toward us and I immediately saw the look in their eyes as they raked their gazes over us. Sergio eyed me with a knowing sneer and I saw him exchange a look with several others. The headlines flashed through my head and suddenly I was very aware of the little camera bots hovering over us.

"Put me down," I said, suddenly panicking. Eleven looked down at me, as if surprised. "Just put me *down*!"

I pushed against the chest of their armor and practically threw myself out of their arms. Eleven leaned trying to keep me from falling, but I was too far gone. I tumbled to the floor in a graceless pile and hissed in pain. Gritting my teeth, I forced myself to stand despite my throbbing ankle.

"Wasn't that spectacular!"

Every muscle in my body tensed at the sound of Cheshire's voice as they strolled into view from between two shelves.

"You did that thing with the books, didn't you?" they asked, emoji face beaming its unchanging smile at me. I nodded. *"Now that was worth some points. Puts*

you right in the middle of the rankings, I think. Quite a climb. I was starting to think none of you were going to figure out how to use the arena properly after Monroe bit it. Good work, champ."

I had no clever retort. I was barely standing as waves of exhaustion and pain washed over me. Cheshire glanced at my rapidly swelling foot.

"Tsk, tsk. That won't do," they said, clucking their nonexistent tongue. *"Can't have you limping around for the next round, can we? The producers won't like that. How long does that take to heal, anyway?"* They turned to Eleven, who gave a quiet answer I couldn't hear. *"Six weeks??"* An exasperated sigh. *"Good lord, humans are inefficient. Whatever. Get that patched and enjoy the break. I'll see you folks in the new year."*

"Go ahead."

Evie looked around uncertainly, then positioned herself against the far wall of the bedroom, magazine cover held directly in front of her.

"Can you hold it a little higher?"

She scooted it a few inches upward.

"Perfect."

The phone camera zoomed in on her. She smiled innocently. "The date is December 1st. Evie and I have decided this is our favorite headline. Can you show it, Evie?"

Evie pointed to the magazine with one finger. On the cover was the photo that had by now been seen by every person with access to the internet or print media in the world—me in Eleven's arms. On the corner of the cover was another smaller photo, a slightly blurry one of me in the process of eating the floor after jumping out of his grasp. The headline read:

TROUBLE IN EXTRATERRESTRIAL PARADISE?

"Intriguing, isn't it? Now if our lovely assistant could open it, we can read what's inside."

Evie dramatically opened the magazine to the centerfold article, which was filled with a dozen more photos of Eleven and me. We already knew what the article said—dozens like it came hot off the presses within hours of us stepping out of Cheshire's library. Every article began with an extremely brief recount of the library events, followed by a ridiculously detailed description of my reaction to Eleven's "affection," then a recap of our "relationship to date" filled with scintillating false details and ending with a guess as to whether our "romance" was at an end or just "hitting a bump in the road."

"Great. Now switch to the one that says I'm pregnant."

For several days after the library, I lay in bed, foot bound and propped up, watching snow slowly build up on the bare trees and windowsills outside. I couldn't believe that I wanted more of these sadistic games to happen, but the thought of spending six weeks anticipating the inevitable nightmare wore me down. To make it worse, my every move in the arena fueled more rumors.

Crish stopped by once or twice at first, but his other engagements kept him busy. Meeting the president, for one. Filming more public service announcements, for another. He always grinned sheepishly when I asked, as if embarrassed for the attention he was receiving. He was the top-scoring contestant, after all, and once upon a time I might have been bothered that he was allowed greater freedom than the rest of us, but after my disastrous visit with Hannah, I was glad not to be in the public eye. In his shoes, I wasn't sure I could hold up a smile nearly as long or genuine.

Of course, the public was obsessed with me regardless. In his first visit, Crish had brought a few tabloids and magazines "for a laugh." There were stories about all of us, but most of the covers bore my face. They sat on the nightstand taunting me, feeding my frustration and ache for another drink, and yet throwing them away somehow felt like letting them "win."

Evie was the one who eventually broke me out of my daze. Aside from the initial unease at her arrival into the game, Evie appeared to have settled into this new way of life better than most of us. After watching me listlessly drift about, she sat next to me, pointed to the magazines, and asked a simple question.

"**Laugh or cry?**"

In the end we decided to laugh. We turned it into a joke and filmed each other holding up the magazines and listing out the most ridiculous of the articles. It relieved the tension somewhat, and for a few hours, I almost forgot about the noises that chattered away in the back of my mind about Sergio, about Eleven, about my father and alleged sister. The day was a little brighter, but as the night fell, I lay in silence watching the videos we made as Evie snoozed away in the other bed, once again filled with mixed feelings that buzzed like static.

A gentle knock startled me. I sat up. Evie was still asleep.

A pause, then more knocking. Someone was at the door. I dragged myself out of bed with some effort and hobbled out of the bedroom on one foot. It was rather late for a delivery to arrive, but not unprecedented. I ought to have a talk with Lydia about scheduling deliveries before bedtime.

More knocking.

"I'm coming!" I hissed, making my way across the sparse living room as quickly as I could, leaning on the lumpy futon they had set up two days after we moved in. Neither Evie nor I ever sat on it as it felt like sitting on a bag of rolled-up socks, but at the moment I was glad it was there as I half-hopped toward the door. Balancing precariously on one foot, I pulled the front door open. "Can you keep it down? Evie is—"

I slammed the door shut. Then, a split second later, yanked it open, grabbed the metal-clad arm, and dragged Eleven inside.

"Did anyone see you?"

Eleven looked at me with what might be amusement as I hopped around the living room, peering out windows and closing curtains. Thankfully the night remained dark and quiet as ever. No news choppers blazed overhead. I let out a sigh of relief.

"What the hell are you doing here?"

"I wanted to speak with you," Eleven replied unhurriedly, looking around the room. I couldn't see their expression behind the blank mask but I imagined a human's living situation must be fascinating to someone alien to the planet. Now they were going to think all humans enjoyed sitting on lumpy futons. "And to your previous question—no, I was not spotted this time. I was able to calibrate your location with greater precision."

"Okay," I said, leaning against the futon. Standing on one foot was difficult, but somehow sitting down felt like letting down my guard. "So what do you want? Do you have another token? Leave it. I'll give it to Evie."

Eleven shook their head. "No, unfortunately no. I came because I had a question."

"What is it?" I asked, wary of their answer. Whatever Cheshire and the "producers" had in store couldn't be good. For a moment I wondered if I had been designated the butt of some joke crueler than the games.

"Did I do something wrong?"

The question took me so off guard I thought I might have hallucinated it. "Excuse me?"

"In the previous round. Did I act inappropriately? I would like to know how to prevent future incidents."

"I—" I started but couldn't seem to finish. "No. It wasn't what you did."

"It was not?"

"No. You didn't do anything wrong. Please just go."

I expected Eleven to teleport right out of there, but they didn't move. Instead, they tilted their head slightly, looking at me like I was a puzzle to solve. "I do not understand."

"You don't have to. Just leave."

"There was obviously a problem. If you—"

"A problem?" An image flashed through my mind—magazines plastered with images of Eleven and me here, alone in the middle of the night, me scantily clad for bed in an oversized T-shirt that ended barely below my hips, and all the headlines that would follow. "My problem is *you*!" I snapped. "Every time I'm seen with *you* there is another story. Every time you touch me there's ten articles trying to guess what weird, nasty things I let you do to me. Everyone is gossiping about me. My face is everywhere. I'm trying to save the damn world and get back to my life, and everyone is making up things about me because of *you*. When this is over, you get to go back to watching your games, hiding your face, and I'll either be dead or go down in history for . . . for . . ." I looked around, picked up the nearest magazine, and threw it at them. It bounced off their chest. The picture of us stared back. "For *this*!"

Eleven looked down at the magazine on the floor. Then, slowly, they bent and picked it up, studying the cover. I sighed and ran a hand through my hair.

"Can you just leave?"

They looked up at me, then back at the magazine.

"Look," I said after a deep breath. "It's not your fault. This is just how humans are. I don't know if your people like this kind of thing, but here, we love our gossip."

"But you do not."

"I don't do well being the center of attention. I'm not made for it. But I'll live. Just leave so I can go back to bed." From the bedroom came a rustle. "And I think we just woke Evie up. You should go before she sees you."

"Not yet." A metal-clad hand closed around my arm. I started.

"What are you doing?" I pulled back in alarm but the hand held tight. "Let go!"

The last thing I saw was Evie emerging from the bedroom. Her sleep-hazed eyes met mine before everything went black.

· · ·

I YANKED my arm free as soon as we landed. Unfortunately I had forgotten about my bum ankle and the motion sent me reeling backward. Eleven was fast, catching me around the waist before I could tumble into a graceless pile, an act that I realized with some irritation seemed to happen a lot. I quickly wriggled free of their grasp and balanced myself the best I could on one foot.

"Where am I?" I demanded, though looking around the stark white dome and black floor, the answer was obvious. "What do you want?"

"Relax," Eleven said, and snapped their fingers in a manner all too similar to Cheshire. A high-backed chair appeared next to me. "Have a seat."

I eyed the chair like it was braided from barbed wire. "So you can do that, too."

"Manipulating the functions of the arena is a basic requirement of my job."

"Sure," I muttered, lowering myself into the seat. It was comfortable enough, but relaxing wasn't exactly the word I'd use. I was also still wearing only a T-shirt and underwear, but I stubbornly refused to be self-conscious in front of Eleven. So I crossed my legs, linked my hands over my knee, and tried my best to look unfazed. "So what now? Is this some kind of special round just for me?"

"No," Eleven said simply. "The arena is not active at the moment. I only booted up peripheral functions in a small area." A wave of their hand and a screen appeared, filled with characters and keys I didn't recognize. I watched Eleven manipulate it with mild fascination. A moment later the large screen vanished, replaced by a row of smaller, rectangular screens that arranged themselves into a circle around me. Each one framed a face, like portraits in an art gallery.

I scanned them. Each portrait had been assigned a number, written at the bottom of the screens. The people—beings—in each one were different, varying widely in age, ethnicity, and number of appendages. I looked from a tentacle-covered face to a pair of bulbous eyes peering out of a beet-red head to what looked like a cyclops covered in fur.

"Who are they?" I asked Eleven, who was standing patiently to the side as I took it all in.

"Past champions from this galaxy."

I moved my hand over the images. They moved in the direction of my gesture and stopped when a familiar face caught my eye.

"This one," I said incredulously as number seven looked back at me, round eyes and smooth cheeks and hair like an onyx waterfall. "This is human. She's human!"

"Her kind has a genetic blueprint similar to your species."

"How is that possible?"

"There exist others like your kind. She was merely the first." Eleven stepped beside me and the images scrolled with a wave of their hand, stopping on number nineteen, an older woman with her silver hair in a tight bun and two streaks of white paint on each cheek. "This is the second." The images scrolled again. Number twenty-seven. A young man about twenty-five years old, with a mohawk and a defiant look in his steel-colored eyes. "This is the third."

"How can that be?" I looked up at Eleven. "How can there be humans on other planets?"

"The champion of the current round," Eleven said, ignoring my question, "would be the thirty-third champion produced by this galaxy."

I scanned the champions. They stared back blankly. "They all look . . ." I muttered, searching for the right word. "Humanoid."

"Humanoid?"

"Yes." I scrolled the faces past. "All of them. Not just the ones like me. They all have a head and eyes and noses and mouths. The skin and hair are different and some of them have extras but . . ." I shook my head. "I don't understand. I just always thought aliens would look a lot more different. Why do they all look like variations on humans? Why are they humanoid?"

Eleven studied me. "Every race has a version of that word," they said.

"What word?"

"The word that lets them describe other races as variations of their own."

"Fair enough," I said. "But why? Why *do* we all look like versions of each other?"

"I cannot answer that question."

"You can't or you won't?"

"My intention does not vary the outcome."

I turned to look at number seven again. She was a lovely girl, with soft, youthful features. Though not of Earth, she looked human in every way; the only noticeable difference was a slight violet sheen to her pupils.

"That one. How old was she?"

"At the time she was crowned champion, she was thirteen by your years."

"*Thirteen?*" I exclaimed. "How can that be? I

thought contestants had to be over seventeen years old."

"The rules of the game have changed over time."

Thirteen. A shiver ran through me as I imagined this child running through a blood-covered maze. She had hard eyes. They all did, in fact, at least the ones who had eyes. Even the ones whose features resembled Mr. Potato Head arranged by a toddler looked like they had seen hell. They all stared back at me, old, tired, and unsmiling.

"What was her name?"

"I do not know. The champions lose their names over time and are identified only by numbers."

"Wonderful," I muttered. "That's just lovely. So what happened to her? After she won, I mean."

"She was viewed as a disgrace by her people."

"You can't be serious."

"As far as I know, she was married as a child, gave birth to her firstborn less than a year before she entered the game, and never saw her child again after."

"Why?"

"Her family cast her out and took her infant as punishment for having made a public spectacle of herself."

I felt sick. Tearing my eyes from the girl's desolate gaze, I turned to another image, a scale-covered being with deep, sunken eyes. "What about this one?"

"Number fifteen. His planet was dominated by two major races that had a long history of racial conflict. When he won the game, his race used it as an excuse to commit genocide, wiping out millions with a holy war waged in his name."

"Was he okay with that?"

"I would imagine not. He was committed to a mate of the opposing race. But that mate, along with their children, were deemed 'unworthy' and killed."

"And that one?" I pointed to another, a long-limbed being with a vertical third eye on their forehead.

"Number twenty. Attempted to seek peace by going into hermitage after the game, but their fame followed wherever they went and they spent most of their life on the move, trying to avoid garnering attention."

"Did it work?"

"Their followers began a new religion in their name."

"And how did that turn out?"

"I believe most of their developed countries have been taken over by the leaders of the religion, who use the champion's name as a 'prophet' to keep the rest of the populace under their thumb."

I shuddered. "Is this what happens to everyone who wins these games?"

"Not all of them. Some do find solace and peace and did good for their planet using their newfound fame, though it did not come easily."

"Why are you showing me this?"

"To show you that no one is 'made for it,' as you say." Eleven gestured at the gallery of champions. "The fact is, your planet is exactly like dozens of others. Sentient beings tend toward sensationalism. It is unfortunate, but it is a fact."

I let out a dry laugh. "Planets full of humans and aliens just like humans. Is this supposed to make me feel better?"

"That is up to you. You can choose to see this as a display of the misery that came before you, or you can see it as evidence that many like you have persevered through this game and continued to persevere through the aftermath that followed, and that your fate afterwards is unknown and open to possibilities both good and bad."

I gave the gallery of champions another look and got shakily to my feet. "I can't fault your positivity," I said, scrolling through the faces once more. Somehow, knowing they'd been down the same path made them feel like old friends. Even the inhuman ones I now looked at with a sense of familiarity. I stopped on one that caught my eye.

His pupils were gold rimmed around a deep blue iris, standing out sharply against his teal-green skin. There was not a hair on him. Instead, thin splashes of iridescent scales adorned the sides of his head and neck, catching light and color and shimmering as if underwater. A crescent of scales cradled the socket of his left eye. His features were sharp and stately. Raised cheek-bones that looked as if they'd been sculpted by careful hands gave away to ears tapered to an almost elfish point.

He looked human, if humans evolved from drag-ons. His portrait, unlike the others, was the only one framed in black.

"This one," I said. "What's his story? Why is his picture different?"

"That one," Eleven said slowly, "was an outlier. The black frame indicates him as an underqualified champion."

"Why?"

"He was the only one to win the games without meeting the point total. His planet was destroyed because of it. He is the last of his kind, a disgrace who only managed to save himself."

"How can you say that?" I said, throwing in a glare for good measure. "I'm sure he fought for his planet the best he could. And he *won*, didn't he? If you ask me, it's not fair that he did everything they wanted and they destroyed his planet anyway. He's not a disgrace. He's like the rest of them. He's—" I glanced at the number under the frame and the words caught in my throat. There was a click and hiss and I found myself face-to-face with those gold-rimmed eyes.

"A champion," Eleven said, the expressionless mask that I'd come to take for granted in his hand. The buzzy filter disappeared from his voice, now smooth and clear and echoed in the empty arena like a soft bass. "But as the last of one's kind, 'disgrace' is an easier title to bear."

EVIE SAT in the living room tapping away on her tablet when we arrived back. She looked up at Eleven and me, lingering slightly on Eleven's unmasked face, curious but unalarmed.

"I will go now," Eleven said, and took a step back.

I reached out and grabbed his wrist before he could disappear.

"No," I said. "Not like that. You can't tell me all that stuff and just leave it there. I have too many questions."

Eleven glanced at Evie, who had set her tablet aside and was now unabashedly watching us. "Questions?"

"Yes," I said insistently. "Like what happened to your planet? What happened to *you*? Why are you working for Cheshire if they destroyed your planet?"

"I'm afraid those questions have very long answers."

"Then answer this one first," I said, releasing him. "Why are you speaking English? I thought the arena was translating, but you're here now and you're still speaking English. Why?"

"My race tends towards omnilingualism. I did not know it was an abnormal trait until I was offered this position. Being able to learn multiple languages in any world is useful in preparing for the games. I studied ten of your most-used languages in order to aid in setting up the arena."

"Ten?"

"Yes," he replied in disturbingly flawless Mandarin. "Including the ones you speak."

I shook my head. "No, no. Go back to English. This is weird enough."

"Very well."

"Is that why you talk like you swallowed a dictionary?"

"I studied the languages academically. It lends to a weakness in everyday vernacular, but provides a solid enough basis for conversation."

"Sure," I said. "I mean, who doesn't miss a few things when they learn ten alien languages at once."

Evie chuckled. I cleared my throat.

"Never mind. Look, come back tomorrow and we'll talk more about it."

"Come back?"

"Yes. It's late. I need to sleep. Come back tomorrow. Don't knock. Just—I don't know—do what you just did, come straight in. So nobody sees you."

"I am not certain I should. Technically speaking, I am discouraged from fraternizing with the contestants."

"A rule you already broke. I'm guessing Cheshire doesn't know about your little slideshow just now," I pointed out. "We have over a month before the next round. You have something better to do?"

"No," Eleven said slowly. "I suppose not."

"So come back tomorrow."

"Alright," he said, though he sounded noncommittal. "Good night."

With that he was gone. I slumped onto the futon next to Evie and let out a sigh, trying to decide where to start telling her about the past hour.

"**Hot.**"

"What is?"

She didn't answer. Instead, she rose, winked at me, and went back to bed.

"Do you ever think about other people who have played this game?"

Crish's blurry face shifted out of frame, then into it again. "Sorry, what did you say?"

I smiled. It seemed the most I saw him in recent history were through these short, blurry video calls. He had become a very busy man. "Nothing. Where are you?"

"En route to San Fran."

"Another appearance?"

"Photos and watching politicians kiss babies. It's hard work but somebody has to do it. Anything exciting back home?"

"Nice of you to call this hole home."

"How's your foot?"

"Taking its sweet time, but getting better."

"You'll be up and about in no time." Someone off screen spoke. Crish looked up for a few seconds, then looked back to me with a sigh. "Sorry, I have to go. I swear it never ends."

I shook my head. "I understand. Don't worry. Do your best out there."

"Hey."

"Yeah?"

"Miss you."

I chuckled. "Miss you, too."

"I'll bring something back for you. I promise." More voices off screen. "Really gotta go. Bye!"

"Bye," I said, but he had already hung up. The timing, as it turned out, was perfect, since Eleven chose that moment to appear in the middle of the living room.

I shut off the tablet and stood, supporting myself on the Formica table. I had no idea what I'd expected of his arrival, but the disheveled suit wasn't it. Up until now, I had never seen him without his armor. At the moment, however, he was wearing what appeared to be a black, nondescript suit similar to the ones commonly worn by the handlers, except he looked like he'd struggled into it the way a reluctant cat was shoved into a holiday costume. The black trousers fit him well enough, but the white dress shirt and black suit jacket hung open awkwardly, and almost appeared to have extra seams and drapes by the way they misaligned.

"Why are you dressed like that?"

He fidgeted with the sleeves of the jacket. "I did not know the customs of your world well enough so I dressed in what appears to be the common uniform for those around you." He tugged at the sleeves. "The materials are somewhat alien to me."

There was that word again. *Alien*. I looked Eleven up and down, an alien in human clothing. He was still looking around the apartment, as if trying to make sense of his surroundings, and I was suddenly very aware that the alien in the room was not the one with teal-green skin.

"You're a long way from home."

Eleven turned back to me. "I beg your pardon?"

"You're on an alien planet. We're all aliens to you, aren't we?"

He paused in the middle of adjusting his clothes, as if the thought was just occurring to him as well. "Yes," he replied slowly.

"You don't have to dress like them. That's not how all humans dress."

"Oh." Eleven looked down at himself for a moment, then removed the ill-fitting jacket.

"You're also supposed to button the shirt," I said, pointing to his exposed midriff.

He laid the jacket aside and fiddled with the tiny white buttons. His fingers were long and slender, with a slight reptilian curve. The nails, I noticed, were dark and on a sliding scale might tend slightly closer to claws than fingernails. Small clusters of scales like the ones on his neck and head also adorned his knuckles, light bouncing off their shimmering surfaces as he struggled with the tiny buttons.

"I apologize," he said, looking increasingly flustered. Out of his armor, he was completely different —awkward, unprotected, vulnerable. "This is all foreign to me."

"You don't use buttons where you come from?"

"None so small."

I stifled a chortle at his effort and decided he shouldn't embarrass himself any further.

"Let me."

I limped over to him, grabbed the shirt by the placket and straightened it. I laid his collar flat and began to do up the buttons one by one. I was halfway done before my common sense kicked in.

What am I doing?

We were standing barely inches apart. My fingers

brushed against his broad chest and taut stomach. The scales snaking up and down his neck disappeared when they reached his shoulders. On his chest, I saw remnants of old scars—souvenirs of the arena.

I'd stopped moving. Did he notice? I quickly started doing the buttons again.

"I'll make coffee," I mumbled as I finished the last button, and hobbled into the kitchen before he could get a good look at my flushed face.

I WAS JUST STARTING to measure out the instant coffee when something occurred to me. I turned back to the dining nook, where Eleven still stood, looking about as uncomfortable as one person could manage.

"Do you know what coffee is?"

"In theory. It consists of beans brewed in hot water?"

"Yes. Do you just default to Wikipedia mode?"

"Most of what I know about the planets where the games are held is learned through academic means. I have gone on excursions to familiarize myself with the local culture, but those have usually been short and discreet." For the first time, I saw a small smile on his face. "And yes, Wikipedia was a most useful tool."

"Not everyone likes coffee." I gestured at the coffee maker. "It's bitter and I personally prefer tea. Coffee's okay with enough milk in it, I guess. Do you want milk?"

"I cannot. My race is what your language would call—" He frowned in thought, a surprisingly human gesture. "I am having a hard time finding the word."

"Vegan?"

"Herbivorous."

"Oh," I said, arching a brow. "I have questions about that, too."

As I filled mugs with hot water and dug out the tea bags, I snuck peeks out of the corner of my eye at Eleven. Matching the person at the little dining table to the intimidating armor-clad figure in the arena was difficult. Though tall by human standards, he appeared somewhat smaller now. Behind the expressionless mask, he'd always held himself still, silent and intimidating in his motionlessness. Now, in the tiny apartment, with nothing hiding his face, I saw the look of worry in his gold-rimmed eyes, as well as the nervous fidgets of his fingers. He was no longer a faceless automaton, but a person with a mind and a story—a person on an alien planet, unguarded and afraid.

I glanced at his hands then quickly turned back to the mugs, suddenly nervous that he would catch me looking. Were those the same hands that left those burns on my arms, and the welts around my neck? The same hands that put Sergio in his place when he threatened me? That pulled Lexi and me up from the edge when we nearly lost our lives on the Pyramid Climb?

A shuffle and I snapped out of my daze. Eleven had stepped behind the kitchen counter next to me.

"Allow me," he said, picking up the mugs and nodding at my bum ankle. "You should sit and rest your injury."

"Right," I muttered. His eyes were a different color today, green instead of blue, though the gold rim was still present.

"Are you certain you want to do this?"

I blinked. "What?"

"I am well aware of how *bizarre* I must look to you. If you are uncomfortable with my presence, it might be better if I left."

"No!" I said, a little too loudly. "No. I just don't know where to start."

"Will your roommate be joining us?"

I glanced at the bedroom door, where Evie usually sequestered herself whenever I spoke with Crish. If she'd heard Eleven arrive, she gave no indication.

"Let me check," I said, and limped over to the bedroom door to knock. Evie opened the door on the second knock and peeked out at me, then at Eleven in turn. A thin, almost sneaky smile crept across her face. She retreated into the bedroom and reappeared a moment later with her tablet.

"**Nice.**"

"What is?" I glanced at the mugs of tea Eleven had just set down on the Formica table. "So Eleven is here; do you want to—"

"**No,**" Evie typed. "**Three wheel.**"

The bedroom door slammed shut again before I could ask what she meant. I gave Eleven a confused look.

"Does she not want me here?"

"No," I replied, maneuvering my way into the seat across from him. "She likes you. But she's hard to understand sometimes. Don't worry about it."

"Alright."

Silence fell over us. I took a long sip of tea and found that I had no idea what to say. When I had insisted that he come back last night, I hadn't given much thought to exactly what I was going to ask him.

"Sorry," he said after a moment. "I am not very good at conversing with . . ."

"Humans? Women?"

"Sentient beings."

"Makes two of us." Desperate to kill the awkwardness, I blurted out the first question on my mind. "What's your name?"

"My name?"

"It's not really Eleven, is it?"

He shook his head. "No. Though I am not sure how it would sound to your ears." He bared his teeth slightly and spoke a phrase that was almost English sounding, but with "s" sounds in unexpected places.

"I won't try to say it."

"Eleven is fine. I have not gone by anything else in a very long time."

"Can't be that long. What are you? Thirty?"

"I have never calculated my current age in your cycles. But I have attended every game in some form or fashion since my own and the time between games was roughly equal. I do know the first champion of your kind, Seven, was roughly of your year 1300, and the second, Nineteen, was roughly of 1650, which puts my entry into the champions list around perhaps 1400–1450."

I stared at him.

"Are you alright?"

"Are you telling me you are—" The numbers ran through my head quickly. "Over six hundred years old?"

"Give or take. Is that the correct phrase?"

"Does your race always live that long?"

"No, our life expectancy is roughly the same as yours. Thirty was probably accurate at the time I entered the games."

"Then why . . ." I couldn't even think through the absurdity of the question.

"The answer to my longevity is complicated."

"Start somewhere."

HE STARTED AT THE ORB, an orb that arrived on a different Earth—it wasn't called Earth, but it might as well have been. There was a reason for this, he paused to explain, as only civilizations that had reached a certain level of social and cultural development could become candidates for the games. It was a world preoccupied with its own problems.

And then the orb arrived, and as one the focus of the populace changed.

The game they experienced was quite different. In addition to being tailored to both appeal to and test the inhabitants of each planet, it had also evolved over time to appeal to viewership. (Viewership by whom? I asked, my mind wandering back to the sewer and that ever-lingering question of who was watching. But he evaded the question.) He himself was selected in the eighth round, an experience he described in chilling, encyclopedia terms. His people had figured out the rules of the game by round three, but it did not decrease the difficulty nor the risk of participation.

Like the masses of Earth, the population of his planet soon became much more enamored with the contestants themselves than the dangers of the situation. The lawmen of his country did not isolate the contestants as Earth did, and soon the media circus was out of control. Showing his face in public was impossible. Family and friends cut off their association to avoid attention. He, along with many fellow contestants, eventually abandoned their homes for slums where they were less likely to be recognized.

"I adjusted," he said. His voice carried a degree of dissociation, as if reciting a story belonging to someone else. "Sleeping under bridges and digging in garbage for sustenance was worth the quiet and anonymity, until I was whisked off to a new round in full view of several others sharing the same shelter. After that I more or less remained on the move."

And it stayed this way until the very end. He changed places, wandering from place to place, trying to time the teleportation into the games for a time when he was safely hidden. Chronic illness was common among the contestants due to rough living conditions and stress. And yet, there was no giving up with the world hanging in the balance. Though some did, he said with a sad shake of his head. Several of his fellow contestants ended their own lives when the inability to find peace both inside and outside the arena became too much. None of the contestants he started with made it to the final rounds.

A few banked on their glory, trading their fame for wealth and luxury. But, he said, they fell into their own traps—thinking themselves to be stars and celebrities distracted them from the harsh realities of the game, and they inevitably lost.

HERE HE STOPPED ABRUPTLY and stood. "I should go."

"What?" I said, panicked. The harsh interruption to his story was difficult to shake off. "You haven't finished. I need to know what happened."

"I'm sorry," Eleven said apologetically. "But my time is up."

"What do you mean? Why?"

He looked away for a moment, as if embarrassed. "The air here . . ."

"Oh. Right."

"The main purpose of the suit was to ensure I could breathe for prolonged periods. Without it, I can remain on the planet's surface for only a short amount of time."

I tried to wrap my mind around his words. For a moment, I had almost forgotten the differences between us.

"I forgot," I said. "I'm sorry."

"It is not your concern."

"You're not going to die if you keep staying here?"

"Nothing so dramatic. It would only be fatal in cases of extreme exertion." He took a step back. "I should be off now."

"Is it hard?" I blurted out.

"What is?"

"Being here." I gestured around the sparse apartment. "By yourself, surrounded by aliens, with air you can't breathe."

He gave me a look that told me it was not a question he expected to hear.

"Dwelling on loneliness," he said slowly, "is not conducive to surviving it."

"Come back tomorrow!" I called after him just as he disappeared.

AUSTIN HEATH LOOKED TIRED. I HADN'T SEEN HIM except for once since settling into the new living arrangements. I had assumed he was so angry over the media riots I'd caused that he was going to deal with me strictly through Lydia going forward.

So when he barged in at barely 7 a.m., looking unshaven and badly in need of a caffeine infusion, I was surprised. He didn't even bother with pleasantries as he walked into the apartment, scanning the narrow space briefly before addressing me.

"Everything alright here?"

"Sure," I said, confused.

"Anything out of the ordinary?"

"No," I said, looking past him at the kitchen counter holding the mug Eleven drank out of less than a day ago. "Nothing."

Heath gave me a hard look. I kept my face blank. Did he suspect something? I had no way of knowing. He usually looked at me with that mixture of annoyance and distaste, doubly so since the rumors about Eleven and me started.

"Alright," he said finally. "Where's Miss Bouchard?"

"Sleeping. It's seven o'clock."

"Is it?" Heath checked his watch. "Shit, I'm still in the wrong time zone." He took off his watch and fiddled with the buttons on the side. "Screw it. I'll do this later." He set it down on a wobbly end table near the door. "I just passed by to do a quick status check. How's your foot?"

I lifted my wrapped ankle. "Getting there."

"Good. Do you need refills on medication?"

"Don't think so."

"You're not overdoing it on the pills, are you?" He tossed a glance toward the bathroom, where my pain and sleep medications were kept. "We have quite enough drama about you in the gossip column, no need to add overdosing to the bastard sibling and alien love affair."

I ground my teeth. "No. I'm managing fine."

Heath turned away from me as if he had no more attention to waste. He knocked three times hard on the bedroom door. Evie poked her disheveled head out after a moment.

"Good morning, Miss Bouchard."

Evie gave him an irritated look and opened the bedroom door. Heath gave the bedroom a brief scan, though I wasn't sure what he could possibly be checking for.

"Looks like you two are doing alright," he said, but the way he looked at me out of the corner of his eye said otherwise.

"Did you expect trouble?"

"I'm sure I don't know," Heath said, raking his gaze over the tiny space. "But I have a job to do, and you understand that after the debacle of your little trip, my performance is under a rather fine microscope."

"I understand." I debated whether to push a little harder. "I'm sure it's hard coming back here to check on us when you're out there parading Crish around."

"You should be thankful for Crish Michaels. He is taking the heat off your little love drama by presenting a wholesome image of the contestants. He is someone the public can look up to and feel safe around. You might not realize it holed up in here, but the people out there need a hero right now."

"Sure. Because being holed up here is *my* idea."

He gave me a scathing look. "You ought to enjoy the peace and quiet offered to you," he said, hands in his pockets as he headed out the front door. "If you were out there with the masses, you'd quickly see that your only worth to them is tabloid fodder."

MY TEA HAD MOSTLY GONE cold when Eleven arrived. I had half expected him to have had enough of my prying after yesterday. He was wearing the same black slacks and white dress shirt, which he managed to button this time— though he missed at least two holes. He slid into the seat across from me at the table and I marveled at how we had slipped into a routine after only one day.

"Your eyes are blue again."

He touched his right eye self-consciously. "Are they?"

"You didn't know?"

"The eye color of my race is dependent on activity level and blood flow. Lighter colors indicate a greater degree of exertion or excitement. Until I encountered other races through the games, I had assumed that was the norm."

My spoon clinked around the still-full mug. "Can I ask you something?"

"If you wish."

"When you were a contestant, still trying to live your life but everyone knowing your name, did you still feel—" I paused. "I guess for you the word isn't 'human,' is it? Your people, did you still feel like one of them? Or like you were something else, because they didn't see you as one of them anymore?"

Eleven drummed his long fingers on the table once, twice. "To be perfectly honest, I do not remember what it feels like to be part of a 'people.'"

"Right," I sighed, inwardly berating myself. "Your planet is gone. I'm sorry. I forgot."

He shook his head. "It's alright. I must have felt it once, before the games. But what you're asking is whether that separation came along with the notoriety of being a contestant."

"Yes."

"It did, I suppose. I have not given it much thought."

"Not dwelling and all that." I picked up the cold mug, took a sip, and grimaced. "So, what happened in your games after you went into hiding?"

"I resigned myself to death."

"Why?"

"Because it felt inevitable. I didn't expect to win. I was surviving the games, but just scraping by. There was another contestant far superior to me in skill. We resided on different continents but we had grown close quickly—fearing for one's lives together had a way of doing that. I fully expected him to win. My body and mind were both ailing and I had no life to return to. I devoted myself to being useful to my friend and seeing to it that he crossed the finish line, because he was the hero our people needed."

I winced slightly at the word "hero."

"But he didn't win."

Eleven pursed his lips and looked out the window. I realized, for the first time, that this was not a story easily told.

"There were three of us in the final round. Then there were two—he and I."

"What happened?"

He didn't speak for a long time.

"It's alright if you rather not talk about it."

"No," he said. "That is not the reason. There is something you must understand—I cannot tell you what occurs in the final round of the games. Aside from the fact that it could be problematic for the both of us, there is nothing I could say that could possibly prepare you for it." He paused, then added, "Should you make it that far."

Those last words fell over us like a heavy shroud.

"What happened to your friend?"

"He splintered."

The word sent a chill through my spine. "Like I did?"

"Yes. And he was killed on the spot."

"But why? Why didn't they snap him out of it, like you did to me? Why didn't the guard, the assistant, whatever, at the time . . ." I drifted off. "There was no guard then, was there?"

"No."

"You're the first one."

"In the older games, splintered contestants were automatically killed, as they were deemed to be no longer of 'sound mind' and therefore disqualified. I became champion by default. Unfortunately, due to the fact that I had spent most of my time in the arena assisting him, my point score was very low. I won the title, but not the safety of my world." Green eyes met mine. "Do you know how agonizingly long it takes for an entire planet to burn?"

I had no words. In truth, I had trouble wrapping my mind around the magnitude of his words. I tried to imagine the Earth on fire—every house, every person, every monument. The little apartment complex I grew up in lined with aspen trees, the office at the university where I worked my first job answering phones and filing reports, the book of stamps my grandmother left me, Tiananmen Square, the Statue of Liberty, the polar ice caps, Niagara Falls; everything I'd ever seen and heard and known, every animal and plant and home, engulfed in flames.

"I'm sorry," I said shakily, feeling like I was suffocating. "What did you do after that?"

"My instinct at first was to take my own life—I had no life left, after all. But they—the producers, as they're called—had taken an interest in me. That was when I learned that my kind's talent in languages was a rare and desirable trait. They offered that since I had no home to return to, I should stay and assist in the games."

"And you agreed?"

"Not at first. I would much have preferred to take my life instead. But they offered something else—a chance to restore my world."

I gaped. "They can do that?"

"To a degree. They claimed they could reseed the planet, create atmospheric, genetic, and evolutionary conditions for my race to be reborn."

"Can they really do that?"

"Truthfully, I don't know. I have no evidence one way or the other. But it's the only shred of hope I have to carry on my people's legacy. We were a flawed, problematic, selfish race, as most civilized races seem to be, but I owe it to them."

I watched Eleven as he looked out the frost-kissed window. At a glance, he was young, and strong, almost intimidating in his stature, but in the gray light of winter, the age he carried on his shoulders and in his unblinking, gold-rimmed eyes was apparent.

"Can I make you some tea?"

He turned to me and gave me a brief smile. For a fleeting moment, that cloud over his face almost lifted. "Let me."

I watched him maneuver expertly around the kitchen. After one day, he'd already figured out the rhythm of the place, unsurprising given that adapting quickly to new surroundings was likely second nature after six centuries. Without a word from me, he took my cup and reheated it as well, and I wondered if he had picked up the mannerisms of humans or if humans inherently carried mannerisms like his kind. When he returned to the table, I saw markings I hadn't noticed before.

"What's that?"

He opened his right palm. In the center, neatly weaved into the shape of a wreath, were eleven strokes resembling those made by calligraphy brushes.

"The winner's laurel."

I took his hand in mine and ran a finger curiously over the symbol. It was flat and smooth, a surprise as I had expected some remnants of scarring.

"Is this a brand? It's not burned in?"

"I do not understand how it was applied. By the time I noticed it, it was already there. Though I do know that it marks deep, down through the layers of skin, flesh, even the bone."

"It marks down to the bone?"

"To prevent the champions from peeling off their skin. As you might imagine, some of the champions would prefer not to wear a permanent souvenir from the games."

"Do they really try to do that?"

"I did. It took some time to get used to, but I've come to accept it." He paused and I saw he was looking along my left hand to my wrist. "I assume there is a story behind yours also. Kintsukuroi, is it?"

"So you can read everything, too."

"Actually, I can read next to none of your languages. I noticed that mark when resetting your shoulder and conducted my own research."

Something in me fluttered slightly, though I wasn't sure why. "The Japanese sometimes fix broken pottery with gold. It's supposed to indicate that something is made more beautiful after having been broken and then repaired." I shook my head lightly. "Honestly, it feels a little pretentious now. I mean, I'm not even Japanese. But I got it after my mother passed and my father drifted away. I wanted to feel . . . I don't know, maybe like I was better for having gone through the trauma, instead of just admitting that my family was broken. Although these days that seems like nothing. I can't imagine being more broken than I am now."

"You will be stronger for it."

"Are *you*?"

"Given a choice, I would like to think so." He started to stand. "I should go soon."

"Oh," I said. "Right. Okay."

"Are you finished with that?"

I quickly let go of his hand, forgetting I was still holding it. "Yes. Sorry."

"You can take a closer look tomorrow if you like."

I looked up at him as he stood. "You're coming back?"

"Unless you have had enough of my rambling."

"No, no," I said, standing. "Come back."

For a second we stood facing each other awkwardly. I suddenly realized I hadn't properly said goodbye to him yesterday.

"What do your people do?" I asked. "When you say goodbye to someone."

I saw him hesitate for a moment. Then, he took a step forward and leaned in, gently taking my arm in his hand. His skin was cool and dry. I let out a small gasp as his sharp teeth nipped the base of my neck. And then he was gone. I sat down heavily in the chair and let out a breath I hadn't realized I was holding.

"Astra!"

Crish's strong arms bear hugged around me as he charged into the apartment, lifting me off the ground and nearly crushing the wind out of me. He spun me around effortlessly and set me down as I tried to shake off my surprise.

"Crish!" I exclaimed at last, looking him up and down. I hadn't seen him in person except for briefly in Cheshire's library and a spotty call here and there. In truth, I hadn't expected to see him at all during this break. He smelled windswept and sandy, marked by the fingerprints of all the places he'd trekked through. "What are you doing here? I thought you were on the west coast somewhere or . . ." I paused. How long ago was that? Two weeks? Three? I had begun to lose track of the days, marking the mornings only by Eleven's visits and the evenings tucking Evie into bed.

"I was. West coast, up north, overseas and back again." I started to close the door behind him but he stopped me. "Come on. I'm busting you out."

I hesitated, looking past him at the quiet units filled with unseen guards. "What do you mean? Shouldn't we talk here?"

He smiled sneakily. "Aren't you sick of being trapped here? Don't worry; I made a deal with the handlers. Come out and get some fresh air."

I shook my head. "You know how well that turned out last time."

"Trust me; it'll be fine." He took my arm and began leading me out the door. Despite my bum foot, I hobbled on after him.

CLEAN MORNING BREEZES caressed my face as we stepped onto the rooftop. I had no idea how we'd gotten here, only that Crish drove with a purpose and destination in mind. I hadn't bothered to wonder what kind of deal he'd made with the handlers, nor how he'd managed to secure a car to himself without their watchful eyes. Honestly, those things felt trivial.

I'd never taken notice of this building before, though now that we were here, I realized it had always been on the horizon. But over time, with all the chaos that went on, it had melded into the background like the rest of the world. As Crish led me into the open air, I felt part of myself opening up, as if waking for the first time after a very long night.

"I found this place the day after we settled here," he said, gesturing for me to join him at the edge of the roof. We leaned side by side over the guardrail. I looked out into the expansive miles and breathed deep.

"You've been out and about, then," I said.

"Yeah," he said, and I could see him squirm under the guilt of having free rein when Evie and I were locked down like prisoners. "It's not all fun and games though. There's a lot going on out there."

I nodded. "I imagine. How are you handling it?"

He shrugged. "It's a lot to process. Every day there's something new. The stock market is swinging like a pendulum, up and down, up and down, depending on what's being said in the news that day. People are struggling with the uncertainty. There's been a run on shops for a while, which is weird, you know? If we lost tomorrow, there'd be no use for any of that stuff."

A run on shops. I tried to imagine it, a regular shop where people were stocking up on everyday essentials. Food, water, toothpaste. Somewhere in between the arena and the isolation, I had begun to forget that everyday things still existed. Those precious few minutes with Hannah had been the only touch of the real world I'd experienced since setting foot in Headspace.

"Do you think other people did this, too?" I asked absently. "The people who came before us, I mean."

Crish turned to me, confused. "Before us?"

"We can't be the first ones. Do you think the other worlds, other planets who went through this, panicked like this?"

Crish chuckled. "You know, I haven't thought of that. Maybe you're right. Maybe there have been others who came before us. The universe is big after all. I can't imagine who else might have done this before though. It's hard. I think I've been too focused on what's in front of me."

"You're doing the right thing," I said, half to myself as I tried to reconcile the reality of Earth with the worlds of thirty-two other champions. Crish laid a hand on my back gently.

"I was thinking," he said as I gazed into the

313

distance distractedly, "all this time being away, and all this chaos, really reminded me of what's important."

"Yeah?"

"Yeah."

I saw him lean down out of the corner of my eye and turned so he kissed me on the corner of the mouth. I gave him a smile and he seemed to pause, then returned it. We stood on the rooftop in the chilly northern wind as he told me of all that went on in a world that grew more distant from me by the day.

IT WASN'T until he dropped me off back at the apartment that I realized what I'd done. My face burned and an apology was too late as his car was already disappearing off into the distance. Plus, I had no idea what I would say even if I tried.

What had happened? When had I become so emotionally divorced from everything that I would turn away from a kiss offered by Crish Michaels, the man who once made me swoon with his mere presence? Who once made my day with a single smile, whose fingers I used to watch dance in the air as he spoke? I hobbled to the futon and slumped into it with a sigh.

Maybe it was that we were far too different. He had always seemed of a different league and world from me, but watching him on the rooftop, talking about all that he was doing out in the world, the gap between us felt like a chasm. He was so connected, so in tune to the churning of the Earth that I had been secluded from—both physically and mentally. Maybe being kept apart had mellowed my initial infatuation for him. Maybe it was simply that the whole overwhelming situation had dulled that part of me. Maybe I'd never know and it was better that I reacted the way I did than mislead him in any way.

Eleven appeared as I pondered this. Evie's door flung open before I'd even had a chance to greet him —she always seemed to instinctively know when he visited versus Crish or the handlers.

"Morning," I said with a smile, getting to my feet.

"Good morning," he replied, and turned to Evie. "Hello, Evie. How are you?" he asked, enunciating and signing as he did, and I watched his fingers dance.

EVIE SLID HER FINGERTIPS ALONG ELEVEN'S PALM, outlining the shape of the winner's laurel with fascination.

"Is this interesting to you?" he asked, signing with his free hand. Within his first few visits, he seemed to instinctively determine what methods of communication to use for her even though I never fully explained Evie's needs.

Evie nodded. She grabbed her tablet and typed.

"**Hurt?**"

"No. Painless," Eleven replied, sparing her the part about having tried to peel off his own skin to be rid of it.

"**Your home?**"

"Similar to yours, but also different."

I watched them converse from the kitchen,

studying with fascination Eleven's curves and differences as he spoke and signed at the same time, pausing periodically to let Evie type out her questions. The stories he told her were different from the one he told me. They were of fascinating sights on exotic planets, exciting competitions, and adventures had over a long and eventful lifetime. He did not tell her about the planet that burned to ashes before his eyes, the disastrous final round that ended in the loss of his everything, or the lonely centuries he'd endured. But then, those were not the questions she asked. She had no interest in the workings of the games, or the tragedies that preceded the crowning of each champion. In her innocence, she saw Eleven and his "career" with pure, open fascination.

We had settled into an odd little routine, the three of us. At times I found myself almost forgetting what awaited us. I listened to him tell Evie about his desert-covered home planet, about the holes he and his friends spent time digging, about his amazement at the immensity of oceans on water-covered planets and the unique and often disturbing ways some races had found to create music. I watched his fingers move, graceful and fluid. When he spoke, my world felt a little bigger than four walls.

"Go?"

"Yes. I should." He stood. He seemed to be staying a little longer each time, pushing the limits of what he could manage in our inhospitable air. I'd learned to read the strain in his pauses and the rhythm of his breaths, as well as the changes in the smoky quality of his voice.

"See you tomorrow," I said.

"Yes," he replied. Despite the fact that I had stopped phrasing it as a question, he still looked surprised every time I told him to come back. "Tomorrow."

"WHERE IS EVIE?"

"In the bedroom." I watched Eleven fill the electric kettle and turn it on. He had familiarized himself to the workings of the apartment for some time now, though he still cast sideway glances at me, as if expecting me to tell him he was doing something wrong. "She is drafting some long, heartfelt letter to the handlers."

"What for?"

"Asking for a Christmas tree. I told her it's probably not necessary, but she's gotten a little obsessed with the idea of writing a letter."

He thought for a moment. I could almost see him

flipping through the encyclopedias in his head. "I'd only read about the holiday in texts."

"It's something of an old tradition, but they've gone fancy with it. These days you can pick up a tree at Walmart in any color you want."

"The live trees are no longer a requirement?"

"Some people go for the traditional approach. I've never been much into it."

"What about the placement of the Star of Bethlehem?"

"You mean the star at the top?" Eleven slid into the chair across from me and handed me one of the steaming mugs. This, too, had become a ritual. "They don't really call it that much anymore, and there's really no limit to what you can put on top of a tree. You know, there's a lot more to celebrating the holidays than what you read in Wikipedia."

"I understand. As I said, my knowledge of most worlds not my own is purely academic." He turned his gaze to the window, a habit he seemed to have picked up from his visits.

"You look at the snow a lot."

"It is a fascinating phenomenon, one not common to the planets I have been to, and certainly not on my home world."

"You still haven't told me why there are other

planets with humans. Or why all the aliens look alike."

"I can't do that. That knowledge is only privy to champions of the games. If you—" He stopped himself. This had also become a habit—we stopped just short of mentioning what would happen if my face didn't end up in that gallery.

"Has Cheshire always run the games?"

"The one you call Cheshire has been master of the arena since before my time, but I do not know if there had been another before."

"But there were no guards before you?"

Eleven tapped his mug in thought. "I haven't been completely truthful," he said slowly.

"About what?"

"My role in the game." He looked almost embarrassed. "There is no 'guard,' as you call it. What I do in the arena has been of my own will, as far as Cheshire would allow. It began when I thought I could find a way to revive contestants who had splintered. Cheshire found this amusing and allowed me to attempt it in the twelfth game. It took until the fifteenth for me to figure out the method to break the splintered state. Cheshire was not particularly pleased with this development. They felt it took some efficiency out of the game proceedings.

However, the producers thought it added an element of unpredictability and I was allowed to continue."

I rolled his words around in my head. "What about when you pulled Lexi and me off the edge on the pyramid?"

"Once I was allowed into the arena for the games regularly, I began to—what's the right word—push my luck, I suppose. It started small—mostly applying first aid to the wounded. Then when no consequences came from that, I began to push further. Much like on the pyramid, I have dragged contestants across the finish line more than once. Initially Cheshire was displeased, but I made the argument that they had technically already completed the challenges and I was only ensuring that more worthy contestants stayed in the games."

"And it worked?"

"For the moment. It is beyond me to put a stop to these barbaric games, but I felt that I could at least ensure those who must play received a fair chance. On some occasions I worry that I will eventually push past Cheshire's limited patience and be banned from the arena, but that is a bridge I will . . ." He thought for a moment, then looked at me. "Burn?"

"Cross. A bridge you will cross."

"Cross. When I come to it."

The thought of quiet, subdued Eleven being a thorn in the side of loud, brazen Cheshire was amusing. "Have you really pushed them far?"

"I have given help to the contestants far beyond what Cheshire would like, though in my good fortune, they have not noticed all of it."

"How did you do that?"

"Discreetly." He gave me a small smile, and tapped his lips twice with the back of his right thumb—the sign for *secret*. "And secretively."

The realization hit me like a ton of bricks. I felt like I was spinning as everything dawned on me at once.

"*You* told Lexi how to play!" I exclaimed. "You signed it to her, when no one was looking!"

"I gave her a hint and she took it the rest of the way."

"She never told me."

"I told her to pass on the knowledge but keep the source to herself. If Cheshire found out, it would have surely resulted in my removal from the arena."

My mouth hung open as my mind frantically replayed that fateful day in the maze.

"Do you know how big a deal that is?" I said, leaning on the table excitedly. "You saved the whole

Earth! If you hadn't done that, no one would've known how to play and we'd all be dead now!"

"No. Because there was another survivor from that game. One who figured out the game without any assistance from me."

"Who?" He gave me a look and I felt stupid. "Oh, right."

"The game would have gone on. You would have ensured that."

I shook my head. The memory of Lexi still stung, and talking about her brought on a wave of guilt. "No. Lexi was amazing. She was a leader. She took care of everyone and made us a team. I couldn't have done that. Crish is doing his best but Lexi . . ." I drifted off. "Lexi is the reason we're all still here."

Eleven studied me. His eyes, a light jade today, seemed to pierce through my skin. "You go to great lengths to convince yourself you're unremarkable," he said, as casually as if stating snow was white.

"What does that mean?" I retorted, offended.

"Nothing." He shook his head. "It is not my place to judge."

"Damn right," I snapped, unable to stop myself. "You're the one who keeps trying to tell me what a 'disgrace' you are when all I'm hearing is you've spent the last five hundred years trying to save other planets from the same fate."

"Makes us birds of a stone then."

"*Feather.* Birds of a *feather.* You *kill* two birds with one stone; you *are* birds of a feather. If you're going to read Wikipedia, get it right."

We looked at each other for a long moment, then a laugh escaped me. Eleven did the same, and though I had never heard him laugh until that moment, it sounded like the voice of an old friend.

"Not what you imagined?"

"Not entirely," Eleven said. The expression on his face was priceless when he arrived and nearly fell into a tangle with the pink, green, and orange abomination in the middle of the living room.

"It's apparently called Unicorn. Evie's choice."

"It's . . ." He studied the colorful four-foot plastic eyesore with almost humorous concentration. "Is there a word in your language for this?"

"You know ten languages from just this planet and you don't have one?"

"Not one that would be . . ." He gestured in the air with a turn of the wrist, as if trying to shake loose something from his massive vocabulary. "Kind."

"The word is ugly."

"I wasn't sure if that was appropriate. The perception of beauty varies widely from culture to culture."

"What would your people say about it?"

He said a word. Most of his native vocabulary sounded like hissing, though I imagined English must sound like gurgling to untrained ears.

"Which means what?"

"Hideous."

"There you go."

He helped me carry two hot mugs into the living room. I dropped heavily onto the futon and Eleven glanced at our usual spots by the kitchen table but said nothing. He handed me one of the mugs and sat down next to me carefully, as if trying to measure what a polite distance between us ought to be. Evie came out of the bedroom, arms bundled with crafting supplies, but let go when she spotted Eleven. I winced as piles of paper, scissors, and glue sticks tumbled to the floor. She hopped over the pile and threw her arms around his neck. Before he could recover from his surprise she was off and back to gathering up her crafts.

"Cup for you in the kitchen," I said. She dropped her things again and bounded for the kitchen. I turned back to Eleven. "She likes you. Do you not do that where you come from?"

"Yes," he said, looking a little stunned. "It was just unexpected." He brought the mug to his lips absently, then stopped. "This is different."

"Something else Evie requested. Hot chocolate. It's a holiday thing. I made yours with water instead of milk." I watched him take a cautious sip. "What do you think?"

"It's interesting."

"Is your race really herbivorous?"

"By your definition, yes. We are not made to digest animal fat and tissue."

"You must think we're very barbaric, killing animals to eat."

"Twelve's race recycled their own dead for food. Their processing plants attached directly to high-security prisons."

I looked down at the dark liquid in my cup. "Well, there goes my appetite."

Evie had returned with her own mug of chocolate. She set it on the wobbly coffee table and began to work at cutting the stack of construction paper in front of her.

"She's making ornaments for the tree," I told Eleven.

"Is that another tradition?"

"Most people buy them. But Evie takes her holidays seriously." I gestured around the apartment. "Not much to celebrate around here though. It's going to be a quiet Christmas."

"I understand this is a holiday that usually calls for gatherings."

I watched Evie cut out neat, colorful strips of paper for a rainbow-patterned garland chain. "I've never been much into the parties. But when I was little, my mother always went out of her way to decorate the house. She would hunt garage sales for things to put up, because she believed in good value, and to her credit, old decorations look just as good as new ones if you put up enough of them."

"When did she pass?"

"Almost . . ." I ran the numbers in my head. "Eight years ago now. God, has it been that long?"

"What about the rest of your family? Will you be allowed contact with them for the holiday?"

I thought of the last conversation with my father. In the past few weeks I had almost managed to forget it, but now it was flooding back.

"It's complicated," I said, and took a long drink hoping to change the subject. "Did you have holidays like this on your planet?"

"Every race finds their reason to celebrate."

Evie paused to show us the intricate snowflakes she had just cut. I smiled at her and looked to Eleven to see his reaction, but he seemed lost in thought.

"I had a large family," he said slowly. "At least that's how I remember it. In the part of the world where I lived, people usually clustered in close communities. I grew up around many people I addressed as family, but most were not blood relations."

"Holidays must've been fun."

"I am ashamed to say my memory of it is sparse. In fact, I cannot remember the names of my own family members. When you asked for my name, I had to take a moment to recall it. I have been 'Eleven' for so long and I speak of my past life so rarely that most of the memories have slipped away."

"You don't remember anything?"

"I remember the last time I spoke to a member of my extended family. I do not remember whether she was a sibling or distant relative or friend." He took a sip from his mug and appeared to hide a grimace. I had a feeling chocolate wasn't exactly palatable to his tongue but was curious to see how much he was willing to drink out of politeness. "I have mentioned her before."

"The one you dug the hole with."

"Yes. She was very dear to me, and when I left my home, trying to avoid harassment from the public, she offered me shelter with her and her children. I was grateful and relieved to no longer be sleeping out in the open, until I woke the first night to find myself surrounded by people taking my photo. Turns out they bribed her handsomely for the chance. They became unruly when I tried to leave. It turned into quite the incident and not in my favor."

"That's awful. Did you confront her?"

"I did, before I made it out the door. It was an ugly scene and I said things that I now regret."

"Sounds like it was her fault."

He shook his head. "Looking back on it, I couldn't blame her. She was raising children alone after losing her partner, struggling to survive and keep her children fed. She took the bribe, I'm sure, as a last resort for her family."

"You don't know that."

"Maybe not. But when you watch the planet burn and wonder if her children are screaming in pain, the reasons why suddenly don't seem so important."

We sat in silence as Evie went about her work. She had moved on to glitter-covered gingerbread men.

"You're trying to make some kind of point."

"Only that one day you might look back on what you've lost, and wish that last conversation had gone differently."

"I'm not sure you're in any place to lecture me."

"You are correct," he said, and said nothing more of it. Later, as he stood to leave, Evie leapt to her feet and gave him another quick hug. He returned it with an arm around her waist and for a moment I thought I saw him smile. Then, quick as she came, Evie was back reabsorbed in her crafts. Eleven turned to me.

I stepped forward and carefully threaded my arms around his waist and for a moment rested my cheek against his broad chest. I felt his hand on my back. It only lasted a moment, but I heard the rhythmic beating of his heart—a heart born in another world.

"See you tomorrow," I said as we parted.

CONVINCING Lydia to allow me another phone call took several more days. In the end, I had to agree to her being present in the room during the call, and to speak to one of their staff therapists if I showed signs of distress. She seemed concerned for my mental stability and worried that I would have a repeat of my previous outburst, though ultimately I think the fear was that my mental state would affect my performance in the arena.

On Christmas Eve, I sat on the lumpy futon, facing our eyesore of a Christmas tree. I had to admire Evie's commitment to the holiday—the tree was now almost completely covered with glittery gingerbread people, marshmallow snowmen, and popcorn garlands. I could even see an attempt at a construction paper Santa and a pair of surprisingly intricate reindeer. A large yellow star had been taped to the top of the tree, and three smaller stars were hung around its base. One had "Evie" scrawled on it. One read "Astra" in my reluctant handwriting —she had shoved a marker and the star at me insistently and pointed at her own star until I wrote my name.

The third read "11." I turned it backwards before Lydia arrived. It was not a conversation I wanted to have with her or anyone else. She seated herself in the tiny dining area, at the same Formica table where Eleven and I had shared dozens of conversations and cups of tea. What would she say if she knew?

I held the phone she gave me, a gray flip type that was quite rare in the age of smartphones. I'd never seen a burner phone before except on TV. The paranoia was real, as if my fifty-five-year-old father who couldn't figure out how to turn on Find My Friends was going to be able to trace my location based on a single call.

I flipped the phone open and closed several times. Truthfully, I had no idea what I hoped to accomplish with this call. Eleven had gotten in my head, despite how hard I'd tried not to let him. What made me call in the end, however, was not the thought of clearing the air with my father, but the little sister I'd never known I had—six years old, living in an uncertain time, hounded by paparazzi everywhere she went through no fault of her own. She looked frightened and confused in nearly every photo I saw of her. Cameras were shoved into her face at every turn. Under different circumstances I might not have bothered to spare her a sympathetic thought, but perhaps the dire situation we were all in had softened me.

I dialed my father's number before I could change my mind. He answered on the third ring.

"Hello?"

I swallowed. "Hi, Dad."

"Astra?"

"Yeah. It's me."

Then, the father I hadn't seen in nearly five years, who could never move a conversation beyond if I'd paid my bills or fixed my car, who couldn't bring himself to tell me he loved me or missed me, who distanced himself several states away when my mother, the last person holding us together, died, began to cry.

ELEVEN ARRIVED a little earlier than usual on Christmas morning. After half a dozen tries, he had finally calibrated the location of the unicorn tree accurately enough not to teleport himself into it. Though this time he nearly stepped on Evie, who was curled up at the foot of the tree under a blanket, snoring away.

"In here."

Gingerly, he stepped over her and walked into the bedroom. I looked up from the bed, where I had been sitting and nursing a whiskey as I watched the sun rise over the fresh blanket of snow.

"She was up most of the night. Too excited about Christmas, I guess. No presents, no problem."

Eleven glanced back at the sleeping shape uncertainly and took a seat on Evie's bed. "Is this part of the Christmas custom?"

"Kind of. Little kids tend to get excited and stay up late for Santa." I took a sip of whiskey. It wasn't my first of the day.

"Is imbibing in alcohol first thing in the morning also a Christmas custom?"

"No. But I needed it." I leaned back against the wall and let out a sigh. "I talked to my dad."

"How did it go?"

"Well enough, I think. He told me a lot of things. I'm still sorting through it." I tapped my finger against the whiskey glass. "That's why I needed this."

He waited for me to continue.

"As it turns out, he and my mother had been more or less separated since I was ten. They stayed together and put on an appearance for me so I wouldn't be a child of divorce. Apparently they got along well and lived separate lives outside the home and it became a new sort of normal for them. He was there for her when she got sick, and stuck by her until she died." I chuckled sadly. "This woman he was with, apparently they'd been together since shortly after he and my mother separated. She was one of my teachers in elementary school. I couldn't believe it, but looking back on it I'm not too surprised. She moved to Florida and after he settled things with my mother's death, he followed. I can't say he didn't do his duty to the family to the end. They didn't plan to have any children, but this girl came and she's a blessing. They just didn't know how to tell me. My dad's never been great at communicating. He last came to see me when she was one and still couldn't bring himself to tell me. A year went by, then another, then another. Now she's six."

Eleven was watching me. I wondered how I looked to him in that moment. "Are you alright?"

I sipped the whiskey again. I hadn't eaten since the previous day and it was going straight to my head, both pleasurable and unsettling. "Her name is Stella. I always thought my mother was the one who loved names that had to do with stars. I spoke to her."

"What did she say?"

"She called me big sister, in Mandarin, and told me good luck. I've been drinking ever since."

"I apologize if I have pushed you into something you regret."

I set my liquid courage on the windowsill,

crossed the room, and sat down next to him. The cool morning light danced between the scales on his neck. I peered into his gold-rimmed eyes and saw they were back to blue today.

"That's not why I was drinking," I said. He was wearing that button-down shirt again. I could see the gentle curve at the base of his neck through the open collar. "I'm still trying to think through everything, including the last few years of my life, but I'm not unhappy about it. I'm glad I spoke to them. And I'm glad I got to talk to my sister, too. It got me thinking about how precarious everything is right now. We have a week before the games start again and no one knows how it's going to turn out. I might never get to meet her in person."

He nodded. I was warm, and a little dizzy. I watched him link and unlink his long fingers.

"And I started thinking about what else I might regret if I didn't have the courage to go for it."

I lifted a hand and traced my fingers over the iridescent scales on his neck, following it down over his throat, clavicle, and to his chest. I couldn't read his expression, but he didn't pull away. I slid my hand back up and pulled him in by the back of his neck. His lips were cool and earthy and I drank him in.

"You know," I said, undoing the buttons on his shirt that probably took him the better part of an hour to do up. "I don't even know if we're *compatible*. Let's find out."

He gripped my hand just as it moved onto the next button and moved it away.

"I should go," he said, and a moment later was gone. I sat on the bed, stunned, my hand still half-raised, trying to understand what had happened.

"Shit."

"Astra?"

I blinked.

"Astra, can you hear me?"

I shook out of my daze and focused on the screen. Disapproving eyes peered back. Crish gave me an expectant arch of the brow.

"Yes," I said. "Sorry. Yes, I can hear you."

"I asked how your Christmas was."

I opened my mouth and found I had no answer to give him. "Fine," I managed after a moment. "It was fine. Evie set up a tree. It was nice."

"Good to hear. How about you, Miranda?"

I didn't know which one Miranda was. I assumed it was the one who answered his question. After weeks of isolation, they all looked like strangers to me. As I sat there, listening to the other contestants exchange pleasantries and stories of their holidays, I realized they had formed a comraderie completely separate from Evie and me. Even now, staring at a screen where almost no one was in the same room, I could tell their eyes glossed over my part of the screen. The only person who occasionally tossed me a nod and a wink was Crish. I was the unpopular kid in class being pitied by the jock.

Even worse, I didn't care.

"The new year is coming up," Crish was saying, every bit the leader. "I think everyone agrees that this break has been much needed. But we have to get back into the swing of things now. The next game could happen as soon as the clock strikes twelve. We need to be prepared."

"Some of us seem to be doing more to prepare than others," Sergio said. There was a round of snickering. I didn't get the joke.

"Keeping *busy*," someone else said. Another round of chuckling. Crish was looking at me.

"Now, guys . . ." he started.

"Just *flaunting* all that effort." A burst of laughter. I glanced at Evie next to me, but she looked just as clueless. Those peeks and sneers were aimed at us— or rather, me.

"Everyone, please," Crish said, a hint of exasperation in his voice. "We have more important things to talk about."

"What's the joke?" I blurted out. Part of me instantly regretted asking. Something about the way they all snickered in my direction dug a pit in my stomach. "What's going on?"

The others exchanged looks. Crish sighed.

"You don't know?"

"Know what?"

More exchanged looks. Crish cut in before anyone else could speak.

"Google yourself," he said in a tone that kept the others from saying anything further on the subject. "But remember—it's just tabloids."

The pit in my stomach became a sinkhole.

GETTING BUSY?? DIAMOND DONNA FLAUNTS NEW LOVER AMID ALIEN AFFAIR RUMORS IN LEAKED VIDEO!

The video was only a few seconds long—grainy, colorless, and shot from an awkward angle. I had to tilt the tablet to get a clear look. Most of the shot was obscured by what appeared to be the branches of a tree—a tree that, had there been color, would've been pink, green, and orange. Beyond the tree I could see through the door to the bedroom. A familiar figure sat on the only bed visible from this particular angle—a tall figure in a white dress shirt.

The top half of his face was cut off. I saw him speak. A moment later I saw myself cross the room and sit next to him. As I sat, I turned toward the camera, just long enough for anyone watching to see my face. Then I turned back to him, spoke for a moment, and leaned in toward him. My face burned with humiliation as I watched myself, drunk and sloppy, snake my fingers down his neck and through his collar, then pull him in for the awkward kiss that drove him off. He leaned back just enough for the video to show the scales around his eye—though in black and white it resembled a tattoo. Mercifully, the recording ended just as I began to unbutton his shirt.

I turned off the tablet, stood up, and paced back and forth in the living room, heart pounding as I looked from the bedroom to the tree, unable to shake the sickening feeling of being exposed. Evie watched me anxiously from the corner of the room, waiting for me to say something reassuring, but I had nothing for her.

Eleven's stony expression was the last I saw of him. He hadn't been back since and I'd thought I was embarrassed enough just having him reject my drunken advances, but now the world appeared to think I had yet another mystery lover under my belt. Site after site shared the video. Millions were speculating who the "new guy with the eye tattoo" was. If anyone didn't think I was a whore before, they certainly did now.

I looked at the tree again. The video was shot from just beyond it. I knelt down behind it and tried to imitate the angle on the video. Could it have been shot from outside the window? I touched the window by the front door. The glass was too dusty. From the wall? There was nothing mounted or embedded in the drywall. I ran my hand over the paint. Not even a hint of a scratch. There was nothing else in the space besides the end table that we never used. The only time it even held something was—

My blood ran cold. I stood and touched the end table. It had gathered a good layer of dust except in one spot, as if someone had set something down on it and then recently removed it.

Like a watch.

I sank to the floor. Evie came over and sat next to me but I could tell she didn't know how to help. I didn't realize I was shaking until she put a hand on my arm. We sat on the floor in silence for a long time.

HEATH WAS NOT WEARING the watch this time. He sat himself down at the Formica table and said nothing. The smug expression on his face told me he already knew what I wanted to ask him.

When I'd called Lydia demanding a meeting with him, I was burning with rage. My mind ran through its angry, indignant speech over and over. But Heath didn't show that day. Nor the next day. Nor the next. By the time he finally came, three days after I called, my rage had deflated into exhaustion. Now, looking at him, I had a feeling that was exactly what he'd intended.

"So," he said evenly. "How can I help you?"

"Why did you record me?" I demanded, too worn out to play games.

Heath chuckled. "Don't flatter yourself," he said. "There was no specific intention for it. Merely a check-in to see if you had anything to hide, and lo and behold, you did."

"If you were watching me, then you know I did *nothing* with him."

"Actually, I don't. The video only recorded short

intervals at random times. Like I said, the intention was not to monitor your every move, but to spot check to see if there was anything to see at all."

"And what does it matter? I was unseen, in private. No one would have known about it."

"Private?" Heath let out an ugly laugh. "You gave up all right to privacy the moment you were taken into custody. What do you think you are right now? You are barely a person. Your worth exists in your ability to play the game and keep the world turning. You are being protected and cared for, all of you, because of that and that alone."

I fought the urge to throw something at his face. "How did the clip get leaked? I thought your security was supposed to be top-notch."

He gave me a look like I was stupid, and everything suddenly dawned on me.

"It's you," I said weakly. "You released it."

He nodded matter-of-factly. "That is correct."

"Why? Why would you do that?" My voice croaked. I didn't know what to think. I could almost accept being spied on—*almost*—but this I didn't know how to handle. "You said it matters how I look to the public. Why?"

Heath stood and pulled out the chair opposite

him. "Why don't you have a seat?" he said patiently. "You're looking a little pale."

I fell heavily into the seat. He settled back down across from me, hands folded.

"The problem with you," he said, "is that you don't think big enough. You never see past the little things—your little life, the little people, even this game. Ultimately, it isn't about whether we win this game—either we do or we don't. It's about *who* wins, and how. You see, people are stupid, ignorant animals who need to be led. They don't just want to be saved. They want a hero. They need a story where there is someone who can lead them and give them hope, a happily ever after. Without it, they'll descend into panic and chaos." He paused and gave me a look that was almost disgust. "And frankly, that hero was never going to be a mutt or a brown chick."

"So you did what?" I bit back, blood boiling at the mention of Lexi. "Bring me down to make Crish look better?"

"Frankly, you brought this on yourself. I was perfectly happy letting you fade into obscurity after Monroe died, but you had to stick out like a sore thumb. If you just fell into line like everyone else, we wouldn't have had to do this. But you kept standing out and drawing attention to yourself, and then that *alien* started cozying up to you. You're not a main character, Donna. You're a sidekick at best, a seat filler. If you're not going to sink into the background, then we have to create another role for you, one that helps lift up the main character rather than distract from him."

"You're making me the bad guy," I said through gritted teeth. "I'm the wild child who makes him look clean."

"It's not personal."

"Does Crish know this? There is no way he would be okay with this."

Heath stood. "Crish Michaels is not your concern," he said, heading for the door as if his interest in me had run out. "This is bigger than both of you. He has his worth and you have yours. At the end of the day, your goals are the same, and you'll be doing everyone a favor by accepting your lot."

CHAPTER 22

A FRIGID GUST PIERCED MY CLOTHING THE MOMENT MY feet met ground. Shivering and bracing myself against the cold, I tried to make sense of the blanket of white before my eyes.

A pair of hands wrapped around my forearm. Evie clung to me as cold winds whistled by. The arriving contestants gasped against the cold as they were printed into the arena. Before us, a frozen tundra stretched vast and uninterrupted, fanning endlessly into the distance, here and there marred by mounds of white and patches of dead grass and dry trees, the only dejected vegetation visible. A heatless sun hung low in the sky, bathing everything in its weak yellow-gray light.

The number of contestants left, including myself,

was sixteen. Compared to the hundred that began this game, we seemed very few.

"Hey." I looked up to see Crish standing over me, a warm smile on his face.

I nodded and returned the smile. At least there was one more friendly face. "Hey."

"Listen, before we start, I wanted to ask you . . ." He bit his lip, as if unsure of himself, an unexpected gesture given his usual confidence. "You and that guy in your room . . ."

I felt shame wash over me again. "It's nothing," I said quickly.

"It's just," he stammered. "I thought we—"

"*HELLO CONTESTANTS!*"

He stepped back as Cheshire strolled onto the scene. A thick red coat with black fur trim hung over their slender frame instead of the usual Edwardian suit, topped off with a thick, multicolored, almost comical scarf. That emoji face smiled as always.

"*Cold, eh? Did you miss me? You can say it. Don't be shy.*"

No response.

"*So pensive*," Cheshire clucked, looking at us each in turn. "*Sergio, looking good. Randy—put on a few holiday pounds, did we? Miranda! Saw that photo shoot you did. Lovely.*"

They said, thankfully, nothing about the leaked video. I waited with bated breath for them to finish the pleasantries and let it out when they were done.

"*Now then, all of you are probably wondering about the new setup. Welcome to the Reindeer Run.*" They clapped their metal hands together several times with glee. "*Sounds fun, doesn't it? I was rather inspired by all the holiday celebrations. For this challenge, you'll be paired up by random drawing. Let's start with that, shall we? Eleven? Where are you? El——*"

A breath caught in my throat as Eleven stepped into view. I had dreaded seeing him again, but nothing prepared me for what I saw. His armor, once bulky and imposing, had been pared down. Gone were the metal platings and helmet, leaving only layers of black and gray material that resembled leather, wrapped around his muscular form and long legs. His gold-rimmed eyes and splashes of scales were in plain view for all to see. Heavy black boots left deep indents on the white snow. Even Cheshire appeared taken off guard by the change in his appearance.

He approached the contestants. I knew all eyes were on the crescent of scales cupping his eye.

"God *damn*," someone exclaimed. "No wonder she's boffing him!"

There was a wave of nervous laughter. If Eleven heard, he gave no indication. My face burned as he drew close. All eyes were on us, waiting to see sparks fly. But he said nothing and neither did I. He held out a small round box filled with thin strips of paper and as I reached in to grab one, he gently, ever so slightly tapped the side of the container. A motion barely detectable.

I stopped and shifted my hand to the next one. He tapped again. He wasn't looking at me, nor me at him. But I changed my selection until he stopped tapping the side of the container. Then, without a word, he moved onto the next person.

"*Partner up, folks,*" Cheshire said, clapping their hands again. I quickly read my paper.

Evie Bouchard

"*Let me explain the rules,*" Cheshire said as Eleven returned to their side and the contestants were all paired up. Their gazes followed Eleven but no one made further comments. "*You will travel down the marked path in pairs. One will be the rider, and one will be the reindeer—I trust you're all able to make that transformation at this stage in the game?*"

Evie shook her head anxiously. "Don't worry," I whispered to her. "I'll be the reindeer."

"*One more thing—the reindeer will be blind.*"

I started. Cheshire winked.

"*You didn't think it was going to be an easy little ride through the snow, did you? All of the reindeer will be blindfolded. As the reindeer, your only job will be to run. The rider must direct the reindeer on the path, avoid obstacles, and deal with some—oh, let's call them inconveniences.*" Cheshire gestured to the horizon. I hadn't noticed until now but a wide path, roughly the width of a four-lane highway, was faintly marked in the snow. "*Your path is clear. You have one hour to reach your destination. The rider must stay atop the reindeer for the entire ride. Falling off your ride before crossing the finish line will cause you to be eliminated. Failing to cross the finish line in time will cause you to be eliminated. Veering off the path will not get you eliminated, but you will want to stay on the path for convenience. And your own safety.*" They spread their hands in an almost ceremonial gesture at the nervous contestants. "*Now, who's ready to ride?*"

AFTER A TENSE, nerve-wracking discussion, Evie and I agreed that I would be the rider. In the end, her inability to speak was the deciding factor. I watched as she struggled with her transformation, a slow and cumbersome effort with several false starts that resulted in what looked close enough to a reindeer but, with its round snout and large eyes, bore a stronger resemblance to Rudolph than anything in the animal kingdom.

At least she got the sizing right. I looked up nervously at the animal's back, which was just higher than the top of my head. I couldn't imagine being perched up there, galloping through the wind and snow. I put a hand on Evie's side gently. She snorted. Even in this form, I could tell how nervous she was.

"Don't worry," I said, patting her gently. "Just concentrate on running and holding your form. I'll take care of the rest."

Most of the other contestants had long finished their transformation and mounted their rides. A few of them had even manifested saddles and bridles. I strongly doubted that either Evie or I had the know-how to produce either. I was trying to decide how to hoist myself onto her back when Crish approached.

"Need a hand?" he asked.

I nodded gratefully. "Yes, please."

He knelt down, linked his fingers on his knee, and when I stepped on, hoisted me up onto Evie's back like I weighed nothing. I balanced precariously on her slippery fur and grasped her antlers. Looking down gave me a wave of vertigo.

"Hold tight," Crish said, and gave me a mock salute.

"Listen," I said before he could walk off. "About before—I'm sorry if I—"

"Don't worry about it," he said, and gave me his trademark crooked smile. Guilt welled up in me as he retreated to his own partner. I pushed it away and focused on the task at hand. I was so far off the ground, and for a moment the awful memory of being five and crying on the back of a birthday party pony came flooding to mind. Evie's back was so high and slippery that I nearly fell off as she took her first step forward.

Eleven was moving again. He approached each reindeer and slipped a black blindfold over their eyes. Evie jerked back as he tried to put it on over her eyes, nearly throwing me off. I held on for dear life as he stroked her face.

"It's okay," I heard him say to her. "You're going to be fine."

She calmed slightly. He glanced up and our eyes met briefly, then his gaze shifted to my death grip on Evie's antlers. He leaned in and whispered something to Evie.

Something snaked around my legs and tightened. I started and looked down. Tendrils of white, sticky webbing had sprouted from Evie's fur and wrapped tightly around my calves, pinning them securely to her side. I wiggled my torso and found it seated much more securely, now tightly anchored. Dots of soft, sticky white appeared on her antlers as well, making for a much steadier grip than the smooth surface. I found a secure hold with my right hand on one antler and tested moving and swinging my left, feeling my confidence bolstered. I looked down to thank Eleven, but he was already gone.

"Contestants to the starting line, please!"

Evie swung her head. I steered her, now blindfolded, toward the start of the snowy path. Riding her was, I imagined, much like riding an elephant. Her weight shifted under me like a living mountain.

"If I pull back, that means slow down," I told her quickly as the eight riders and reindeer lined up. "I'll try to steer you in the direction you need to go. Don't rush. We can do this."

She snorted, though I couldn't be sure if she heard or understood. I wished desperately to be the one blindfolded to spare her the terror she must be feeling, but being unable to see when she was mute and openly exposed to danger on my back was not likely the better option.

Sergio stood to the left of the line, mounted on his partner. Next to him was Crish. I steered us to the right.

"*Ready?*"

Cheshire's voice snapped me back to attention.

"*Set.*"

Evie shifted nervously under me. I braced myself, tightening my grip on her antler.

"*Go!*"

The reindeer next to me reared up like a horse and slammed into Evie's side on their way down. The rider's elbow struck me square in the face and for a moment I saw stars. If not for the glue strings around my legs I would've gone tumbling to the ground, ending our run before it even began. By the time we steadied ourselves the other riders were already far ahead. I patted Evie's head to let her know I was okay. Then, slowly, steadily, she began to march forward.

THE GOING WAS slow at first. Convincing Evie to ease into a trot took time and patience. We lost sight of the others quickly and I had no idea how long the path was, but I couldn't rush Evie. Blind, awkward, and anxious, she shambled onward. I figured out quickly that every snort was a request for reassurance and that the best way to signal directions to her was not with the antlers but with gentle nudges of my legs on either side of her. The tundra, once we settled into our rhythm, was peaceful and breathtaking. Miles and miles of snow caught the faint gray-blue of the sky in their nooks and folds. All sounds were muffled save for the crunching under Evie's hooves as we passed. If not for the circumstances I might have enjoyed this stroll, but it was not long after we picked up the pace that I spotted the first body.

It was completely black, like a scorch mark upon the white snow. I initially mistook it for a pile of ash until we got close and I saw the vaguely human shape lying with its back to me. Not enough of the face was left to identify the figure, but based on the few patches of hair that retained their original color, I guessed it was Miranda. I tugged on Evie's antler and she slowed her pace with a snort. I patted her side.

"It's alright," I whispered, not daring to speak up. We passed the body just as a half-howl, half-shriek barreled through the air. Evie started in terror. I grabbed hold of her antlers to keep myself steady, scanning the horizon anxiously. A shape reared up in the snow—a reindeer rapidly losing its girth and fur as it reverted back to its human form. Before it could gain traction, half a dozen sleek black forms were on it, pushing it back down into the snow. Another scream—disturbingly human this time—rose and suddenly cut off. I tried to level my left hand to shoot but could not for the life of me form the gun's shape in my mind.

One of the black shapes turned toward me. It was an odd thing, faceless and vaguely canine shaped. Its movement left no mark on the snow, nor did it produce a single sound as it moved. It slithered towards us and an invisible bubble of cold accompanied it. The hair on my arms and neck stood up.

"Run," I said to Evie. "*Run!*"

She broke into a desperate gallop. I held on with every ounce of strength I could muster, steering her the best I could to keep her on the path as the rest of the shapes left their prey and sped after us.

One broke from the pack and ran parallel to us. Even up close, I could make out no discernable features, feathers, or fur. It looked like a hole in space, cut out in the shape of a wolf or dog. It lunged and nipped at Evie's ankle. I pulled her to the side and she nearly veered off the path. I corrected her quickly, just as another one leapt onto my back from behind.

The intense cold that struck me was like pins puncturing my skin. I instantly knew that what took the contestants half a mile back was not fire but frost so frigid it turned them to dry bark. My joints and muscles clenched against the sensation. I gritted my teeth and willed the thing off my back.

Diamond spikes shot from my skin. I grimaced against the pain and turned just in time to see the creature hit the snow behind me, several gaping but quickly closing holes in its body. The cold lifted immediately and I urged Evie onward. The black shapes were hot on our heels. We soon passed another pair of fallen contestants and two more black shapes paused their feeding to join the pack. I counted six total and they were drawing nearer every second. The path curved. I kept Evie heading straight as long as I could but soon twists and turns forced us to slow our pace. Frozen ponds began to appear to the left of the path and the right dropped off into a steep slope.

Evie galloped beneath me. Landing a shot aiming backwards on a moving steed was out of the question. They had already wised to my trick and were now flanking us from both sides instead of chasing from behind. I pulled Evie in a zigzag pattern, keeping her out of range of their nipping teeth. It wouldn't be long before they landed a bite, and if Evie fell they would be on us in a moment and we'd be another charred shape in the snow. I wished, desperately, that I had something to work with, like the books in the library.

And I did.

I grasped Evie's antlers with both hands. "Just keep running," I said to her, hoping she could hear over the sound of her own hooves. "You're going to feel this. Just ignore it. Keep going!"

She snorted and I hoped it was an affirmative. Gripping her with everything I had, I concentrated on the environment around me, searching for the same hum of connection as I heard from the books. It was there—faint, near indetectable, but there. I grabbed hold of it, focused on it, and pushed.

A bubble. I couldn't see or hear it, but I knew it was there.

I pushed again. Evie barely missed being bitten as the creatures redoubled their efforts. It was now or never.

A geyser of snow shot out from the ground to our right. Evie stumbled but did not fall. The three creatures to our right screeched to a halt in surprise. Another geyser shot out to the left, sending one of the dark shapes into the sky with a *boom*. The rest paused their pursuit for a single second, giving us just enough time to get out of the range of their nipping teeth.

I didn't dare stop. The geysers of snow boomed alongside us like a tidal wave as we ran. Chunks of snow fell all over Evie and me as we raced toward the finish line. If I stopped, I feared I would lose that hum of connection and our only protection would be gone. I concentrated on Evie's thundering hooves, the sounds of exploding snow, trying to keep my focus sharp enough to steer. Red spots swam in front of my eyes, then black, then static. I saw the finishing line through blurry, snow-covered eyes, just as Evie stepped through the ice.

We were off course.

I hadn't noticed until now, but rather than following the curve of the road, we were running toward the finish line in a straight path, over a large frozen pond. I heard the crack of the ice as Evie's back hoof went through, but she pulled it out and kept going. Before I could even straighten, she stepped through again. Her front hooves scraped against the slippery ice and miraculously were able to hold on once more. She heaved herself up and tumbled forward. The others gathered around the finish line scrambled to get out of the way. The glue threads around my legs loosened and with one desperate jerk of her massive body, Evie threw me. For a terrifying moment I was airborne. My hands flailed helplessly as I grabbed empty air and my back slammed into the ground. I rolled over, panic welling up as I searched for Evie.

She was on the ground, mere feet from the finish line. As I watched, she rose, planted her front hooves, and shakily pushed herself up. Then, with a thunderous crack, the ice beneath her gave away. I scrambled to my feet, shrieking her name as her antlers disappeared beneath the ice. I dove after her without a thought.

The cold that struck me was excruciating. Pain rendered me blind and numb for a split second. I forced myself to steel against it and focused on the ocean course, where Evie and I first met. My spine creaked and lengthened and I flapped my tail fin before it was even fully formed, diving downward.

I saw her. The reindeer shape had mostly fallen away. Her terrified eyes—human once more—peered up at me. As I drew near I saw that her legs were still in the shape of the animal, kicking uselessly against the freezing water. I went down, hand stretched toward her. Our fingertips touched and I pulled her close. She was running out of air, and I was running out of strength. I struggled, turning my tail as hard as I could to move upward, only to realize that I could not see the hole in the ice above me.

Where is it?

I searched desperately. Evie went limp. I shook her, gesturing at my own tail, hoping she would transform, but she was too far gone.

Where?

I couldn't hold on anymore. A sharp pain pierced the side of my head, nearly knocking the breath out of me. It was a familiar pain, one that doubled the fear growing inside me. My skin tingled and grew hot. It was a feeling I'd felt before. I fought it, but the heat grew. The exit was nowhere in sight and the panic was winning. I struggled. I gasped. Evie's eyes closed.

A strong arm slipped around my waist and I felt myself being hoisted upward rapidly. I held on to Evie for dear life, fearing if I lost consciousness she would slip back down into the darkness for good. My head broke through the water just as my form unraveled. Half a dozen hands dragged Evie and me out of the water and onto the cold snow. Shivering, gasping, I flipped Evie over to make sure she was still breathing. A pair of boot-clad metal feet stopped in front of us. I looked up at Cheshire standing over us.

"That was interesting," they said, but the words weren't aimed at us.

Soaked head to toe, Eleven dragged himself to his feet and faced the arena master, who regarded him with lines for arched brows.

"They had reached the finish line," he said to Cheshire, in a tone that almost dared them to challenge. "They were safe from elimination."

"Is that so?" Cheshire said, eyeing Evie and me, two wet, dripping, pathetic forms hunched in the snow. I held Evie close to me, rubbing her arms and legs in a futile attempt to warm her up. "Cutting it a bit close for me, but I suppose I'll trust your *judgment*." They snapped their fingers. "Come, contestants. Let me count you up and see who's left."

Slowly, the others drifted off after Cheshire. I made sure Evie was breathing, stood, and took a deep breath.

"Thank you," I said to Eleven. "I—"

He rounded on me. "What were you *thinking*?"

What?

"Why did you jump in after her? You were at

your limit! What do you think would have happened to you both if you splintered?"

I gaped at him in shock. Was he really berating me?

"What was I supposed to do?" I bit back. "Let her drown?"

"I would have gotten her. That is my job!" he said. The way he spoke roused my anger, like a parent reprimanding a child. "I would have retrieved her without you in the way."

"It *isn't* your job!" I snapped. "You said so yourself! How can I rely on you when you don't even know what your job is? I wasn't going to leave her behind!"

"Then think about what's going to happen to your planet if you died taking the risk! Seven billion who need every possible chance to stay alive. Do you not value your worth as their champion at all?"

Those words struck me like a ton of bricks. Austin Heath's smug face floated in front of my eyes.

He has his worth and you have yours.

My hand pulled itself into a white fist and sailed in a short, tight hook into Eleven's face, cracking against his cheek bone and snapping his head to the side. The impact surprised even me. The other contestants watched from a distance, stunned, but none more than him. He straightened, touched his cheek, and looked at me with shock in his gold-rimmed eyes.

"You don't get to decide who's worth more," I spat. "*Alien.*"

I'D REALLY DONE IT NOW.

If there were a tabloid that wasn't screaming "Diamond Donna" before, they were certainly shouting it now. If anyone had had any doubt that something was going on between Eleven and me, they certainly didn't now. The recording of our very public row became the most viewed video clip in history within twenty-four hours. By the end of the second day it had been made into dozens of memes, fitted to a variety of auto-tuned music, remixed with six popular songs, and turned into an extremely popular gif.

Eleven's striking features also didn't go unnoticed. Now that his name could be matched to a face, the speculations about our relationship increased tenfold. **#HotAlien** was trending on all fronts and the poll was already out on what our "couple name" should be—unless, some speculated, we were already broken up, given that I'd just cracked him one in front of the entire world.

Locked in a daze, I couldn't stop replaying the sound of my fist against Eleven's face. I paced the apartment over and over, restless and agitated. Even Evie stayed out of my way. This continued for two days, then on the third, as I turned around to start yet another one of my thousands of passes through the living room, I nearly ran into him.

WE FACED but did not look at each other. I couldn't help noticing that he had finally managed to close up that dress shirt without missing a button. I tried to say something, but he beat me to it.

"You should have taken the token."

I lifted my gaze in disbelief. "That's all you want to say to me?"

"It's the truth."

"I punched you in the face," I said. "I kissed you and you ran off, then we fought in front of the whole world and I punched you. And that's what you want to say?"

"I am not concerned with any of that." His

stony demeanor was getting under my skin. "I am telling you *this*—you should have taken the token when the opportunity came. You should have left here, gone back to your life, and skipped this misery."

"I *know*," I said, exasperation welling up. "I *know* I've been a misery. I'm sorry. I'm sorry I made a move on you. I'm sorry I kept taking up your time and dragging stories out of you. I'm especially sorry I was pissed at someone else and took it out on you. That's on me. Just walk out of here and I'll never bother you again."

He looked away from me and shook his head, then lifted a hand and pinched the bridge of his nose as if frustrated - a very human gesture. For a brief moment I saw a crack of emotion in his mask.

"That is not what I meant," he said slowly, pushing the words out with obvious difficulty.

"I know what you mean."

"No, you *don't*," he said, taking a step towards me. I was suddenly reminded of how much taller he was. "Do you know how difficult it is to exist in solitude for hundreds of years? To keep from connecting to any living being so you never feel that loss when they are inevitably gone? Do you know where the last person I allowed myself to become friendly with is? The last contestant I dared to grow close to, over ten games ago?"

I swallowed. "Where?"

"Not in the gallery." He ran both hands over his face and drew a deep breath, as if trying to contain himself. "You don't know anything. You don't know what an absolute *misery* it is to watch you walk into that arena every time not knowing if you'll walk back out, to see you throw yourself against the odds over and over, to know I'd been *foolish* enough not to learn my lesson the first time and get attached again. And you"—he gestured at me—"you could've spared yourself this humiliation of being associated with me, of the world gossiping about you, and nearly making a drunken mistake that you surely would have regretted later."

I gaped at him. "Excuse me?" I scoffed. "I was not making a mistake."

"I *know* what I look like to your people," he went on, as if not hearing me. "Have you never wondered why so many of your characters in your stories and films—the monsters, the creatures, the *aliens*, look like me? It's because your people remember me. I've been on this planet before, many times, scouting and learning its culture and people for the games. There are some who have seen my face. They remember me. It always happens. This isn't the only planet filled with images of green-faced abominations. Because of these games, my likeness is everywhere in this galaxy. It is one of the reasons I began to cover myself completely—because every time I turned around, there were more monsters wearing my face. I am too old, and have been at this too long, to delude myself otherwise. I might be a novelty to you now, but it's something you will only regret later."

"There may not be a *later*!" I snapped. "I could be dead in the next round, or the next one, or the next one. And whether or when I die doesn't matter, because you don't get to tell me what I did was a mistake, or that you're just a *novelty*. You don't think it's a misery for me to work up the nerve to make a move and then be rejected? You don't think it's a misery to read everyone speculating all the things we're supposedly doing to each other and not actually getting to do it? Your solution to everything is to sacrifice yourself. You don't think *that* is a misery for me?"

My outburst caught him off guard. I watched a parade of emotions play over Eleven's face, as if he was trying to decide which was the correct one. I closed the distance between us gently. He didn't move back. I reached up to touch his face and he stopped my hand with his, but didn't move it away. "You should stay away from me," he said, sounding like he was trying to convince himself instead of me.

"Is that what you want?" I said. "Because I want you. I wanted you then, and I want you now. Do you want me or not?"

He scooped me up as if I weighed nothing. The moment my body pressed against his, something quaked through me—a craving, a hunger. My lips found his and in a moment we were wound together like roots and vines. He tasted like wine and meat after years of water and twigs.

"You won't be in trouble for this?" I asked in between breathless seconds.

He pressed me down onto the futon. The color of his eyes was rapidly changing, a gold sheen taking over both pupils. "Let's find out," he breathed.

Then he was buried in my neck. I felt his teeth and tongue against my skin. A thin trail of scales led from the space between his shoulder blades down his spine. I raked my fingers over it and felt him shiver. My other hand snaked to his collar and pulled the buttons open one by one. The world was so small in that moment between the lumps of the futon and the weight of his body on mine.

Click.

We both froze. I scrambled to crane my neck and peered behind me. Evie stood at the bedroom door. She hadn't made a sound this whole time and I had completely forgotten that she was only one room away. She looked from me to Eleven, then back at me again. For a moment I felt like a teenager caught with the neighbor boy's hand up her skirt.

"You finish fighting?"

I cleared my throat in embarrassment, face burning as I slid myself out from under Eleven, who self-consciously lowered his head as he retracted his hand from under my shirt. Evie watched us untangle ourselves with a completely neutral expression on her round face. I couldn't tell whether she didn't understand what was taking place or was teasing us intentionally.

"Yes," I said, trying to keep my composure as we eased into sitting positions beside each other. "We're done." Evie nodded her approval.

"Tea." she declared, and siddled off toward the kitchen.

I covered my mouth with my hands to keep the fit of laughter from bursting out. Looking beside me, I saw Eleven hiding a smile behind his hand. We looked at each other and could barely contain our chortles as Evie banged around the kitchen behind us.

"So," I said after we took a moment to collect ourselves, "why did you take off the suit?"

He shrugged. "I'm not sure. I think it bothered me to think of the assumptions being made that you were with anyone other than me."

"That's pretty petty."

"I know." He chuckled. "But also, you were right —you don't have the luxury of hiding your face. I suppose I felt that, being the other half of the rumors, I should do the same."

I reached over and helped him button his shirt back up. As I finished the last one, he took my hand, brought it to his lips, and gently kissed my fingertips. And we sat, the three of us, as we had done so many times. When he left, he hugged Evie and kissed me on the cheek and lips. Evie immediately gestured that she also wanted a kiss on the cheek, which he gave.

For a moment, in that chilly little apartment, I foolishly allowed myself to feel happy.

THE NEXT ROUND SAW US BACK INTO THE ARENA. THE old arena, with black floors below and white dome above. The only difference this time was the circles covering the floors, hundreds of them, each roughly eight to ten feet across. As I walked around them curiously, I saw that there was palpable tension among the contestants as they entered one by one. Only twelve of us were left now.

Eleven kept his distance as usual. The moment the others spotted him, I saw eyes darting back between him and me. I had no idea whether Heath had recorded any more footage of us, or whether it was released. But I found it difficult to care. Whatever he would have recorded was no worse than what the rest of the world already thought. In fact, the populace would be sorely disappointed to know that all we'd managed so far was two minutes of clumsy fumbling that ended with Evie walking in.

Our eyes met briefly and I quickly broke the gaze as memories of his fingers cupped against my bare skin flooded back. Evie, however, waved to him happily the moment she was printed in. He waved back with a thin smile. The others could make of that what they wanted.

"*Hello contestants!*"

Cheshire strolled into view from out of nowhere as usual. By this point all of us had grown disturbingly accustomed to their presence. Most of the others looked weary, almost bored of this charade. Cheshire looked us over one by one.

"*How's my final dozen? You who have made it this far should be very proud of yourselves. We are entering the final rounds of the games now, and this is your chance to get truly creative.*"

A pause. Then, the emoji face turned to me.

"*Of course, I understand some of us have gotten more creative than others, both on screen and off.*"

A wave of snickering from the others. This was becoming the norm. I looked past Cheshire at Eleven, expecting to see him annoyed or angry at the arena master's insinuations, but what I saw was neither. Instead, he was looking at me with an expression that I now recognized far too well. It was one of resignation, an apology, the same expression he'd had when he told me I was better off without him. He was, once again, apologizing to me for bearing the brunt of the humiliation because of him.

I ground my teeth.

"*Well, are we ready then?*"

"No."

Cheshire turned to me in surprise. "Oh?"

I marched past them, straight to Eleven. I grabbed him by the collar and yanked him down eye-level to me.

"You," I said, loud enough for everyone to hear, "should wish me luck," and crushed my lips against his. He hesitated for a brief moment, then pulled me in tightly. The kiss lasted two seconds—the first for the audience, the second for me. When it was over, he didn't let go.

"Get inside a circle," he whispered.

I nodded, pulled away, and walked back to the other contestants. My heart pounded and my face flushed. Ignoring the stares, I grabbed Evie's hand and pulled her next to me, into the middle of the nearest circle.

"*Wasn't that amusing?*" Cheshire said, their voice dripping with sarcasm. I had a feeling that, for the first time since the orb landed, one of us had truly gotten under their metaphorical skin. That emoji face, though still smiling, looked a little colder than usual. *"If you two are done with your little floor show, the rest of us would like to proceed with the real game."*

"Sure," I said dismissively.

The emoji face flickered, sending a chill of alarm down my spine. Cheshire pulled their attention from me in an almost exaggerated swivel, as if making a big show of snubbing me.

"Needless to say, we only need one champion," they said. *"So from this point forward, we'll be dealing with eliminations a little more, shall we say, aggressively. Be ready for surprises, and as always, use your head."*

The floor disappeared. I hadn't even had time to react when three people fell screaming to their demise in the gray, misty depth below. Those standing inside the white circles remained safe, and several people who were lucky enough to be close to one or had quick reflexes grabbed onto their edges and pulled themselves up. The ground between the circles was gone. The circles floated on air, with nothing but thick clouds and fog below. We were down to nine, just like that.

The ground beneath us wobbled. I instinctively grabbed Evie.

"*Did I forget to mention?*" Cheshire quipped from their platform. "*Only certain platforms will support more than one person. They will have red rims. If more than one person stands on the other ones for more than a minute, shoop!*" They mimicked a platform falling with a swoop of the hand.

The ground wobbled again. I let go of Evie and leapt onto the nearest platform, landing on my knees painfully.

"*There you go.*" Cheshire paced their own platform unhurriedly, eyeing the rest of us. I looked around the arena. The circles didn't extend indefinitely. Instead, they seemed to form a loose path into the distance, roughly twenty circles wide. Eleven stood on one at the outermost edge, the starting point. The white dome above was also covered in mist. If we weren't standing on the circles, I would have trouble telling up from down, as if we'd been swallowed by a thundercloud.

"*The goal is simple—stay on the circles; don't fall. But keep moving. Like I said before—the red circles will support more than one person, but once we start, the other circles will also fall if you stay on them for more than three minutes. So long as you keep moving, you'll be fine. Easy enough, yes?*" They surveyed our tense faces. *"Oh, and I shouldn't have to say this, but—no flying."*

Vanessa's wide, dead eyes floated through my mind.

"Now for the truly interesting part." One slender hand lifted and counted off each of us. *"There are nine of you left, and we only need a maximum of seven for the next round, which means two of you will have to go. Except, you see, there are no obstacles this time besides the platforms themselves. No monsters, no traps, no big fishes trying to eat your faces. Which begs the question of how exactly two of you will be eliminated. That is where it gets fun—push, shove, sabotage! Go wild! No time limit and no rules on how you knock someone off as long as you do it. The round will end once there are only seven remaining on the platforms."*

"Wait!" I turned to see Crish raising his hand.

"Questions?"

"Are you actually telling us to push each other off?" he asked incredulously. "You can't be serious."

Cheshire cocked their head to one side. *"Look at you. Such a boy scout. Don't worry; we understand that all of you have a reputation to consider. After all, we promised you fame and success, and we don't want to start that off with a bad image, do we? All of your identities will be obscured for the folks at home. They won't be able to tell who's who until the game's over. Just a little fancy camerawork to help you relax."*

The hair on the back of my neck stood up. The contestants regarded each other apprehensively, but one particular pair of eyes was on me—Sergio, whose excitement was written all over his face as he stared straight toward me, one corner of his lip quivering with anticipation. I pretended not to see.

"Ready?"

"Hey!" Crish yelled, but Cheshire had already lost interest in him.

"Set!"

"You can't—"

"Go!"

A bullet sang through the air. I heard it whistle past my ear, barely missing. I swiveled to face Sergio, but he was midjump onto another platform. The others were on the move, too. Someone else had taken a shot at me. I drew a frightened, shaking breath.

THE FOG THICKENED the farther we ventured down the path. Soon we were disappearing and reappearing from each other's views. I couldn't see more than two platforms away from me and several times

I lost my sense of direction. Thankfully, Eleven followed us, and I knew to always put him behind me to move forward, but eventually he disappeared from view, too. In the eerie, soupy fog I saw only gray and circles. Though I heard the movement of others, I could never tell how far away they were, only that they advanced in the same general direction. Once in a while a camera bot buzzed into view, circled me a few times, and wandered off.

A shout. A male voice. The cameras careened in its direction. I looked toward it but the fog blocked my view. Shuddering, I kept on.

A shot soared over my head. I turned just in time to see someone dart sideways into the fog.

The number of circles decreased as I moved forward, becoming farther and farther apart. Jumps became increasingly difficult. I saw someone appear through the clouds, flapping awkwardly on what looked like pigeon wings and barely making it to the edge of the next platform. A real gamble considering what happened to the last person who flew, but Cheshire appeared to be permitting the little winged skips and hops given the growing distance between platforms.

I landed on a new platform only to find the next one much too far away to jump to. I considered wings. After much straining and concentrating, pigeon wings sprouted from my back and immediately fell apart into a useless pile of feathers. Bat wings flapped oddly and uncontrollably and nearly dragged me off the platform sideways. With my weak understanding of them, wings were simply not an option, which meant I had only one possibility left.

I reached out to the fog. At first nothing changed. Then, slowly, tendrils of thick gray mist began to drift toward me. They moved sluggishly, but they came, and I heard the faint humming.

Bridge.

The fog gathered, thickened, and formed its shape before me. A few long moments later a foggy bridge connected my platform and the next one. I eyed it suspiciously. Memories of crossing the wobbly book bridge made me shudder. At least the books were solid. I had no idea if this fog bridge could even support me or if I would simply fall through on the first step.

"*Stop!*"

My head jerked up, in the middle of trying to make up its mind. I quickly looked around but realized the voice wasn't meant for me. It came from behind, to my left. Through the fog I could barely make out two shapes.

"*Let go! Don't! D*—" The voice was female. After a brief pause, I heard it switch to a scream that quickly disappeared as it fell below. I shuddered and stepped resolutely onto the bridge. There was a terrifying moment as my foot sank down ever so slightly, but it held, with a slight give like suspended silk. Arms out to my side like a tightrope walker, I moved forward and tried not to look down. One step at a time I approached the next platform.

A thump to my left. I focused on moving.

Another thump. Someone was catching up.

Muffled voices. Several camera bots shot in and out of my peripheral view. I looked behind me. Most everything was covered in fog. I kept putting one foot in front of the other.

"*And we have eight!*" came the voice from above. I nearly fell out of surprise. "*One more and we'll have our final seven. Get tussling, contestants!*"

A bullet zinged past an inch in front of my face. I stumbled backward and barely managed to catch myself. Several more shots rang out but luckily aiming was difficult in the fog.

Armor.

A layer of diamond crystals formed on my left

side, creeping like ice across water and covering the left side of my face, shoulder, arm, and leg. A bullet struck me square in the head and bounced off the diamond crust, nearly knocking me over but thankfully doing no harm. Walking was difficult with my left leg stiff in the diamond armor. Bullets barraged me from the left side as I plodded forward, mercilessly hitting my head and torso. Two camera bots zoomed into sight and hovered nearby. I looked up and Sergio was on me the moment my foot hit the next platform—one bearing a red rim.

He knocked into me from the side and I threw myself forward, crashing painfully onto the platform. He grabbed my hair and yanked me backward. I swung my left arm and the hard diamond armor caught him on the side of his jaw. His grip loosened briefly and I tried to crawl away, but he grabbed me by my unarmored right arm and yanked me toward the edge of the platform. The diamond shield over my left hand sprouted claws and sank into the surface. I anchored myself as hard as I could as he tried to drag me off the side, clinging on for dear life. One of his arms changed into an enormous ax that smashed down on my arm. I cried out in pain as my bones quaked inside the diamond coating.

It couldn't end here.

The ax came down at me again. Would he cut my arm off to throw me off the edge? Before it came down a third time, I released my anchor and yanked my entire body backward. The ax struck the surface of the platform, leaving a crack several inches long. I swung my armored arm again and caught him on the back. Sergio wobbled as if to fall, but recovered quickly and spun around, right as I put up one hand, fingers held in the gun position, pointed directly at his forehead.

We froze.

For one extremely long, tense second we stared at each other, him with his ax raised, and me with my gun pointed at his head. I could hear my own breath rasping in and out.

I'd never managed more than one or two successful shots. The odds were against me. If he swung right now, he would crush my head. My mind unhelpfully conjured up images of Mikale James's brains all over the sewer floor.

Did I have it in me to pull the trigger?

Neither of us found out the answer as another shape sailed out of the nearby fog. I saw the surprise on Crish's face as he spotted us on the platform, already midleap. I watched him flail as if in slow motion, try to change directions in midair, fail, and crash right into Sergio.

The two men went sprawling. Were the platform just a bit wider, Crish might have caught himself with ease, but he rolled and slid over the side before he could stop himself.

Sergio was on his back, dazed from the impact. I scrambled over him and caught Crish before he completely lost his grip. The look on his face was one of surprise and incomprehension, as if he hadn't fully understood what had happened. His weight dragged me almost immediately over the edge with him, but I managed to anchor myself with diamond claws that sprouted from my legs and sides.

His grip was slipping, as was mine. Both our hands were covered in sweat and I could feel my joints creak. I manifested layers and layers of diamond around our hands to lock in the grip, but he was dangling precariously in the air now, and I felt dizzy just looking down at the foggy depth. The concentration required to keep the diamond intact was taking its toll and black spots began to dance before my eyes.

"End the round!" I screamed. My voice was practically swallowed by the void. "It's over! *End it! End it now!*"

The fog suddenly disappeared. The ground beneath us solidified. Crish's weight was off my arms and I allowed the diamond layers joining us to shatter. We collapsed on the solid ground, panting and gasping. I lifted my head to see the other contestants not too far away. In fact, it seemed they had been closer than I realized. I was relieved to see Evie only a few circles away.

A hand lay gently on my shoulder. I looked up, struggling to catch my breath, to see Eleven. He helped me stand and before I could fully get on my feet, wrapped his arms around me and squeezed tightly. For a moment the stoic facade he showed the world fell away. I hugged him back, trembling. As I stood, I still felt like the ground could give out at any moment.

"*Seems we have a cheat here*," came Cheshire's voice as they approached. I felt Eleven stiffen protectively. "*What's all this then?*"

"I didn't cheat." Still breathing hard, I faced them. "I followed the rules. You said the round ends when seven people are still on the platforms. He wasn't on the platform."

Cheshire tilted their emoji face one way, then the other. My heart pounded. Behind them, I saw Sergio and Crish rise to their feet apprehensively.

"*Clever one, aren't you?*" they said after a long moment, sounding genuinely impressed. "*Very well. I'll let this one slide. The next round will belong to the final eight. But be aware—an extra person will only make the game harder.*"

Then, in that same exaggerated manner that left me with no doubt that they were done with me, Cheshire turned to Eleven. One thin, metal hand lifted and rested on his shoulder and I saw Eleven flinch and grimace. Cheshire's needle-sharp thumb was buried at least an inch into his skin, right under his collarbone, through his clothing and flesh. He struggled to keep his expression blank as Cheshire squeezed their hand tighter. A dribble of dark blue blood dripped down along his chest.

"*Consider this your only warning,*" said Cheshire in a voice that shook me to the core, "*Eleven.*"

CHAPTER 25

ELEVEN DID NOT VISIT THE NEXT DAY, NOR THE DAY after that, nor the days that followed. While I couldn't pretend to know the inner workings of the games and what rules he might have broken, I feared that things were worse than he had let on so far. His absence served as yet another stark reminder of how little control I had—any of us had—over the situation.

I woke the morning before the next round to a sound in the living room. I glanced at Evie's sleeping form, then checked my phone. It was only just past three. I considered going back to sleep, but the rhythmic sound coming from outside the door didn't stop.

Thunk.

Thunk.

Thunk.

As if someone was tapping a flat surface.

I got out of bed and hurried to the living room. Part of me leapt at the hope that it was Eleven. But when I opened the door, a strange sight greeted me.

Someone was lying on the futon. I could only see the top of their head propped up on the armrest from where I stood. The lights were off and the only source of illumination was the window. They were throwing a small rubber ball at the ceiling and catching it as it fell.

Thunk.

I closed the bedroom door behind me gently.

Thunk.

They had to have heard me, but said nothing. The ball went up and came down again.

Thunk.

"Crish?"

The hand throwing the ball stopped and dropped down.

"What are you doing here?"

He didn't answer me. Instead, I saw his hands toss the rubber ball up and down. Up and down.

"Do you check in to the outside world at all anymore?" he asked in a strange voice.

I took a step toward him, but he didn't turn. "You mean go online? No, not really."

"The hottest debate right now is whether you're 'hot' enough for your boyfriend. The general consensus is no."

"I don't need to see internet trolls talking about my looks."

Crish sat up, still not looking at me. I watched him toss the ball back and forth between his hands.

"That's what's wrong with you."

I blinked. "Excuse me?"

"Small picture. All you see is yourself, your little world. You can't stop focusing on what people are saying about you because that's all that matters. You can't ever open up your eyes and see everything else going on."

"What are you talking about?"

"Do you know what's happening in the world right now, besides the little stories about you and that *thing*?" Crish stood, but his attention was still on the ball. He tossed it in his hand. Up and down, up and down. "Of course you don't. You're too busy getting dicked by E.T."

A surge of anger coursed through me. "Is this about Eleven and me?" I asked hotly, trying to keep calm. "I'm sorry if I led you on or—"

"Don't flatter yourself," Crish interrupted. He tossed the ball above his head, almost to the ceiling, and smoothly caught it again. "I have no interest in you. Have you looked at yourself? Put you in a crowd and you'd disappear without a trace. If it weren't for this goddamn game you wouldn't get picked out of a lineup. I knew from the day I laid eyes on you that you were nothing special—surviving that first round was just a fluke. I've met millions like you. They usually chase me down in the streets and park themselves in tents waiting for a smile and a nod. And that's what I usually give them—a smile and a nod and they snap themselves in line and walk away satisfied. But you"—he gave me a quick glance and was back to the ball again, as if I wasn't worth a second look—"just aren't smart enough to take that smile and nod and go back to your place. So I had to push a little harder. A little flirt here, a little hurt there, a little kiss and a little 'I thought we had something.' No harm intended, just enough to keep you in your place and out of the spotlight. I honestly didn't think it would be so hard. I went into every round sure that it'd be your last, but you've certainly proven your resilience." The ball stopped. He met my gaze at last. "Even with Sergio nipping at your heels."

A chill ran through my veins. "You know about Sergio?" I asked, a quiver in my voice. "Did you tell him to go after me?"

"Oh, not just him." The ball went into the air, then dropped down again. "There were others. He's just the most aggressive one. Desperate to be famous, that one, but so young, easy to sway."

"He killed Mikale James."

"I didn't tell him to do that, but it was appreciated. Having another big name in the game would've split the audience. Sergio knew that. He's clever when he wants to be."

He took a step towards me. A casual, nonchalant step that unnerved me regardless. I was suddenly very afraid. The apartment felt cramped and stifling. "Why are you doing this? Aren't we all fighting for the same thing?"

The ball stopped again. Crish pointed at me. "No. That is what you're missing here. We are absolutely not fighting for the same thing. *You* are fighting for your little life. You—or at least some part of you—think that when this is over, you'll get to step back into your pathetic little life, do the sad little things you've always done, and pretend nothing ever happened."

I said nothing. He wasn't wrong.

"Like I said, you have no idea what's been going on out there. The life you had, the one we all had, is gone. The world is changing. Do you know how many countries are militarizing? Or the number of major political scandals surfacing because the people behind them are afraid they'll meet their maker with dirt on their conscience? Did you know there are regions where murder and rape are rampant in the streets, and vigilante justice is at an all-time high, because the 'end of times' means both the good guys and the bad guys just don't give a shit anymore? Third world countries are invading each other's borders. Over a dozen states have legalized hard drugs and prostitution with at least dozen more on the way. Everyone's rushing to the altar or abandoning their families because what the hell, the world is ending anyway, right? What's it matter if you marry the douchebag you met last night or ditched your brats in the back alley?" Crish let out a dry laugh. "Oh, I could go on and on. You don't know all the things I've seen and heard these last couple of months. It's enough to drive a man mad."

"What am I supposed to do about that?"

"Nothing," he said. He was smiling in a way that I didn't like, as if he was privy to some cruel joke that I didn't know the punchline to. "That's the point.

None of this has anything to do with you. You see, it's a hopeless mess out there, and when this is over, someone is going to have to sort it out. People are going to lift their heads out of this fog and find that they've really shit the bed. Not only that, they're going to find that they'll never feel right again, because their whole world, literally, has been threatened. There are going to be a lot of unsettled, perturbed, terrified people looking for a direction, and someone's going to have to give it to them."

"And you think that's you?" He was moving towards me, a slow pace. I took a step back for every one he took forward. I wanted the futon between us, though I wasn't sure what that would do if he really meant me harm.

"Don't get the wrong idea." He tossed the ball again. It made its gentle *thunk* against the ceiling. "It's not like I came into this intending to be some savior of the world, but when I walked in here, and saw that a mutt, a brown chick, and a bunch of nobodies were all we had to work with, I knew it was a cross I had to bear."

A mutt and a brown chick.

"Noble of you," I said, trying to keep my composure. "I take it Heath agreed with you."

Crish shrugged. I glanced at the bedroom door.

Evie was still sleeping. "I know you and Austin don't exactly get on, but you shouldn't cut him short. He's under quite a bit of pressure from the powers that be. Trust me—they know exactly what they're doing. Did you really think they locked us away to protect us? It was to control us, so that they could have the final say over what the public saw of us and how our images are used. I'm fine with that. It's the unwritten part of Austin's job to find an idol for the people, and you and that Scot didn't exactly give him a lot to work with." He gestured in my direction casually. "But despite that, you went on to cause an extraordinary amount of distraction for a nobody. That whole diamond thing, so flashy. Getting it on with E.T.—well, no accounting for taste for either of you. Though I did enjoy watching you deck him one on camera." He clicked his tongue. "But really, it's all just a cheap distraction. People would rather talk about your little soap opera than focus on what's important—crime, economy, keeping peace. I can go on and on, making speeches and appearances and going on goodwill missions and meeting presidents, but it doesn't matter—because at the end of the day, all everyone wants to know is if you're getting green dick missionary or doggie style." He walked around the futon. I backed around the other way. "Still, you've proven to be a challenge. I really thought by now you would've either died or at least lost your nerve and faded into the background. Even that thing with your sister didn't knock you off your block."

I stared at him. My mind felt like pieces of a puzzle sliding into place. "You told the paps I was at Hannah's house. It wasn't her boyfriend posting on Facebook. It was you and Heath."

"Blame your boyfriend. His flashy entrance at the first safe house provided us a bit of inspiration."

I felt dizzy. Crish made his way towards me again and I nearly tripped over my own feet getting away from him. That smile on his face never wavered, the same smile that charmed me and most of the world. "Why are you telling me this now?"

"You know, I'm not sure," he said, tossing the ball back and forth in his hand. There was something restless about him. Something bubbling and simmering underneath the surface. "Maybe it's disgust from seeing you stick your tongue in E.T.'s mouth—you're shameless, you know that? But mostly I think I'm just tired of pretending, especially when you're nearing your last round."

"What does that mean?"

"Figure it out."

"I saved your life."

"And don't think I'm not appreciative. I am. Especially now that I can make a big show of mourning the 'woman who saved my life' after I walk out of here. You should thank me—I plan to give the people an *epic* tale about you, fix your reputation. You're going to leave a hell of a legacy. Little Stella is going to grow up proud of the big sister who died a hero."

"Thanks."

"You're welcome," he said, and tossed the ball to me. I caught it instinctively. He walked past me, hands in his pockets, to the front door without a look back. "Later, Diamond Donna."

I looked down in my hands and in the dim light from the windows finally saw that what he had been handling was a transparent super ball. The little green alien figure inside smiled and waved at me, the same way it did back when it sat in my little home library.

CHAPTER 26

WHEN THE TELEPORTATION VERTIGO WORE OFF, I WAS alone in a tiny, unlit space with rough walls. Immediately claustrophobic, I felt blindly in the darkness until I found a doorknob. It pushed open surprisingly easily and I stepped out of what appeared to be a closet in a dilapidated building. The walls and floors were stone and the hallway I now stood in curved into the distance. On the opposite wall were several steel-framed windows. I stepped up to one and peeked out.

The structure resembled an old stone keep castle. Tall tower walls reached into a dark sky. Above, I saw the familiar red letters that read **16:00**. Was this round only sixteen minutes? Either way, the countdown had not started. I was on the third or fourth floor. Below me were murky, moving waters and sky bridges that connected various parts of the castle. Every step I took sounded thunderous in the eerie silence.

I saw no one else. If we had been dropped in different locations in this vast building, it would take significant effort for us to find each other. Something skittered to my left and I jumped, but it turned out to be a camera bot, crawling around on eight legs like a spider instead of hovering, little feet clicking against the stone rhythmically.

Something weighed against my skin. A cuff had been wrapped around my right wrist. It looked like metal, and released a tiny spark like static electricity at my touch. I concentrated and tried to manifest diamonds under it to break it apart.

Nothing.

I tried again, concentrating hard.

Still nothing. A wave of dread spread over me. I looked around to make sure no one else was around. Suddenly, I felt very vulnerable.

Shield.

Nothing. No diamond crystals appeared over my body. That sense of manifesting, the little tingle that went with growing something outside one's body, simply wasn't there. Every time I tried, the cuff sent out another little spark and I felt a slight sting on my wrist that traveled up my neck.

"*Hello contestants!*" Cheshire's voice resonated from the walls. "*Welcome to the Castle. We will be leveling the playing field a little bit for this one.*"

A sense of dread crept over me.

"*First, the rules—in this round we will be taking the number down to the final four, which means the game will end when we have eliminated four contestants. You have the entire castle to yourselves—well, almost. You may encounter some of the other inhabitants, and they're not terribly friendly. Here's the trick—this round will be double blind. Meaning not only will the folks back home not recognize you, you will not be able to identify each other. All of you will look the same to each other as the other inhabitants. How will you be able to tell who's who? That's where those fashionable little cuffs come in.*"

I looked at the cuff, and just as I did, a slender, featureless figure stepped into view, accompanied by tendrils of smoke. It spotted me at the same time I spotted it. Neither of us moved.

"*The other contestants will be wearing the same cuffs. But they're awfully hard to see unless you get close, and the other inhabitants may not let you get close enough to take a look. So if you see something coming at*" *you? Well, you'll have to take your best guess whether to fight, flee, or cooperate."*

The thing took a step forward. I took one back. I raised both hands to indicate I had no aggressive intentions, but I had no idea if it understood. I couldn't see if there was a cuff around its arm in the dark.

"There is another part to the cuffs; that's where the level playing field comes in. I'm sure most of you have discovered by now that your manifesting abilities are being hindered. The cuffs are providing a minor shock to your system, just enough to disrupt your thought processes and prevent manifestation from completing. Don't worry; there shouldn't be any permanent damage."

It raised its hands, too. I pointed to the cuff on my wrist and hoped it would do the same. It did, but something about the way it pointed bothered me.

"The cuff is a handicap that will deactivate after a set amount of time. The length of time you will be handicapped depends on your ranking in the game. The lower your score, the longer the handicap."

It was mirroring me. Instead of pointing to its right hand, where my cuff was, it pointed to its left. I pointed to my left wrist, and it did the same, slowly moving closer as it did.

"Once the timer starts to count down, your handicap will be as follows."

The timer hadn't started. Maybe that was why it wasn't making a move? I took a step back. It took a step forward.

"Evie Bouchard, ranked in eighth, sixteen minutes."

I shuffled backwards, trying to put more distance between myself and the apparition.

"Donna Ching, ranked in seventh, fourteen minutes."

Had I dropped back toward the bottom again? So much for the points the book birds earned me. It didn't matter. The thing moved with a soft slither over the stone floor, following me.

"Crish Michaels, ranked in first, two minutes."

Did I miss the ones in the middle? I wasn't paying attention. What number was Sergio? I remembered Crish's words with a shudder. Who else was gunning for me in this round? I might have no friends besides Evie in this arena.

"Ready?"

I picked up my pace to a full run.

"Set."

My hand hit something not stone. I looked to see the door to the closet I started in. I was back where I began. I yanked it open and threw myself inside.

"Go!"

I pulled the door in and held it closed as hard I could. For a thick, silent moment nothing happened. Then, I heard the slithering down the hall, past the door. It passed me over, then back the other direction, searching.

It tapped on the door. I held my breath.

Tap. Tap. Tap.

I didn't dare move a muscle. It pressed against the door, like a serpent constricting around its prey.

Tap. Tap. Tap.

The knob turned in my hands. I held as tightly as I could, fighting the thing's grip. Feeling my resistance, it redoubled its efforts. Teeth clenched, I willed myself not to let go, but little by little my sweaty palms lost their grip.

The door ripped out of my grasp as the thing tore it straight off the hinges. With an unholy shriek it pounced on me, swallowing me in thick, dark mist. My mouth and nose filled with a soot-like substance as it enveloped me. I struggled and suffocated, fighting to push it off, but touched nothing but smoke.

Shield.

The cuff shocked me. My body jerked but I tried again. I couldn't breathe and my lungs were packed with smoke.

Shield. Shield. SHIELD.

The cuff shocked me again and again. Pain quaked through my arm but I barely felt it as consciousness threatened to escape me. The smokey thing shoved me back into the tiny space in the closet, pressing me against the cold stone wall. I felt desperately around but there was nothing to grab onto.

SHIELD!

Pain seared the entire right side of my body. There was a loud *crack*. The thing pulled itself off me and slithered into a quivering pile on the ground. I clutched my now-numb right arm and drew a sharp breath. The air smelled like electricity. The thing reared up, hesitated, then slithered into the shadows.

I stayed in place for a long moment. The right side of my body couldn't seem to unclench. Gritting my teeth, I forced myself to stand. The cuff on my wrist sparked. Whatever I did to it, it shot off enough power to scare off the creature. I felt slightly comforted to know my options in a pinch, but whether my body could take another jolt was anyone's guess.

I pried myself out of the cramped closet and headed down the hall, in the opposite direction of the creature. I passed the steel-framed windows again. The numbers in the sky read **14:49**. Only a little over a minute had passed.

No more creatures crossed my path, though every now and then I heard the unnerving slithering coming from the shadows. Some of them might be observing me, hesitant to approach and always just out of sight.

At the very end of the hall I found a spiral staircase descending down to the next floor. I could see very little but with no other paths before me, I made my way down, one step at a time, both hands feeling the stone walls around me. I counted the steps to keep myself steady. At number forty-six my foot hit the bottom. This floor was brighter, fed with gray and red light from dusty windows. And it was by that light that I spotted the body.

There was no doubt the unfortunate contestant was dead. Their body was in full view, metal cuff rhythmically flashing on one limp, swaying wrist. It was a man. I racked my mind for his name. His body had been pierced through at least a dozen times by the crystal cluster holding him up, displayed at eye level like a macabre piece of art. The body was fresh. Blood had not even seeped to the ground over the crystals. I'd seen enough of it to know that the clusters holding him up were diamonds.

I gave the corpse a wide berth. A shadow creature slipped into view, saw me, and quickly moved on. My chest tightened for a moment thinking it might have been Evie.

I found more stairs and kept making my way down. From the windows I looked up at the countdown in the sky. Nearly eight minutes had passed now. Several people should have regained their manifestation, unless they'd already met their maker. The bottom floor gave way to a wide, windowed door. Through it, I found myself in a desolate garden. The sky cast its gray light down at me and for a moment it almost felt peaceful. A paved path wound through patches of nightshade and belladonna. At the center of the garden, surrounded by overgrown shrubbery, was a stone statue in the shape of a crouching angel. Where its face once was, however, was a cluster of diamonds. Beneath its pedestal was another large cluster, and I had a sinking feeling in my chest when I took a closer look.

Another one of the contestants was splayed on top of it, hanging face down, as if the crystals had caught her by surprise from below. One arm was pushed above her head by a shard of crystal through the wrist and the rest of her was bent in unnatural angles, folded like a mangled sheet. I was grateful for the long hair covering her dying expression. Something moved and a shudder coursed through my body. Three minutes remained on my handicap.

A lot could happen in three minutes.

A shadowy form moved into view, looking at me from behind the bushes and shrubs but not backing down when I looked back like the last few did. I raised my hands and pointed to the right wrist. It glanced at my wrist, then up at the sky.

03:56

I looked around. The thing and I were alone. It moved a little closer to me. And looked up at the sky again.

I spun around and made for the door. It gave chase immediately. I managed to run inside and slam the door behind me, but the thing was only a second behind. It moved very differently from the others. Wide, loud strides instead of soft slithering. I ran up the stairs and to the second floor hallway. There was only one door in sight. I stumbled inside and locked it behind me.

I was inside what looked like an old ballroom with gilded walls and chipped bannisters. Rotten golden drapes hung from the walls. The door rattled behind me and I pressed my back against it. It rattled again. The thing behind it was throwing its weight against it. Through broken windows on the other side of the room I saw the time now read **03:12**.

Another rattle. I felt the weight of the metal cuff on my hand, my last hail mary if I could survive the jolt. Frantically searching the room for anything to use as a weapon, I spotted a broken curtain rod on the ground. As I tried to decide whether I could get to it, the sound behind me changed.

The cough of an engine, like a lawnmower, filled my ears. I pushed myself off the door and dove forward just as the blade of a chainsaw plowed through the door, splintering it in all directions. I scrambled to my feet and ran to the center of the ballroom just as what was left of the door slammed open.

The shadowy, faceless creature stood there. On its right arm was the metal cuff, but unlike mine, it was not blinking. The shadow advanced on me without hesitation.

"I'm a contestant," I said loudly, holding on to one last thread of hope that perhaps whoever it was didn't realize who was in front of them. "I won't hurt you. I'm a *contestant*!"

They struck me across the face so hard my jaw rattled. The floor rushed up at me and I managed to catch myself. How much longer was the handicap? Killing me would not take but a second. A hand tangled itself in my hair and pulled me up to my knees.

"I know exactly who you are," said a low voice I'd come to know much too well in my ear. "It's too bad I don't have much time to enjoy this, but it's going to be the longest thirty seconds of your life."

I sank my nails into the skin of his hands, desperately trying to pry him loose. Crish swung his hand and slammed the side of my face into the stone floor. At least one tooth rattled loose.

"You told them to use diamonds," I gasped through the pain.

He slammed my face down on the floor again. "Don't think you can waste time talking."

"Fuck you."

My face hit the stone floor with a sickening crack. Wet, warm fluid gushed out of my nose. Everything tasted metallic. His hands came around and cradled my chin.

"This will hurt," I heard him say with what sounded almost like giddy anticipation.

I braced myself for that moment when my neck snapped, but it didn't come. The hand in my hair released and I collapsed onto the floor. My shattered nose struggled loudly and painfully to draw air. I turned my head just enough to see Eleven standing a few feet away, between me and Crish.

A few more seconds. I just needed a few more seconds.

Crish, still looking every bit the shadow creature, lunged at Eleven, who caught him by one arm, side-stepped out of his way with practiced precision, and threw him across the room with his own momentum. As Crish got back up, I saw him rapidly cycle a variety of manifested weapons in and out of his hands.

"I," he seethed, facing Eleven. "Am *so sick* of *you*."

He took a step forward, then stopped. Something was happening to his body. His shoulders and arms blew up like balloons. The shadow fell away like shed skin, revealing the form underneath that looked less human by the second. His forearms swelled up like Popeye, and his shoulders were rapidly looking more like a gorilla's. Eyes wild and unfocused, he lowered his head toward Eleven as if intending to barrel through him like a raging bull.

"Oh god," I gasped through my split lips. The splintered form of Crish shambled toward us. Eleven looked at me over his shoulder, and I saw anger burn in his gold eyes as they landed on my bloody face.

No, I wanted to say. *It won't end well.*

But all that came out was a bloody cough.

With a roar more animal than human, the thing that used to be Crish charged. The muscles in its swollen neck and shoulders clenched as it raised its fist. Eleven leapt nimbly out of its way and in a small, quick movement barely noticeable, he cut it across the arm with the tiny curved blade that manifested and changed shape even as he moved. I saw it become a hook for a very brief second and then change back to loosen itself from the flesh it was buried in. The wound was short but deep. The gash it left in Crish's forearm sprayed fresh blood all over the floor, but if he felt it, he gave no sign. His face was swollen, too, as if his muscles were growing too big for his skin. His eyes were nearly buried in the mountain of bulging flesh.

The castle disappeared around us. The walls fell away into pixels like a computer program deleting itself. Three other contestants appeared, trading confused glances at each other and the disappearing castle, but soon all eyes were on the commotion in the center of the arena.

The remaining camera bots gathered. Every eye in the world was on Crish Michaels.

· · ·

THIS MATCH WAS unlike anything I—or anyone else —had ever seen before. Seeing Eleven move against Crish made me realize that none of us knew what we were doing in this arena. Despite his raw power, Crish wasn't even able to land a glancing blow on Eleven, who moved around him with impressive agility, like a tamer dancing around an awkward beast.

Not only did he switch the size, shape, and type of his weapon with every move to maximize speed and blocking, he manipulated the arena itself to his advantage. As Crish charged, the ground beneath Eleven's feet suddenly shifted upward, boosting him into the air to jump easily over Crish. Every turn Crish made, little rocks and bumps appeared under his feet, tripping him and slowing him down, leaving openings at every turn. Changes to the arena that took monumental efforts for the rest of us were only parlor tricks for Eleven.

However, even for all his skills and advantages, the fight was at a stalemate. I could see him buying time, trying to figure out how to disable Crish and shock him out of his splintered state. Crish was attacking too quickly and violently for him to pin down, and even if he could, I wasn't sure he could hang on to Crish's swollen neck long enough to make a difference. Crish was becoming faster and stronger as his splintered state continued to grow out of control. Skin began to tear apart on parts of his body as he barreled through the arena like a tornado. By contrast, Eleven was slowing down. A terrifying realization hit me as Crish landed his first blow, square in Eleven's chest, knocking him backwards.

He can't breathe.

I saw Eleven clutch his chest as he rose to his feet. I'd gotten so used to seeing him out of his armored suit that I had forgotten its most important function. He was drawing short, rapid breaths and I wondered if he'd also just realized what a precarious position he'd fallen into. Crish charged at him and he scrambled out of the way, but I could see he was approaching his limits. He flicked his wrist and the weapon in his hand changed into a claw-shaped knife.

Crish came at him again. Eleven slid under the massive, swinging arm and cut Crish's ankle. Crish went down to one knee and Eleven was on him in a second. The knife changed into a metal chain, which he swung skillfully around Crish's neck like a cowboy hog-tying a calf. For a moment it seemed he'd gained the upper hand as Crish reeled, choking and gagging. But then one giant, meaty hand reached back, grabbed Eleven by the shoulder, and slammed him down onto the ground.

Eleven drew a deep, pained breath as he hit the hard surface. Crish's fists came crashing down at him over and over. He manifested metal and stone shields one after another to protect himself but they broke quickly under Crish's blows. With each manifestation I saw him struggling harder to breathe.

Finally, his manifestations could no longer hold form. Crish let out a triumphant roar and reared back with both hands clenched into fists, ready to put an end to the fight.

"*No!*" I screamed.

There was a pause, a very slight one, as Crish instinctively looked toward me. But it was enough. Eleven was on his feet in an instant and the curved knife was back in his hand. I gasped as the blade disappeared into the underside of Crish's throat.

For a moment, no one moved. Then Crish raised an arm, but it fell uselessly back down again. He stumbled once, twice, and fell forward. Eleven caught the falling form as it descended and changed shape, becoming smaller, thinner, more human. By the time he lay still against Eleven's arm, he had returned to normal.

Gently, respectfully, Eleven laid Crish on his back. The knife buried in his neck disappeared. Eleven took a shuddering, exhausted breath and fell to his hands and knees beside Crish. Shaking the shock from my mind, I pushed myself to my feet and hurried to him. As I wrapped my arms around his shoulders to steady him, his breathing was disturbingly shallow.

The other contestants gaped at us, trying to understand what had happened. Aside from Evie, I recognized Sergio and a contestant from Eastern Europe. Out of the three, only Evie appeared surprised at the sight of the three bodies propped up by diamonds.

Cheshire appeared, but without their trademark smug grin. In fact, they had no face at all. The blank space above the Edwardian collars was somehow more frightening than any face of anger. Fear burrowed its way inside me like an ugly worm.

"Justify yourself."

Eleven drew a deep breath. His lung crackled. He pulled himself to his feet with strength he probably didn't have. I stood and opened my mouth to defend him, but he squeezed my arm firmly and pushed me behind him.

"I cannot," he said simply.

Cheshire's tented fingertips tapped together. Once. Twice. "*Is that so? No reasons? No excuses?*"

Eleven shook his head. He was swaying on his feet. "No. None."

"*I don't suppose you want* her *to pay for your infraction?*" Cheshire asked, glancing at me with their invisible eyes.

"No." Eleven shielded me with one arm. "I take full responsibility."

Cheshire looked from him to me. My entire body was numb. Blood flowed out of my broken nose. Cheshire's face flickered back on. There was something cold about that emoji face, with its lined eyes and mouth spread into an enormous, almost circular grin. They gestured nonchalantly toward the other contestants.

"*You're done*," they said, and with a snap of their fingers the others were teleported out of the arena. The bodies and crystals disappeared as well. Cheshire shifted their gaze up. "*Visuals off*," they said to the cameras buzzing about. I heard soft clicks as they switched off one by one. There was no one left in the vast, endless arena except Cheshire, Eleven, and me.

Cheshire's metal hand shot out and seized Eleven around the neck, lifting him off the floor as if he weighed no more than a kitten. That smile remained as they turned to me with the glee of a child torturing a bug.

"*Tell me, Diamond Donna,*" they said teasingly. "*Did your boy here tell you the real reason his people wouldn't leave him alone?*"

I shook my head. My hands moved reflexively. Diamonds spread over my fingers and curved into sharp tips, like a cat drawing its claws in alarm.

"No!" Eleven gasped, barely able to choke the word out beneath Cheshire's grip. "Don't."

"*The reason they were fascinated with him, you see,*" Cheshire continued, "*wasn't because he was interesting, or talented, or even made for good stories. No, it was because he was a sideshow.*" They jiggled Eleven like a rag doll, pulled him close, and traced the crescent of scales around his eye with their other hand. "*See, his people, the rest of them, are covered in scales. But once in a while, you get a freak like this one, who can't grow them properly. Instead, they get the scales in ugly little patches. They're usually outcasts, stared at in the streets, and forget about finding a mate. And his people, oh you should've seen the look on their faces when they saw him in the game. They were so excited to see how far the naked mole rat would make it. It was such a spectacle.*" They pulled Eleven even closer, until his face was inches away from their lined eyes. "*We gave you a place here. I let you into my game, and this is how you repay me.*"

With a swing of their arm Cheshire threw Eleven to the floor. He landed heavily and as he tried to push himself up, Cheshire pushed him back down with a foot on his back.

"*I didn't want you here. I told the producers you were trouble. But they found you amusing. They insisted you'd be useful.*"

They reached down, metal fingers wrapped around Eleven's left arm.

"*I've been fed up with you for a long time, you bothersome reptile.*"

Something sizzled. A tendril of smoke rose from beneath their grasp.

"*I'm going to enjoy this.*"

What happened next I could never be sure. All I knew was that a burst of heat struck me in the face and for a moment Eleven's entire left side was on fire. I couldn't tell if the screaming in my ears was me or him. Then, as quickly as it came, the fire was out, but the aftermath left me weak in the knees. Eleven's entire arm was black, charred beyond recognition. What was left of his clothing melded with his skin, impossible to separate where one ended and the other began. The burn extended up his shoulder, to his neck and face, nearly reaching the crescent of scales around his eye. Cheshire opened their fingers and Eleven's arm fell lifelessly to the floor. Bile retched up in my throat at the smell of burnt flesh and leather. I covered my mouth tightly but couldn't stop gagging. My body convulsed as it tried to eject its organs and more blood gushed out of my nose.

"*There is one thing I liked about these lizards*," Cheshire said, addressing me as casually as if we were conversing at Sunday brunch. "*They're very resilient, both physically and mentally. Much more so than you hairless apes. They can regrow body parts, even whole limbs given enough time. You should see the game we had in his home world. Oh, the things you can do to them before they finally give up the ghost.*" A shrug. "*Of course, just because they don't die doesn't mean it doesn't hurt.*"

The diamonds were sprouting out of all my fingers now. I couldn't help it. Something in my head was screaming, shrieking, begging to rip that infuriating smile off their face.

"*Now, now,*" Cheshire said unhurriedly. "Control those things. *You're looking pretty battered as it is. You wouldn't want him to suffer for nothing, do you? Be a good girl and put that away.*"

Trembling, I forced the diamonds away. The claws shattered and fell to the ground in shining pieces.

Smiling, Cheshire turned Eleven onto his back with a kick to his side and sank the tip of one razor-sharp finger into his torso, pushing down with agonizing slowness. My body tightened in phantom pain at the sight of it disappearing one millimeter at a time into Eleven's body. Eleven gripped Cheshire's wrist with his remaining hand, but was powerless to stop it as Cheshire dragged it across his body like a surgeon eviscerating a cadaver. He opened his mouth and instead of screaming, he sputtered blood in gurgling spurts. My knees buckled and the next thing I knew I found myself kneeling in a pool of dark blue blood. Still smiling, Cheshire stepped back from Eleven's limp body. For a moment I thought he must be dead, but then, with shuddering movement, Eleven rolled onto his side. I half-ran, half-crawled to his side and cradled him in my arms, trying hard not to look at the gash that ran the entire length of his stomach and what his remaining hand was struggling to hold in. He raised his head slightly and seemed to be trying to say something, but when he opened his mouth all that came out was blue and more blue that pooled quickly in my lap. I held him tightly and could not control my own sobbing. Grief, guilt, and fear ran together. I was drowning.

Darkness took over for a brief moment, as if someone turned out the lights on the world. I blinked.

Again, like a shutter clicking. Cheshire watched me with a wide grin.

The sensation was familiar. My body suddenly went cold, like my blood turned to ice. Then it burned. I moved my arm and felt my body crackling as diamonds filled my veins. The skin on my right arm protruded like something was trying to break free. I heard a faint tinkling sound, like crystals clacking against each other.

"*Well*," I heard Cheshire say in amusement. "*This'll be entertaining.*"

Nothing hurt anymore. Suddenly, I felt no pain, no sadness, and no fear. Power coursed through my body, aching to burst out. I looked up at Cheshire and an image of myself tearing them apart with bare hands flashed through my mind with a shudder of pleasure. Would they scream? I would love to hear them scream. The crackling was filling my entire body now, and I felt myself giving in to it. It was triumph. It was pleasure. It . . .

"Don't."

The world swam back into focus.

"Don't splinter."

I looked down. Eleven's golden eyes looked back at me. He was barely able to manage a whisper through the blood filling his mouth, but it was enough. I tightened my grip on him and held his head against my chest.

"I won't," I said, breathing deeply to collect myself. The crackling sound slowly faded. "It's okay. I won't."

Eleven drew a shallow breath and I shivered. How did we get here? Were we just in each other's arms less than a dozen nights ago, blissfully and naively thinking it was as simple as the two of us being together? The next time I held him was not supposed to be as he lay dying.

"*How disappointing*," Cheshire said, hovering over us. I could almost hear the crackling in my veins again. I gritted my teeth and pushed it away. "*Well, if that's all, then sorry to break you lovebirds up. You're done for the day, Diamond Donna.*"

"No!"

Evie jerked back as my eyes snapped open. My arms were still cradled in front of me, but Eleven was no longer in them. I looked down and around for him frantically, but even as I did it, I knew he was no longer within my reach. My clothes were covered in blood—mine and his.

Evie grabbed me by the shoulders, feeling my face, neck, and head. The tiny apartment was filled with people. Heath was there, as were Lydia and several others I didn't know who appeared to be conversing rapidly just out of earshot, all wearing a mixture of apprehension and disgust. I heard Heath call for medical personnel.

"Are you OK."

I turned my head stiffly. Evie was typing frantically into her tablet.

"Are you OK. Couldn't see. Heard screams. What happened. Are you OK."

Everything came crashing down at once. The last half hour replayed a hundred times in a moment. The castle. The corpses propped up on diamond clusters. Crish's hand in my hair. Eleven struggling to breathe, pulled away, gutted like a fish before my eyes.

Was he dead?

I didn't know. Was he still there in the empty arena, left to die because he dared to protect me?

How did this happen?

How did I let him get dragged into this fight that wasn't even his?

Why couldn't I just step back into the shadows and know my place like Crish said? None of this would've happened.

"You may need to make a statement."

I looked up. Heath was looking at me and shaking his head.

"And here I thought you couldn't be any more of a PR disaster, you go and . . ."

"**Shut up.**"

We all started. Evie held up her tablet. She clicked the volume button repeatedly until it was as loud as it could go.

"**Shut up. SHUT UP. SHUT UP.**"

Heath narrowed his eyes. "Now see here, young lady," he said sternly. "You friend here may have just been responsible for the death of the man who was the only—"

"**SHUT UP.**" Evie typed furiously, fingers flying over the keyboard. "**Crish was shit. Never like him. He hit her. You don't care. SHUT. UP.**"

She turned back to me, concern all over her face, and typed.

"**Are you OK?**"

I wanted to answer, but couldn't. I didn't know

the answer to that question. For a long moment, no one spoke. Then, eyeing my blood-drenched clothes and pursing her lips, Evie typed again.

"He OK?"

I opened my mouth but only a choked sob came out. Evie's arms folded warmly around me and I fell into her embrace, tears mixing with blood.

THE DOCTOR RESET AND SPLINTED MY NOSE AND checked me for concussions. I knew without looking in a mirror that my face was a bruised peach. He kept asking me questions but they all sounded very far away.

I couldn't eat or sleep. Everything smelled and tasted metallic. Every time I closed my eyes all I saw were Eleven's charred arm and his other hand trying to keep his insides from being outside. At night everything ran together—Lexi, Bella, Eleven, Crish, bodies on top of diamonds, and I woke covered in cold sweat, convinced my lap was full of blue blood. Heath hinted more than once of aggressive medical treatments to keep me from becoming dehydrated.

For days I moved around like a husk. They brought in a psychologist who tried to talk to me about trauma. For the first time, there seemed to be a genuine concern for my well-being, though I had suspicions that it stemmed from fear that my current state would result in poor performances in the arena. They'd lost Crish, their savior, and they were paranoid that losing me would pose a very real chance that planet Earth may lose this game. The psychologist was nice enough, but I had nothing to say to her. We sat in the living room across from each other. She asked me questions and I studied her neat clothing and pearl earrings. She looked like me—same brown hair, same pale skin, same thin frame, but like me before the arrival of the orb, back when I still lived a quiet life on an Earth where every person didn't either curse or praise my name, a whole other life ago.

I waited for her to ask her questions, then politely told her I had nothing to say. She wanted to know about the exact nature of my relationship with Eleven, saying it would aid her in helping me process my trauma. I told her I didn't know, which was the truth.

The outside world buzzed with gossip. Vigils were being held for Crish all over the world. I had no idea what the cameras showed them, but chances were even in death, he won. The story, I was fairly sure, was that I found a way around the handicap to kill the three contestants, then when Crish confronted me, Eleven stepped in, and the rest was history. No one saw him smashing my face into the stone floor over and over. If I stepped outside the facility right now, there would be stones thrown at my head and effigies burning in my image. He was, after all, the only contestant to have amassed over one hundred points so far. His victory would have ensured Earth's survival. Now it was once again up in the air. Even if I were to emerge the champion, it probably wouldn't be enough to redeem me in the eyes of the public. I might forever go down in history as the whore who doomed her planet.

And yet, I was strangely calm.

There was a sense of peace in knowing there was no kind of life waiting for me after the games. Crish, in all his mad ambition, was right about that—the world would never be the same again.

I allowed myself to imagine what it would be like if my life were to end when the games did, and found it a comforting thought. There was something very soothing about having nothing left to lose. I thought of Bella and Erin and Stella. This world no longer belonged to me but I could still win it for them. Lexi's and Eleven's sacrifices wouldn't be in vain if I finished what they'd started.

Raising my tablet to eye level, I opened the Headspace webpage for the first time in months and reviewed the current scores. In the little time we'd had together, and through his sacrifice, Eleven had shown me how this game was truly played.

All I needed now was courage.

I STEELED myself against the possibility that, upon entering the arena again, the first thing I would see was Eleven's body on the floor. But thankfully that was not the case. The arena was pristine as always, as if the atrocities of the previous round never happened. I scanned the peripheries, half-hoping to see Eleven standing there as always, restored just as the arena was. He was not.

Evie touched my arm. She had stuck close to me ever since that last round. Not far from us, whispering to each other and looking surreptitiously our way, were Sergio and a red-haired man from Italy whose name I couldn't recall. Crish was quite the inspiration and leader to the younger contestants, and I could see the bitterness in their faces that I was the one who survived instead of their idol. I already knew that my enemies in this round extended beyond whatever Cheshire dropped on us.

"*Well, well, well.*"

Cheshire's voice sent panic through me. For a brief instant I saw it all playing in front of my eyes again.

"*My final fabulous four. How are you doing today?*"

None of us said anything. Cheshire looked each of us over and settled their gaze on me.

"*You have a question,*" they said, studying my battered face in amusement. My nose was still bandaged and my face was covered in angry purple bruises. I must've looked a sight. "*I can tell. Go on; don't be shy.*"

"Is he alive?" The voice that came out of my mouth was stronger and steadier than I expected.

"*Excellent question.*" Cheshire grinned. "*Technically, yes.*"

"What does that mean? Where is he?"

"*Oops, sorry. One question only.*" Cheshire spun their walking stick playfully in the air. "*Tell you what, if you win the games, you get all the questions you want.*"

I took a deep breath. The crystals in my veins were already crackling. I tried to quiet them. "If I win," I said, looking them straight in those lines that made for eyes, "I'm going to make you regret ever picking me."

"*I like that fire,*" Cheshire said, unfazed. "*Keep it burning. You'll need it.*" They turned and paced around us in a circle. "*Which leads me to the next bit of news. You see, your boyfriend interrupted the previous game before it was concluded; therefore your win was nullified. As determined by the producers and myself, you will receive no points for the last round. If you want to earn back those points, you will play in a special penalty round today. Solo.*"

"Solo?" I looked toward the others. "You mean, by myself?"

"*Precisely.*" Cheshire seemed positively giddy. I had a feeling they were the one who convinced the producers to find a way to make me pay for Eleven's misstep. "*But don't worry; there will be some perks. You see, the standings on the scores aren't exactly stellar for you folks right now.*"

With a wave of their hand, a screen appeared in the air, with four names displayed.

Sergio Lopez 79
Crawford Ricci 68
Donna Ching 57
Evangeline Bouchard 51

"*As you can see, the way it stands now, none of you have enough points to stop the big bang. It would be such a disgrace to let you come out ahead only to have your planet destroyed anyway.*"

The word *disgrace* echoed in my mind.

"*But, do well in this round, and we'll reward you with a nice chunk of points. Based on performance, of course. Who knows, it may even be enough to get you over that hump.*"

All eyes were on me. I tore between uncontrollable panic and eerie calm.

"Okay," I said.

"*Questions?*"

"What are the rules?"

"*Take down the target.*"

"That's all?"

"*You want more?*"

I said nothing. A large red circle appeared on the floor. The other three contestants quickly stepped out of it, though Evie had to be dragged out by Sergio. My veins crackled.

"I'm ready."

"*Good.*"

I clenched and unclenched my hands. My joints popped and cracked. Cheshire turned and walked away from me.

"*Go*," they said, and snapped their fingers.

The ground quaked as an enormous creature fell into the arena. The impact nearly knocked me down. Squaring its powerful haunches, it let out a thunderous roar from one of its two heads.

UNTIL NOW, I had only seen chimeras in picture books and mythological texts, though the thing barreling down toward me was more like a blind man's interpretation. It stood tall as an elephant, with one main head that looked like the face of a lion stretched over the skull of something definitely not a lion. On its right shoulder a second head in the vague shape of a ram barked, baring long, glistening fangs. Rearing up at the end of its coal-black body was what appeared to be a red cobra.

"Shit!" I heard one of the others shout. The chimera turned and pounced in their direction, but slammed into an invisible wall that stopped it from exiting the circle. The mock lion head shook off its daze and turned towards me.

I did nothing. Standing in my spot, I rotated my head slowly. The crackling was getting louder and I was warm all over. The chimera examined me. I heard it move. I felt it breathe. Diamonds pricked their way out of my skin, one at a time. Each one sent a wave of strange, bitter pleasure through my body. Crish must have felt like this in his final moments.

The chimera centered on me, eyeing me in suspicion, then approached, a little more cautiously now that it had had one run-in with the unseen wall. Its footsteps vibrated against the floor. First slowly, then faster, then full speed it barreled toward me, its dark, bottomless maw wide open. I focused on the crackling in my veins.

It bore down on me, unhinging its jaw to swallow me whole.

I shot one fist upward into its mouth and for one second every vein in my body burst open. My joints popped like fireworks and tiny diamond spikes emerged from my face and scalp. But there was no pain. I felt nothing but warmth and excitement as my body shifted on its own.

The beast paused in confusion. The diamond cluster sprayed from my arm into its mouth, filling it and hooking it in place in the space of a second. It struggled but I held tight. The strength I commanded in a splintered state was shocking even to me, and I held on to the alien pleasure of it. I pulled back and the beast moved with me. It tried to free its jaw but the diamonds were already growing inside its mouth.

Shining, transparent spikes pierced its cheek, emerging from its eyes and ears. The cobra tail reared up and struck at me and with one swift motion I sliced its head in half with my free hand, my body moving of its own will. The ram head was still barking, but now panicked and fearful.

More diamonds emerged from its body. With each passing moment its torso became more of a pin cushion. Diamonds began to pierce the ram head, cracking its horns as they grew from within.

The world blacked out for a second. I shook my head.

Again. Like a shutter.

The beast was beginning to slow its movement. It dropped to the ground heavily.

Click. Black.

I was nearing my limits. The splinter was taking over.

The chimera fell onto its side, its body riddled thickly with diamonds. I drew a breath.

Don't.

I heard his voice.

Don't splinter.

I held on to it.

Gradually, the crackling sound began to go away. The diamonds in my eyes and face collapsed. I dropped to my knees and closed my eyes. I remembered the feeling of holding him in my arms and hearing him whisper to me. The diamonds on my arm fell away, too, shattering like glass. I pushed away the pleasure, the excitement, and forced myself to feel the present—the cold floor against my legs, my exhausted breathing. The high of the splinter reluctantly receded. My body craved it, hungered and begged for it, but I pushed it away.

"One minute and twenty-four seconds."

I opened my eyes. Cheshire had entered the red circle. They poked the chimera with one long finger.

"Now that's a record." Cheshire bent over me. My head swam. *"Partial splinter. I haven't seen one of those in a very long time. Good job, Diamond Donna."*

"Astra," I said, struggling to keep breathing. Black spots appeared across my vision. "Stop calling me that. My name is Astra."

Cheshire waved me away. *"Sure, sure. Whatever you like."* They leaned down, patted my head condescendingly, and lowered their voice. *"You're playing a dangerous game, but I like it."*

The world turned black.

· · ·

I WOKE up to voices all around me and a splitting headache hit me the moment I sat up. I grimaced and looked around to see the doctor, Heath, and several other handlers.

"What's going on?" I asked. My throat was dry and itchy. Someone handed me a glass of water and I downed it gratefully. The others exchanged a worried look amongst themselves.

"You've been asleep for almost twenty-four hours," the doctor said.

My mind couldn't process this information. The room felt very bright and I thought I might pass out again. A dull ache emanated from my body and coursed down my right side. My right eye was blurry.

"Twenty-four hours?"

"We were beginning to think you weren't going to wake up at all," Heath said. "You missed a very important broadcast from the orb."

"I did?"

"While you were passed out, Cheshire made another appearance. He only had one thing to say."

"What's that?" I shifted slightly on the bed and immediately felt dizzy.

"The next round is the last."

"The last," I muttered weakly. "Can you all . . ."

Words seemed to escape me. "Leave? I just—it's very loud."

They exchanged another look. Heath made a gesture and the handlers filed out. The doctor was the last to leave, after forcing me to peer into a little white light so he could look at my pupils, then saying he would check in on me again in an hour. As the room finally silenced, I managed to get shakily to my feet. Through the bedroom door, I could hear them speaking to Evie. My head was full of wet cotton and a wave of nausea hit me. I stumbled to the bathroom and vomited into the sink, though little came out but bile.

I ran cold water and washed my face. The right side of my scalp ached and when I rubbed it with one hand, a clump of hair came loose. I stared at the dark limp strands around my fingers, unsure what to make of it, and wound up dropping them into the toilet. My joints creaked and popped with each movement.

If I splintered again, would my veins fill up with diamonds until I became a statue? The face in the mirror had no answers.

THE THUMP IN THE ROOM JERKED ME AWAKE. I HAD NO
memory of when I fell asleep again. Something
touched my shoulder and my arm swung out in a
knee-jerk response. Someone backed away. The
lights came on, blinding me. Evie stood a few feet
away, holding one eye.

"Oh god!" I gasped. "I'm so sorry. I thought—"

She shook her head and smiled to show she was
okay. Then, her face changed to a worried
expression.

"What time is it?"

Evie held out her tablet. **"Four. Couldn't sleep.
He dead."**

"Who is?"

"Other guy. Crawl."

My mind reeled. Then, it clicked.

"Crawford?"

She nodded.

"Dead?"

Another nod.

"How?"

Evie typed. "**Sood.**" She shook her head in frustration. "**Sod. Sooey. Side.**"

"Suicide," I repeated numbly. "Why?"

"**Don't know.**"

Evie and I sat down at the Formica table. As I set up a conference call on the tablet, Eleven and Crish looked at me from the same chair they'd both occupied at different times. I took a deep breath, willed them away, and waited for the call to connect.

The first face that appeared was Sergio's. I started slightly at the sight of him and avoided his gaze, hoping the others would distract from me. But no one else appeared, and it took a moment longer for me to remember that there was no one else left. A group once over thirty was now three. Sergio stared at me—unmoving, silent, and cold.

Another screen popped up after several moments of awkward silence. Heath.

"So," he said, looking exhausted. "I received

some grim news. As of an hour ago, Crawford Ricci was found dead in his quarters at the Turin facility."

No one said anything.

"They've ruled out foul play. It was obviously suicide. He left a long, rambling note that was definitely in his handwriting. It's a piece of work. He's quite the poet, they say. To sum it up, the pressure finally got to him." He cast an almost accusatory gaze at me. "He names you specifically. Says he saw what you can do and that he doesn't even think you're human anymore. Says if what happened to you and Crish is what's necessary to win, then he's out. Rather hang himself on his own terms."

Sergio was still staring at me. Heath folded his hands in front of his face thoughtfully.

"There is speculation on our end that this is foul play of some kind, but it's unlikely. We are down to the wire here, four people—now three—against the end of the world. It wouldn't be a smart move to take away one extra chance to win us out of this nightmare." He let out a heavy sigh. "Either way, it's all down to the three of you now."

He paused, looked at us each in turn, then focused on me. "You," he said, "Donna. You've got a chance to redeem yourself, if you want it. Once news gets out that Ricci bit it, there's bound to be a bit of a panic. The world needs a hero right now and unfortunately that's you. You're leading in scores by a damn wide berth after that last round."

I blinked. "I am?"

"You didn't know?" He sighed again. I watched him tap off screen for a few seconds. A moment later, he held up his phone to the screen. On it were the latest scores and rankings. But the website had changed. All the other contestants had been removed. Instead, large red letters read **COUNTDOWN TO FINAL GAME** at the top. Below were the last three contestants.

Donna Ching 107

Sergio Lopez 79

Evangeline Bouchard 51

I STARED AT THE NUMBERS. They didn't seem real.

"You mean they gave me ..."

"Fifty points for taking down that thing, which puts you at the top." Heath pursed his lips. "You know, there is a push for the other two of you to throw the last round."

"No!" I blurted out. "You can't do that. You don't know how they'll change the rules for the last round."

"We're aware of that," he said dismissively. "That is why no decisions have been made. Of course, ultimately, once you're in the arena, it's all up to the three of you. Just keep in mind that ultimately, the goal is to save the world, not grasp for glory."

Sergio still hadn't said a word. I had a feeling he wasn't listening to a word Heath was saying.

"Anyway, we're holding the press conference as soon as possible, which means this afternoon. A team will be over to prep you."

"Prep me?"

"The public needs to see a presentable hero, and this is the only chance you'll get to address them directly. You need to look—and sound—the part. If you want to walk out of here with any sort of reputation other than the whore who spread her legs for the enemy, you'll be smart and do as you're told."

"Maybe I'm fine being the whore," I bit back.

But Heath had already hung up. After a moment of silence, Sergio hung up, too, not having uttered a sound the whole time.

I took a deep breath. Evie looked at me inquisitively. I gave her what I hoped was a reassuring smile.

"**Scared.**"

"Don't be. It'll be okay."

"**No**," she said. "**You. Scared.**"

HOW DID I GET HERE?

As I stood behind the thick green curtain shielding me from the cameras already flashing away, surrounded by security personnel, my face plastered with makeup, hair squashed underneath an itchy wig, I found myself disoriented and lost.

Voices chattered all around me. No one was talking to me but everyone was talking about me. The speech they gave me threatened to slip through my fingers several times. Being watched by an unseen audience in the arena was one thing; to face them was another.

My back ached from hours in the makeup chair. Half a dozen meticulous hands had transformed me into my current state, one I didn't recognize in the mirror. Gone were the purple bruises and heavy bags under my eyes, hidden under layers of foundation and blush. A thin, hard splint was fitted over my nose and covered with a flesh-colored film that could pass for skin at a quick glance. The wig they'd selected matched my natural hair color perfectly. In fact, it was smoother and carried a better sheen than my own hair, which had been falling out in intermittent patches. My eyebrows were teased to within an inch of their lives. My chapped lips were coated with gloss. They even covered the scratches and scrapes on my neck and hands.

I'd never considered myself a particularly attractive person, or even skilled at grooming beyond basic hygiene and a layer of lip gloss in the winter. But at the moment, I had to admit, I looked radiant. Perhaps even beautiful. I looked the part of the people's idol, the hero who could see them through these dark times, a leader they could follow to the light at the end of the tunnel.

And I'd never felt so fake.

"Are you ready?"

I nodded, though it was a lie. Lydia had stayed by me for most of this process, and for that I was grateful. I would've preferred to have Evie nearby, but they felt it was too risky to have both of us out in public at once.

"I know you didn't exactly have time to rehearse, but just try to relax and read what's on the paper."

The speech.

I looked down at it. The sheets of paper were thrust at me this morning as I was ushered out the door. I'd only had time to glance at it on the ride here—*here where? I'm not sure*—but I had gotten the gist of it. It was a good speech, not too long and not too short, succinct, patriotic, and reassuring. I heard someone say that presidential speechwriters had been drafted to pull it together overnight. That same person then commented in a low voice that the speech itself was worth more than a dozen of me. I couldn't argue—all of this was way, way beyond the value of my life and person.

Did I not scold Eleven for thinking the same way of himself? Perhaps I was beginning to understand him a little better. What would he think if he saw me now? Would he still find me "remarkable," all dolled up to play the part they gave me?

Heath marched up to me. "Remember what I said," he said, for the ten millionth time. "Go up, read the speech, thank them for coming, don't answer any questions."

I had nowhere to run, so I said, "Okay", and forced my legs to march forward.

· · ·

ALL EYES WERE on me as I approached the podium. I walked stiffly, keeping my eyes forward and my face blank as cameras chattered. As I stopped at the microphone, the sounds died down. I took a deep breath, laid the speech on the podium, and looked up.

They were writing.

That was the first thing I noticed. Dozens of pens and pencils were scribbling furiously. Why were they writing? I hadn't said anything yet. I glanced at my handlers offstage, hoping for a clue, but was only given urgent gestures and nods to carry on. I turned back to the reporters, and that was when I noticed their faces.

It was all too familiar. Those sly smiles, the smug glances, the little looks exchanged and tiny whispers over shoulders. I'd seen it before, and now I was seeing it again. It was the look of judgment, the look of people who thought they knew me because they'd seen me for five minutes on a screen, the look of the other contestants as they jeered behind my back. It was the look Cheshire gave Eleven and me, until we got too far underneath their metal skin.

It was the look that said what I wore or said didn't matter—they'd already made up their minds about me.

The urge to turn and run overwhelmed me and for a moment I couldn't breathe. To read tabloids was one thing, but to stand here and be judged, open and vulnerable, was something else entirely. I stared dumbly at the room full of men and women in their pressed suits, pencils and tablets poised. How many more were watching on cameras? On the internet? They were broadcasting, livestreaming, recording. Every pair of eyes in the world, in this moment, was looking and passing judgment on me.

My chest tightened.

Every muscle in my body clenched.

I heard Heath hiss, "*Talk!*"

I couldn't. I opened my mouth and nothing came out.

I can't do this.

I can't change everyone's mind about me with one speech, no matter how good.

I can't.

I can't.

I forced myself to draw a deep breath and let it out. The world swam back into focus as the realization slowly dawned on me.

There was absolutely nothing I could do. I was not their idol. I was not their hero. I was not Crish. They would pass their judgment no matter what.

They would twist my words, manipulate my image, do whatever they pleased to fit me into their mold.

No matter what I did.

"*Talk!*" I heard the whispered hiss again. The audience leaned forward expectantly, waiting for me to choke.

No matter *what* I did.

I raised a hand, tangled my fingers in the strands of the meticulously placed wig, and pulled. A wave of gasps rippled through the crowd as my own thin, messy hair, bald in patches here and there, appeared. As cameras flashed, I grabbed my sleeve and wiped it across my face. Lenses and screens all over the world zoomed in on my bruised face and misshapen nose as the fabric sheared off the layers of foundation.

"Ladies and gentlemen, thank you for coming," I said into the microphone. The prepared speech slid off the podium and landed by my feet. "I will now take all questions."

DONNA "ASTRA" CHING STUNS PUBLIC IN SHOCKING INTERVIEW!

"Can you comment on the accusations that you

were responsible for the lives of three contestants in the castle?"

"I didn't kill anyone." I met the man's eyes steadily. "You can choose to believe me or not, but it doesn't change the facts."

DETAILS OF THE HEADSPACE ARENA REVEALED!

"Are you saying that the united front presented by the contestants is false?"

"Our images are dictated to us. The truth is not so pretty." I gestured at my bruised face. "A fellow contestant did this to me. The line between friend and enemy is thin in and out of the orb."

WHAT IS THE REAL RELATIONSHIP BETWEEN DONNA CHING AND THE ALIEN ELEVEN? THE ANSWER MAY SURPRISE YOU!

"What exactly is the nature of your relationship with Eleven?"

I knew this question was coming. They all leaned forward expectantly, waiting with bated breath.

"He listened to me," I replied. "He trusted me and valued me for more than my ability to play the game, which is more than can be said for the rest of the world." Was there a slight downturn of eyes in shame? I wasn't sure. "And when things turned ugly, he defended me when my fellow humans wouldn't." They waited for more. "And I don't care if that's not the answer you hoped for."

DONNA CHING REVEALS PREDICTION FOR FUTURE OF EARTH IN FIRST EVER PRESS BRIEFING

"Do you think Earth will win?"

There it was. The real question. The only one I wanted to answer. I could sense my time was almost up. The shadow over Austin Heath's face had grown darker and darker and I could almost hear steam hissing out of his ears.

It was alright. It didn't matter anymore. *I* didn't matter anymore.

"Yes," I said, and my voice echoed all around the globe. "I don't know what price it will come at, but I believe we will be victorious."

And if we weren't . . . well, no one would be around to call me wrong.

. . .

MAYBE IT WAS a little too dramatic.

Maybe it wasn't enough.

Maybe I should've said more about Eleven.

Maybe I should've said less.

Maybe I shouldn't have let them take so many pictures of my bruises and patchy hair.

Maybe I should've said no to the makeup in the first place.

As I scrolled through the thousands of videos, pictures, and articles, I felt a sense of calm and peace that I hadn't felt in what seemed like an entire lifetime, though I wasn't sure why. Possibly because I was finally able to face the public as myself, or maybe because I finally got under Heath's skin and there was a certain satisfaction in that—he was, as expected, extremely unhappy with the turn of events.

But most likely, it was because the tone of the world had finally changed.

Feelings on the press conference were quite mixed. On either end were extremists, eager to call me a saint or a liar. But for the most part, the populace fell somewhere in the middle, discussing the debacle in hushed, serious tones and trying their best to reframe the last few months. Everyone had a different interpretation of my words, body language, and clothing. Medical experts excitedly analysed the bruises on my face and my potential state of mind. Not that long ago it would have driven me crazy, but now, watching it all unfold before me, I didn't feel the slightest stir of unease or disgust.

Because they were finally talking about *me*. The me I chose to present to them, rather than a version spoonfed the public by the handlers or the camera bots. I was, at last, a person and not a mere name and face in the gossip column.

Hannah sent me dozens of messages, as did Addison. As did my father. They approved, they praised my courage, but they were worried, and I couldn't reply to reassure them that I was okay, that I was better than I had been in a long time. I held on to the thought that at least my words meant something to them, even if I had no idea if they really reached anyone else.

At least, until I woke to the tablet ringing a few nights later.

INCOMING CALLS WERE rare and it took me a long moment to realize the sound was real. I expected Heath, but when I picked up the tablet, it showed a number I did not recognize. After a brief debate, I answered it. A woman's face appeared. She looked to be about forty, with wide, tired, watery eyes, and was dressed in a worn gray polo shirt.

"Oh my god," she said when she saw my face. "I thought they might've given me a fake number. It's really you."

I didn't know what to say. Her face was full of emotion, like someone seeing a long-lost friend for the first time in years.

"I begged," she whispered. "I begged so hard. I really thought they'd give me the runaround."

"Hi," I said awkwardly. "Do I know you?"

She shook her head. "No. No, you don't."

"Can I . . . do something for you?"

She looked down and for a moment I thought she would burst into tears. "My name is Danielle Monroe."

The name crashed down on me like a pile of bricks. "You're Lexi's wife."

"I am. Well, ex-wife technically." She shook her head and seemed to be trying hard to swallow her tears. "We're actually divorced, but we never really went our separate ways. At first we were just staying together for Bella, but after a while we realized neither one of us was really going to leave. We kind of failed at divorce, I guess you could say."

"How's Bella?" I asked gently.

"It's been tough. She has nightmares. I didn't let her watch it but it's hard to hide. I mean, the whole world saw it. I'm trying to get her in with a good therapist, but without Lexi here . . ." She dropped her head and buried her face in her hands, shoulders jerking sharply as she sobbed. I ached to reach through the screen to lay a hand on her back.

"I'm sorry," she managed to say between sobs. "I tried so hard to get to you. I just wanted to talk to the last person who was close to her before she died, and now that I'm here, I don't know what to say."

"How did you get hold of me? I didn't think anyone could."

"There are these support groups out there. They're families and friends of people who died in these games. We get together and try to support each other, even across the pond. I attended a few meetings, and that's where I met Aaron."

"Aaron Hale?" I hadn't thought I would hear his name again. In fact, I had completely forgotten about him these last few weeks.

"Yeah. Really nice guy." Danielle wiped a tear from her eye. "He spoke to us and talked about the game. He told us about you. Said you were kind, and that you're trying so hard, and how you saved his life by giving him your ticket out. He got real emotional, talking about how his kids have a daddy because of you." She smiled slightly. "We all saw you speak, you know. We saw you wipe off that makeup and show your face, and talk about the real stuff. There's such a want to make the contestants into some idol or stigma, and you broke that. I've never seen anyone so brave."

My face warmed at her compliment. "Thank you."

"No," Danielle said insistently. "Thank *you*. You're in there, and you're fighting. They say such horrible things about you sometimes, but I don't believe them. Lexi knew good people, and I can tell you're good."

Thinking about Lexi made my eyes sting. "She was a hero," I said sincerely. "She was the first one to figure it out, and she made us a team. None of us would have gotten to this point if it wasn't for her."

"She has that way about her, doesn't she?"

"She does."

"Can you . . . tell me about her?" Danielle looked to me hopefully. "Just, those last few weeks, when she was there. Can you tell me what she did? How she sounded?"

I did. I told her about the very first call I had with

Lexi, about how she insisted on talking to me in private, how she looked out for me and figured out the tricks of the game while I was still panicking about being away from home. I told her about the next round, how she took charge of a directionless group and made them a team, how many people she saved right off the bat. I talked about her leadership, about her bravery, about how she never backed down no matter how much others tried to question or crush her. I told her as much as I could in the time we had, and she listened with an entranced, loving look in her eyes.

"Thank you," she said after I finished. Then, pursing her lips, she sighed. "Listen, your friend . . . I'm sorry about whatever happened to him. No one knew him like you, obviously, but it looked like he acted out of love, and you just can't blame a man who protects the one he loves. I hope things pan out for you. Somehow."

I forced a smile. "I hope so, too."

"Listen, Miss Donna . . ."

"Astra," I said. "I go by Astra."

"Astra then. You got one thing wrong in your speech."

"I did?"

"He wasn't the only one who saw you for more

than the game. There are some of us—a lot of us—out here in the world who see you for that brave, amazing person you are. You got a friend in there?"

I looked up. Evie was standing at the door, watching and listening with a concerned look on her round face. "Yea, I do."

She nodded approvingly. "When you get out of there—and I *know* you'll get out of there—you got friends out here, too. I just wanted you to know that."

THREE OF US ENTERED THE ARENA.

The space felt strange with only three of us. It was almost hard to remember what it felt like when there were so many of us. But that wasn't the only thing that was different.

We examined the dome and floors, trying to figure out what had changed. The white dome above us was lower, and the horizon, which used to extend infinitely, was actually visible. I could see where the dome connected to the floor. It felt like a room now, rather than an endless, surreal space. Though the arena was still at least the size of a football field, it felt strangely claustrophobic.

We each tested out manifesting weapons and shields. Nothing seemed to have changed there. Sergio's eyes flickered to me as he held his hand in the shape of a gun, as if trying to decide whether to off me right there.

"*Hello, finalists.*"

I didn't even see where Cheshire came from. They simply appeared between the three of us, looking over each in turn.

"*Lost one, didja? Well, no guts, no glory, am I right? We've got no room for weaklings around here.*"

Several camera bots buzzed our way. Cheshire turned to them. I rarely saw them directly address the audience during a round, and something about this act gave me a sense of finality.

"*Thank you for sticking with us this whole way,*" they said in the game show host voice that started this whole thing. "*I'm very excited to reintroduce your three final champions for Earth. It's certainly been a crazy ride, but here they are!*"

They strolled to Sergio and grabbed him by the shoulders from behind. "*Sergio Lopez, a solid performer. While he's never been quite the top standout contestant, we've seen some very ambitious moves from him. Who knows, if you folks are still here after this round, maybe we'll release some bonus footage. Boy, you should see what this guy can do when he sets his mind to it.*"

I saw Sergio suppress a flinch. He was wondering

what they had caught on camera, but was keeping his cool. Cheshire moved to Evie, who seemed to shrink within herself when they leaned against her. "*Evie Bouchard. Last in score but first in effort. And one of our youngest finalists to date. She's kept a low profile and played it safe, but she may have to step it up for the final round.*" They tweaked Evie's nose. She grimaced. "*Low and safe won't do it for a champion, little one. Get ready to bring the pain.*"

Finally, they turned to me. With a slow, dramatic flair, they circled me twice before settling behind me and pushing me to face the cameras. "*And lastly, one of the finest in the bunch. Astra Ching. What a dark horse she's been. One might expect her to blend into a crowd at first, but look at her—so inventive, so scandalous, so fun. If you're placing bets, this might be the one to pay off.*"

I eyed the horizon.

"*Now, if you're all ready, we're going to discuss the final round.*"

The arena was smaller than it was a few minutes ago—a subtle but noticeable change. The space was shrinking even as Cheshire spoke.

"*Usually we have more than three in the final round. Higher numbers make the game more interesting, but we can make do with three with a little extra excitement thrown in. I think you probably noticed some changes to the arena. We don't break out this little feature unless we have three or fewer in the final round."*

Eleven's words echoed in my mind. *Nothing I could say could possibly prepare you for it.* I shuddered.

"This is an elimination round. Last one standing is the champion. As potential champions, you're obviously equipped to face only the best of the best."

The space was still shrinking. The hair on the back of my neck stood on end.

"Which is why the final round, as is the tradition of Headspace, is battle royale."

All three of us turned as one. Evie's eyes were full of terror. Cheshire oiled their way around us.

"No holds barred. Tear each other apart. Indulge in those dark fantasies we all know you've had about each other. But do it quick. For every minute more than one person is standing, you lose more space. I figure you have about thirty minutes before you're all up in each other's personal space, and let me tell you, getting crushed to death with your face up someone else's asshole is most unpleasant."

I saw Sergio move his wrist out of the corner of my eye. He was smiling.

"No room for sympathy here. No friendships. And remember, if no one survives, boom! No more blue planet." Cheshire stepped in front of me. They were

still addressing all of us, but looking only at me. "*Certain past participants have had a very hard time with battle royale. They get it in their heads that they can get through these games and keep their hands clean. But that doesn't make for good ratings, does it? They resist and try to find ways around it and generally try to cheat their way out, but that's just wasting time. In the end, that survival instinct kicks in and they do what they have to do, no matter how much they mope about it later.*" They dropped their voice to where only I could hear.

"*Your boyfriend was a real mess after his final round. But you've got harder eyes than him. Don't disappoint me.*"

I swallowed thickly. Sergio moved again, ever so slightly, still smiling.

"I have a question."

"*Yes?*"

"How many points are we each worth?"

Cheshire tilted their head curiously. "*Points?*"

"Yes. We have points," I said. "You can't tell me now that they don't mean anything. I'm the only one with over a hundred points right now. What happens if one of them wins and can't come up to the point total? Why should they fight if they can't?"

That emoji smile widened. "*Excellent point,*

Diamond Donna." They gave a cartoonish shrug. "*Personally, I don't give a damn whether the champion comes up to the total or not, but since you mention it, let's make it interesting. You are each worth twenty-five points. Which means, no matter which one of you it is, if you kill the other two, you will make the point total.*" They glanced at Evie. "*Keep in mind, only direct kills will go toward your total.*"

I nodded. "Alright."

"*Let's get started. Fight. Win. Kill each other.*" Cheshire turned their back to us and began to walk away. A few yards down, they raised one hand and snapped their fingers. "*Go.*"

I shoved Evie out of the way and raised a shield of diamonds in front of myself at the same time, just as Sergio fired from his right hand. Two bullets bounced off my shield, where Evie's head would've been. Evie stumbled back. Sergio rounded on her and I saw his determination—he was set on taking her out first so he could go toe-to-toe with me.

I slammed into him and knocked him several steps back. His right fist came at me, now coated in a thick layer of metal, and vibrated against my shield. I manifested the first weapon that felt right, which turned out to be a replica of Eleven's curved hunting blade. I slashed at Sergio and caught air as he fell back and came at me again.

Through all these rounds, I had never stopped to think until now that hand-to-hand combat was not my forte. In fact, I knew next to nothing about fighting. Not once did I take on an opponent one-on-one aside from the chimera, which I only defeated by taking a huge gamble. I didn't know how to jab or parry or predict the moves of my opponent, nor did I have Eleven's agility and experience. I could copy his weapon, but wielding it was an entirely different matter.

My veins crackled. I suppressed it. I couldn't splinter. Not this early. I had no idea what would befall Evie if I were to lose control. Eleven was no longer here to pull me back.

Then there was the harsh reality of it all—was I really going to kill Sergio in cold blood? And if I did . . . would I have to do the same to Evie?

My saving grace was that Sergio did not appear to be significantly more skilled than me. If he were Crish, neither Evie nor I would be standing within a minute into the round. But Sergio was still faster and stronger, and though I managed to catch him off guard to start, he was now driving me back.

I shielded myself and swung back when I could,

but my strikes found no target. I had no idea what I was doing and I couldn't pause long enough to manifest anything else. Sergio's face split into a triumphant grin as he saw me on the defensive more and more.

The blows let up for a moment. I swung and missed and Sergio took the opening. What felt like a lead hammer struck my shoulder and something shattered inside. The pain blinded me for a moment. I clenched my teeth against it and willed my bones to hold together. A series of rapid crackling filled my body and I had a feeling my shoulder blade was now knitted together by a web of diamonds. It only took a second, but that second was long enough for Sergio to turn from me and take aim at Evie again. I reached out toward her and a cluster of diamonds exploded into form in front of her, just in time to block the bullet, but in doing so I lost control of my weapon and shield and they crumbled out of existence before my eyes.

Sergio turned on me again. I managed to create another shield and back some distance away from him. My back hit something soft and a surge of freezing cold enveloped me immediately. With a startled cry I threw myself forward and felt my body pull out of something thick and sticky. I turned just in time to see the arena wall ripple like a disturbed pool of water before falling still again.

"*Oh yes*," came Cheshire's voice from above. "*Watch out for the sinkholes on the wall. Fall into one, you're done for, and nobody gets the points.*"

There was now only as much space as a small gymnasium around us. The walls closed in before my eyes. Sergio advanced. I managed to pull a tiny bump out of the floor in front of him as he stepped within striking range. He tripped and I took the chance to scramble aside. A bullet missed my face by inches and disappeared into the sinkhole.

I couldn't concentrate. The shrinking space and Sergio's relentless attacks muddled my mind. My shoulder ached. Diamonds ground against bone against flesh.

And the real problem, I knew, was that I still couldn't commit myself to killing him. Every time that hesitation rose, I felt my manifestations weaken. Sergio caught me across the jaw and I heard bones crack. Once again I willed my body to hold. He hit me again. I lost consciousness for a very brief second and he kicked me in the stomach.

My veins crackled. My skin pricked from the inside out.

He grabbed me by the collar and lifted me to my

knees, then hit me across the face again. The space around us had shrunk to the space of a medium-sized den. We were losing ground fast.

"I'm so sick of this."

I looked up. Sergio was talking to me. It was a little difficult to hear over the growing crackles in my veins. I pushed them down, refusing to let them take over.

"I'm going to kill you, and then kill the mute girl, and walk out of here."

I could feel the diamonds pricking out of my skin. If I splintered, I would tear him apart in a second.

"I'm done with this shit."

For a moment I heard the crack in his voice, and through the blood and sweat on my face I met his eyes. They were red and swollen.

"He was going to take me with him."

He looked the way Eleven did as he'd told me about his lonely existence as a champion. Broken. That smile that had stayed on his face since day one had crumpled to a pair of lost, desperate eyes.

"We were going to walk out of here together. Usher in a new era. That's all wrecked now because of *you*!"

I swallowed hard. "I don't know what he

promised you," I whispered around a mouthful of blood. "But it was never going to happen. There can only be one champion."

"He was going to find a way. I believed in him."

"You all did. That doesn't change the rules of the game."

"Shut *up*!" He punched me again. All I heard was crackling. My insides felt like an overfilled bag of beads, rattling and churning, trying to break loose. Sergio raised his hand, fingers formed in the shape of a gun. He pointed it at my forehead. I had a brief memory of Lexi, standing like the hero she was, gun raised, after taking down the metal marble. The crackling in my veins was getting louder. I couldn't manifest anything anymore. If I splintered, would I survive?

I closed my eyes.

The shot never came.

I opened my eyes.

Sergio had lifted his gun from me. He stumbled backwards.

Evie clung onto his back, one hand over his nose and mouth. White, sticky glue bubbled from her fingers, quickly covering his face. Sergio struggled, yanking at her arm and hair over his shoulder, swinging his body, trying to throw her off as his face became an angry red. Evie hung on for dear life, even as he punched her eye and tore out chunks of her hair. More and more glue appeared from her hand, filling Sergio's mouth and nose and even covering his eyes.

Sergio flailed and fought. His face was completely covered now. He was frantically trying to tear the white substance off but to no avail. The horrific scene seemed to go on forever.

Finally, he fell, twitching in a disturbing manner, Evie still clinging to him. She panted hard, knuckles turning white. She held on long after he stopped moving.

I got shakily to my feet and went to them. Her hand was still stuck to Sergio's face. I pried her trembling fingers loose one by one. She collapsed against me and burst into tears. I held her tightly. The space around us was closing in. We were now sitting in the equivalent of a walk-in closet. Time was running out fast and we were uncomfortably close to Sergio's still-warm body.

What now?

The answer was obvious. Still holding Evie, I grabbed her hand and bent her fingers into the shape of a gun. She was breathing hard, sobbing, as she watched me. I pointed her finger at my forehead.

471

"Go ahead."

She shook her head so hard I thought I heard her teeth rattle.

"You did great. Perfect. Take me, then you can win."

She shook her head again, opened her mouth, then closed it and swallowed, concentrating as if she'd just become aware of her own tongue.

"**No**," she said, gagging around the word as it came out. Though it emerged from her mouth, the voice was a mechanical one, the same one emitted by her tablet—the only voice she'd ever known as her own.

"Do it."

"**Not—**" She gagged again. Her mouth wasn't used to speaking. Whatever she'd manifested to make the words come out was lodged uncomfortably in her throat. "**Not. You.**"

The ceiling was lowering. If I stood, I would hit my head. Time was almost up.

"Hurry, Evie."

"**No!**" She pushed me. A mass of gluey web shot out of her hands and covered me, gluing me to the floor.

"We don't have time for this! You have to hurry!"

"**No**," she said again, this time a little more

clearly. More webbing was flowing out from her. My left hand was stuck to my thigh, which was stuck to the ground. I tried to shake my right hand free and she grabbed it with both hands. Within a second my fingers were swallowed by sticky webbing and I couldn't pry my fingers apart.

"Evie! Stop it!" I cried. "What are you doing? We're running out of time!"

The room was barely big enough to contain the three of us now. Sergio's body was pressed against my leg. Evie held my face in her hands and cleared her throat.

"**Not. You.**" she said again, clearer this time. "**I watched. You.**"

"Evie," I said insistently. Sergio's head had disappeared into the rippling wall. A sinkhole. "You have to listen. You have to kill me now or we're going to be crushed."

"**I know.**" With each word, she seemed to increase her grasp on speaking. "**I am slow. Not stupid.**"

"Hurry up and shoot me!"

"**No.**" She shook her head. "**You. Are not. Listening.**" She stood. Her head nearly hit the ceiling. There was barely any room left now. She took a step backward and behind her was the sinkhole. **"You protect me. I. Protect you."**

"Don't do this!" I shouted desperately. "You're supposed to win!"

Diamonds began to pierce out of my skin, pushing through the webbing, but the sticky substance was difficult to break. My heart and stomach sank as she blew me a kiss.

"Thank you," she said, and without another look back at me, walked into the sinkhole.

I BLACKED OUT FOR A MOMENT.

The next thing I saw was light. The space around me had returned to normal. I flexed my fingers. They moved easily. Evie's glue was gone. The endless black floor once again extended into the horizon. I couldn't help but notice that the arena looked exactly the same as the first time I'd stepped inside it. Except, for the first time ever, I was completely alone.

"Looks like we have a champion!"

I didn't look up as Cheshire's shadow fell over me. Cheshire scooted their ginning face toward me.

"They're cheering for you. Don't think you can hear it from here, but trust me. You just saved the world.

Granted, that ending was a bit anticlimactic, but get up and take a bow, will you?"

I didn't move.

"You hear me?"

Just a little closer.

"Yoo-hoo. You alive? We're gonna have to blow the Earth if you died on the home stretch."

One long finger extended toward me. I held still.

Closer.

"Hello?"

Closer.

"Earth to—"

My hand shot out and grabbed Cheshire's wrist. They started a little in surprise but didn't pull back immediately. In that second they hesitated, I let the crackling take over. It exploded through my veins and diamonds burst from my skin.

In a moment their entire arm was coated. The thick diamond layer climbed over the rest of them, covering the Edwardian suit, down their legs and over their shoes.

"*Hey!*" they shouted, before the diamond engulfed them completely. I held tight and pushed the crystals forward. The emoji face flickered and disappeared. The headless form was encased in an enormous block of diamond like an insect in amber.

It crashed to the floor, quaking the entire arena. The camera bots raced to our side to capture the event.

I got to my feet and stood before the crystal. The camera bots circled us, as if hesitating to approach.

"Turn off the cameras," I said to them. "*Now.*"

For a moment I thought it wouldn't work, but one of the camera bots shut off with a click, followed by another. One by one, they flew away. For a moment, nothing happened.

"*You didn't actually think that would do any good, did you?*"

I shook my head. "No. That was just for the audience."

"*Dramatic. I like it. You have my attention.*"

I looked at the headless form inside the diamond crystal. The voice was coming from every direction and I had no idea which direction to face, so I spoke to the robot.

"I want to talk to the producers."

I SAT ON THE ARENA FLOOR, BACK LEANING AGAINST the crystal encasing Cheshire. I tried to manifest a clock to watch time tick by, realized I didn't know how clocks worked, and settled for a metronome.

No one was watching me now. The camera bots had gone and Cheshire—the real one—had supposedly gone to talk to the producers. It occured to me that they could leave me here indefinitely, but I didn't think that was the case, not when there was something worthwhile at stake.

What was going on in the world right now? Did the human race see what happened? I didn't know if they were cheering for the win for Earth, cursing the fact that I was the one left alive, or speculating about what was going on after I seemingly trapped Cheshire. Bit of all three, perhaps. It must be quite the chaotic scene behind these walls. I raised one hand to eye level and cracked my joints. Miniature clusters of diamonds grew out of my fingertips, then disappeared again at my will. When I got out of here, I might miss the feel of them.

"*So.*"

I lifted my head. "Yes?"

"*I've spoken to the producers.*"

"And?"

"*They're willing to give you a shot.*"

My heart leapt. "Really? It's doable?"

"*Don't get too excited. Doable is one thing—organic beings are only flesh and memories. But there is a limit to what they can grant without compromising the integrity of the game. Not to mention bonus rounds are few and far between. In fact, I don't think one has been done in this particular galaxy.*"

"Which means what?"

"*It means you better be ready to deliver a hell of a performance. Feeling confident?*"

I wasn't. But it didn't matter.

"I need a guarantee," I said. "I need to know that, when I do what I promise, you'll guarantee me *something*."

"*I don't have to bargain with you. In case you haven't noticed, you're not exactly holding many chips.*"

"You've gone to your producers and sold your case that I'm going to deliver some serious entertainment. Are you going to go back to them and welch if I back out?"

There was a pause. *"Aren't you a clever one."*

"It's just basic business. I want a guarantee on Evie Bouchard."

Another pause. *"Very well. She was second place. Deliver a good performance, and I'll push for her to be restored."*

"And Alexis Monroe."

"Unfortunately, that one is less likely. The producers don't see the value in restoring a contestant who washed out in the first half. You can argue all you want, but I recommend saving your breath. You know by now that your opinion is valued at precisely nothing."

"What about Eleven?"

"Ooo, sorry. That one is not yours to bargain."

I swallowed my disappointment. It was bitter going down. "Fine. Evie. How can you prove you can bring her back?"

A moment of silence. Then, a single beam of light descended into the arena. Where it hit the floor, it began to print a pair of naked feet, followed by bare shins, knees, hips, and up and up until a complete person, naked as a newborn, stood before me. She looked just as she did in life, except . . . new. Her skin was without a single blemish. Gone were the scars and marks from the games. Her hair was shiny and smooth and her eyes were closed as she stood there, still as a mannequin. A strangled sob threatened to escape me.

"Evie." I started stepping towards her, but the disembodied voice stopped me.

"*Don't touch. She's still settling. Besides, she's empty. I haven't downloaded her memories yet.*"

I looked her up and down. Every detail was there. It was Evie, in the flesh.

"How is this possible?"

"*Didn't I tell you? Organic beings are just flesh and memories. Deliver in the bonus round, and I'll finish her off, package her up, all ready for you to take home.*"

"Alright."

A dozen camera bots flew into view and clicked on. A door appeared in front of me, standing on nothing and held up by nothing. It was dark brown, wooden, slightly worn, with two skinny panes of clear mosaic glass, and somewhat familiar-looking, though I couldn't place it.

"*The arena has been prepared. Are you ready?*"

"This isn't the arena?"

A chuckle. "*Oh, no. The bonus round calls for a very*

special arena. We only just finished preparations. I think you'll enjoy it. We certainly will."

"If you say so."

"*Just a reminder—you can quit any time you want, but do, and your friend goes bye-bye forever.*"

"Of course."

"S*tep through, eliminate the target, and you're done. There are only a few rules. This arena will be a little different. No boundaries. No time limit. And* **no manifesting.**"

I started. "What?"

"*In you go!*"

The door swung open and a strong gust of wind pulled me in like an astronaut into a vacuum. My feet left the ground for a brief moment and the door swallowed me. When I steadied my feet again the old arena was gone. The door slammed shut. The new surroundings took me so off guard that for a long moment I thought I must be hallucinating.

My couch was still piled with blankets. Boxes sat against the walls, some half-opened and still on the floor. The geology book was opened up to the property of diamonds. Facing the couch was the old TV that had followed me from my parents' house to my college dorm to my first apartment to this house. My beautiful little library sat in the corner, beckoning my tired mind and body.

I was home.

The TV switched itself on. I saw Cheshire's face appear, just like it did that first fateful day.

"*Hello contestant,*" they said. "*Welcome to the Dead Earth Challenge.*"

A WARM, familiar scent filled the house. The home-owners' association had given me a bowl of cheap potpourri as a welcome gift and its flowery scent still lingered in the air. I opened the boxes against the wall one by one and fished out item after item. Framed pictures, diplomas, old T-shirts from college career fairs. . . . Had I just woken from a dream? Did the last few months really happen? I moved to the library and flipped through every book. Pieces of my life, a life that had been so far away for so long.

An orange lay on the kitchen counter, one that I had started peeling at some point that day. It was still fresh, like I had never left. Because I hadn't— I'd only been dreaming for a very long time. I picked it up, finished peeling it, and placed one wedge into my mouth. It was tart and real. Everything I'd eaten since that first round had tasted like damp cardboard. When did I stop tasting and smelling? I couldn't even recall what I'd eaten, or done with my time. All I remembered was the arena, and the feeling of being surrounded by the gossiping voices.

I sat down carefully on the couch, as if my body was afraid it would vanish on contact. But it stayed, solid and comfortable. I lay down, suddenly exhausted. I remembered Cheshire's words. I remembered their face on my TV. I remembered something about a challenge. But at the moment, I couldn't bring myself to care. My body and mind begged for rest. There was a rhythmic thumping in the air. My head hit a pillow and I was asleep instantly. A deep, dreamless, peaceful sleep for the first time in what felt like an eternity.

WHEN I WOKE I couldn't quite remember where I was, but then the world swam into view and I remembered I was home. There was an orange on the counter and I ate it. It was tart and sweet at the same time. I wrapped myself in a blanket and went to my library, where I sat on the floor and flipped through every book in turn. Every page was the touch of an old friend. When I could read no more, I lay back on the couch. Everything felt right. Warm and soft and comfortable. Like home.

I DIDN'T KNOW when I fell asleep but when I woke up I was sore and hazy and lying sideways. Was the television on? I'd thought I fell asleep watching it but I must have turned it off. The boxes were an eyesore. I should unpack some more after I took a shower. The curtains were drawn and the room was comfortably dim. I debated opening them, then decided against it. I shambled to the bathroom and took a shower. The mirror was fogged over but I didn't need it anyway.

There was an orange I'd started peeling earlier and I took one piece from it. It was tart and sweet and delicious. I wrapped myself in my favorite robe and settled on the library floor.

I WOKE up unsure what time of day it was. There was a dim, gray light coming through the curtains. It must be foggy outside. No point opening the curtains, then. The mirror was fogged over as I headed into the bathroom to take a shower.

I work tomorrow. Don't I? Where is my work bag?

After my shower, I sat back on the couch and finished peeling an orange I'd started earlier.

IT WAS STILL GRAY OUTSIDE.
The mirror was fogged over.

THE ORANGE WAS fresh and tart.

THE BOXES by the wall needed to be unpacked, but there was plenty of time. *I'm home now.* Somehow I felt like I'd been away for a very long time, even though I'd never left. On this long, lazy afternoon, I was just glad to be home.

I OUGHT TO SHOWER. The mirror was fogged over. But I didn't need to check myself anyway.

I READ books and ate my orange. *Have the days always been this long?*

. . .

I SHOULD GET to unpacking later.

I WOKE up on the library floor. I must have fallen asleep reading. I should take a shower. I got up and became disoriented for a moment. Yawning, I reached out to the nearest shelf for support and my fingers hit something, knocking it off. I looked down to see a little green face looking up at me, smiling from inside a transparent super ball.

WAIT.

CHAPTER 31

I MARCHED INTO THE BATHROOM AND SWIPED MY
entire upper arm over the fogged mirror. The right
side of my face still had the remnants of the bruises
Crish and Sergio had put there and my nose was
scarred and slightly crooked to one side. I moved my
arm and my shoulder cracked and popped, as if the
bones had been broken and knitted back together by
clumsy hands.

On my right arm, between the elbow and shoulder, were five pink welts roughly the shape of
fingers. The skin had wrinkled in its attempt to heal
and the scars might never go away.

For that, I was grateful.

I ran my fingers over them. They were the first
marks he had left on me. I pulled my robe open and
touched the spot where he nipped me the first time,

that first goodbye we said as friends. My skin chilled at the memory of his blood in my lap, and my lips yearned for the taste of his. My mind had forgotten in its haze, but my body remembered.

There was that thumping again. It sounded like construction work being done far away, but I knew better. It was the thing I'd been hiding from in my little cocoon.

I took one last shower and took time to dry and tie back my hair. I went to the bedroom, which I'd somehow never stepped into the whole time I'd been here, however long that was. The pajamas I wore in that first round, still freshly stained with blood, lay in a pile on the floor. I opened the closet and was unsurprised to find only one set of clothing —the uniform I'd worn to nearly every round of Headspace, clean and ready on a hanger. I put it on, taking time to straighten each corner, and returned to the living room.

Something looked different now. Perhaps because I'd finally broken my pattern. The room had reset itself. The pillows and blankets were piled as they were when I first entered. The half-peeled orange sat on the counter. The geology book lay open. The super ball retook its place on the shelf. I pulled open the curtains for the first time since I arrived. Someone had spray painted a little green alien with a bulbous head and a prominently erect member on the outside of the glass. Beyond it was a foggy, barren landscape.

I went to the door, put one hand on the knob, and looked back at the room. My home. My library. The one I had wanted to return to for so long. I allowed myself one moment of sadness before pulling the door open and stepping out into the mist.

THE DOOR CLOSED BEHIND ME. I didn't have to look to know there was no building or house. The door was just a door, standing in the vast emptiness. At first glance it looked like an endless, lifeless desert, gray and still. The sky was cloudless. The ground beneath me was hard and cold. The thick mist parted as I stepped forward and soon the source of the thumping was visible to me.

It was enormous. At first I mistook it for a mountain, but then it moved, lifting each immense limb with patient slowness. I couldn't get a good estimate of its size, but it would certainly be noticed barreling through downtown. It paced the horizon, the ruler of this barren world. As it turned, I saw that, like a joke, a huge red target had been painted onto its side.

But the beast, whatever it was, was not the only interesting thing before me. The more the mist cleared, the more I saw that the shapes I initially took for dead trees or rocks were actually something else entirely. I took a few tentative steps that quickly changed into a run as I approached the nearest one.

"Lexi?"

My arms threw themselves around Lexi's shoulders before I could stop myself. I squeezed for a long second before admitting to myself that something was wrong. She didn't look at me. Her eyes were blank and her pupils oddly shrunken. I touched her face. She was cold. I grabbed her hand. Her fingers were stiff. Under her chin was a large, dry wound.

She was dead. A corpse propped up on her feet.

Behind her, countless people filled the plain, stretching into the distance. Hundreds. Thousands. Millions. They all stood in their odd, stiff way. I went to the next person. Crish. He stood unmoving, gazing at nothing. His face had a sickly gray tint. Beside him was Evie. And Crawford. And Miranda. And Sergio.

I moved farther, passing one person after another, moving faster until I was running. Uncomfortably familiar faces greeted me. I found my father, and Hannah. I found Bella and Danielle. I found little Stella. The farther I went, the fewer familiar faces there were, but the bodies didn't stop. Men, women, children, elders. And on and on and on. I ran until I had no breath left in my lungs and still the bodies went on. I dropped to the ground and buried my face in my arms.

Dead Earth.

What have I done?

I waited for Cheshire's voice to resonate from the sky, to guide me or tease me or laugh at me for having doomed the entire planet in my gamble to save a few. But nothing came. I sat in silence, surrounded by standing corpses. Eventually, I looked up at the sky. In that moment, I knew I could sit in despair forever, never moving from that spot. Instead, I stood up.

The apparition in the distance lifted one gargantuan forearm, then slowly put it down again. It was vaguely shaped like a gorilla, with a seemingly eyeless head trailed with long tentacles. I walked as close as I dared to it—close enough to see its leathery, elephant-like skin, covered with scars and moss around the trunk. It moved tiredly and heavily like an old god, one forgotten by time that had moved at its own pace while the rest of the universe came and went. On this dead Earth, it and I were all that was left.

I held up one hand and flexed it. My veins crackled but nothing came out when I tried. No crystals appeared from my skin; no weapons formed for me to use.

The creature took another step. The ground shook. A dry chuckle escaped me. Bonus round indeed.

I sat down again, standing corpses all around me, and watched the creature move, majestic in its way. *Here I am*, I thought to myself, having opened my mouth and boasted that I would take whatever came, and now I had no idea what to do except maybe walk forward until that thing crushed me without a pause in its slow stroll.

I longed for Eleven. He would know what to do.

I longed for Evie. She always brought smiles.

I longed for Lexi. She was brave.

I peered over my shoulder, then got to my feet and retraced my long walk back to the floating door. Lexi was the one closest to it. Even in death she looked brave and determined.

"What would you do?" I asked her, and gently cupped her cold face in my hands.

A humming filled my head the moment my skin touched hers. I pulled away in shock. Lexi didn't move.

Carefully, slowly, I put my hands on her face again. The humming returned, like a distant voice singing. I held her and the humming grew louder. I heard her song as it told me a story. Her story. I touched my forehead to hers and the song exploded in my mind. Every word she'd ever said, every emotion she'd ever felt. I heard it.

What would you do?

I lifted my head from her. For a moment her song echoed in my head and her memories played before my eyes. I opened my eyes and she had moved. Instead of staring ahead, she was now looking over her shoulder, toward the lumbering beast in the distance.

I went to Evie and held her close. Head to head, hand in hand. She hummed softly. She didn't talk. She wanted to show me. I watched her life fly by, and felt the final choice she made—a choice that brought her immense joy.

"Thank you," I whispered to her. "Can you save me one last time?" When I opened my eyes, she was looking toward the creature.

I went to Crish. Even in death, he didn't enjoy my

company. He was too tall for me to touch my forehead to his, so I tried his chest instead. It worked, and his mind was noisy. I heard a lot of shouting, voices and demands pulling him this way and that. He was a very busy man, with heavy expectations on his shoulders. He smiled so broadly, but inside, he felt dark and jaded, like a room full of invisible, prickly things. He didn't so much show me his memories as tore them apart and threw them at me. I caught them and tried not to wince as his anger and ambition bombarded me alternately.

"I know," I told him. "But no ambition of yours will see the light of day if this world stays dead."

I looked up. He had turned slightly.

"Come on," I said. "Be our savior."

His head creaked as if turning on a metal joint. He turned until he was also looking toward the creature. I looked behind him at the endless bodies in the tundra. This was not a challenge of power or cleverness, but one of endurance. Quit any time, Cheshire had said, but I had no intention of doing so. Not when I had all the time in the world.

All the time in the world, I thought to myself with a wry smile, and headed to the next nearest person.

. . .

I WALKED across the plain that never seemed to end. The sun, if there was one, never set, as if the Earth itself had stopped turning. The day languished in gray, lazy, early evening light. Ugly little gray bushes dotted the plains, the only source of life aside from me and the beast. I ate their miserable-tasting berries, not worried about whether they were toxic, as they were clearly placed there to sustain me on the journey stretched before me. I slept wherever I lay, though I was never sure for how long. Time stood as still as the dead planet, and occasionally the beast in the distance rested. In those peaceful times, I was the only thing moving, a single dot across endless space.

I'd lost track of where I had started long ago. There were no days or nights or seasons. How long did it take to listen to the stories of millions of people? Was everyone on the planet standing dead, waiting for me? I didn't know. I just knew what I had to do, and I had to keep going. Time passed. Or rather, I passed time. I kept walking, and I kept watching the beast on the horizon. It slept for long periods of time, then woke to pace, then slept again. Sometimes I lost track of it as my path led me farther away, but ultimately it always came back into view.

A coastline greeted me. I walked along it, took off my shoes, and let the gray waves lap at my bare feet. There were no clam shells or hermit crabs scurrying on the sand. I sat on the colorless beach and watched the ocean. On this unturning planet, there was no rising of the tides. The beast moved into the shallow waters and slept, head pillowed on its haunches. I washed the sand off my hands in the salty water and marveled at the wrinkles and veins that had begun appearing on the backs of my hands.

Still I walked. I spoke to every person and heard their story. They all had something to say, and each one was as fascinating as the next. They all had stories of their own worries and fears during those terrible months of watching and waiting for the world to end.

I walked on.

I crossed the endless landscape. My hands grew old and my joints ached.

I walked on.

My clothes lost their color but did not tear and my shoes held the best they could. My hair grew gray and I couldn't quite see the beast as clearly as I used to.

I walked on.

The people on the beach stood. Timeless,

preserved, forever young. I watched my hands grow a little older, a little more wrinkled, a little more yellow, with each face I touched.

I walked on.

THE BEAST WAS SLEEPING when I finally approached it. It was magnificent, a sight to behold for one as insignificant as me. After untold time in this unchanging world, it was the one thing I could truly relate to.

"Hello," I said, standing at the edge of the waters. It was resting a short distance from shore, water lapping at the beach around its enormous body. "I'm sorry for what's about to happen."

It didn't move. Of course not. I was nothing but a speck to it. But specks add up. I looked it over one last time.

I turned my back to it. On the beach and beyond, millions and millions of faces turned toward me, toward it. I'd heard their voices, songs, and stories, and spoken to each and every one of them. I knew their names and their lives and what each one of them did during those fateful few months when no one knew if we would live to see another sunrise.

"Take back your world," I said to the people, and began to walk.

As I passed them, they moved. They walked stiffly, but steadily and with purpose. They marched past me in hundreds, thousands, millions. I kept walking, my hands in my pockets, away from the beach. I already knew what was about to happen, and I didn't need to see it.

Behind me, I heard the beast stir as they swarmed him like ants. At first it swatted them away. I heard its fists land in the water, splashing the shore. Then the movement became faster, more frantic. The ground quaked with each strike and I kept going.

They keep coming. They were small but there was power in numbers. Enough ants could devour a lion. I heard it roar behind me. It was in pain, but they wouldn't stop.

I walked on.

The sounds behind me continued for a long time. Then they began to slow. I heard the beast's last mournful bleat. The people were still walking past me, toward the scene. Toward where the last breath of life sighed out of the old beast.

I walked on.

I went until the sounds behind me ceased. I went

until I felt the exhaustion finally begin to take over. I went until there were no more people to walk by and I was completely and utterly alone in the world.

The landscape around me gave way to white. The sky and horizon merged. I seemed to be walking on nothing. The cracked ground of the plain turned smooth, then white.

Still I walked on.

I had no idea where I was going, only that I was done. I would walk forever if I must.

This was it. This was where I got off the ride.

"You think it's over, don't you?"

I stopped. I hadn't heard the voice of a living person in what felt like an eternity.

The newcomer walked into my field of vision, tan skinned and dark haired, with wide, bright eyes that tinted slightly toward violet. She peered at me and smiled. I knew her face.

"Hello, Thirty-Three," she said. She was young. Very young. No more than early teens, dressed casually in jeans and ankle boots, hands tucked in the pockets of a gray tweed jacket. "I could speak in Mandarin if you like, but Eleven said you prefer English."

"English is fine." I studied her face. "I know you."

"Yes, you do." She looked me up and down, an expectant smile on her face, waiting for me to connect the dots.

"I saw your face."

"You did. Eleven showed you. He thought he was sneaky, but nothing in this arena escapes me."

"You're one of the champions."

"As are you. Congratulations, Thirty-Three. You can call me Seven. Or, if you like, you can use the name your people gave me."

I nodded. "Yes. Hello, Cheshire."

"You don't have to keep looking at me like that."

"Like what?"

We were walking together in an endless white landscape. She had started and I had followed and now we were walking like a pair of friends having an afternoon stroll.

"Like you're confused about whether you want to rip my face off. You're welcome to try and rip my face off."

I shook my head. "I just have so many questions."

"Consider this your orientation. It's part of my job as the arena master. You are now a champion. Congratulations." Seven—Cheshire—spread her arms in a familiar gracious fashion. "It's a hard-earned victory and you played well. Don't think the producers didn't notice. You are one of a kind and they are *very* excited to have you join the gallery. But I'm getting ahead of myself. Let's start at the beginning, shall we?" She grinned. "I always love this part."

She snapped her fingers and the white suddenly faded to black. I started in surprise as I found myself standing in the black of space. Distant stars blinked all around us.

"In the beginning, there was the universe, and the first beings who lived in it. They were far beyond what we can comprehend, so all you need to know for our purposes is that they existed. In your terms, I suppose you can call them 'Gods.'"

"Gods?"

"The Gods existed for a very, very long time. Then, when they'd learned everything there was to learn, and done everything there was to do, they became bored. So they began to create. They created planets, and they created other beings. Lesser beings. Beings who, while they cannot function at the level of the Gods, are still pretty darn entertaining.

"Creation is a long process, you see. But the Gods have time. They spent eons moving the pieces and shaping the environments, experimenting and testing to make the perfect races. Today, we call it evolution."

Another snap of her fingers and we were on Earth, hovering hundreds of feet above the ground. Looking down, I saw herds of animals running across a wide savanna. Another snap and we were under the ocean, though I felt no water. An enormous shark swam by us without a pause.

"You see, when you are an ageless being, a few billion years putting together a race of beings intelligent enough to provide some entertainment is nothing. Kind of like casting some chumps for a reality show, or slapping a bag on the village fool's head for a laugh."

"You're telling me the whole human race was created for the entertainment of some alien race."

"Is it really that surprising? Many like to say they're created in God's image, but they have no idea how right they are. Age doesn't necessarily make you saintly. We are as the Gods are—petty, sensationalist, cheap entertainment over deep thought. Our value to them lies in our ability to entertain. And guess what—we're good at it."

I shuddered.

"And we're not the only ones."

The ocean disappeared. We were now standing

in the middle of a busy, bustling street. It looked quite a bit like Times Square at first glance, but everything was just a little different. I didn't recognize the language on the billboards, and the skyscrapers were built using a material with an odd golden tint, as if made with sand. A pair of hot suns beat down on the people milling about—people covered in iridescent scales.

"This is Eleven's planet."

"Was."

I regarded the bustling civilization around me and couldn't help feeling a wave of sadness. "You burned his whole world."

"Rules are rules."

"Are you really going to recreate this planet?"

"That project is still in proposal stage."

I shook my head. "I hate the way you talk about this, like these people's lives weren't worth anything. They were living beings, not stage props."

"Wrong." Seven snapped her fingers again, and we were once again back in the arena, with its white domed ceiling and shiny black floors. "That's exactly what they were. It's what they were made to be, built from the very fiber of their being. Have you not stopped to consider how a species from an entirely different planet as you could somehow evolve to possess the same physical blueprint as you, have similar social customs, cultures, habits, and even mating compatibility?"

"I asked Eleven that, yes." I paused. "Mating compatibility?"

She stared at me for a moment, then sighed. "So after all that drama, you didn't even take him for a ride."

My face flushed hot. "We haven't had the chance."

"If you had, you would know that your species and his practically occupy the same branch of evolution, with only one minor shift—his species was reptilian in origin, and yours mammalian. Your cultures, like most in this galaxy, had been shaped to be as similar as possible through time. Aside from the minor physiological differences, like those between walking lizards and hairless apes, you're all exactly the same."

"But why?"

"Drama. Have you not figured it out yet? The show is much more interesting when the lizards, apes, and octopuses can love and bone each other."

I studied her face. There was something unsettling about the idea that I was speaking to Cheshire, who for so long had been a headless robot with an emoji for a face. But I couldn't deny the similarities. No matter what she said, the stony smile in her eyes never changed. "Why do you say it that way?"

"What way?"

"Like you're not a 'hairless ape.'"

The smile wavered very briefly. It reminded me of that flicker of anger when I spoke dismissively to her several rounds earlier. "Don't compare me to those wretched things," she said, her mouth still smiling but her eyes no longer.

"Why not?" I prodded. Either I had nothing left to lose or making Seven lose her cool felt like a tiny, minute victory. "You're from another Earth. You're human. Don't you care what happens to us? Eleven worked for hundreds of years trying to restore *his* people, and all you want to do is torture yours?"

Seven let out a sharp, almost angry laugh. "Maybe I should've saved myself the trouble and left you in the jar."

"What jar?"

"Your house. We call them jars—pocket spaces made to simulate the environment the person finds most comforting. Some champions of the games never make it out of the jar. It's easier to stay in there than face reality. A few even chose to go back into the jar after their orientation." She looked to me.

"You won't want that. I can tell. Although I'm kind of tempted to shove you back in right now."

"What's the point of the jars?"

"Call it an escape route we offer the champions. Some people prefer to hover in their comfy little limbo after the games. They can treat it as an adjustment period, or stay in there. I think Four is still in theirs."

"What would've happened if I never snapped out of it?"

"If you couldn't break out of the jar, you had no chance in the bonus round. Organic beings, no matter their species and shape, value a good escape."

"You're doing it again. You're an 'organic being,' too."

Seven's dead smile was making me nervous, but I struggled to keep her from noticing. "I am so much more than them."

"Are you? Because one hairless ape to another, we sure look a lot alike."

Something heavy struck the side of my head, knocking the wind out of me. I saw stars for a moment and nearly fell over. Before I could straighten, it struck me again. This time across the face. By the time my vision cleared, my nose was bleeding. I raised my gaze to Seven.

"Champions though we both are, don't forget that I'm still the master of this arena."

"Fine," I said. "Fine."

"I am different from them," Seven continued, biting each word. "For that matter, I am different from *you*. You've only won the game. You haven't earned your place among us yet. You've still got a long way to go."

I wiped blood from my nose. "A long way to go doing what?"

"Working the games."

"Why would I do that? I don't know what sadistic high you get from this, but I have no desire to torture other humans. Or anyone."

She clicked her tongue, like a parent frustrated with a child. "Do you think there is any chance that you could go back to your old life?" she said. "Your house, your friends, your family, and the world that's been whispering shit about you while you were risking your life to save it? You will never have peace again. The world will continue to be cruel to you for the rest of your life. They will watch you, and gossip about you, and you will never be able to escape."

"No," I said slowly, watching the shift on her face. "You do it because they hurt you. You do it because . . ." Realization dawned on me as I recalled the face of the sad, frightened girl in the gallery of champions, and I had a feeling she could tell. "Because they took your baby."

Silence fell over us. I watched pain, anger, and resignation play in Seven's eyes.

"Yes," she said. "That is how it began. But it is also so much more than that. You do not know how ugly a world can be until it takes your child from you. You think you've seen the worst of it. That is, until you realize that every other world out there is just as ugly."

I nodded. "I understand."

"No, you *don't*. That's the point." She gestured at herself. "Do you know what I am? I am memories. Organic beings are nothing but flesh and memories, and flesh can be replaced. Old age? Not an issue. Disease? Nonexistent. But the arena giveth, and the arena taketh away. You may look the same, but with every replacement, you feel a little less like yourself, a little less connected to who you used to be, because whatever they're replacing you with, it's not what you were originally made of. What do you think is holding your broken bones together right now?"

I shifted my shoulder slightly. It crackled. Seven smiled smugly.

"The champions who still live are a different breed altogether. We are not what we started as—we are more than the common, ugly beings in their common, ugly worlds. *I* am more, more than the little girl who sobbed over what she lost."

"Sounds to me like you're less. You've lost who you used to be, when you had a home and a name instead of a number."

Seven snapped her fingers and turned from me. "Come. Walk."

We walked. Our surroundings changed as we did. I saw cities and spires rolling by, followed by little burgs and villages, then mountains and deserts and oceans and lakes, and grassy fields filled with alien flowers. I saw people—humans and not—going about their lives on the surfaces of unfamiliar worlds.

"You think we've lost something," Seven said as we walked past the rolling landscapes, unraveling alongside us like filmstrip, "but those of us who choose the game see it as we've gained. We gained perspective to reality, to what our fellow beings are truly like. We've gained distance from the ugliness and pettiness and found a manner of peace unparalleled. We've seen sights you can't imagine, done things beyond your comprehension. We are more."

"Agree to disagree," I said shortly, and pointedly ignored the annoyance on her face. "Where's Eleven?"

"Alive. More or less. He needed to be put in his place, but I couldn't off a fellow champion without approval from the producers. They rather like to collect the champions, like pinning butterflies."

"Flattering." A little village of four-armed beings scrolled by. I watched their young offspring play in the dirt, stubby fingers working what looked like a wooden top with surprising dexterity. "But not what I asked."

"Let me tell you something about your boyfriend," Seven went on, continuing to ignore my question. "Some people are born to be outcasts and he's one of them. He was an outcast among his own people and he's an outcast among the champions. He thinks empathizing with the contestants will make him feel like he belongs, but he's wrong. No one thanks him for what he does, and the producers allow it only because they find him amusing, especially when he gets caught. This wasn't the first time I've ripped a hole in him and it won't be the last. Stubborn one he is—more of him has been replaced by the arena than not, and yet he just won't quit. One day another arena master may take over for me, and he'll give them reason to rip him apart, too." She gave me a slanted look. "Didn't tell you that, did he? Guess the number of times he's lost his guts doesn't make for a good date night story. Bless that idiot for how hard he tries."

"If you insult him one more time," I said as we stopped at the edge of an endless ocean. Deep red waters lapped at a dark brown beach. "I *will* rip your face off, master of the arena or not."

Seven shrugged uncaringly. "Fair enough."

"NOTHING in this game happens by accident."

I watched the waves come and go. The inhabitants of this world appeared to be amphibious, with skin like pearl and wet, lidless eyes. "Somehow I'm starting to get that feeling."

"Everything that happened in and out of the arena was carefully orchestrated. That first visit Eleven made to you to deliver the token? I made sure he didn't land anywhere near you. Where would the fun be if he did?"

"Nowhere, I suppose."

"Would you be surprised to know the contestants were carefully selected?"

I turned to Seven. Like Eleven, she looked much older close up than from a distance. "We were?"

"Yes. Ever since I took over as arena master, at least. This game has been refined many times, all for the purpose of entertainment."

"You have a knack for this."

"I do. I am clever, creative, and have no regard for the wellbeing of my own species."

"You made it so no child as young as you would ever step into the arena again."

"Don't think you can make my heart grow larger by pointing out one single act of pity."

"Kindness isn't pity."

"You and Eleven were made for each other." Seven bent down, picked up a smooth gray shell, and skipped it into the ocean. "I found that randomly selected contestants lacked a certain chemistry with each other. They didn't blend together to make the most interesting interactions possible. I watched the civilized beings of each planet, studied them, even steered their cultural and social growth to experiment and find out the best personality types and situations."

"We were all picked to make the best possible show?"

"Most of you. There were some fillers, but once in a while the fillers surprise you. Alexis Monroe was a filler. So was Sergio Lopez."

"And Evie?"

"She was my bet to win."

I turned to Seven in surprise. "Evie? Evie Bouchard?"

"Humans have a tendency to overlook the underdogs. All of you were so focused on her shortcomings that no one noticed she was the most competent player by far."

The ocean disappeared, replaced by a series of screens, each showing Evie in a different round. Evie feeling her way around the sewers, leaving a trail of glue-covered rats behind her. Evie guarding herself with a shell of white glue as a structure collapsed over her in the Hollow City. Evie listening intently as Crish spoke to Sergio and several others, filling their heads with dreams of fame and freedom.

"No one suspected her competence and she knew this. She had gone her entire life slipping under the radar, escaping notice, and being underestimated, and she used it all to her advantage. She watched and listened and kept her strengths close to her heart. While her fellow humans were busy over-looking her, the Gods were betting on her to win."

"And she would have. If she didn't choose to save me."

"The drawbacks of kindness." Seven paused. "Go ahead, ask."

"Was I a pick or a filler?"

"You were a pick. But not mine."

"Then whose?"

The screens disappeared. A jungle appeared before us. We followed a dirt path winding slowly downhill. "You have to ask?"

"I thought only you got to pick the contestants."

"I let Eleven have his input once in a while, just for laughs really."

"And he chose me?"

"He paused."

"Meaning what?"

"Meaning while scrolling through hundreds of thousands of contestants, he paused on you. Only for a split second. In fact, I wonder if he even remembers. But I saw that pause. I didn't know what it was about you that made him pause, so I thought I'd bring you in and find out. Lo and behold, you didn't disappoint." Exotic birds squawked overhead, though I couldn't make out their forms in the dense foliage. "Of course, some of the champions working the games prefer a close, personal touch."

"Personal touch?"

"They go as far as disguising themselves, ingraining themselves into society, getting close to the contestants of their interest, and nudging them one way or another on a personal level. A lot of work, but highly entertaining if you're into that." She winked at me. "Understand now?"

"Yes," I said slowly. "I do."

"Is the Earth really dead?"

"No. I could've razed the Earth just to set up the bonus round, but I didn't. Restoration would've thrown the next show off schedule. What you experienced was an extensive simulation."

"How long was I in there?"

"About a week."

"Was any of this real?"

"Unfortunately, yes. You haven't been living a coma dream. Any other questions?"

"What happens now?"

"The aftermath of the games, most likely. A traumatized planet will always suffer fallout—war, social upheaval, cultural revolutions, and such."

"And what happens to me?"

"That's up to you. Join us, or don't. You have the rest of your life to decide."

"Does anyone actually take the rest of their life to decide?"

"Some do. Others decide quickly."

"How many champions work for the games right now?"

"If you join us, you'll know."

"I still have so many questions."

"I know." Seven reached out and laid a hand on my shoulder. The arena had returned to black and white. "But now's not the time. Orientation is over. Welcome to the ranks of champions. And good luck, Thirty-Three."

She pushed me, and I fell backward into darkness.

I WOKE TO A DIM, QUIET ROOM.

Once my eyes adjusted, I held up my hands. They were young and smooth and covered in IV tubes. The room was unfamiliar and simply furnished. Against the window, sitting across from each other and speaking quietly, were two familiar faces. They looked up when I cleared my throat.

"Welcome back," one said.

I studied them as closely as I could through bleary eyes. I had never examined their faces closely, but now, behind the wigs and makeup and whatever concealed the extra eye, I recognized them beyond a doubt.

"What are your numbers?"

They exchanged a look.

"Ten," said the man who called himself Austin

Heath. "I can't say I'm not disappointed. I thought I fed Crish Michaels everything he needed to hear to win this one."

"Thirty-One," said the woman who called herself Lydia Porter. "And looks like I bet on the right horse."

They had set up Evie in the room next to mine. No one knew why exactly she was still alive and I didn't feel the need to enlighten them. Not yet. She slept like an angel, not a mark or scar on her smooth, round face. No one could tell me when she would wake up and after a few days I stopped asking. I sat by her bed every morning, watching the sun streak across her strawberry-blond hair, and thought about all that I had to tell her when she finally opened her eyes. She had to be the first to hear this story.

A vigil was held outside the hospital. People lit candles and said prayers for us, which now seemed very humorous. They allowed immediate family to visit. I finally met Stella.

Government officials visited. It seemed to be a formality. They thanked me for my service and enumerated all the honors the government was prepared to grant me. I listened without a word, and after they left, spent a long time thinking about Eleven's words about the title of "champion" versus "disgrace."

The Earth, as it turned out, did not witness the bonus round. Though I couldn't bring myself to watch the recordings, I was able to piece together through hearsay that the broadcast turned off after I attacked Cheshire, and the orb remained silent for the week I spent walking the dead Earth. Speculations were wild and I didn't correct them. The voices —and the world—felt very, very small.

Offers for book deals, movie rights, and interviews on late night shows came through every day. I turned them all down. The love the world wanted to lavish on me was cheap. A week ago it was cursing me for being a traitor and whore. What would it call me tomorrow, if I told them what I now knew?

THE IDEA WAS FLOATED for a rally to be held on my discharge, but I made sure it did not happen. Heath came through on that—courtesy of one champion to another, he said. Instead, a ride was arranged for me, and a plane to wherever I wanted to go. I bid goodbye to the doctors and nurses, stopped to kiss

Evie goodbye, and promised I would return to see her soon.

Then, I went home.

MY LITTLE HOUSE was exactly how I'd left it, minus a few boxes worth of stuff that had accompanied me to the safe house. Figure out if I'm getting those back —add it to the list. I expected the naysayers to have left me some graffiti and toilet paper rolls, but it looked like Heath had come through on his promise that my home and belongings would be protected. I unlocked the door and stepped inside. The house was warm and stuffy. Power and water had been shut off long ago. Boxes and clothes lay strewn around the floors, covered in a thin layer of dust. I went into the bedroom. The pile of bloody pajamas was still where I left it. I shoved them into the nearest plastic bag I could find and sat down on the bare mattress as the sun sank beneath the horizon. I was alone for the moment. How long did I have before the paparazzi caught on that I was here?

I turned on my phone, which had been reconnected to the world. I'd spent my time in the hospital clearing the thousands and thousands of messages and emails that had built up. But they kept coming.

Change my number—add it to the list. I texted Hannah.

I'm home

She responded less than a minute later.

On my way

I sat for a while longer, reveling in the silence. As the night fell, I finally moved to my library. There, I sat on the floor and picked up the old, dust-covered geology book that started it all. The pages crinkled as I turned them slowly, and when I looked up, he was standing in my living room, as if he'd been there all along.

"I watched you in the bonus round."

"How did I do?"

"Remarkable. But I never doubted that." His left sleeve was rolled up, and I saw the remnants of burns winding their way up his wrist and arm. I patted the space next to me. He crossed the room and joined me on the library floor. I opened his buttons and the jagged scar that ran the entire length of his stomach stared back at me. Gently, I traced it end to end with my fingertips.

"It's not a dream."

"Would you prefer that it were?"

"No. Never." I pulled his lips to mine. The taste of them woke me from the daze that had accompanied me since the dead Earth. "Are you in trouble? Did they finally kick you out of Seven's arena?"

He laughed. It was a tired, resigned laugh, the kind of sound that one made when they couldn't think of what else to do. The same laugh I laughed when the doctors gaped, baffled, at the X-rays showing veins of diamond holding my shoulder blade together.

"The producers offered to make my position in the arena official."

"They did?"

"It would appear that your people were not the only ones fond of your story—and my part in it." He took my right hand and opened it. There, on the center of my palm, was the winner's laurel, thirty-three intricate strokes in the shape of a round wreath. "Congratulations, champion."

"It doesn't feel like a victory."

"It never does."

"I didn't like orientation."

"No one likes orientation."

I leaned against the wall. He did the same. I sighed and buried my face in my hands.

"Something wrong?"

"I just realized Hannah's going to be here in

twenty minutes and when she sees you, she's going to have questions."

"Questions?"

I raked my gaze over him. I wanted him close, held tight. My body and heart ached to consume him, drink him in, make him part of my world and me part of his. There was time for that now. All the time in the world.

"Don't worry about it."

"Alright."

"How do you deal with it?"

"With what?"

"Feeling so old inside but looking so young. I walked among the dead for so long, but I don't see those years on my face."

"I live. A day at a time. As will you."

I leaned against him and hooked my fingers into his. "What now?"

"That's up to you. You have a lot of decisions to make."

"I don't even know what I want to do tomorrow. Or tonight. I can't see past the next day or the next hour. I can't imagine making decisions that affect the rest of my life." I touched his face. I knew he understood, but had no answers for me. In a world that looked increasingly like a cardboard diorama, he was real.

He opened his hand and laid it next to mine. Our winners' laurels stared back at us, side by side. Outside, I heard singing wind, passing cars, and the voices of playing children. The world rolled on as we sat still, and for now, that was alright with me.

FIGURE OUT LIFE—ADD it to the list.

Hey reader,

We hope you enjoyed *Headspace.*

Authors live off reviews. If you enjoyed this book, please leave a review on the site of your choice (e.g. Amazon, Goodreads, Barnes & Noble)

Also, want a free book? Get one when you sign up for J.D. Edwin's newsletter. Sign up at jdedwin.com.

ACKNOWLEDGMENTS

This book is dedicated to Jason, who always supported me;

to the team at Story Cartel Press, who believed in me;

to Alice, who found all the typos, inconsistencies, and misused punctuation;

to everyone who took the time to read this book and live for a moment in the crazy world inside my head;

and to Mr. Sanders, who told me in 11th grade that I was a good writer.

Before Earth, before Cheshire, there was a very different:

Master of the Arena

The Prequel to Headspace

Coming December 2021

Nasmi Kol is a slave. Her existence is small and simple ... until the black orb comes to Maeda.

Suddenly, she finds herself the champion savior of her world, only to be cast out by her family. Having nowhere to turn, she is taken in by the master of the Headspace arena, H'otto, and the former champions of the game. Strange as her circumstances may be, she finds a renewed sense of purpose with her new family, as well as a new name —Seven.

But things are not as simple as they seem. As the days and years wear on, Seven slowly begins to realize that the arena is filled with secrets, and that the truth behind eternal life is not so holy or beautiful. A cruel fate awaits all champions, and if she wants to help the ones who came after her, she has to take matters into her own hands.

What will it take to save not only herself, but those she loves as well?

Read on for a sneak peak of the upcoming prequel . . .

CHAPTER 1

Run.

    Survive. Manifest. Bleed.
    Thorns.
    Champion of Maeda.

I opened my eyes.

I had grown used to the dreams, and as usual, no matter how vivid they were in the dark, when light arrived, they melted away like a flake of ice on a hot stove. Tears hung from my eyes, but whether they were tears of sadness or merely the last remnants of sleep, I couldn't tell. As I sat up, the last of the dream fell away, shaken off as easily as if it were a leaf that landed on my shoulder.

Tam smiled at me from his spot on the ground, where he'd been chewing on a rag doll I'd painstakingly stitched for him from scraps of old cloth. He babbled and reached for me.

"Did Mama doze off?" I cooed as I picked him up and tickled his chubby feet. His joyful laugh rang against the walls of our tiny bedroom. "Come, let's put you to bed."

And so I washed and dressed him, and laid him down for the last time in the little cot across from mine. He wiggled, smiling up at me as if my face were the most amazing sight in the known world. I smiled down at him until he closed his eyes, then sat down next to him and stroked his hair.

Has this scar always been there?

Long, ugly, and red, it snaked over most of my left forearm. It must've been quite a painful ordeal, whatever caused it, but it couldn't have been that bad. After all, I couldn't recall it.

Just like this one.

On the palm of my right hand was a series of marks like pen strokes. I'd tried to wipe them off several times, but they refused to budge. Seven strokes formed a perfect circle on my skin, dark red as if left from an old burn, but I stared at it and remembered no pain. I spent a moment pondering these scars, as I always seemed to do before bed. But the effort gave me a mild headache, like staring into a bright light for too long. So I lay down in my own cot across the narrow room and watched Tam's little chest rise and fall. I used to worry that he might fall out if he rolled, but not anymore. Because I already knew he would wake laying on his side, bright violet eyes fixed on me. And when he saw me wake up, he would smile, and reach to be picked up. We would spend the day inside, playing and laughing on the floor, curtains drawn to hide the thick gray mist outside. I would play him his flute, and though my skills at stringing together a tune were atrocious at best, he would still smile at every screechy, off-key note.

Tomorrow would be the last day.

So would the day after that.

And the one after that.

Voices drifted through the closed door to our room. The main room of Mama Dorma's house was abuzz with conversation and music. A gathering was taking place, and I could hear Santi's throaty laugh in between intermittent chatter. Mama Dorma was doubtlessly showing off the stone vases in the hall and how well her jasmium flowers were blooming in the front garden. The spicy scent of her meat stew, which had been cooking all day, wafted through the door and my stomach growled, but to show my face would only lead to trouble. I hoped someone would remember to slide a plate in for me.

A pair of feet shuffled near the door. I heard arguing—Santi wanting me to join the festivities, and his mother, the matriarch of the family, vehemently cursing him for even thinking of allowing a Kol out in the presence of honored guests. I pretended not to hear—I had no interest in being paraded before judging eyes. This tiny room with its little cots, brown floor, and colorful tapestries depicting cheerful scenes of women wearing sunhats and picking summer fruit on the walls—this was where I preferred to be, just me and Tam.

Finally, as the sound of the festivities began to die down, the door opened and a bowl and spoon were pushed through. The root vegetables were cold and the rich soup had begun to congeal, but I was grateful for it regardless. I ate sitting on the cot, trying and failing to keep Tam from grabbing at every bite. He had been well fed before the gathering, and this was the first proper meal I'd had all day. I swallowed every soggy bite without complaint and set the bowl out of Tam's reach on the small bedside table. That table won't be out of his reach much longer, not once he learned to walk, which would be any day now.

Night would soon fall. I would doze for a while in the evening and dream, then wake without remembering what the dreams were—though somehow I knew it was the same dream over and over. And I would put Tam to bed again. For the last time.

The hundredth last time.

The thousandth last time.

Each time was the last, or so I told myself, then I woke up and did it all again. No matter how many times I played that damned flute, that same damned song, I never seemed to get any better. That same cold bowl was pushed through the door, day after day. That same shuffle of feet in the hall, those same curses. That same gray mist rolled past the curtains. The curtains I never opened. I studied those scars and they made my head hurt, so I watched Tam sleep. It was all a play. An endless pantomime.

My baby will never grow.

My baby will stay small and lovely.

My baby will never change.

My baby will stay, so long as I stay.

I slept, then woke up and repeated it all again. For the last time, I told myself as I held him tightly, smelling his milky goodness and feeling his chubby arms around my neck. The very last time.

If only he didn't feel so real.

I cried on the final night. The real, true, final night. I wasn't entirely sure why I cried, because I didn't know what lay beyond, only that it loomed so frighteningly close, like a dark, silent, stalking thing breathing down my neck. When the tears dried, I pulled back the curtains and watched the gray mist roll by. Then I sat and stroked Tam's hair, remembering the feel of every dark fiber. He wiggled and cooed and fell asleep gazing up into my eyes. I leaned down and kissed him, took two steps back, and tore my eyes away. If I looked at him, I knew I would lose my courage again. I would rush back to the cot and pledge to spend eternity by his side, whether he was real or not.

The bowl from the thousandth last meal we shared lay on the floor. I kicked it. It slid across the floor and clattered against the wall. Through the bedroom door I could hear the party winding down, though I knew there was no one on the other side. If I opened the door and turned around, would I see Tam melt away, like the dreams that haunted me so relentlessly? I wrapped my fingers around the knob, took a shuddering breath, and pulled.

The cold and metal that greeted me was jarring but unsurprising. The warm browns and reds of my husband's family home were nowhere to be found, though I never expected it to be there. I didn't need to turn to know the room behind me, along with the phantom of my son, was gone. I took a step through the door, into the familiar chill of the arena—a chill I'd come to know so very well.

Run. Survive.

I shuddered. Breathing suddenly became a struggle. The scar on my left arm began to hurt and I looked down to see I was digging the fingernails on my right hand into it. I forced my fingers loose and looked up at the metal dome above me. It was different, alien. The chill penetrated me to the bone. I looked down and saw not a sandy beach, nor a paved road, nor a mountain path, nor any of the stages upon which I'd run and screamed and bled in this arena. Instead, it was a surface of metal plating, stained here and there with dark spots that I hoped were rust and not something worse. I moved slowly in a circle, holding myself and shivering, feeling as if I'd been swallowed by a giant metal beast. I had only known the games, each one a different stage, a different terrain, a different world.

Is this really the arena in its true form?

My head spun and for a moment I couldn't feel my body in space. Flashes of sights and sounds assaulted me from all directions and I forced air in and out of my lungs. I heard screaming, the faraway voice of the dead. Lives lost. Everything spun faster and faster. The scar on my left arm stung and when I looked down, blood spilled out of it in rivers.

I have to get out.

Explosions. Screaming. I heard it all. Every hair on my body stood up.

I won. I get to leave. I have to leave.

Blood everywhere. Teeth in my flesh. I couldn't breathe.

Have to leave. Have to leave.

"I was beginning to think you preferred stasis."

The voices disappeared as if a door slammed shut. The sudden silence was deafening. I looked at my arm again expecting to find torn flesh and flowing red, but saw only a dark, dry scar. Running a finger over its surface, I wondered for a moment how much time had actually passed. The circle on my right palm remained unchanged.

"The winner's laurel will not go away so easily."

I started and searched for the source of the voice. Scanning the arena, I nearly missed him as my eyes ran over where he stood—his fur blurred almost seamlessly into the brown rust of the dome. Short and stumpy, standing a whole head shorter than me, he was definitely not what I expected. Two short arms linked behind the back of his pudgy body, and two more were folded in front. Dark, round eyes rolled over my form, taking me in from head to toe. The wispy brown fur on his long, floppy ears quivered. A wide, friendly mouth spread into a smile beneath his round button nose.

I shuddered despite his disarming appearance. He resembled the little friendly puppet I played for Tam, or the sweet, harmless wild hoppers that snooped around Mama Dorma's yard, searching for vegetable scraps that I sometimes left out for them behind Mama's back. But though I had not seen his face until now, I knew beyond a doubt who he was. His voice had haunted my every waking moment since the orb landed on Maeda. The need to flee overcame me and I instinctively reached for the door I had just come through, but my fingers grasped empty air. I stood there with my hand raised, feeling like a fool.

"Welcome," that terrifying voice said. My skin crawled hearing it soft and gentle out of the mouth of this creature instead of booming from above. "I am H'otto, I speak for the gods."

"Kol knows," I blurted out, taking a large step back as he took a small one forward. "Kol wants to leave."

"I imagine you do," H'otto said, unhurried. His eyes blinked separately from one another. "You are welcome to leave any time. But why would you want to?"

Unable to decide between fear and confusion, I said, "Kol wants to go home."

"To the home that forces you to call yourself 'Kol'?" he chuckled. I realized I was still holding the nonexistent doorknob and lowered my hand stiffly. "If you wish. But first, won't you take a walk with me, Seven?"

Made in the USA
Las Vegas, NV
22 July 2021

26864477R10321